A DAMIEN HUNTER ACTION NOVEL

GHOSTS IN THE FOG

NATHAN BEST

First published 2023

Big Sky Publishing Pty Ltd
PO Box 303, Newport, NSW 2106, Australia
Phone: 1300 364 611
Fax: (61 2) 9918 2396
Email: info@bigskypublishing.com.au
Web: www.bigskypublishing.com.au

Cover design and typesetting: Think Productions

NATIONAL LIBRARY OF AUSTRALIA
A catalogue record for this book is available from the National Library of Australia

Title: Ghosts in the Fog
ISBN: 978-1-923004-09-2

A DAMIEN HUNTER ACTION NOVEL

GHOSTS IN THE FOG

BIG SKY PUBLISHING
www.bigskypublishing.com.au

NATHAN BEST

'Put the bass up, will ya?'

Lemmy Kilmister,
Motörhead

For veterans who are struggling with the darkness of mental illness, may the shadow lift and you be in the sun.

For Steph, always.

CONTENTS

CHAPTER ONE

Damien Hunter

Shtokman Gas Field
Nevzgody Gas Platform
325 nautical miles north of the Kola Peninsula
September

As the hands of his scratched Military Navigator watch moved to 4am, Damien Hunter slipped on his helmet. He glanced across at the disinterested faces around him. Five men crowded into the confined space of the doghouse. He had no idea who they were. Like many things in Russia, the man was just part of the greater machinery of the state.

He pulled the exit hatch open and stepped onto the drilling floor. Sleet and wind swept across the open deck and slammed into him. He tucked his head deep into the hood of his heavy jacket, then pulled a thermal face mask up, exposing only his eyes. Damien could just feel the sub-zero temperature of the

Arctic through the thick layers of his clothing. The safety glasses he wore thrummed lightly against his face in the wind. Glancing up to the helicopter deck to his left, Damien saw the tails of an AgustaWestland AW189 and an older Kamov KA-32S.

As he strode quickly up to the drilling platform, Damien glanced across at the control room and saw blank, bored faces staring impassively back at him. These were the men who had no wish to be out on deck.

Damien drew in a lungful of frigid air. It reeked of oil and grease. He took over from the chainhand going off shift. Damien inspected a section of rusting drilling pipe where it sat in the mouse hole. The noise on the deck was deafening.

The next pipe section dropped out of the derrick above. After it was lowered into position, Damien grabbed a brush thick with dope and wiped it quickly through the coarse threads. He tightened the connection with a pair of hydraulic makeup tongs, then stepped back as the new section hauled clear of the mouse hole and connected to the main drilling pipeline. He hefted a heavy set of slips and dropped them either side of the pipe to guide it on its path.

Mud splattered against his jacket and Damien frowned. He could not remember so much mud being on the drilling floor. His clumsy boots slipped slightly on the surface. Glancing around at the other men on the deck, he saw they had noticed it. A grunted yell in Russian reached out to him. He looked over at the angry, overweight toolpusher. The man was indicating for him to spin in the next section of drill pipe. The stabbing of the toolpusher's hand towards him forced a rise of annoyance in Damien's throat. Nodding, he reached out for the tongs and pulled them across.

Movement in the control room caught his eye. Damien snapped his head up to look through the sleet at the men inside. He could see them yelling and gesturing frantically at each other. He felt the deck jump slightly beneath his feet. He started to back away from the drill hole. The toolpusher came down from his perch and started screaming and waving his arms at Damien. The man's face was bright red with anger.

An ear-splitting siren crashed through the thick atmosphere of the drilling floor and warning lights started flashing. Panicked Russian erupted over a speaker.

The toolpusher pulled up short. His face lost its redness, replaced by a pale tinge as he turned to move his bulk towards the nearest ladder.

Damien spun away, heading for the door of the doghouse. The drill floor jumped again, and a roar filled the air. Glancing back, he saw mud and debris erupt into the air as the rig suffered a kickback.

Engulfed in mud, the toolpusher disappeared into the murk.

Damien could see other workers rushing down ladders and escaping to the main rig deck. Mud and water coated the control room windows, obscuring the view of the men inside. They were working frantically to regain control of the drill head.

Damien shook his head.

He charged back into the maelstrom.

Small chunks of rock and clay mixed with mud hammered down on his helmet. Damien wiped his safety glasses clear as he searched for the toolpusher. He slipped over on the slick deck plates, landing hard on his right side. His head bounced off the steel deck and his helmet spun away into the gloom. Stars spiked in front of his eyes for a moment. Then he was up and on his feet.

He shuffled forwards to where he had last seen the toolpusher and saw the vague outline of the man squirming on the deck. The toolpusher was trying to drag himself clear. Moving carefully forwards and ignoring the debris falling around him, Damien clutched the back of the man's jacket. He tugged the toolpusher over onto his back, then dropped to his knees and looked the man in the eyes. The blankness of panic greeted him.

Plucking an abandoned helmet from the deck, Damien jammed it over the toolpusher's face and leaned into the man's weight.

Slowly, Damien dragged the man over the drilling deck and

towards the doghouse. He could hear faint shouting and looked over his shoulder. The hatch was open a crack and he could see a blurry face and hand encouraging him to hurry. Struggling with the heavy Russian, Damien continued to pull and slip on the slick deck plates. His ears rang with thundering noise. His nose was full of mud where the thermal face mask had slipped down. Locking on to the sound of the shouting, he kept moving and forced his way out of the danger zone.

Suddenly, he felt a hand grip his jacket and drag him through the hatch. Damien tripped over the lip of the opening and landed in a muddy heap on the doghouse floor.

The men crowded in the room helped the toolpusher to his feet and guided him to safety.

Left by himself, Damien lay on the floor in a tangle of discarded clothing and equipment.

'Typical,' he said, out of breath. Laughing to himself he rolled onto his hands and knees and dragged himself upright. He felt the pleasant tingle of adrenaline spread through his body.

Damien dropped back the hood of his jacket and pulled away the safety glasses to wipe away the mud from his face and hair. He shrugged out of his heavy weather gear and pushed them into his locker. There was no point cleaning them. His next shift would be in the sleet anyway, which would carry away most of the grime. He strode to the door set into the rear wall of the doghouse, pulled it open and surveyed the rushing men in the corridor.

Sirens were still blaring warnings in Russian.

Damien could feel the effects of the kickback through the walls and floor as he moved out into the corridor. He was making for his emergency station. He was one of the station's medical technicians. He was heading to the infirmary to collect his gear. Damien's training and experience far exceeded the requirement. He had chosen to write down just enough information to satisfy the position. There was no need for anyone to know anything more about his past.

Tromping mud and water along the hallway, Damien cocked his head to the left as he heard the warning sirens suddenly fall silent. Stopping to listen, he heard the all clear given. The warning lights winked out. The voice shouting over the PA called the next drill shift to the floor. Stood down, Damien's shift clocked off to clean up and rest.

Smiling, Damien reversed course. Five minutes later he arrived at his cabin. He stripped out of his wet clothes, strode over to the shower, set the temperature, and stepped inside.

As the hot water hit his face he was suddenly disorientated.

His mind assaulted him with the memory of the stench that was the burn pit at Tarin Kowt, in Afghanistan.

It's only another flashback, cried Damien in his head.

Forcing the feeling from his tortured mind, he opened his eyes and focused on the wall. Drawing deep, calming breaths, he formed a ball in his mind and started spinning it. Old habits die hard. He was sure to calm down if he followed his pre-mission ritual.

The water sluiced away the mud and sweat; Damien allowed the warmth to soothe him. The need to shower multiple times a day had never left him.

Afghanistan was two years in the past. Damien had spent a year recovering from his injuries and then spun into a drug and alcohol-fuelled depression of which he had almost no recollection. The loss of his friends ground at his mind.

In a rare moment of sobriety, six months earlier he had been sipping on a cup of thick black Australian Warfighter coffee when a message appeared on his mobile telephone. The SMS simply contained a number to call. After a week, curiosity made him dial. It had turned out to be an American Green Beret he knew. Damien had worked with the operator before he joined the shadow private military company known as the Taipan Organisation. It had briefly occurred to Damien that the operator had managed to acquire his unlisted mobile telephone number. Everyone in the community had their ways of finding each other. The operator had simply stated that he heard Damien needed a new start. There was a job opportunity he thought Damien might be interested in.

The conversation had been quick and gave Damien an option, a lifeline. His acquaintance had contacts in Russia. There was a position in their harsh and unforgiving oil and gas industry. An energy company was looking for a roughneck and medical specialist, no background questions asked. Damien had argued that he was unwelcome these days in Russia. The operator had countered that it would be handled.

Suffering a moment of clarity between drinks, Damien had taken the chance and signed up. Plane tickets and a working visa arrived in his email 12 hours later. After four days of grinding international travel, he boarded a Plyos Energy Kamov KA-32S, with its unique twin main rotors, as a chainhand bound for a remote gas platform. He had found the place he wanted to be. No-one knew he was here. No-one would try to contact him. Damien sobered up and worked hard to put the demons of his military and contractor life behind him.

Carefully, Damien closed his eyes and searched his mind for any mission flashbacks which might be lurking, waiting to surge forward to haunt him. Smiling as he felt nothing, he scrubbed his body clean, turned off the water and stepped out of the cubicle. As he towelled himself down, his eyes chanced on the thick lines of scar tissue which snaked over his torso. His toes were misshapen and painful from the beating Rainer Toussaint had delivered to them in Afghanistan. Like many things, Damien tucked the discomfort into a box and filed it away. He had always found it easier to hide pain than to deal with it.

Dressed, Damien clipped a radio to his belt, opened the door and looked cautiously up and down the passageway before stepping outside. The flashback had triggered his hypervigilance. Damien felt on edge. A gentle tremble coursed through his body. Taking a deep breath to calm himself, he headed for the mess room. His stomach growled. Another downside to working on a Russian rig in the middle of nowhere was the poor food and total lack of ice cream.

Barents Sea

Russian Sector

Captain Yuri Brusilov sipped from his cup of coffee and eyed the massive floating liquid natural gas facility, *Boris Gakkel,* off the port quarter. Brightly lit against the perpetual twilight of September in the Arctic, the *Boris Gakkel* was 350 metres long and 60 metres wide. Stretching up from its deck was a massive complex of derricks, pipe work and walkways extending to a long skeletal finger at the bow. From its end point a constant flame roared into the sky as excess gas and hydrocarbons burnt off into the atmosphere. The *Boris Gakkel* automatically processed gas from three well heads below and the distant production platform, Ispytaniye.

The *Boris Gakkel*'s working lights looked to Brusilov as if he was approaching a small city. He had first seen the glow of the lights as he commenced his approach two hours earlier. The glow reflected off the band of cloud which seemed to permanently cloak the area. It made very little difference that it 4:30am. It could have been midday. The weak attempt by the sun to illuminate the Arctic would have resulted in the same dim twilight.

By pumping warm water into the ocean surrounding it, the *Boris Gakkel* kept a 100-metre radius around its hull clear of ice. Broken ice floes continuously threatened to push in and close the narrow opening which allowed ships to dock with the massive facility.

Brusilov was the master of the liquid natural gas carrier *Leonid Khabarov*. A new generation icebreaking ship, the *Leonid Khabarov* was 260 metres long and 42 metres wide. With its distinctive spherical Moss tanks hidden under a façade which rose proud of the deck, *Leonid Khabarov* was the flagship of the Plyos Energy fleet. Capable of breaking through up to 2.5 metres of ice, the ship was truly at home in the Arctic. Even so, directly ahead of the ship was the nuclear-powered icebreaker *Yamal*.

The *Yamal* had been clearing a path through the thicker ice floes which were beyond the *Leonid Khabarov*'s capacity. Brusilov was grateful to have the powerful icebreaker along as insurance.

The *Leonid Khabarov* along with her sister ships, *Isa Umarov* and *Khasan Idrisov*, traded a routine and mundane route from the *Boris Gakkel* to mainland Russia to offload and return for more product. It was mind-numbingly boring.

Russia's most distant gas field, Shtokman, was situated high in the Arctic, constantly battered by storms and heavy weather. No matter the time of year. Men and equipment were under constant strain as they worked and struggled to survive in the harsh environment. The platforms which drilled the field were the first generation of ice-hardened facilities. Designed to be icebound throughout the year. In Russia's favour, the platforms were out of reach of environmental activists who dogged any oil and gas exploitation in the Arctic.

'Rudder midships,' Brusilov instructed.

His polished accent gave away his privileged upbringing in the Petrogradsky district of St Petersburg. At 66, Brusilov was in the prime of his career. His chiselled face was smoothly shaven. Brusilov was well known for the hard, professional glint of his grey eyes when he turned them on someone. He had served his time in the Russian Navy as a young man, which ignited his passion for the sea. Working his way up from rusting tramp ships which plied the Russian coast he had spent time with Maersk Moll on container ships. Once he had held command for 10 years, Plyos Energy had contracted him to be the captain of the *Leonid Khabarov* on her maiden voyage. Three years later he was still on board.

'Rudder midships,' repeated the helmsman.

'Thank you. All ahead slow,' advised Brusilov. He was calculating his approach speed to ensure it was not too fast for the tugs which were approaching from the starboard shoulder. He intended on coasting up to the connection point and letting the tugs do the rest of the work.

'All ahead slow,' responded the chief engineer.

Ahead of them the large ocean-going tugs *Kulak V Perchaake* and *Moguchiy Molot* stood ready to assist the ship.

'All stop,' instructed Brusilov. He waited for his engineer's reply and picked up the radio handset. 'Tugs attending, this is the *Leonid Khabarov*.'

'Good morning, Captain, you have *Kulak* and *Molot*,' responded the captain of *the Kulak V Perchaake*.

'Da, good morning. We are all stopped. Approach and put your lines up,' replied Brusilov. Both tug masters answered quickly. Plumes of diesel smoke erupted from their exhausts as they manoeuvred towards the gas carrier.

'First officer are the men ready to take the lines?' asked Brusilov as a squall of sleet hammered against the bridge windows.

'All is ready,' responded the first officer from the starboard side of the bridge.

Nodding, Brusilov walked over to the covered port bridge wing and studied the approach. He had little time for his first officer. Brusilov considered the man to have risen too quickly through the ranks. He lacked the experience and understanding necessary to hold the position he had clawed his way into. There were better men in the fleet, but the company had decided on him.

Brusilov stood at a console embedded into the deck of the port bridge wing. The console gave him full control of the ship for berthing. The wide windows gave him a clear view of the space between his ship and the *Boris Gakkel*.

'*Leonid Khabarov*, forward tug has line up and ready for orders. Stern tug is the same. Ready to work,' called the tugs as they lay just off the slightly rounded hull.

'Both tugs take up slack and lay back quarter power,' ordered Brusilov.

As the powerful tugs applied braking pressure to the ship, Brusilov spotted the flashing light above the manifold he had to aim for. The light was situated just forward of the midship line of the *Boris Gakkel*. He could see men moving on the deck as they readied the connection.

Slowing to a stop, the tugs held the *Leonid Khabarov* in

position, 20 metres from the *Boris Gakkel*.

'Good morning, Captain, we are ready for you to complete berthing and start pumping,' radioed the controller on the *Boris Gakkel*.

'We'll be all fast in about twenty minutes. We will come up onto the fenders momentarily,' responded Brusilov.

Pushing hard up against the ship's hull, the tugs eased the gas carrier into position.

Berthing complete, Brusilov walked to his seat and glanced down at the two electronic chart displays which flanked his chair. He could see the targets for the two gas platforms 50 nautical miles further into the ice-bound sea. The nearer one, Nevzgody, was in the last stages of drilling well heads to commence pumping gas to the *Boris Gakkel*, the underwater pipes lain and connected. The more distant rig, Ispytaniye, was already pumping gas. In a few months it would disconnect from the well heads and towed to a new location.

A momentary break in the clouds and sleet gave Brusilov a fleeting view of a brilliant finger of excess gas as it burnt off from the Nevzgody platform. He was more than pleased to be on a safe and warm bridge. There was no way he would want to be one of the men working in the hell of the Arctic on either of the platforms.

Damien

After dropping down a series of passageways, Damien arrived at the hatch which led into the mess. He looked left and right along the passageway, assessing any threats, before opening the door and entering.

A wall of heat assaulted him. The noise of laughter and conversation roared in his ears. The room was full of workers either going off shift or getting ready to start. Management staggered the start and end times of different shift gangs around the rig to free up space in the mess room.

Damien did not see a friendly face anywhere in the sea of workers. Over at the servery, he greeted the attendant in flawless Russian, with a Polish accent. The attendant stared at him impassively as he dumped an overflowing ladle of Solyanka into a tray and passed it over. Solyanka's peculiar combination of sweet and sour flavouring mixed with meat and pickled cucumbers was the least pleasant dish the cooks served. Damien was convinced that it had the potential to be more palatable if an actual chef made it.

Damien thanked the attendant and poured himself a cup of coffee, which he already knew was going to taste terrible. He was unable to procure his favoured coffee in the Arctic. No matter how he tried, it never turned up. Damien was sure there was a Russian border guard somewhere in the system enjoying a cup right now.

He picked a table and snaked through the workers toward it. He spotted the toolpusher he had saved during the kickback and nodded a greeting. The toolpusher stared at him, his mouth slightly open as if to reply. The man slammed his mouth shut and turned back to his meal.

Shrugging, Damien took a seat at the least crowded table and greeted the other men who sat there. They ignored him. Damien was the only non-Russian on the rig. He arranged his tray exactly in the centre of the space in front of him. He set his coffee cup 8 centimetres from the top left edge and spaced out the spoon, 3 centimetres from the left centre edge. Smiling lightly, he took up the spoon and wandered it through the Solyanka looking for something which might be worth eating.

Placing the full spoon carefully into his mouth, Damien steeled himself for the taste. He was surprised to find the cook had succeeded in making it slightly less awful this morning.

He sensed a person walking directly towards him. He placed the spoon on the table and looked up.

Steaming towards him was Fedor Davydov, a person Damien had no liking for. Fedor was a bear of a man. A long career in oil and gas had shaped him into a cruel and unpleasant man. Damien regarded him quietly. Fedor was the offshore operations engineer, a position he liked to exercise the power of. Damien took a deep breath as Fedor halted across from him. He planted his feet on the deck and moved his chair back slightly. He investigated Fedor's face impassively. Damien waited for the man to make his play. This was not the first time the two men had had a confrontation. Damien was continually amazed that Fedor never seemed to learn after each failed encounter.

'Get off my rig!' roared Fedor in Russian, slamming his hands down on the table. His eyes filled with hate and anger.

'Good morning, Fedor. What's the problem this time?' asked Damien. His Russian was smooth. He lingered on the last part of the sentence for effect. Fedor missed his tone.

'Ah, the little Australian speaks our language. I hate your stinking Polish accent. I want you to leave. You are not welcome here.'

'Fedor, we have been down this road before. You're choosing your path right now. I am eating. Leave me alone,' countered Damien and watched Fedor's face grow redder. The man huffed aggressively.

'I don't like you.'

'I know, Fedor. But I have no problem with you,' said Damien.

The men sitting at the table quietly picked up their trays

and moved away. The mess room grew quiet. There was a pregnant pause as everyone waited to see what was going to happen between the two men. It was well known that Fedor hated Damien, though there was never an apparent reason for it. Damien was not Russian, but he worked hard and did not mind being ignored, so the other men were indifferent to his presence.

'I am a made man. I work for powerful people. You will respect me,' bellowed Fedor. A long-standing member of the Solntsevskaya Bratva mafia family, Fedor maintained his position to further the criminal endeavours of his Pakhan. Fedor was not a man who had the capacity to think for himself. Damien knew this was a show of force to encourage other workers to join him. The Solntsevskaya Bratva family were pushing their sphere of influence into the Arctic oil and gas industry.

'I know who you are, Fedor. What do you want?' responded Damien. He could see the man was weighing his options. This was the most forceful confrontation Fedor had initiated towards him since he had started working on the rig. Something new was happening here.

'You caused that kickback and injured my friend. He had to save you and haul you off the drill floor!' said Fedor. He turned to indicate the toolpusher, who dropped his head silently to look at his food.

'You're misinformed, Fedor. Anyway. What do you want?' asked Damien.

Fedor's face clenched. He drew himself up to his full height. Swinging his right fist high above his shoulder, Fedor snapped it forwards, aiming for Damien's nose.

Reacting instantly, Damien slid back his chair. He carried himself to the right and easily dodged the clumsy punch.

'Are you sure you want to do this?' asked Damien calmly, eyeing Fedor for a reaction.

Bellowing, Fedor pushed around the table towards Damien, who moved lightly out into a gap between the next row of tables. Men struggled to get out of their way.

'Stand still!'

'You don't want me to, Fedor. You don't want that at all,' replied Damien, a menacing tone dropping into his voice.

Rage clouded Fedor's mind. He rushed at Damien.

Calmly eyeing the approaching man, Damien stepped in towards the freight train of muscle and lifted his fists up beside his face, adopting his fighting stance. Smiling, Damien dropped his head slightly and focused his whole being on defending himself.

Fedor registered the change in Damien's stance. The smile on his face slipped. He knew something was not right, bound by his own momentum, Fedor was committed to his assault.

Before the Russian could react, Damien placed three fast, well-aimed punches into Fedor's nose, spreading it out across his face. Fedor staggered but continued forwards. Damien dropped and swept Fedor's legs out from under him. Fedor went sprawling face first onto the deck. As he tried to twist upright, Damien slammed a boot between Fedor's open legs and crushed down on his testicles. A roar of pain erupted from Fedor, and he squirmed. Damien moved forwards. He dropped a knee into Fedor's back, gripped his hair, lifted his head back and slammed his face into the unforgiving steel deck.

Damien looked up to see if anyone was coming to Fedor's aid. After scanning their faces, he knew Fedor was on his own. He crashed the man's face into the floor again.

Damien heard Fedor groan a few words. His voice a weak tremor. Stepping off, Damien moved to stand beside Fedor's feet and watched the man slowly roll over. Fedor's face was a mass of blood, his nose mashed flat across his face. Confusion and pain filled his face and Fedor eyed Damien carefully.

'Is this ended?' asked Damien calmly.

Fedor mouthed something unintelligible.

'I can kill you, Fedor. You should know that now. I'm not the man you think I am. I will kill you if you try this again. You're warned. I will not tolerate you again. I don't care who you're aligned with, mate. I have met worse men than a simple bully like you. Do you understand? I am being kind to you, Fedor. Remember what happened here the next time you think about taking me on.'

Fedor spat blood and spittle at Damien.

Smiling, Damien balled his left fist and readied it. Fedor looked up, a tremor of fear rippling over his face.

Flashing up his hands in a show of surrender, Fedor relaxed on the deck.

Nodding, Damien moved back to his table. He sat down and continued trying to find the edible parts of his Solyanka.

Immediately, the conversation and laughter in the room resumed. Fedor was not a popular man on the rig. Some of the workers looked at Damien with a new respect; others maintained their indifference.

Fedor groaned and rolled into a sitting position. He reached out for the arm of the nearest man to help him. The worker shrugged him off. Growling angrily, Fedor got painfully to his feet and looked around. There was no support for him in the room. He seethed as he stalked between the tables and headed for the door.

The same impassive-faced attendant who had served Damien arrived with a mop and bucket. Reaching over to Damien's tray he placed a ring of sweet Sushki bread down carefully and nodded a quiet thank you. He started cleaning up Fedor's blood.

Nikolay Voronoi

Port of Murmansk
Kola Bay
North-western Russia

Staring at the wharf far below him, Captain 3rd grade Nikolay Voronoi sipped at his black tea and was happy to be in the warmth of the ship's bridge. Along the wharf, men moved in the cold as a light flurry of snow drifted across the water. The shoremen were finalising the preparations for the ship's departure. The snow was not something he had expected when he awoke in his cabin at 4am. The weather in Murmansk was unpredictable. By 6am, Nikolay stepped onto the bridge, accepted the tea from his steward and began to quietly contemplate his life. Nikolay liked nothing about Murmansk, but it was his home for the time being.

Nikolay wore a sad face. It had been his curse since childhood. He never looked happy even when he was. Always sad to the eyes of strangers and family alike. At an early age he had decided to prove himself through dedication and hard, professional work. That had been the key to his initial success. No women ever seemed to take interest in him. He struggled to establish social friendships when those around him effortlessly excelled at it. Nikolay had always thought of himself as more intelligent, interesting, and skilled than any of his peers. That trajectory ended with the assignment which had landed him on this ship. Not everything in his life had gone to plan.

He crossed to the centre of the bridge, glancing at the chief engineer sitting off to one side in his seat. The man was yawning with boredom. Shaking his head, Nikolay was more pleased to see that the helmsman was standing ready at his station. The rest of the bridge officers clustered around the computer at the rear of the bridge. A soft giggle of laughter came from the group of young men. For a moment Nikolay considered going over and finding out what was going on. He chose to mind his own business. The upcoming sortie was going to be unpleasant enough without Nikolay coming down too hard on the men. They were wary of him already.

'Do I have engines, Chief?' asked Nikolay.

'Engines ready, Captain,' replied the chief engineer, not bothering to look up.

'Thank you. We throw lines in fifteen minutes.'

'Da.'

Nikolay was the captain of a mixed bag of a crew; some were unhappy to have him on board and some were so inexperienced they barely knew their way around a ship.

It was the ship that made him truly unhappy. The *Aysberg*

was one of the oldest of the Ivan Susanin class diesel electric icebreakers, armed with twin 76-millimetre guns mounted forward and two 30-millimetre AK-630 close-in weapons systems just forward of the stern helicopter deck. The ship was an antique. The *Aysberg* belonged to the Border Service of the Federal Security Service of the Russian Federation, a branch of the Federal Security Service of Russia. Anchored 15 years previously, the decommissioned ship rotted while the government looked for a new owner or a suitable mission. Unfortunately for Nikolay, the Border Service found itself short of ships capable of patrolling along the edge of the Arctic ice floes. The *Aysberg* found itself pressed back into service.

Nikolay could not be sure if the *Aysberg* had had anything done to it during a short refit other than a thin coat of paint. Everything appeared rusting and neglected. He had worked his crew hard over the month allocated to bring the ship to readiness for its first sortie into the north. The *Aysberg* was as good as he could get it in the short time allocated. Not one of the crew thought the ship was in any fit state to go anywhere near the ice floes, but that was where they were going.

The crew could deal with the issues of the *Aysberg* but were most dismayed with their captain. They were aware of Nikolay's past service and the reason he had come to be in command of the icebreaker. Two years previously, Nikolay had been a captain first class in the Russian Navy, proudly commanding a Udaloy I class destroyer in the Pacific Fleet. He had been a man on a gentle but positive career trajectory. The curve was dropping below where Nikolay felt he should have been, but upward all the same.

That career trajectory had taken a sharp downward turn during a sortie to support a fleet exercise with submarines. Nikolay had been rash. His inexperience had shown during night manoeuvres. He gave poorly considered instructions to the night watch and retired to bed. Nikolay had placed his ship in the path of the approaching submarines and support ships moving into the exercise area.

Waking early, Nikolay had come to the destroyer's bridge and eyed the thick fog piled against the bridge windows. He had accepted a cup of black tea and went through the status of the ship and their course with the officer of the watch. Querying why the destroyer was outside of its assigned position, Nikolay had reacted angrily when advised that it was he himself who had issued the orders and lain the course. Each subsequent watch had followed his instructions without question. At the radar console, Nikolay studied the contacts. In his rush he failed to adjust the range to enable him to see the approaching fleet.

He ordered a course reversion and all ahead on the engines,

then settled back into his chair. Nikolay was angry at himself and the incompetence of his crew. Unknown to him, Nikolay had ordered a course which placed them into the path of the oncoming fleet.

An hour passed. The fog seemed to grow thicker. Nikolay continued to sip at the tea, lost in his thoughts. The third officer shouted a collision warning. Nikolay had leapt from his seat and issued an emergency course change to port. His destroyer turned quickly into the path of a submarine support ship and sliced away its bow. The renting of the collision and the screaming of alarms and yelling on the bridge rattled Nikolay. He had been unable to think. As his destroyer passed through the open water where the bow of the support ship had been, his damage control officers yelled at him for action. Shaken, Nikolay had fallen back on his training and issued orders to secure the ship and called for all stop on the engines.

Still haunted by the forlorn sound of the support ship's foghorn sounding and the distress calls it was sending as the crew fought to save their ship, Nikolay struggled to sleep.

One poor command decision had cost the lives of 20 sailors, damaged the support ship beyond repair and injured his own destroyer. His career was over. Nikolay's previously good record had reduced his prison sentence to two years. Then he had taken a transfer into the Border Service due to a lack of qualified captains. As penance, he was to patrol the north in the harshest conditions his superiors could find.

Accepting his lot in life, Nikolay found himself on a recommissioned rust bucket, heading for ice floes with a crew who had no faith in his decision making. He could not have hoped for a worse way to continue his seafaring career.

Nikolay never left the ship. He preferred to keep to himself and pay for his mistake by ostracising himself from society.

'Shore party advises they have completed their work. We're free to leave,' stated Nikolay's second officer.

'Very well. Is the ship ready in all respects?' Nikolay responded.

'We are ready, Captain.'

'Thank you. Give me engines, Chief,' instructed Nikolay, continuing to relay his orders for unberthing.

The second officer communicated the captain's instructions to the mooring teams via a handheld radio.

'Slow ahead, Chief.'

The light rumble of the engines thrummed through the decks. Nikolay visualised the thick black smoke issuing from the exhausts.

'Prepare to head for sea,' ordered Nikolay. The *Aysberg* swung away from the wharf and started navigating the river which opened the port to the sea.

Ustrada

Chechen Republic

'We will embarrass the Russians on the world stage. We will damage their economy. My friends. My comrades. We will bring them to their knees. My informants have discovered that the Russians are not protecting their Arctic oil and gas fields with enough ships. Chechnya can exploit these vulnerabilities. We, gentlemen, will be the lever which brings celebrations to the streets of our country. We will do these things. Our mission and fight are a just cause; we will prevail. You are the wolves who will take the fight to the Russian oppressor. Loyal and selfless men of the cause like yourself sacrificed all for the glory of Chechnya. Allahu Abkar!' grandstanded Sheikh Taimieov.

He held the room in his steely gaze and took in the reaction of each man to ensure it conformed. Sheikh used every bit of his 190-centimetre muscled frame to reinforce his will on the men before him.

Sheikh's reputation as a cold, ruthless operator had ensured his rapid rise from a private in the first Chechen civil war in the 1990s to the leader of the second largest Sunni freedom fighter group in Chechnya.

A standard with the proud lines of a Chechen Wolf dominated a banner behind him. Across it in scripted Chechen were the words Itt Stag. Sheikh had named his group after the 10 men he had fought with against the Russians. Only he and his second-in-command, Talhig Chechenskiy, had survived an assault on Russian T-72 tanks in the streets of Grozny. It was in their honoured memory that Sheikh justified his terrorist attacks on Russia. With tales of valour and glory during the assault, Sheikh would whip his soldiers into a fanatical fervour.

Sheikh carried his 55 years easily, though his greying hair hinted that age was catching up to him. A fanatically loyal fighter for Islam and the Sunni Chechen way of life, Sheikh was no less ruthless and domineering in his older years. His anger and hatred fuelled with every act of oppression the Russians committed against his country. Sheikh had remained relatively unknown to Russian intelligence – just another rising soldier in a long list during the wars. This had been his gain. He was now able to strike at the weak crown on the Russian Bear's head. Sheikh would destroy the Arctic oil and gas fields which Russia held so dear and cripple the military supported economy which continued to threaten his country. Sheikh believed his name would be forever linked hand in glove with the coming catastrophe and relished the thought of it.

A rising roar of shouting and whistling greeted Skeikh's words. The small crowd of his closest commanders rose to their feet, applauding his speech. Sheikh gave a satisfied clap to his men. He dropped down in his seat behind the large table around which they all stood. He motioned for his men to sit.

Sitting comfortably in the same dark camouflage uniform the men wore, Sheikh moved his AK-12 assault rifle to one side to give himself some more space. He was the only person permitted to have a weapon in the room. Sheikh never fully trusted even his closest men.

'Are preparations in order?' he enquired, looking at the man who sat opposite him.

Talhig Chechenskiy nodded and fixed his commander with an unwavering look. The two men had fought together for decades. Talhig's face carried scars from a knife fight in his first battle. Shrapnel from a Russian bomb dropped by an Sukhoi SU-25 ground attack aircraft which he had been trying to shoot down had cleaved away any further attempts at being handsome. Talhig's face was an ugly mess of scar tissue. He used it to inspire the men below him. Never with fear, always with pride. He accepted the wounds in the defence of Chechnya. His motherland.

'All is in order, sir. I have pre-positioned the fifty assault troops for the mission just outside of Murmansk. They are under the cover of a religious gathering to promote the virtue of a Sunni life. The Russian infidels are watching them closely. The helicopters are already in position to pick up the assault team. The man that the Solntsevskaya Bratva family kindly gave to us on the Ispytaniye gas platform is in our pocket as much as theirs. Contact's established with him. He is currently on the Nevzgody platform but will transfer over in the coming days. He is at the ready to assist us when we arrive. I see no issues, sir. All is in order,' outlined Talhig.

The mission planning had taken years to formulate and cost the lives of many men to pull together the equipment needed. Skeikh's decision to gently link with the Chechen Mafia and their connections with their Russian counterparts had stood them in good stead. It had been a simple exercise to procure the two Mil Mi-26 and two Mil Mi-17 helicopters they required to transport the assault teams to the gas platforms. Weapons and support equipment easily purchased.

'We have decided not to procure the transport aircraft. It was not favourable to try and secure an airfield for it to load and take off from. The Russians would have easily detected our movements. I have sourced an asset for the sister mission. Though not adequate, it's most likely to be a one-way mission and will suffice,' continued Talhig.

'Did the Bratva present any problems? I have spoken to them at length to arrange this. I assume all is in good order. Was it as it should have been? What were their final demands for the help they extended us?' asked Sheikh.

'It was as simple as an exchange of money and the additional promise of their inclusion in the final victory spoils. We will hold the gas platform long enough to rig it for demolition. The next phase of your plan can then commence. Once achieved we will escape by flying the helicopters to a position well clear. Our friends have arranged for a small freighter to pick us up once we have ditched in the ocean. We will survive in the water long enough for rescue, I'm assured.'

Sheikh nodded. He fully believed that the Russians would roll over after his men had carried out the strike. With their gaze elsewhere, an uprising to oust them could take place. Russia would weather the storm that was just about to break on them, shut out the rest of the world and go back to business. What Sheikh was looking for was the moment Russia looked to its north and relieved the pressure in Chechnya. Then he could begin to agitate and coerce other groups of freedom fighters to rise and push the Russians clear past the borders. Sheikh secretly harboured ideas of a good slice of the land and resources which lay beyond Chechnya's traditional sphere of influence. He wanted it as a spoil of war to sweeten his rise to full power in the country.

'Good, good my friend.' Sheikh grinned with pleasure. 'You will accompany the helicopters, Talhig. You will be my eyes and ears. Bring us glory.'

'Very well, sir,' replied Talhig. He had hoped Sheikh would

allow him to participate in the battle to come. His heart was full of pride.

'Be under no illusion. In the next few days, we will make history. Many of our men will lose their lives to ensure victory, but we will be successful. We will be victorious. One Chechnya for its people to be free of the oppressive yoke of the Russian hand. Freedom!' bellowed Sheikh.

He stood up and raised his AK-12 high above his head. More cheering greeted his ears. 'Do not forget Grozny. Never forget our beloved capital. That is why we fight. Russian blood soaking into our soil. That is what we want. Dismissed. Talhig, a moment please.'

Talhig stood behind his chair and waited patiently for the others to leave. As the last man left, he moved to pull the door closed. It was not unusual for Sheikh and Talhig to speak in private.

'Sir?' started Talhig.

'Take coffee with me, Talhig. We are old comrades,' replied Sheikh in a quiet voice bordering on paternal.

Smiling, Talhig accepted the offered cup and sat back down.

'You did well not to mention the sister plan to the operation, my friend,' said Sheikh pointedly.

'It's the business of ourselves and Dasha the captain. The missile boat is enough to achieve the secondary target. The secret of it is safe with us. Two missions are more likely to succeed than one,' replied Talhig.

'Doubts?'

'Never.'

Sheikh regarded Talhig silently for a moment and looked down into the black surface of his coffee.

'What of the other matter?' he asked. 'Do we have him?'

'I have contacted his handlers. They have given me his mobile telephone number. I have a time to call him – tomorrow. Then I will put the plan and idea to him.'

'What have you planned if he does not accept?'

'To be honest, my old comrade, his presence is not essential any longer. We can easily operate without his specialty. I have substituted other weapons.'

'Very well. Call him regardless. Advise me when you have been in contact and of the outcome.'

'I have faith in you and this plan, Sheikh. What do you think our chances of success are?' queried Talhig. He instantly saw a cloud of annoyance settle over Sheikh's face.

'Victory's assured until the Russians react. We know they will use the hammer and anvil to stamp out our operation. The Russians are predictable if nothing else. They will attempt to storm the gas platform, kill everyone, and quietly dispose of the evidence. That you can be certain of. It's Dasha's mission which will add the blaze of glory to the history books and take the Russians to the international stage for their crimes.'

'A bleak outcome,' responded Talhig, quietly looking down at the table. He suddenly felt his years and that his own death was speeding towards him.

'What you achieve this week is the diversion for the true objective of swinging Russia's gaze to the north and not on what is happening here in Chechnya. You and only you know this to be true among the men who sat at this very table. There's glory on all fronts. I do not want to stab at the side of the Russian Bear. The deaths of a handful of civilians in the streets of Moscow under the guise of terrorism is not enough. I applaud those brave brothers who have taken the fight to the Russian homeland in the past, but it is not my way, Talhig. Not my way in any sense.'

'I understand, Sheikh, but I don't want to waste the lives of the special forces men I have assembled for this mission. Maybe we should have used lesser experienced men if they are expendable.'

'No men other than those you have trained would be able to handle the harsh conditions they are going to experience. Lesser men would break and doubt their commitment to the cause. They might consider laying down their weapons for the Russians to take from their still living hands. No, you have chosen well. The success of your operation hinges on the fanatical devotion of all men involved.'

'I have women in the teams. Asma and her soldiers are coming on the mission,' said Talhig, smiling at Sheikh. He was not the blind chauvinist that Sheikh was. Talhig believed in the way of the warrior. Gender had never come into his view. He had fought alongside women whose depth of hatred and dedication to killing Russians was an experience. It had squeezed his heart tight at the things those women did to captured soldiers. Their screams echoed in his ears all these years later.

'Your love of female soldiers is of no concern to me, Talhig. I am aware of your liberal thoughts and approach to things. Asma's fighters strike fear anywhere they go. Think nothing of my words. You have chosen the best of what we have and trained them for the battles ahead. Your women will do you proud.' Sheikh smirked at Talhig and regarded him.

For a moment he detected weakness in his second-in-command's voice. Uncertainty. This was not the Talhig who had bravely destroyed tanks in the streets of Grozny all those years ago and forged out of the smoke and devastation by his side when the battle ended.

Could his resolve be weakening with age? thought Sheikh.

If that was the case, then he would need to cast around for a new second-in-command. The suicidal nature of the operation into the Arctic might be the perfect opportunity to clean house.

'It's not love. It's the understanding that a man or woman in uniform can kill just as well as each other.' Talhig was defensive. Sheikh's tone had stung him.

'Be that as it may, my dear friend. As soon as you land on Ispytaniye and report that you have secured it for destruction, I will contact the other freedom fighter leaders and push them to react. Only we know about the missile boat and the attack on the gas ships. That's our trump card, Talhig. No-one else knows.'

'It'll take time for the Russians to organise a way to fight us on the platform. That'll give time and an opening for the missile boat to commence its attack and take them by surprise. Russia will bring its full military to bare on Chechnya as soon as the other groups rise,' replied Talhig.

'I am counting on it, Talhig. It will be the world governments and global environmental organisations who will bring the most pressure. While we strike to expand Chechnya's interests and free ourselves, the rest of the world will not care. I will use the power of the disaster to justify the uprising to the others. The troops are ready and supported. This plan will be the crowning glory of our lifetime.'

'Very well. To us,' replied Talhig, raising his cup.

'Allahu Akbar!'

Sheikh laughed and raised his cup to clink against Talhig's.

Private Mahmud Isaev

'I'm going for a cigarette,' said Private Isaev. He stood up and made for the door of the Itt Stag headquarters. Isaev had joined Taimieov's Chechen freedom fighter group five years earlier, training as a radio operator and low-level cryptographer. The post ensured Isaev was close to every move the glorious leader made. Isaev drank in the wisdom and power of the man.

Worn out, Isaev was stiff from hours of preparing and planning. His body felt like he had not slept more than an hour in the last week. The complexity of communicating with a team in the Arctic from mainland Chechnya was a nightmare. Isaev was across the primary communications plan. His job was to ensure the secondary high frequency network was available if the primary means failed. He often wondered who and why people still used HF radios. Isaev hated the static and strange electronic noises which hammered his ears each time he tried to hear the faint voices of other stations. There was an art to using and listening to the staticky HF airwaves. Isaev did not feel that he tuned into it like his sergeant. The man could hear the faintest voice on the radio but appeared completely deaf most other times.

Radio equipment, thick cables and power supplies cluttered

the table he worked at. HF was still a successful tool to communicate with stations in the higher latitudes of the Arctic Circle. Isaev often wondered if the equipment irradiated him with each transmission.

'Okay, don't be long. There'll be plenty of traffic the boss wants us to transmit soon enough,' instructed Warrant Officer Aslan Maskhadov. He did not bother to look up from his work. Maskhadov was a veteran of the Chechen struggle. He was a hard and gruff veteran forged in the brutal cauldron that had been the early 1990s conflicts. Isaev felt they had a personal connection by the occasional kind word of advice Maskhadov directed at him.

'I will,' replied Isaev passively. He picked up a pack of Marlboro cigarettes from the desk and walked to the door. Isaev pulled the heavy door of the communications bunker free of its jam. The bunker was decades old and a reminder of more violent times in the city. He stepped through into the muddy light of another cloudy and depressing day in Chechnya.

He pulled a cigarette free and lit it. Drawing deeply, he walked slowly away from the bunker, looking at seemingly interesting things like all smokers do. He headed down the road towards a low brick fence which encircled a ruined children's playground. Isaev wondered why the community had never rebuilt it. There was no need for it to be like it was. Many years had passed since war had pressed its hand against this part of Chechnya.

Isaev casually slid a mobile telephone from his shirt pocket. He checked to make sure he had signal, unlocked it, and opened WhatsApp. He selected a chat group about Land Rovers and typed, 'Hello'. Immediately, a question mark appeared in the reply box. Isaev nodded slightly to himself and closed WhatsApp. He opened a hidden file container. After copying the contents, Isaev reopened WhatsApp, pasted the file and pressed send. A second later a smiling emoji appeared. Isaev sniffed to himself, kept his head low, looking at the telephone, then lifted his eyes to glance slyly around himself.

He felt he was alone.

Isaev locked the mobile and dropped it back into the shirt pocket. He drew deeply on his cigarette and stared absently around himself. He confirmed he was alone on the street. But someone could be watching him from the grimy windows of the apartment buildings which dominated the area.

Private Mahmud Isaev was Captain Boris Godunov of the Main Directorate of the General Staff of the Armed Forces of the Russian Federation. He was an intelligence agent seconded to the ruthless assassination teams of Unit 29155, embedded in Chechnya 10 years earlier and left to sleep or rot as he felt, until activated. When Sheikh Taimieov first rose to power five years earlier, Godunov found himself activated. His handler steered him into the low-level communications position. His ability to access information and, on occasion, Taimieov himself ensured Godunov maintained his value to Unit 29155. He would assassinate Taimieov if the command came. In the meantime, he sent a continuous stream of intelligence back to Moscow. The GRU followed every move of the Itt Stag group.

He stalked back to the entrance of the bunker, dropped the cigarette butt on the ground and stamped it out. He exhaled a cloud of blue smoke from his lungs, pulled open the door and stepped inside.

Godunov had just sent his handler the complete plans for the Chechen assault on the Shtokman gas field platform. In addition, he had outlined the plan to agitate an uprising among the other freedom fighter groups across Chechnya.

Presidential Cabinet

Senate building
Moscow Kremlin Complex

President Konstantin Petrov looked up from his laptop at the sound of rapid knocking on his office door. He nodded at his secretary, who was sitting across from him, to answer the intrusion. The woman strode towards the double doors. Petrov heard a soft clunk as someone forced the lock.

Both doors flung open.

Petrov sat back in his chair, ready to defend himself.

Where are my security men? he thought.

'What's the meaning of this!' he shouted. He stood up to receive the two men rushing towards him. They pushed his secretary aside as she moved to block their advance. After recovering, she rushed from the room. Petrov assumed she was going for help.

'Mister President. Please excuse both of us but you must hear this immediately. There's an emergency in Chechnya,' exclaimed General Pyotr Zakharov-Chechenets. He was the Chief of General Staff of the Armed Forces of the Russian Federation. Beside him stood a man Petrov had seen by Zakharov-Chechenets' side on several occasions.

'Sit,' ordered Petrov, indicating the two chairs across from him.

Taking his own seat, Petrov looked up as five security men rushed into the room, weapons up and menacing.

'It's okay. A misunderstanding, nothing more. Go back to your posts.'

The guards looked at him uncertainly.

'Go back to your posts!'

He dismissed the men with a wave. Behind the guards his secretary stood uncertainly, peering in at the intrusion.

'Tea,' ordered Petrov. He fixed both men with a steely look.

He would have their heads if this was not a national emergency.

'Mister President, have you met Major Vladimir Sokolov? He is head of Intelligence for Unit Two Nine One Five Five,' said Zakharov-Chechenets introducing the man with him.

'No, but I have seen you, Sokolov. What is the meaning of your intrusion? What's this emergency?'

'Go ahead, Sokolov,' said Zakharov-Chechenet. He leaned back in his chair as if to distance himself from what was coming.

'Thank you, sir. Mister President, do you recall the Chechen freedom fighters of Sheikh Taimieov's Itt Stag movement?' asked Sokolov. He showed no nervousness in front of the most powerful man in Russia.

'I do,' replied Petrov, his interest piqued.

'We have received advice from an asset embedded with the group. Taimieov has planned to execute an attack on Russia,' supplied Sokolov evenly. He could see the President glaring intently at him. The man was taking in the information and processing the political ramifications.

'What are the details? When is the attack?' asked Petrov. His tone was deeply serious. Terrorist actions against Russia were not uncommon, especially those coming out of Chechnya.

'Taimieov is planning to highjack a Plyos Energy platform in the Shtokman gas fields. They will set it for destruction and cause an environmental disaster to attract the attention of the international community. This they hope will swing blame on us and divert your attention. While that attack is underway, Taimieov will gather all Chechen freedom fighter groups. Then commence an offensive against our forces to regain power in the country. This could be the prelude to another civil war.'

'Calm yourself, Sokolov. Pyotr, how are we positioned to deal with an uprising in Chechnya?' asked Petrov as he rolled the implications of Sokolov's plan around in his mind.

'The Chechen uprising hinges on the gas platform attack, which we are expecting to occur in the next five days. I can order an immediate deployment to contain any efforts by the terrorists to activate in Chechnya. We have a large enough force to quell anything. In addition, our asset in their group has supplied their entire order of battle and movements. I see no issues,' replied Zakharov-Chechenet confidently.

'As I expected. Do we know which platform is the target?' asked Petrov.

Signalling for Sokolov to pause, Petrov waved his secretary forward as she entered the room. Quickly, she crossed the space, lay a tray of black tea and sweet biscuits on the table, spun eloquently, and left, pulling the double doors closed behind her.

'It will be the Ispytaniye platform. It's the most northern and is operational. Currently pumping gas to a processing ship approximately fifty nautical miles away,' replied Sokolov.

Nodding absently, Petrov poured tea for each in turn and picked up a biscuit.

'Plyos Energy are responsible for their own security,' he replied.

'They are, sir, but rely heavily on our military to assist. There are arrangements in place for the use of our armed forces if needed,' replied Zakharov-Chechenet.

'Advise the President of Plyos Energy of the threat. Order the Commander of the Northern Sector Command to assist in any way the company may require. This will be an FSB operation. Bring an Alpha unit online and monitor any Chechen movements. The terrorists must enter our borders somewhere before they can get onto the gas fields.'

'The intelligence packet we received indicates that the Chechen terrorist force are already in Russia. They're currently located near Murmansk, sir. Border control flagged an entry a week ago. A small FSB Alpha detachment is monitoring them. With this additional information, we believe these men are the assault force. They are here under the guise of a religious mission.'

'Clever. Keep them contained. How're they getting to the platform?' asked Petrov, taking a small bite of the biscuit.

'That was not in the plans. Our man inside was unable to verify their method,' responded Sokolov.

'No matter. I'll have to assume it will be either by ship

or aircraft. There are no other options. These are my orders. General, bring your forces to readiness to counter the threat of uprising in Chechnya. Pass responsibility for the protection of the gas platform to Plyos Energy with assistance from the FSB as I stated. Make it so,' ordered Petrov. He returned to his laptop. He placed the unfinished biscuit back onto the tray among the others.

Dismissed, Zakharov-Chechenet and Sokolov took their leave and walked quickly from the room.

Petrov looked up and sipped his tea thoughtfully as the doors closed behind the two men. He was considering what the next week would bring.

CHAPTER TWO

Damien

Damien shifted uncomfortably in his bed. Sweat slicked his skin as the nightmare bit into his fragile mind.

'Come on, Stayer, keep going, mate! We're almost out of it. Not long now and we'll be in the tree line. Keep up, mate, please,' yelled Damien above the crash and roar of the battle which hammered around them.

The air seemed to be full of dust, smoke, bullets, and the screams of dying men.

Suddenly tired, Damien fought the urge to drop into the dust and wait for life to end.

Stayer fell to the ground next to him and stared up at him. Further down the slope, Wuz yelled at them to keep running. A bullet whizzed close by Damien's head.

'Get up, Stayer. I'm not leaving you here. Not in this fucking place!' yelled Damien, tugging at the dead weight of Stayer's body.

'It's time, Damo. It's okay, mate. I'm happy for it to finish here. I like this place,' replied Stayer in a strangely distant, dreamlike voice.

Deep mocking laughter drifted through the chaos of battle. Frowning, Damien looked across the polluted air at a figure standing massive and black against the terrain. There was a giant on the battlefield. The figure continued to laugh as it stepped free of a group of boulders. It lifted a massive rifle into a broad shoulder.

An ear-splitting boom filled Damien's ears. He looked down at Stayer. A massive projectile crash into his friend's chest plate. Stayer exploded into a massive eruption of blood and flesh.

His throat working noiselessly, Damien turned to look at Wuz, who was calmly waving to him in the distance.

Harsh laughter echoed through the valley.

Damien felt himself rooted to the spot. Stayer's blood dripped down over the brim of his ball cap. His face was thick with its sticky wetness. Damien opened his mouth and quickly slammed it shut.

A scream was building there.

Damien let out a wheezing sound of horror instead, spun on his heels and threw away his rifle. He careered down the slope, trying to get away from the battlefield. Damien stripped away his equipment and dropped it in his wake. Focused only on escape.

Finally, the scream of terror tore free as Damien ran as fast as he could. Laughter followed him. The report of the massive rifle hammered again through the air. Damien looked up to see a projectile heading towards him.

Time froze as the giant projectile hovered a centimetre from his nose. Damien slammed his eyes shut.

Damien snapped his eyes open and surged upright in his bed. He looked wildly around the dark space of his cabin, trying to orientate himself, fighting back the urge to vomit.

'Fucking nightmares. I've fucking had enough,' said Damien quietly into the darkness.

He reached over for the bottle of water on the nightstand beside the bed, rolled off the lid and took a long pull of the cool liquid. It tasted lightly of oil and salt. The desalination plant did not work well when the rig was ice bound.

Lying back down, Damien allowed his body to settle.

For decades Damien had endured the nightmares of combat and dying men. The dreams he had now, since his last mission in Afghanistan, were crippling. He had spent a year self-medicating after recovering from injury. The deep pain and hurt of losing his friends bit into his mind and hammered against his skull each day.

Being the sole survivor of the final Taipan 16 mission had done nothing but drag out the pain he had suppressed. Damien felt like he was losing his mind as he scrabbled in the dirt, bleeding out as Simon Brown dragged him to a waiting helicopter, then whisked him back to Tarin Kowt and safety.

Brief snippets of his Taipan handler, Don Murphy, looking down at him, flashed in and out of his mind as doctors worked to save his life. Damien had not seen Don again. In fact, he had not received any contact from the man he had spent years working with. The Taipan Organisation had cut Damien clean away like a crippled, candling parachute. Damien had been stabilised in Tarin Kowt, then transported to Australia. He was to spend his recovery in a secluded private hospital in the farmlands west of Sydney.

Damien had not heard of the facility before. Its discreet driveway and entrance belied the patients inside. Damien, isolated for the first six months, entered the last stages of recovery. He discovered he was not the only patient. All seemed to have mental illnesses of various diagnosis. He was the only one to have physical injuries as far as he could tell.

A hard-faced psychologist tried to lead Damien down a path to enlightenment. Damien knew he was wasting his time. There was nothing wrong with him. Everyone else was weak and disturbed. He needed to get back on his feet and he would be good to go. The psychologist thought differently. It was not up to him. Damien considered himself rock solid. Soon it had been time to leave.

Just under 12 months following his rescue, a car had pulled up at the hospital's entrance and Damien stepped inside. Simon Brown had been in the driver's seat and gave him a quiet nod but did not engage him in conversation. Simon handed him a small backpack. Inside Damien found 10,000 Australian dollars, a Heckler and Koch USP Compact 9-millimetre pistol and a set of keys. By the look they belonged to a car and a house. A parting gift from the Taipan Organisation. At least they had let him live.

Simon had not spoken a word during the three hours it took to arrive at the front door of a small cottage in the expensive suburb of Sydney's Double Bay. As Damien looked through the driver's window, Simon had turned quickly, given him a smile and thumbs-up. Damien climbed clear of the car. Immediately, Simon gunned the engine and disappeared down the road and disappeared.

Damien stood in front of the cottage, confusion tugging at his mind. This was not his house. He had an apartment on the Lower North Shore. He had never thought about living in Double Bay. The icing on the cake from the Taipan Organisation.

Damien was a chaotic and unkempt mess as he endeavoured to remember as little as possible for the next year of his life. Drugs and alcohol drove his spiral. Damien was unsatisfied by the numbing buzz two bottles of Captain Morgan Gold a day afforded to his mind. He searched for effective ways to kill off the nightmare.

Cocaine was the fuel he discovered.

Damien had cut off contact with his son, Ryan, and refused to visit Stayer's wife and children. Damien visualised Stayer's grave site but could never bring himself to make the short journey to see it. He distanced himself from Wuz's family. Damien learned from a news report they were all killed in a car accident. He had waited for it to affect him, but the feelings were as distant as Afghanistan. To compensate for his out-of-control life, Damien maintained the cottage to the level his OCD demanded. Damien was in a waking cocaine nightmare, with no visible light at the end of the tunnel.

Tripping over a rare moment of clarity, Damien came to the realisation he needed to stop, reset, and regain himself. His strong, unbending mind struggled to the surface. Damien decided to take the lifeline thrown to him by his American acquaintance. It was time to disappear from his life. He locked the cottage's door, leaving behind his dependence on the drugs and alcohol.

As soon as Damien stepped foot in Russia, he'd taken the option to move from rig to rig and not return home after each swing of duty. Damien transferred like cargo between the Ispytaniye and Nevzgody gas platforms each month. It suited him perfectly. Shortly, he would be heading over to the Ispytaniye platform. Sighing, Damien sat up and swung his legs clear of the bed. His feet lightly touched the cold floor.

He showered to wash away the lingering effects of the nightmare.

After towelling down, Damien slipped on faded overalls, pulled on his boots, and clipped a Gerber Gator drop point folding knife into his pants pocket. He glanced at his watch. The scratched glass and battered case looked a lot like he felt.

7am.

Grimacing, Damien realised he didn't have time to eat. He grabbed his handheld radio and clipped it to his belt.

Damien made his way up the flights of stairs and along the corridors which would lead him to the doghouse. As he dressed in his dirty heavy weather gear, Damien could hear a growing wind hammering against the walls outside. He noted a drop in the temperature.

Storm coming, he thought as he opened the hatch to the drill floor.

Nikolay

Nikolay climbed the last stair to the bridge and opened the door to let himself into the darkened and quiet space. It smelled of stale tobacco and coffee. His first officer turned to see who had arrived and nodded briefly before returning to his duties. Nikolay acknowledged the greeting. He noted that the man had turned away before he could have seen the response. Sighing, Nikolay reminded himself that this was his lot in life. He had to make what he could of it. He walked across to the left hand Transas Electronic Chart Display, or ECDIS. He checked their position and the laid course. He saw that the first officer had made a minor correction to bring them closer to an oil platform at the southern end of the Shtokman gas field. Their assigned patrol area was a further 200 nautical miles to the north-west of the platform. The course variation would add a few hours to their passage.

Out the bridge windows the dim morning light shone on the Arctic Ocean. Soon a permanent darkness would descend over the water, and it would not be this light again for many months.

Twenty-four hours into their passage, Nikolay had guided the *Aysberg* safely through the congested waters surrounding the entrance to Murmansk. The ship doggedly pushed through the military traffic and the merchant fleet moving goods and product between Russia and the world's ports. They had finally made it into the upper latitudes. Nikolay was happy to be in the open ocean, even if it was the Arctic. Already the ship's stabilisers were struggling to maintain some form of comfort as

5-metre waves rose to smash into the tired, reinforced hull of the *Aysberg*.

The port engine had broken down twice since leaving Murmansk. The first time the cooling system had failed; the second, a valve stem sheared. The engine had emitted a heart stopping whooshing sound and sprayed diesel throughout the engine room before shutting down. Each repair had taken a few hours. The fact remained that they needed both engines running perfectly if they were to take on the ice floes in their patrol area.

'Why have you changed the course?' Nikolay asked his first officer as he slowly walked towards the man. The memory of his fatal error years ago came to the front of his mind.

'Headquarters asked us to do a run past the rig. To show the flag they said. It was a valid order. I saw no issue with it, Captain,' responded the man quickly. He had no respect for the disgrace who stood beside him and called himself a captain. The command of the *Aysberg* should be his.

'Why did you not inform me?'

'You were sleeping, Captain. Did you wish me to disturb you?' The first officer smirked slightly.

'That's the normal process for a course correction. Especially one ordered by headquarters. So, yes, you should have woken me,' said Nikolay quietly. Their conversation was only for their ears. The two lookouts turned slightly but kept their posts on either bridge wing.

'I'll keep it in mind for next time, Captain.'

'Please do.'

He strode back to the centre of the bridge, seething inside but maintaining a calm exterior. Nikolay knew he should dress down the first officer and report the violation of written procedures. He breathed deeply for a moment, considering, then realised that his reminder about procedure would have to suffice. The first officer was looking for a confrontation with and Nikolay had removed it. The Arctic was a large place. He was under no illusion that the odd unpopular captain had slipped below the surface over the years.

In the next 24 hours they would arrive at the edge of the main floe. The two most northern gas platforms, Nevzgody and Ispytaniye, were a further 10 nautical miles into the ice pack. The Plyos Energy company operated them. Ice bound for much of the year, both platforms were the first of their kind.

Life must be hell for the men working on them, thought Nikolay.

He considered the warm and comfortable bridge a perfect location for him. His world could have been much worse. At least he was still at sea and in command.

A shrill alarm sounded from the console in front of him. An ancient red light started blinking.

'Port engine over speed, Captain,' called the engineer on duty. He reached past Nikolay to silence the alarm.

'Yes, I can see that, thank you.'

Nikolay leaned forwards and plucked a dull grey telephone from its cradle.

'Chief, what's the problem with the port engine this time?' he enquired as soon as the disinterested man answered.

'I'm still investigating, but I think the governor has failed, Captain. I have shut the engine down. We will need to continue only on the starboard engine until I can affect the repair.'

'Very well, Chief. Thank you.' Nikolay turned to face the first officer. 'Call me when we are on both engines. Or, if the repairs will take longer than three hours.'

'Yes, Captain.'

'You do understand my order?' said Nikolay, pushing the point.

'Yes, Captain,' replied the first officer sullenly.

'Thank you. Please do not make any more course alterations without first informing me,' said Nikolay. Calm but firm. He saw the two lookouts shifting uncomfortably on their feet. Both men had picked up his tone.

'I will, Captain.'

'Good watch,' finished Nikolay and turned to leave the bridge. He paused for a moment to look through the windows at the mounting seas. The *Aysberg* was going to be a handful in the coming days and the month-long patrol ahead of them. Taking a deep, almost happy breath, Nikolay opened the door and headed down the stairs. He was still pleased to be in command. Even if it was on a temperamental tub like the *Aysberg*. As he left the bridge, he realised he had forgotten to enquire for more details about the course change. No matter, an order was an order.

Kirovsk

175 kilometres south of Murmansk

Major Georgiy Urvantsev took in the bleak town butted up against the Khibiny Mountains. Kirovsk was a town he had never intended on visiting, let alone spending a week in its confines. Georgiy was a member of the Federal Security Service of the Russian Federation. He commanded a Directorate 'A' of the FSB Special Purpose Centre or Alpha detachment. He turned his gaze from the town, letting his eyes drift across the spur of the mountain range then down at the compound the Chechen religious men were occupying.

The air smelt clean, and its dryness tugged the moisture from his sinuses.

Georgiy was in command of a small detachment of 20 men,

split off from the main battalion to work security for an event he found curious. Fifty Chechens entered the country to speak and display the virtues of living a Sunni Islamic life in Russia. Georgiy was intrigued as to why the Chechens had chosen this little town far from Murmansk as their base. With a population not much more than 28,000, it did not provide rich ground on which to sow the seeds of Islam in Russia. There was a very small local Islamic community, who seemed to have separated themselves from the Chechens. It must have been a political minefield to allow this event to take place. The bad blood between the two countries ran deep. Georgiy had no love of Chechnya. He had served in the fourth offensive of the Chechen civil war and remembered the brutality of both sides.

In the week they had watched the Chechens, the detachment had noted that the Sunnis were of fighting age, engrossed in their religion and exercised constantly. Georgiy was not sure what constituted a religious spectacle. The Chechens had ventured out of their rented compound twice since arriving. The demonstrations of faith he had discreetly watched were weak and obviously staged for anyone who was observing. With each passing day Georgiy grew more suspicious about what was happening in the compound.

Georgiy was authorised to use any surveillance assets he required for the mission. He was wary of relying too heavily on electronics. He had chosen to order the 24/7 top cover of a single armed Kronstadt Orion RPV. Before the arrival of the Chechens, Georgiy had ordered the compound fitted out with microphones and concealed cameras. Still, all that the surveillance had revealed was that the men prayed up to seven times a day and discussed the aspects of Islam which empowered them. The eerie undulating tones of call to prayer echoed against the mountains each day. He saw no signs of military equipment. There seemed to be nothing which belied that the men were in Russia to do anything other than to celebrate Islam. Georgiy was not surprised that they ate, shat, and slept the same as any man. Georgiy could not shake the feeling that the Chechens were waiting for something to happen.

He stepped back into his UAZ Patriot SUV.

Chechen terrorist acts had threatened Russia's security for decades. With such a strong force of men these Chechens could strike a significant blow against Mother Russia. The compound they had chosen was on the outskirts of the town. It let out onto an open, unused stretch of cleared land. The Chechens exercised in the open section next to the compound. If nothing else, they were physically fit.

'Back to base,' he instructed pulling the four-wheel drive's door closed.

The driver had been enjoying the warmth of the cab while his commander conducted his daily observation of the town and compound. The major was always looking for that something extra which would tell him what might be happening. Electronic surveillance could not tell the whole story. In the back of his mind, the driver was also looking forward to a coffee and snack. His stomach growled. His attention needed caffeine to refocus it.

Georgiy struggled to keep his men on task and interested. No action and what was rapidly becoming a babysitting assignment caused frustration. The coming winter was not far away – September was unusually cold this year. Georgiy had always been a supporter of physical eyes on a target, but the frigid conditions at this time of year meant the electronic means in the compound were very popular with his men.

The driver parked across the road from the tall clock tower. He lined the Patriot up with the other vehicles of the detachment and shut it down. As one, the men opened their doors. With practised ease they exited the vehicle and were inside the building before they could present a target. Before the Chechens had arrived, the FSB had commandeered the lime-green five-storey building across from the clock tower as its base of operations.

'Anything to note?' asked Georgiy as he walked into what had originally been the dining room. It was now their operations centre. Five of his men worked the portable consoles which filled the space and controlled the surveillance assets. Behind the operators stood Georgiy's second-in-command, Lieutenant Yakov Davydov.

'One thing. Minor, but when an operation is this boring, you notice things,' stated Yakov. He stood a little taller than Georgiy, his hair was short, and his thick muscles strained to escape his uniform. Compared to Georgiy's medium athletic frame, Yakov was a body builder. Yakov was new to the FSB and Alpha teams and was glad to be cutting his teeth on a simple surveillance operation. He had been pleased to learn that Georgiy was to be his commander. Georgiy's reputation as an effective and efficient operator was legendary. Yakov watched and learned everything he could.

'Dazzle me, Yakov. Surely, something has happened?' responded Georgiy brightly. He liked Yakov and saw a significant future for the man. Pulling off his gloves, Georgiy accepted a mug of tea from a passing soldier. He nodded his thanks.

'Ten minutes ago, a group of three men left the compound and crossed to the open ground.'

'Hardly new,' replied Georgiy, looking carefully at Yakov. He was trying to ascertain if his understudy was inventing action to test himself.

'We've seen this before, yes, but normally at least twenty men go in turns to exercise. These men did not exercise. They walked a very precise pattern across the ground, stopping frequently, talking, and pointing.'

'Interesting. They know we're watching.'

'They do. We have not tried to hide our presence particularly. I only note this because it's different. It could mean the men just wanted privacy to talk or it could mean a change in their behaviour. I am not sure yet. They have returned inside and no-one else has come out.'

'Good work, Yakov. Keep a weather eye on it. Report to me if there is anything else of note.'

'Da,' responded Yakov beaming.

'When does their purported religious leader arrive from Grozny?' asked Georgiy, changing the subject.

The FSB intelligence apparatus via the GRU had noted a request from Chechnya for a cleric leader to arrive in the next 24 hours. Once in Kirovsk, the cleric would commence the program in earnest to convince the local people that the Sunni way was the future. Georgiy doubted the inhabitants of the little town would listen.

'He arrives in Murmansk tonight. A Chechen vehicle will collect him tomorrow morning for the drive here. We have a team at the airport to tail him to his hotel, keep watch and then follow to Kirovsk. We have a name, but not a face.' Yakov read off a ruggedised tablet in his hand. 'There's intel that the cleric will leave Grozny under the guise of a businessman employed by a Chechen textile company. There's no supporting information,' said Yakov, a slightly bemused look on his chiselled face.

'We shall see what this brings,' replied Georgiy.

He turned and headed towards the office he had commandeered. Georgiy wanted to discuss his feeling that something was building with his superior and mentor. He took the stairs to give his cold body some exercise, rather than take the elevator. The machine looked like there had been a long time between servicings. As he reached the door to his makeshift office Georgiy's mobile telephone started ringing.

He didn't recognise the number.

'Da?' he answered cautiously. Georgiy hoped it was not one of the many scam calls which seemed to dominate the world these days. Even FSB-issued mobile telephones had numbers that scammers could access in their bid to fleece people of their money and time.

'Major Urvantsev?' came the reply.

'Da.'

'I am Major Vladimir Sokolov. Head of Intelligence for Unit Two Nine One Five Five. We have not met,' replied Sokolov. A flat tone cut his words.

'Nyet, we have not. It wouldn't be common that our paths would cross, Sokolov,' replied Georgiy gravely. A chill of worry settled down his spine. Unit 29155 were well known in operator circles. The unit of government-sponsored assassins and their shadowy reputation for violence was a poorly maintained state secret.

'As you say. There's a change in your mission, Urvantsev.'

'I do not take my orders from you. I'm sorry, Sokolov,' responded Georgiy, annoyed at the inter-service push and shove. He had always tried to maintain his distance from it.

'You will receive an authorisation shortly from your headquarters. In the meantime, I have information for you. Are you alone?' Sokolov recognised the other man's veiled and cautious tone. His unit's reputation preceded him.

'Go ahead, I'm alone.'

'Go secure.'

'Stand by,' replied Georgiy. He pulled the telephone away from his ear and opened an application to secure their call. 'Line is secure.'

'The Chechen religious delegation you are babysitting aren't who they seem. We have received credible intelligence that they are going to undertake a terrorist act to the north. Imminently,' said Sokolov. He stressed the last word.

'What are the new orders?' requested Georgiy. He had known something was not right about the Chechens.

'They're cut and forwarded. It includes a full briefing. As you know, the Chechen cleric leader is due to arrive. This man is in fact the commander of the assault team. We don't know how they will be leaving their current location to launch the attack. Be vigilant. I will not need to call you again.'

'Da,' replied Georgiy and hung up the call.

Georgiy paused briefly, huffed to himself, then walked slowly out into the hallway. He called for Yakov to assemble the men as he made his way down the stairs.

Talhig

Grozny Airport

Talhig stepped around the border force desk, fishing his mobile telephone from his trousers. He had dressed in a dark business suit and overcoat. He carried a battered brown leather satchel to complete the disguise. Everything about his appearance matched his cover of a Chechen businessman flying to Murmansk to negotiate a textile contract. Talhig even played a tired and worn expression across his face. Just another of the many men trying to make a living across the political and cultural minefield between the two countries.

It was Talhig who remained oblivious to his compromise. The GRU and FSB knew his identity and destination. They were tracking his every move.

Talhig casually looked around. He found a deserted spot near the windows which overlooked the main runway. A mix of different sized aircraft were taking off and landing as people went about their travel. Military helicopters flitted along the perimeter fence. The machines of oppression were making for the heliport opposite Talhig. He unlocked the telephone. Satisfied he had enough privacy, he tapped in a telephone number and put the handset to his ear and waited.

The call answered on the second ring.

'Yes?' Came the reply, heavy with a deep French accent. Talhig could hear a slight slur in the man's voice. As if his mouth were misshapen and warped. Talhig called up a mental picture to visualise the man. The image was as ugly as his own face. Maybe this man had experienced life much as he had.

'My name is Talhig. You're expecting a call from me?' he asked in equally accented English.

'Yes.'

'Do you have time to speak?' Talhig asked, buying time. The background noise on the man's end was confusing. Talhig was sure he could hear the high buzz of insects and the distant call of birds.

'I will be busy in five seconds. You will need to hold until then,' instructed the voice.

'Very well. I'll hold.'

'Thank you. You will hear a gun shot,' the man advised. Talhig heard the telephone placed carefully onto the ground.

Talhig waited and looked at his watch. Exactly on the fifth second, he heard the distinct sound of a supressed rifle firing a single shot. Just as the man had stated.

'Okay. What is it you would like to talk to me about?'

'I'm told you are a skilled specialist in many tasks. One I'm particularly interested in.'

'I can guess which one. It's been much in demand over recent years. I think my reputation is growing. As does my fee. What's the target?'

'A Russian asset in the Arctic. We require a man such as yourself to assist with the outcome.'

Talhig was deliberately cagey. He had no intention of discussing the upcoming operation. Except for the crew on the missile boat, none of the freedom fighters had a complete picture of what was to unfold in the next few days. There were Russian ears in the airport surrounding him.

That he was sure of.

'Maybe you misunderstand my skills. I'm not a cold weather specialist. My talents may not fit your purpose. A basic question, Talhig. Do you represent a terrorist or private organisation?' asked the man. Talhig could hear him disassembling a rifle.

'Neither.'

'Have my employers suggested I can help?'

'They only suggested a conversation. No guarantee of services.'

'Not that they can in any case. But I must decline this one job, Talhig. I can see many issues with the environment. The main issue is my own safety. The Arctic is unkind and unforgiving. The weight of the Russian military will come against you. That, my friend, is not survivable. Are you aware of this?'

'I am. I've dedicated people. We will damage Russia with a disaster they cannot hope to recover their reputation from internationally,' preached Talhig. His voice rose slightly in volume and pitch as the fever of commitment came to the fore. Catching himself, he stopped talking abruptly and looked around. The nearest person was 20 metres away and lost in their own mobile telephone.

'Another reason for me to pass. The Bear has never much cared for the lives of those who oppose them. I am sorry you have wasted your time, Talhig. I wish you the best with your operation. I will hopefully read about you in the news. That way I'll know you have succeeded.'

'I've a supplementary plan in case you refused the job. I would have been happy to pay whatever price you asked. Does that change your mind?'

'No, Talhig, it does not. I'm not a man short of money or in need to make more. I enjoy my work. I also enjoy living. I see death for a specialist who accepts your offer. I am available for other work in the future if you live. You have my number.'

'I will not call you again.'

'Good luck. You will need it, my friend.'

The line went dead in Talhig's ear. He slipped the telephone back into his trouser pocket. Sighing, Talhig stared at the Sukhoi Superjet 100 which would take him to St Petersburg. From there a connecting flight to arrive in Murmansk.

He had flown with Azimuth Airlines when it had been Rossiya Airlines. Not fussed on their level of service, Talhig had few choices. Azimuth were not as interested as Aeroflot in the backgrounds of the passengers who boarded or where their plans took them.

Hearing a call to board announced over the loudspeaker above his head, Talhig hefted his almost empty satchel. He checked his ticket. Like any tired and harassed businessman, he shuffled towards the gate. Keeping his eyes low, he showed his ticket to the steward who ushered him down the air bridge. At the aircraft door, another steward directed him to his seat at the rear. Talhig waved away the offer of headphones and made his way down the aisle. He missed the furtive look the steward gave him.

Talhig stashed his satchel under the seat in front of him and settled into the window seat. He looked around briefly then closed his eyes. As soon as he stepped off the plane in Murmansk, he would take on the persona of a cleric. The head of a group of worthy and dedicated men in the town of Kirovsk, two hours' drive to the south. An Alpha team watched over the compound. It did not matter to Talhig. The assembled team had no idea of their mission, only the details of their cover story. The arranged helicopters would bring in the mission equipment and clothing.

Talhig felt the aircraft push back and heard the stewards laboriously working through the safety briefing. Talhig knew security was tight at the compound. Details of the mission remained secure from the prying ears and eyes of Russian intelligence.

Before the Superjet had reached the main runway, Talhig was asleep. He would have precious few hours of rest in the coming days.

Talhig felt he had nothing to fear.

Mys-Chyorny

250 kilometres East of Murmansk

Dasha Amayouv gazed out into the sleet which hammered against the windows of the UAZ-450 four-wheel drive van. He hoped the day was going to get better. The drive from the outskirts of Murmansk had started five days earlier. It had been a test of the strength of man and machine for both to have arrived at Mys-Chyorny safely.

Crammed into the interior behind him were his crew. They were the bare minimum needed to operate the ship he could faintly see riding on anchor 100 metres offshore. All experienced and previous sailors of the Russian Navy each man could be relied on not to waver in his duties. Dedicated to Sheikh Taimieov's cause. His crew formed the linchpin of the coming operation. Having made their peace and embraced Allah in their final days, the men were ready to commit the ultimate sacrifice. If it came to that.

Mys-Chyorny lived up to its name of 'black cape'. Perched on a freezing peninsula, it was a harsh and remote place with fewer than 10 people living in the area. Dasha found it perfectly located to take charge of the vessel, quickly shake down any issues and head for sea. Time was short and he felt the pressure of everything needing to be in good order. There was no time for repairs or forgetting anything.

Amid the gloom of the low coastline near the end of the muddy road in front of them, a bright torch turned on and circled in the air.

'Drive to him,' he instructed the driver, his missile engineer, Mikhail Reznov. He was the only member of the crew competent enough to negotiate the rough terrain they had had to endure to make it to the jump off point.

Without answering, Mikhail gunned the engine and negotiated the last 200 metres, aiming for the torchlight in the gloom. Soon the weak beams of the van's headlights impaled the shapes of two men in heavy weather gear, their faces cowled against the sleet. The man with the torch lowered it and gestured for the sailors to get out.

'Stay here. I'll go,' instructed Dasha. He pushed open the passenger door and plunged into the weather. He walked over to the men and stood, waiting for them to speak. When neither did, he shook his head in frustration. Dasha was tired and sore from his journey.

'I'm Captain Dasha Amayouv. You're expecting me and my crew. Is that our boat?' Dasha indicated the vessel. As the sleet cleared for a moment, he frowned and squinted to better see the vessel. 'Is that an Osa?'

'Da. It is an Osa Two,' replied the man holding the torch. His voice sounded like a wolf growling. He glared grimly at Dasha.

'It's an antique!' replied Dasha, not believing his eyes.

The last Osa missile cutter rolled out of the Vostochnaya Verf shipyard in the early 1970s. At 38 metres long, the cutter was not the vessel Dasha wanted to take into the Arctic at any time of the year. Two large missile containers sandwiched the small, armoured bridge which jutted like a chin out from between them. Another two crowded the rear deck. The cutter looked top heavy and unstable as it rocked and pitched on its anchor.

'It suits the purpose you need it for. The Osa's paid for.'

'Is it armed, fuelled and provisioned?' enquired Dasha. He knew he had no choice but to accept the cutter.

'We have procured at great expense four Termit anti-ship missiles. They are very hard to find these days. We have a friend who deals in these things. The forward thirty-millimetre cannons each have two thousand shells. The stern cannon is not operational. You're fully fuelled and have provisions for five days. I received orders not to load food or water for any longer than that.'

'Five days will be sufficient. Thank you. Can you ferry myself and my men to the cutter?'

'Da.'

'Have the engines been serviced?' asked Dasha.

'The run here was good enough. They work very well considering their age and the condition the ship arrived in. I have had a team of men readying it for your operation. The engines will work long enough,' answered the man simply. He turned to walk towards a small launch pulled up onto the shore.

Dasha turned to the van and indicated for his men to join him. Immediately, the doors flew open and the sailors piled out with their bags.

'We'll take care of the van. There are rifles on board for each man also. AKs. Is this acceptable? They're cheap.'

'Da, they'll be fine. We know how to use them.'

'I expect you do. You're Chechen?'

The man almost spat out the word.

'Is that going to be a problem?' asked Dasha, slowing his stride and steeling himself for a fight.

'Money exchanged hands. I assure your safety, Dasha Amayouv. But I don't have to like you.'

'The feeling is mutual. Shall we go?'

Dasha's men arrived and crowded around them.

'Get in the launch,' replied the Russian in a low growl.

Ten minutes later the launch, driven by the second Russian, bumped up against the hull of the Osa II missile cutter. A narrow rope boarding ladder hung down the port side. Waving them to get off, the first Russian grunted as he threw the sailors' bags onto the wet deck.

'Is the bridge open?' asked Dasha, sleet stinging his face. He had no intention of being unable to access the bridge. He was quite sure that as soon as his crew all stepped on board the launch would disappear, never to return.

'All is open and ready for you. Get off. We can spare no more time here. Our window has closed. We must leave. Get off. Hurry,' urged the Russian, waving his arms in the air.

'Everyone off and to the bridge, quickly now. We must get underway and head for the target area,' urged Dasha as he took the first rung of the ladder and climbed on board his new command. It was a far cry from the Kirov Battlecruiser, *Pyotr Velikiy*, which he had served on as a fresh-faced 18-year-old.

Dasha strode around the deck to the hatch set into the starboard side of the casement which let into the small bridge. He heard the Russians gun the launch's engines. In seconds the launch disappeared into the sleet and gloom, heading east.

Stepping into the narrow companionway, Dasha was pleased to see that the lights were on. He could hear the comforting hum of the generator running below decks. Entering the bridge validated his initial fears. This Osa was an antique. The air smelt of diesel fuel and damp waterlogged panelling. Pale light blue paint covered everything. The surface of each piece of equipment was flaking. Screens scratched or damaged fitted into the consoles. Reassuringly, despite their condition each screen glowed softly.

The crew came in behind him and looked around with the same distaste.

'Listen up. This cutter could be our final home on this earth if Allah is to will it. We're entrusted with a glorious mission. One which'll help to bring the Russian Bear to its knees. Our comrades in arms will leave for their mission tomorrow. I will need all power and speed for the duration of the transit. Fuel is not a concern. We must be on time. There'll be no excuse for not being in position for mission commencement.' Dasha investigated the eager faces around him for any trace of concern. 'Our comrades are counting on us to be successful. We must do our part.'

'Do we have missiles and guns?' asked Mikhail, glancing around the bridge.

Dasha noticed for the first time how wet and tired the men looked. He would need to find time for them to rest on the passage north. The cutter was going to be uncomfortable for everyone. Especially if they wanted to sleep, eat, or perform any duty other than cling to their seats or beds.

'Four Termit anti-ship missiles in the containers. The cannons have two thousand rounds each. More than enough for the assigned mission. We go to glory, men. We have been comrades for many years. We will bring pride and joy to Chechnya. We will not fail.'

A roar of cheers greeted his ears. Dasha felt a surge of pride in the men he considered his friends. They were the only team entrusted with the complete plans of the mission. Sheikh

Taimieov's trust in them was absolute. Dasha had no intention of breaching it.

'I want us to be underway in one hour. No delays. Any problems that we can deal with on the way, we will. Only bother me with those things which we cannot sort out before departure. To your positions, men. We leave as soon as we are able,' ordered Dasha, turning to survey his bridge.

As the sailors filed out, Dasha made his way to the centre of the cramped space and looked out of the armoured windows. The cloud base had dropped low to the water and sleet pounded the glass. He could see it bouncing off the deck plates. Noticing that the radar display was on but not energised, Dasha knew he would have to chance the passage without operating it. If it became too dangerous, he would activate it. The fewer ships who could detect their movements the better. A small modern automatic identification system receiver was screwed to the console beside the radar display. The screen showed distant targets. It was the AIS that Dasha would use to monitor which ships were around them.

Dasha flicked on the VHF radios and adjusted the volume. Silence issued from the speakers. Frowning, he considered where they were and figured that there were no other vessels around them transmitting. He would need to keep a close eye on the radios to ensure they were operational.

Settling into the captain's chair, Dasha continued to study the interior of the Osa. He felt a further surge of pride. This was his command. His last, but his command. This unnamed cutter was now his responsibility. He was undertaking a mission of such importance that it formed 50 per cent of the total plan. Dasha and his 10 men were the anvil on which Sheikh Taimieov would hammer at the Russians. In two days, history would change.

Forty-five minutes later, the crew reported the cutter ready to go to sea. Dasha ordered the engines engaged and the fastest possible speed maintained for the duration of the passage.

The Osa surged through the rough coastal water. The hull tried to cut a clean wedge through the waves. Already the small ship was beginning to pitch and roll in the 3-metre swells. Dasha knew the sea state was going to get worse. Pushing the conditions and danger to the back of his mind, he focused on navigating the course he had planned over the last six months. In just 300 nautical miles, he and the crew would see action in a fight that would form stories told to the children of Chechnya for years to come: the time 10 courageous sailors fought against the Russian oppressor and smashed them into the sea.

'Allahu Akbar,' said Dasha quietly and felt the conviction of his faith.

Plyos Energy Headquarters

Arkhangelsk

An aged 40-foot shipping container sat in a sectioned-off part of the dirty carpark at the rear of the Plyos Energy company headquarters. The exterior bore the damage of many Russian winters, its paint flaking and streaked with rust. A thick umbilical cord stretched out from the main building and disappeared into a large grommet embedded into the front of the container. Near it, an entry door opened through the original swinging doors. Parked next to the container was a near new pale-yellow Lada Niva four-wheel drive. A worn path snaked through the muddy slush from the car to the door. The only indication the container was in use.

Alexi Chirikov leaned back in his chair and adjusted the lightweight headset he wore. He studied the 10 large screens mounted on the back wall of the shipping container and relaxed. He took a sip from his fourth can of Red Bull since starting his shift at 9am; Alexi was buzzing nicely at the midpoint of his 14-hour shift. Polar white paint covered the interior of the container and the banks of LED strips in the ceiling cast a dazzling light. Designed to confuse the controllers' bodies the lights helped them cope with long shifts.

The screens displayed a panoramic electronic view of the

Arctic oil and gas fields including the platforms which serviced them. It was Alexi's job to ensure the platforms and production ships were safe from natural and manmade hazards. Alexi had worked as one of four security controllers for the Plyos Energy company over the last three years. The most exciting things he had experienced were ice floes and Greenpeace activists threatening production. Both had been easy enough to deal with.

Alexi scanned left to right in a practised, smooth motion across the main screens and then down to the terminal mounted into the long console. A soft *bing* announced a new email had landed in the inbox. He touched the trackball mouse set into the flat desk of the console and scrolled across to highlight it.

Just another intelligence report from the FSB about the Chechens hundreds of kilometres away, thought Alexi.

It seemed the Chechens were doing nothing. Just like they had been for the last week. Alexi closed the email and filed it. He had hoped the FSB would uncover a plot to destroy a platform. Then he would have something exciting to do.

An electronic screen to his right housed the radios and telephones. Everything in the container was soft. No physical radios or telephones had a place in this secure and advanced space.

An alert sounded on the third screen and Alexi looked up to see what the issue was. A large red circle surrounded an oil platform servicing the East-Prinovozemelsky field. A thick red bar flashed across the top of the display.

Alexi called the screen down to his terminal and clicked on the alert bar. Immediately, his screen flew across to the source of the alert. A ship shape on the screen was blinking red. A proximity warning block had opened beside the contact. Alexi noted the name of the vessel heading towards the platform. He turned to his radio console and selected the channel for the area.

'*Ostashkov Three*, this is Plyos Energy Control,' Alexi called over the radio. He hovered his mouse pointer over the ship shape. He called up the vessel's automatic identification system data. Alexi could use a combination of radar and AIS data to track any ship within the oil and gas fields. *Ostashkov 3* was a 200-metre container ship on its way to Murmansk for discharge. Alexi was sure the captain had decided to take a shortcut through the field. Sometimes they misjudged how close they would come to the platform. The container ship was 10 nautical miles out. Plenty of time to correct the error and get it back on course.

'Plyos Energy, this is *Ostashkov Three*, go ahead,' responded the officer on watch. Alexi detected a Ukrainian accent.

'*Ostashkov Three*, you are about to enter a restricted area. You're instructed to alter course to pass well to the south of the platform ahead of you.'

'We'll be okay. We will not pass too close. We are late for our discharge and need to make up time,' replied the officer. The man's tone told Alexi he had no intention of complying.

'Negative, *Ostashkov Three*. You are to alter course immediately. Do you require me to supply you with a course to steer?' Alexi understood merchant vessels tried to save money and time by cutting close to the platforms. Normally, they complied soon after detection.

'I'm comfortable with my course, Plyos Energy Control. No need to give me further instruction. I will pass clear in good time.'

'*Ostashkov Three*, instruction, you are to immediately alter course.'

'Negative. We will hold our course.' The officer's resolve was stiffening.

'Stand by, *Ostashkov Three*,' instructed Alexi.

He punched a speed dial number on his communications console. A direct connection to the Soviet Navy's Northern Fleet Air base operations centre at Severomorsk near Murmansk.

'Lieutenant Tereshkova, operations,' came the curt answer.

'Good afternoon, Lieutenant Tereshkova. It's Alexi Chirikov from Plyos Energy oil and gas platform security.'

'Da,' answered Tereshkova. He knew this company had a security arrangement with the Air Force, in particular the Maritime Aviation wings.

'I see you have a Tupolev maritime surveillance aircraft to the north of the East-Prinovozemelsky field.'

'We do. They are midway through their sortie. Is there something you need help with?'

'I do. The container ship *Ostashkov Three* is not complying with my instructions and is about to enter a restricted area.'

'I will task the aircraft to assist. To what level do you need?' enquired Tereshkova.

'We'll start with a low over flight and see how the vessel reacts.'

'Estimated time of intercept, five minutes.' Tereshkova easily calculated the distance between the large four engine maritime patrol aircraft and the target he had for *Ostashkov 3* on his bank of screens.

'Thank you.'

Alexi terminated the call and watched the data block for the Tupolev TU-142MZ reverse course and head towards *Ostashkov 3*'s track. In minutes the two data blocks came together. Then the TU-142 continued to the south before swinging slowly back to its original on-station position.

'Plyos Energy Control, this is *Ostashkov Three*. We will alter course and comply with your instructions,' said a new voice. The officer on watch had called the captain to the bridge. As the captain stepped foot onto the bridge, the TU-142 appeared over the top of the waves forward of the ship. The massive aircraft roared directly for them, lifted over the containers, and thundered low over the bridge. The captain's decision had been easy to make.

'*Ostashkov Three*, thank you for your cooperation. Good watch,' responded Alexi as a smile played across his lips. He called Lieutenant Tereshkova to thank the Air Force for its assistance and noted the event in his log. In addition, he sent a short email to the board of Pylos Energy advising them of Lieutenant Tereshkova's assistance. He included a suggestion that Tereshkova receive something to encourage his continued support.

Happy at the light relief from his dull shift, Alexi leaned back in his seat and drained his can of Red Bull. Absently, he reached into a small refrigerator next to his seat, pulled out a fresh can and popped its top.

Seven hours to go, he thought and settled in.

CHAPTER THREE

Talhig

7am. Talhig stepped out of his hotel looking the part of an Islamic cleric heading out to speak to his flock. He strode to the waiting car, resplendent in a black traditional jubbah over a striped caftan. One of his soldiers arrived from Kirovsk to collect him. The driver leapt from the car and rushed to open the passenger door in a flourish of respect. Talhig nodded, hid a smile, and dropped into the warm interior. He had recognised the driver immediately.

Asma Maskhadan returned Talhig's smile as he settled into the passenger seat. Asma was a professional soldier and the only woman to rise alongside Talhig to be his right hand. Her long black hair pulled back and hidden in a tight bun beneath a cap, Asma made herself look as close to a man as possible. But there was no hiding her attractive, slightly chiselled features. Talhig knew that beneath her loose clothes was a fit and well-formed body. The pair had shared a brief and fiery encounter many years earlier. Talhig had always praised Allah for allowing him to survive the breath-taking and punishing encounter. He well remembered the warm pleasure of it.

Asma was ruthless on the battlefield and earned a reputation for cunning and abstract fighting. A master of weapons and hand to hand combat, she was a deadly soldier to have by one's side. Which was why Talhig kept her there. Better to see her in the light than have Asma sneak up on you in the dark.

'Three security men in the car half a street back,' said Asma. Her voice was husky and alluring. She took the steering wheel and slowly guided the car out into the street. In the rear vision mirror she spotted a car pull out and accelerate before maintaining a safe distance.

'The same men who have been tailing me since the airport and all night I suspect. I would hate to be in that car. The smell must be terrible.' Talhig chuckled.

'Are you happy to be followed, Talhig?' asked Asma.

Asma saw advantages in being familiar with her commander.

'Yes, yes. Let them come along for the ride. We have nothing to hide. The mission will start in less than twenty-four hours.

The Russians will have no idea what's happening, until it does,' stated Talhig. 'How far to Kirovsk?'

'Two hours,' responded Asma. She split her concentration between keeping an eye on their tail and gaining the motorway which would take them to the small town.

'How are the men treating you?' asked Talhig. His tone softened with concern. His less evolved brothers were still living in the dark ages when it came to women.

'Their throats are still intact. My girls are keeping their distance and being careful not to generate any feelings which may impact the mission. They are loyal and devoted, Talhig. As you know,' responded Asma quietly. She had detected the change in Talhig's tone and felt a surge of affection towards him. She had not forgotten their encounter either.

'Good, good. As I expected, Asma. Wake me when we're close to Kirovsk.'

Talhig closed his eyes and immediately fell asleep, a talent he had developed early in his military career.

Damien

Damien spread his legs wide and struggled to keep his footing on the slick drilling floor. He tried to brace himself against the wind that howled through the superstructure. Like a banshee the wind screamed, twisted, and wound itself around the drilling deck. It threatened to send the crew sprawling. The Arctic storm which had quietly raised its head earlier in the morning hammered against the platform. Its growing ferocity had postponed all outside work except essential drilling. Damien figured the weather had to be serious if the Russians refused to work in it.

He had wondered ever since stepping foot on these platforms why the designers had insisted on an uncovered drilling floor. A simple roof would have provided much improved working conditions for the crews. Damien could only put it down to cost or the hardness of the average Russian oil and gas man. Either way, Damien thought it was a crazy and unsafe way to work.

He pushed against the wind to seat the makeup tongs around the next drill pipe section, then spun it home. Damien had found a small part of the control room wall which gave him a partial lee and used it to his advantage. The thermal face wrap pulled up under his eyes was barely doing its job. The clear safety glasses he wore rattled steadily on his nose in the howling wind.

There were 10 sections of drill pipe to go, then the job would be complete. By the next morning the Nevzgody drill teams would have concluded their task. The well head would connect to the main gas pipe a week later. Plyos Energy had decided not to change out the Nevzgody platform once the final drilling had taken place. It was too expensive and difficult. Plyos changed the role of the rig from exploration to production and work continued. Ever the thrifty Russians.

'Hey!'

Damien turned to look towards the control room door which led onto the drill floor, searching for the source of the yell.

'You. Come here!' shouted one of the controllers as he struggled to keep hold of the door.

Nodding, Damien caught the eye of the toolpusher he had saved two days previously and indicated the controller. A curt nod came as a reply. The toolpusher turned to watch the next section of the drill string cut deeper into the ocean floor.

Damien approached the controller, gesturing with his arms wide to ask what the problem was. Talking was pointless.

'In the doghouse. I'll talk to you there,' yelled the controller. He walked unhappily across the 5 metres of open deck to the hatch and yanked it open, disappearing inside.

Damien followed the man into the tight interior of the doghouse.

'I couldn't talk to you out there. You're the Australian?'

'Da,' replied Damien, pulling his face wrap down and dropping back his jacket hood. The man flinched at the sound of Damien's perfect Polish accent.

'You the one who made a fool of Fedor?' asked the man.

'I'm the one. Why?' enquired Damien. The doghouse was the perfect place for an ambush. He glanced quickly around the room to take note of everything he could use as a weapon. He set his body to react immediately to any threat.

'He deserved it. Good, good. That isn't why we are here. Like I said. I can't talk to you in that fucking weather.'

'Okay.'

Damien relaxed a degree and waited to see what was going to happen.

'Main office had you flying to Ispytaniye at eighteen hundred today. They are having problems over there and they want a good man to help. The weather is too bad to fly. You will be staying here until we are able to get the helicopters into the air again. The pilots say they will not fly. I can't see what their fucking problem is. A bit of fucking wind.' The controller gestured at the ceiling dismissively. 'Is that going to be a problem for you?'

Damien knew in no uncertain terms that the weather was extremely poor to be flying in. He had extensive experience and thousands of hours in the back of and at the controls of helicopters. The controller seemed to think otherwise. But he was not going to be the one in the airframe when it ploughed into the ocean.

'Nyet,' said Damien. He relaxed his body. He wouldn't be shifting locations this evening. He had not even bothered to pack his few possessions.

'Good. Go back to work,' said the controller brusquely and pushed passed Damien and back out into the storm. Before Damien had even stepped out of the doghouse hatch, the controller was closing the opposite door to the control room and was safely inside and out of the weather.

Back on deck, Damien could hear the toolpusher yelling at him to get onto the next section of pipe. Damien made his way carefully over to his station.

Dasha

Pounded by the unforgiving sea, the small cutter was almost impossible for Dasha to keep on course and upright. The weight of the missile containers on the topside of the superstructure acted like a giant pendulum. They rolled and twisted the ship hopelessly from side to side. Most of his crew where either sick or terrified. Only his engine and missile men were absorbing the conditions. A bucket on the floor was full of Dasha's own vomit and anything else he did not have time to leave the bridge for. The man he had recruited to be on the helm, though very experienced, was out of his league in these conditions. Dasha had taken over.

Driving into an oncoming swell, the bow punched deeply into the dark water. It rolled up the deck and smashed into the bridge windows. Dasha instinctively ducked as he heard a loud cracking sound. Snapping his head up to look at the windows, he could see the outboard port hand window had a long split running through its centre. Cursing, Dasha scowled at the seawater which was already pushing past and onto the floor.

'Get below and find something to shore up that window!' he yelled above the howling noise of the ocean pounding the cutter. He directed the order at the helmsman who had burrowed as deeply as he could into the engineer's chair.

'What?' the man replied. He had heard Dasha but did not want to leave the relative safety of the chair.

'You heard me! Now go!' shouted Dasha harshly.

Shaking his head violently in anger and fear, the helmsman released his seatbelt. He was immediately sent diving onto the bridge floor. He gave Dasha a baleful look as he picked himself up and left through the rear of the bridge. He bounced off equipment as he went.

Alone on the bridge, Dasha took stock of what was happening around him. The Osa was a good vessel in calmer water but a pig in this type of weather. The cutter was taking on a steady stream of seawater which the pumps could just keep up with. The starboard aft missile container was damaged. Someone would need to take a suicidal walk along the outside deck to repair it. Dasha had instructed his missile men to fix the problem as soon as they were in the lee of the production ship, their destination.

He tried to focus on the Transas satellite AIS display which the Russians had installed for him. The screen displayed the target vessels. The production ship, *Boris Gakkel*, and an LNG carrier, the *Isa Umarov*, with two large tugs were 100 nautical miles away. If Dasha maintained their current speed, they should be in striking range in just over six hours. He noted another gas carrier heading towards the mainland from the same location.

Dasha prayed to Allah for fairer winds in their approach to the target. There was no certainty that the guidance system on the cutter would cope with the sea conditions. Dasha needed to have completed the mission by dawn tomorrow to ensure all went to plan. He had no wish to upset Sheikh Taimieov's time frame and incur his wrath. Dasha picked up the telephone from the console and called down to the engine room.

'Da,' answered his unhappy chief engineer.

'Can you give me more speed?'

'Nyet. You have all I can give you. Any more and the screws will pitch out of the water. If we get an overspeed and the engines shut down we are going to die, Dasha,' he responded gravely.

'Okay. How's the fuel?'

Dasha had hoped the chief engineer could squeeze more out of the engines. As it was, they would make their objective around 9pm that night. Plenty of time until the second phase of the operation commenced.

'We're drinking it like a sailor. But we have plenty left for the time we will be on this earth. The starboard engine is operating within parameters but is troublesome.'

'Thank you.'

Dasha heard a curse and turned to see the helmsmen stumbling back onto the bridge. Blood was streaming from a wide cut across his forehead. Under his arms he had a roll of thick canvas and a hammer.

'It's all I can find,' said the man as he passed Dasha. Blood flew into the air with each word as it ran into his mouth.

'Close the opening and then I will look at your head,' instructed Dasha. Nodding, the helmsman set to work trying to keep on his feet. He began to hammer the canvas into place along the wooden inner frame of the window.

Georgiy

The CCTV display showed the car with the Chechen cleric turning into the main street of Kirovsk. It headed towards the compound. Georgiy watched and waited. The information he had received about the imminent terrorist attack had sent him into a state of hypervigilance. He had gone over hours of footage and audio recordings. There was nothing to back up the intelligence report. He had fought against Chechens and respected their spirit and ability to conceal their intentions. Like ghosts they could strike almost at will. As terrorists they were known for their ability to appear and inflict casualties without the intelligence community noticing. This team of supposed freedom fighters appeared disciplined to the highest degree. Georgiy knew better than to underestimate them.

'Did they stop along the way from Murmansk?' Georgiy asked as he turned to look at Yakov.

'No. The driver kept to the speed limit, obeyed all rules, and drove steadily to Kirovsk. The drone footage showed the cleric sleeping the entire way. Neither man spoke after an initial conversation. A quiet trip down to see their comrades,' replied Yakov. His chest squeezed with tension as his mind changed gears from babysitting the religious faithful to the prospect of engaging terrorists.

'Have the team stand by. I want us ready to respond when they make their move. I have a feeling, Yakov. But I can't place it on anything. Thoughts?' asked Georgiy.

'The intelligence could be correct or could be wrong. We have seen it before. There has been no additional confirmation on their plans. It might be as the Chechens say. A celebration of their faith. The means to recruit from the locals here in Kirovsk. That's their stated purpose.'

'Or?' said Georgiy pushing.

'Or it could be cover for a large-scale operation against the state as reported by intelligence. I just don't see why they would be based in Kirovsk to do it. There's basically one road in and out. Apart from that clock tower there is very little of value here. Certainly not of political or military value. I'm at a loss, same as you are, sir.'

'Oh, Yakov, I'm not at a loss. They have chosen this place for exactly the things you stated. It makes sense to me. I just haven't nailed down the finer details,' stated Georgiy as he turned back to the monitors. 'Ready the men,' he said quietly.

Yakov called the Alpha detachment team leaders and advised them to stand the men to and be ready for action.

The car passed through the compound gates. Two men had rushed from inside the main building to throw them open as the car approached. By the way the two men carried themselves they were excited to see their cleric. The driver guided the car to a gentle stop near the front door of the building, climbed free and jogged around to open the passenger door.

The cleric stepped out of the car, looked around slowly, surveyed the ground and turned to peer up into the sky. Georgiy took a half step backwards. The man was looking directly at the drone as if he knew it circled 1000 metres above him. Georgiy took in the man's damaged face. He wondered if the cleric had been in one of the many civil wars of his country. The cleric certainly carried himself like a military man as did the others in the compound. That was not surprising. Most of Chechnya had served in the military at some stage of their lives.

'Send the image of his face to headquarters to see if there's a match,' ordered Georgiy after the cleric had disappeared inside. 'I want to know who that man really is.'

Nodding, an operator captured the upturned face from the footage and transmitted it. Ten seconds later he received a response.

'Sir, the man is Talhig Chechenskiy, second-in-command of the Chechen Itt Stag freedom fighter group. He's listed also as a cleric of Islam,' relayed the operator.

'An interesting development and a further confirmation of the information we received. Keep tracking him as he moves through the building,' instructed Georgiy, a light smile on his face. He could feel the first tendrils of adrenaline moving into his system. He took a sip from his ever-present mug of tea, found it cold and drank it anyway. He had long ago lost the aversion to eating and drinking anything meant to be hot. Operations came first. The bank of screens in front of him changed to show the interior of each room in the compound.

'He seems to be heading for what I believe is a dining room. The men have assembled in there. There are four men on the outside perimeter of the compound. They appear to be on watch. An escalation, sir?' queried Yakov.

'Maybe, but I think not. They know we're watching. If they were aware we had compromised their mission, there would be a different reaction. Their very important cleric just arrived. They are being cautious to maintain their cover story. We would be the same if we shared their mad obsession. It's just in our favour this time.'

The hidden microphones picked up the steady pace of the cleric as he walked, escorted down the hallway which led to the dining room. They all moved at a very military, measured, and consistent pace.

'Do you hear the sound of his footwear?' asked Georgiy.

'Sounds like he has hard-soled shoes on, sir.'

'Boots, I think. Isolate it for me.'

'Da,' responded Yakov. He scrolled a mouse pointer to hover over the sound isolation icon on the terminal he was using. Immediately, all other conversation and noise ceased. The sound of footsteps played through the speakers.

'I think the cleric is wearing military boots. I know that sound. They make a very similar sound to the boots I wear,' said Georgiy pointing down to his special forces issued winter boots.

Distinctive by the two thick buckles which closed a flap over the boot top.

'Good pick up, sir. You could be right there,' replied Yakov, reinforcing his commander's call. He was amazed at the connections Georgiy could make with the most obscure information. The hallmark of an effective operator.

'A guess only, but I think a good one. This Talhig Chechenskiy is not the cleric he is making out to be for our cameras. Assign a man to go back through the footage and study the boots the other men are wearing. Not too far back. Just enough to confirm what they're wearing. Then conduct a closer search for any sign of weapons or equipment. They must have camouflaged their combat load somehow. How else will they conduct a mission?' said Georgiy wondering aloud as he watched Talhig enter the dining room.

'Sir.'

Yakov turned and assigned the job to the Alpha team's specialist communicator, Private Lazarov, who sat next to him. In five minutes, they had an answer.

'Sir, all of the men are wearing military style footwear,' relayed Yakov excitedly.

'Available anywhere on the battlefields of Chechnya, any surplus store and issued to both Chechen and Russian forces and allies. I want to know if the men on guard start acting differently. Restore the sound.'

Immediately, the sound of singing and rejoicing burst from the speakers. The cleric was standing in the centre of the dining room, received as if he were a national hero.

Georgiy stared at the man, wondering what Talhig wore beneath his juddah.

Alexi

Staring intently at his watch and then the large clock with its bright red digits mounted on the wall, Alexi wished he was at the end of his shift, not the start. No amount of willing would cause his shift to go faster. In 14 long hours, he would head home to his small and basic apartment. After a quick freshen up and a bite to eat he would be out the door again. He was hoping to hook up with a blonde and very attractive woman he had met the previous week. She had given him the address of a small jazz club and told him to be there by 10pm tonight. He intended on being there. He had 90 minutes to get there after his shift ended. Opportunities were never to be missed out on as far as Alexi was concerned. At 28 he was feeling the need to find someone and settle into family life. He was not as good at finding that person as he thought he would be.

Shifting his gaze to the main monitor on the wall, he watched the small, intermittent track the off-going operator had detected.

Alexi created an inset window and locked it to track the vessel. It displayed no AIS, nor was it emitting any radar energy or making radio calls. The track was silently and steadily punching north towards the Shtokman gas fields. The only sensor Alexi was able to track with was through a satellite radar feed he took from the navy. It was a good tool, but not always reliable. The target he currently had was dropping out every 30 minutes, only to reappear again further north.

By the size of the radar return the vessel is small, thought Alexi.

He was unable to tell its exact size. The radar feed was not that accurate. Either way, he wondered what madman would be out in the storms rolling through the area. The most northern, ice-bound gas platforms had reported an Arctic storm battering them. The open ocean was not a safe place to be in any size ship.

When the off-going operator had first noticed the target, he had taken little notice as it was still 100 nautical miles from the nearest Plyos asset. Now it appeared to be closing in on the production ship which serviced the Shtokman gas field.

Time to take some action. Alexi sighed. He pushed the blonde's face from his mind and focused on his job.

'Unidentified vessel approaching Shtokman gas field; this is Plyos Energy control, over,' called Alexi over the radio. He had selected a radio frequency which serviced the area the vessel was moving through.

Silence.

'Unidentified vessel approaching Shtokman gas field; this is Plyos Energy control, over,' repeated Alexi.

Silence.

'Unidentified vessel, respond immediately. You're heading towards a restricted area. I am authorised to engage Naval Aviation assets to confirm your identity. I will enforce a course change for you to pass clear of the restricted area. Acknowledge.'

Alexi was not sure which air assets would answer his call this time. He could see a TU-142 well to the west and an FSB IL-76MD-90A patrolling along the coast near the Swedish border, but nothing close to his target.

A garbled, jumbled rush of static and words erupted into his ear.

'Unidentified vessel, say again?' he replied.

'Plyos Control, this is *Stenka One Eight, Stenka One Eight*. Do you receive me?' The response was full of static and frustratingly faint. Alexi raised the volume for his headset.

'*Stenka One Eight*, you're barely readable. Sir, you are heading into a restricted area. State your vessel type. You are not displaying any AIS or radar.'

'Roger, Roger, Plyos Control. We are a naval patrol vessel making our way to the edge of the ice floe for an extreme weather exercise.'

'*Stenka One Eight*, I do not have you as scheduled traffic for that sector. I am unaware of any military exercise that far north. How many vessels are in your group? State your vessel type,' replied Alexi. He was going to push the point. This was something that he had not experienced before.

'We are a destroyer. Udaloy class, steaming alone.'

'*Stenka One Eight*, the radar target I hold for you is too small to be a Udaloy destroyer.'

'I do not know what you want me to do Plyos Control, that is what I am,' came the calm reply.

'Stand by,' advised Alexi and consulted his database. He could not find any Udaloy class destroyers called *Stenka* and the use of digits after the callsign denoted it was a root callsign. Something was not right. '*Stenka One Eight*, you're not in the database. There's no Udaloy destroyer called *Stenka*. *Stenka One Eight*, reverse your course and await inspection by air assets, over,' insisted Alexi.

'Plyos Control, you are unreadable. What do you want?' The speaker had a disinterested tone.

'*Stenka One Eight*, comply with my instructions immediately.' Alexi had rolled upright in his chair and was sitting on its edge. He could feel his adrenaline rising and heart pounding against his chest.

Too much Red Bull.

Silence.

Alexi repeated his demand.

Silence.

Pausing, Alexi checked his equipment, retuned his radio and sent a call to *Stenka One Eight.*

Silence.

Cursing, Alexi picked up the telephone and dialled the number for the Northern Fleet Air base operations centre at Severomorsk near Murmansk. A different man was in control of the shift who did not receive Alexi as well. After 10 minutes of arguing for an immediate response to what was obviously a threat to the production gas ship, Alexi hung up on the man and stared at his console. Naval Aviation had never refused a request before. Maybe the officer on watch was new. Either way, Alexi was without immediate options.

After selecting the telephone number for the head of Plyos security, he waited for the line to connect. His heart was racing.

Dasha

Dasha dropped the radio telephone onto its hook and looked out into the twilight. He knew he had played his hand. There was no way he could risk an over flight by a naval aircraft, he had to respond to the radio call. The dark night sky was ominous beneath the heavy clouds which crowded it. In his mind, fighter jets were already roaring down the runway at Severomorsk, loaded with missiles and hungry to destroy the little cutter. There was no time left. He had to bring his part of the operation forward. A whole 18 hours forward. Looking at his watch, Dasha calculated he would be on station in two hours. There was no time to loiter and bob around in the ocean waiting for the scheduled commencement time. He was too early. The Russians had changed the plan.

Securing himself deep into his chair, Dasha plucked a satellite telephone handset from the console. He jammed his thumb on the power button and waited for the unit to establish a satellite connection. He typed in a short text message and pressed send. Dasha had informed Sheikh and Talhig of the compromise and that his part of the plan was launching early.

'Chief!' he called as he pushed the satellite telephone back into its cradle.

Silence.

Picking up the internal telephone, Dasha pressed the button for the engine room. He was not sure why he had called out for the chief. He was not on the bridge. Fatigue and stress were biting into his mind.

'Da,' responded the chief engineer.

'Give me all the power you have. We're manoeuvring to attack early. The Russians have found us. Pass the word.'

'Okay. You have all the power I can give you, Dasha. Allahu Akbar!' shouted the chief excitedly.

'Allahu Akbar,' responded Dasha. He looked across at the helmsman.

'Get me Mikhail and sound general quarters. We're moving to attack.'

Nodding, the helmsman leapt from the safety of his chair. As he passed the bridge command console, he twisted the knob to sound the alarm. Instantly, alarms started sounding throughout the cutter. Men ran as best they could in the violent seas to their battle stations. Minutes later Mikhail arrived on the bridge, panting. His eyes were shining with excitement and a little fear.

'How long until you can have the forward missiles ready for launch?' enquired Dasha.

'Thirty minutes. Do we have targets?' responded Mikhail as he caught his breath.

'Missiles for the tugs. Then we will close on the LNG carrier and attack it with the cannons. Take the production ship intact with no damage. That's very important. I have the ship targets on my screen; you will in the fire control centre as well. You're cleared to launch when ready. I am making best speed to close the distance. Get two men up forward to inspect the cannon to ensure all is in order. We will need it.'

'The ocean is too rough to launch. The guidance systems will not work,' pleaded Mikhail. He worked his hands in front of himself. Success would be on his head.

'Make it work. I don't care how. Go!' Dasha dismissed the missile engineer.

'All men are at their stations. All sections report ready for action, Dasha,' advised the helmsman.

'Good. We go to glory. Inshallah.'

Nikolay

Nikolay found himself called to the bridge by the third officer and frowned at the radio exchange he listened to. He consulted the ECDIS and searched for the suspicious target Plyos Energy Control was in contact with. The display held nothing in the reported area. He was not surprised. Nikolay had steered the *Aysberg* to the east as he approached his patrol area. The distance between himself and the contact was increasing with every second.

In five hours, the *Aysberg* would start to close on the ice floe and commence her duties. The port engine was still making its own mind up when it wanted to work. The going was slow with little headway in the last few hours, and the lack of progress and rough ride were wearing on the crew. Nikolay was not looking forward to the next five weeks of patrol if it was all going to be like this.

'Confirm we have no destroyers call *Stenka*, please,' Nikolay said to his third officer. The man raced to the rear of the bridge and returned with a thick leather-bound book. He struggled slightly under the weight. Dropping it onto the table next to Nikolay, he thumbed through the text until he arrived at the Udaloy I class destroyers.

'Nothing, sir.'

'Interesting. If you were trying to hide your identity, why pick such an easy fact to check? I don't think we have a Udaloy class destroyer for company out here. Apart from commercial ships, we're the only government vessel this far north,' said Nikolay. His mind was racing through options and what this might mean.

At the back of the bridge, the satellite telephone started ringing. His frown growing deeper, Nikolay lifted it to his ear.

'Da, Captain Voroni.'

'Nikolay, Admiral Unkovsky,' came the gruff and firm response.

'Sir, to what do I owe the pleasure?' asked Nikolay.

Admiral Unkovsky was the commander of the Northern Sector for the FSB and Nikolay's ultimate boss. The use of his first name was instantly worrying. Unkovsky was not known for being on first name terms with his staff. Nikolay had never met the man.

'There's the possibility of a developing terrorist situation in the Shtokman gas field. A group is planning to attack the Ispytaniye platform. You're the only on-water asset I have close enough to observe and render assistance if required.'

'What are your orders, sir?' asked Nikolay. He tried to digest the rapid-fire information Unkovsky hammered at him. Pride swelled in his chest. This could be the chance to break free of his crippling reputation.

'You are to proceed at best speed towards the ice pack which is to the south of the two platforms and await orders,' replied Unkovsky. His voice continued to be gruff and hard. He had become aware of the plan for the attack on the Ispytaniye gas platform an hour earlier. A careful man, he did not want to launch too large a response in case the terrorists became aware of the compromise.

'We will proceed as ordered, sir. Another thing. We overheard radio calls between the Plyos Energy controller and an unknown vessel heading towards the Shtokman gas field. Could they be related?'

'There're no reports that the terrorists have a vessel involved. I will pass it on. Thank you, Nikolay. Is there anything that will impede your ability to carry out your orders? What's your estimated time on station?'

'We're having port engine problems, and are five hours from the ice floe, sir. I estimate twelve hours to close with the edge of the ice floe nearest to the platforms. We will need to burn a lot of fuel to get there quickly.'

'Make it so, Nikolay. We'll send you a tanker when you need to bunker in the coming days. There are broken ice floes along your course. Be careful, even though you are ice rated. Again, you are the only asset we have in the area. For your information, the icebreaker *Yamal* is leading a gas carrier to the mainland from the production ship. If you loop to the south, you will pick up their path. It will make it easier for you. We have no air assets currently available due to weather.'

'Should those vessels be warned away from the area, sir?' questioned Nikolay.

'Nyet. They are at no risk or danger of being involved in the attack. That's the assessment. Trade will continue as their company sees fit.'

'Very well, sir. We will change course immediately and make best speed for the area. I'll keep you informed.'

'Yes, you will. Good luck.'

The line went dead in Nikolay's ear. He pushed the satellite phone back onto its hook. He paused for a second to collect his thoughts. Nikolay spun on his heel and rushed to the chart table, calling his third mate as he went.

Damien

Damien collapsed onto his bunk. His head was swimming, and he could not grab any of the thoughts swirling in his head. The crying face of his son kept flashing before his eyes. He struggled to maintain himself.

'Get a grip. This has happened before. Stay in charge. You're in control,' said Damien quietly. He dropped his head into his hands.

Trying to breathe as a heavy weight squeezed his chest, Damien fought to control the emotions welling up in his throat. His feet danced on the floor and his legs twitched and jumped of their own accord. Pain flared behind his eyes. He slammed them shut to keep out the dim light of the cabin. The drone of life on the platform hummed through the walls and drove into his head.

Biting back tears, Damien stretched against the wall and tapped his head lightly against it.

Then he leapt to his feet and began pacing back and forth.

'Control, Damien, control. Tuck it away. Get on mission. You must get back on mission,' he muttered as his hands started to shake.

Damien had felt the first tendrils of an episode forming in his mind as he finished his post-shift meal. He barely made it back to his cabin. His mind triggered while he ate the bland food in the mess room. He caught sight of Fedor staring at him. Venom dripped from the man's eyes. They were like darts stabbing at him. Fedor's smashed nose plastered and stretched across his face. Deep purple bruising flushed his skin. The threat was clear: Fedor had not learnt from their last encounter. Damien needed to end this before he became the victim. He was never the victim. He was the one who delivered death and destruction. It had been another life, but he was a highly trained operator. He had been Taipan 16.

A surge of anger and hatred had roared through Damien before he could catch it, and almost took over his mind.

He had bitten down on his lip to generate the pain needed to stop the urge to kill Fedor. All he achieved was a break in the skin and a bead of blood forming along his bottom lip. He had made to stand and leave before he acted on his instincts. His legs refusing to move until they started to twitch. Damien knew he was in trouble. The twitching was the first sign he had begun to slide.

Gathering his resolve, he had vaulted from his seat, drawing the attention of everyone in the room as he knocked his metal tray to the ground. With a crash the tray spilt what remained of his meal, scattering it over the floor.

Immediately, a kitchen hand had appeared, picked up the tray and cleaned away the mess.

Damien abandoned the table and made for the door. Careering down passageways, he bounced from wall to wall, off kilter. His felt like the deck of the rig was pitching and heaving. Sliding down the final stairs to his cabin, he had been unable to breathe as he yanked the door open. Hurrying inside he'd slammed the door closed behind him.

Focus. I need to focus.

He lifted his face clear of his hands and looked around the cabin. His eyes dropped onto the bedside table beside his bunk. A hardcover copy of *Ice Station* by Matthew Reilly sat on the table. Damien always carried one of Reilly's books with him.

Suddenly tired, he dropped back onto the bed. He tried to find the calming ball in his mind and failed. His stomach lurched as though he was going to be sick. He saw Stayer's face flash in front of his eyes; Damien's son, Ryan, stood in the background. Damien groaned. Wuz's pale face, his beard full of blood and saliva, floated up to greet him, empty eyes staring up at him.

Curling into a ball, Damien shook as though he was cold. Sweat poured from his skin and he could smell his own distress. Faces flashed passed his eyes. The faces of men he had killed. The blank faces of those lives he had destroyed remotely with bombs and missiles. His ears filled with the screams of children.

A piercing, shattering pain stabbed into his mind.

Damien passed out.

Dasha

'Are the cannons online?' yelled Dasha as he struggled to hand steer the missile cutter towards the soft glow of the production ship's lights. He could see them against the horizon.

'Cannons are ready. Control is with Mikhail!' shouted the helmsman above the roar of the engines and the storm. He had left the safety of his chair and was trying to keep his feet. The cutter pitched and rolled in the heavy seas at the edge of the broken and deadly expanse of ice floes.

'Mikhail, do you have a firing solution?' called Dasha towards his missile man. Mikhail sat hunched over a console in the fire control room at the bridge's rear. The three steps that led down in the room were slick with water from the damaged window.

'I cannot get a good lock. I have detected multiple radars painting us. In this clutter, I don't think anyone can detect us. The boat's moving too much, Dasha! I need calmer water. The guidance system for the missiles topples and fails. We need calmer water!' stressed Mikhail. Sweat poured down from his brow and kept getting into his eyes. He had activated the MR-331 Rangout radar system to support the missile firing five minutes earlier. The radar managed to achieve only intermittent contact with the tugs he was trying to target. Dasha had passed him the positions of the vessels via the AIS display to speed up the process. Mikhail felt like he was fighting against treacle.

'So, the tugs are using their radar?' asked Dasha.

The cutter took a massive wave over the port bow. It drove the vessel deep and twisting into the dark water. Rolling up the deck, the wave crashed into the bridge windows and stove in the temporary repair, seawater exploding through dowsing the bridge. Crying out, the helmsman dropped to the floor clutching his arm. Dasha looked down at the man as the water swirled around the floor. The twisting motion of the cutter was hurling the helmsman roughly from corner to corner.

'Da. I can see it on the Nikhrom display. I can isolate and target their emitters,' replied Mikhail. He snapped out his hand and caught hold of the helmsman as he tumbled down the steps into the firing station. He jammed the wayward man under the console. 'What's wrong?' he asked the distressed sailor.

'Glass from the window cut my arm. I haven't even started the battle and I'm already injured. Twice!' cursed the man bitterly. Dasha had tried to stitch close the cut to his forehead. In the pitching seas he had only managed to create large looping sutures which looked like a child's handy work.

'Can you get back on your feet?'

'Da. Give me a moment,' replied the helmsman. Blood poured from his forearm and added a dull pink hue to the seawater which swirled around the deck.

'Secure that window!' shouted Dasha. He turned and saw the helmsman slowly pulling himself out from under the targeting console. Waving vaguely, the man disappeared out the back of the bridge. He embarked on what he felt would be a fruitless search for something to stop the influx of water.

'Mikhail, how are you going?' called Dasha. He could hear the production ship, *Boris Gakkel*, calling out to them to identify themselves on the radio. Ignoring the enquiry, Dasha continued with the mission.

'Locking onto the tug radars now. I still need calm water, Dasha. Can you find it?' replied Mikhail.

'I'm heading into the ice floe to the south, it will be calmer there,' replied Dasha. 'Five minutes and I want those missiles in the air. We must succeed!'

Aiming for the path cut by the last icebreaker, Dasha guided the cutter between the tonnes of ice which mounted up either side. If he connected with even a glancing blow to the ice, the Osa's hull would cleave open, ending the mission. Pulling back the throttles, he dropped the cutter's speed to 15 knots and entered the opening. Blocks of ice dotted the sea in front of them. Dasha was glad for the constant twilight of the Arctic to guide him. He was sure the reflected glow of the production ship's lights on the clouds was helping as well.

Almost immediately, the cutter stopped its crazed pitching and rolling and came onto an even keel. Dasha heard a loud cry of happiness from behind him.

'We're among the ice, Mikhail. Fire the missiles!' yelled Dasha.

Ice and water whipped up by the howling wind as it roared through the shattered bridge window stung Dasha's face. The helmsman rushed past. He started hammering a light steel square into place over the opening. It looked to be a perfect fit. Dasha figured the man had not looked particularly hard earlier.

'Missile lock! Stand by for firing. Range, ten nautical miles. Do I have permission to fire?' called Mikhail.

'Fire! Fire the missiles, Mikhail. Then get the cannons targeted on the gas carrier alongside the *Boris Gakkel*. I want its bridge disabled as we get closer.'

'Firing!' yelled Mikhail. He mashed a finger down on the launch button for the two forward missiles.

Instantly, the two protective outer doors on both missile containers flicked open, exposing the nose of each of the P-15M Termit anti-ship missiles. The port missile engine fired first.

Smoke and flame erupted from the rear of the missile container. The massive anti-ship missile shot into the air.

Heat, smoke, and flame poured in around the temporary repair the helmsman had made with the bridge window. The heat scorched the paint, and everyone was coughing out the toxic fumes which flooded the bridge. Dasha blinked his eyes furiously to clear them as they teared and stung.

A thick cloud of smoke enveloped the missile boat.

Passing clear of the cutter, the weapon accelerated towards its target. A second later the starboard forward missile leapt from its container and followed its brother towards its designated target. The twin exhaust plumes from the rocket motors announced the launch. The Termits skimmed 25 metres above the ocean, accelerating to their terminal speed of just under Mach 1.

The cutter emerged from the thick smoke of the launch with its forward deck scorched and blackened. Dasha stepped over to the hatch set into the starboard side of the bridge and yanked it open. Frigid air poured in and whipped the smoke and fumes into a furious eddy which roiled around the space. Mikhail opened a rear window. The bridge cleared in seconds. Dasha drew in a deep breath of cold, crisp air and then slammed the hatch tightly shut.

'Missiles are tracking. Good track. They're on target. Seekers are active. Good lock. Impact in five, four, three, two, one,' advised Mikhail. He stood and rushed to the windows to watch the destruction.

Dasha and Mikhail could just make out the superstructure of the massive production ship on the near horizon. The missiles closed in and impacted the tugs a few hundred metres to the north of the *Boris Gakkel*. Both tugs exploded simultaneously. Flame and debris arced into the air. The vessels broke in two and quickly disappeared below the waves.

All Dasha and Mikhail could see of their handiwork were twin plumes of flame raising into the twilight sky.

'I have a mayday call being made by the gas carrier and the *Boris Gakkel*!' called the helmsman.

'Commence barrage jamming,' responded Dasha.

Mikhail rushed back to the targeting console and dropped heavily into the seat.

'Jammer online and transmitting.'

'Have you shut them down?'

'Da. They are still sending but no signal is strong enough to get more than a few hundred metres. No-one can hear them,' supplied Mikhail. He narrowed the jamming band to cover the frequencies the two ships were attempting to use.

Dasha increased the speed of the cutter and guided it towards the two surviving ships. He could see black smoke pouring from the gas carrier's exhaust stacks. The master must have decided to get underway.

A plume of white gas erupted into the air. The hoses used to fill the carrier blew away from the manifolds, retracting quickly back to the production ship. Warning lights flashed on board both ships.

'Target the bridge of the gas carrier, Mikhail. Do not hit the production ship or the hull of the carrier. Only the bridge, Mikhail. Can you do it?' stressed Dasha.

'See how we go, Dasha. Stand by.' The closer they came to the large vessels the easier it was for Mikhail to lay the targeting icon over the gas carrier's bridge. 'Firing!'

The twin 30-millimetre cannons rapidly fired five rounds each.

Dasha locked his eyes on the gas carrier.

A split second later he could see the cannon shells impact the superstructure of the ship. The heavy shells shredded the bridge. Smoke continued to pour from the ship's exhaust.

'Good shooting, Mikhail. Good man. We'll close and take the production ship. Get the men ready to board.'

'The gas carrier is heading away. Still looks to be under power,' informed the helmsman. In the calmer water between the ice floes, he was able to use binoculars to observe the targets. 'Men are running on the decks of both ships. I'm not sure what they are doing. Ah, there are men on the production ship going to launch its lifeboat. Da, they are launching it now.'

'Mikhail, target the lifeboat with the cannon. Range fifteen hundred metres,' ordered Dasha.

'Firing.' Mikhail's voice was mechanical. There was no trace of regret for the fate he was dealing out to the innocent men attempting to escape.

The deck thrummed with the rapid shots from the cannons. The deadly shells arced through the twilight sky.

A bright orange lifeboat on the *Boris Gakkel* fell clear of its mounts and stabbed deep into the ocean, driving a few metres under the surface before the buoyancy of the boat took over and forced it rearward to the surface. As it settled, the crew engaged the engine. The first 30-millimetre cannon shell splashed close by. Mikhail found the range and the heavy shells bracketed the vessel, smashing it to pieces. Destroyed, the lifeboat sank beneath the surface, taking the crew with it.

'Boarding team prepare,' called Dasha over the ship-wide intercom. From below, the five men assigned to assault the production ship donned their equipment and charged to the deck. The assault team moved past the bridge and assembled next to the forward twin 30-millimetre cannon mount.

Shoving the throttles to their stops, Dasha called for everything the engines could give him. The cutter rocketed forwards, cleaving a deep trench in the ocean as the stern ducked under the acceleration. With communications jammed, Dasha was powerless to communicate his intentions to either ship's crew. He decided to demonstrate his demands with force.

'Mikhail, fire an illumination round over the production ship's bow. Do not hit it. We don't want any accidents,' called Dasha.

Mikhail spun out of his seat and charged up the steps. He grabbed a large flare pistol from its bracket near the port door and sorted through the flares until he found a white illumination round. He pulled open the hatch and joined the shivering men near the 30-millimetre cannons.

Dasha spun the wheel as fast as he could and cut through the frigid water in a snap port turn. Closing on the *Boris Gakkel*'s stern, he passed clear of it by less than a coat of paint. As the cutter pulled wide passed the bridge, Dasha could see men staring down at them. He ran the cutter down the length of the ship to the bow, flicked it around the point of the ship, then continued the turn to spin the cutter into a ground loop. The engines rumbled as the cutter settled in the water between two large pieces of ice.

'Fire, Mikhail!' shouted Dasha above the howling wind through the open bridge door. He kept his eyes locked on the ice floes either side of them, ready to gun the engines to keep clear.

Immediately, Mikhail straightened his back and pointed the

pistol to the sky and fired. The shell arced high into the air. Seconds later the flare ignited 100 metres over the *Boris Gakkel* and exploded into a brilliant white light. Descending under a large parachute the strong wind grabbed hold of the flare and sent it northwards. The flare slowly fell towards the ocean.

'Prepare to board!' shouted Dasha.

He gunned the engines. The cutter shot forwards, emitting a cloud of exhaust smoke. Closing midships on the starboard side of the *Boris Gakkel*, Dasha guided the cutter in close to the ship's hull and pulled the throttles to idle. The two vessels lightly bumped together. The smooth water lee provided by the *Boris Gakkel* finally settled the cutter's uncomfortable rolling pitch motion.

'Board. Go, go!' commanded Dasha.

Leaping into action, two men of the assault team lifted Bastelle Tactical Air Initiated Launch grappling hook launchers and fired them up along the hull. Rising high in the air, the grapples looped down and over the railing which circled the production ship. The men disconnected the ropes from the launchers, then pulled down with all their strength to test the hold. Satisfied, they anchored the ropes to the cutter's deck and called forward the first of the assaulters.

With their dark helmets tightly pulled down and a black thermal wrap hiding each man's face, the boarding team looked like machines. They dressed in heavy black fatigues against the cold with AK-74Ms slung over their backs. Only their eyes showed as they stared out intently, steely and determined. The first two men fitted electrically powered scaling harnesses to the grapple ropes. As quickly as they could they initiated the climb, lifting off the deck to slide up the ropes. When they arrived at the railing they swung themselves over, pulled their AKs free, and covered a section each of the walkway. Finding it devoid of life, they moved towards the bridge. Behind them the rest of the team appeared at the railing and joined them. Unstoppable machines, they jogged to the stern accommodation.

The team were making for a series of exposed stairways which would let them onto the rear of the bridge. A choked cry from above drew the attention of the team leader. Looking up he saw a crewman pointing a fire hose at them, perfectly positioned to force them off the stairs with the weight of the water. The crewman held a moment of power. Snapping up his rifle, the team leader fired a single shot, hitting the crewman between the eyes and dropping him lifeless to the deck. The team continued the charge up the stairs and arrived at the bridge.

Through the windows they could see frantic activity as officers tried to send distress messages and make telephone calls. Ship-wide announcements tried to warn the 100 workers of the production ship of the boarding. Pulling on the hatch which led to the bridge, the team leader found it unsurprisingly locked. He called forward the last member of his crew, pointed to the hatch and indicated he wanted it blown.

The assaulter quickly placed small squib charges against the door's hinges and locking handle. After inserting remote detonators, he signalled for everyone to move back, paused for a second, then initiated the charges. A dull clanging boom sounded. The door dropped off its mounts and clattered to the deck.

Charging inside, the team sighted on each crewman firing deliberate shots into them. After killing the defenceless bridge crew, the team cleared the bridge. Happily nodding, the team leader rushed onto the starboard bridge wing and looked down. He spotted Mikhail standing near the 30-millimetre cannons. He waved a triumphant arm above his head. Immediately, he saw the cutter pull away and head out to sea. They were going to chase down the drifting gas carrier as it slowly steamed itself towards the unforgiving ice pack to the north-east.

'Clear this trash off the bridge,' ordered the team leader. Blood splashed across the consoles and pools of it leaked from the 10 men who had tried to seek safety on the bridge. A Chechen leaned down and started dragging the first body out the open bridge door. He tossed it over the side. He would repeat the process until the space was clear.

Eyeing the three unoccupied members of his team, the leader stalked quickly up to them.

'Clear the ship. Kill them all. Keep hunting and killing until you have them all. There are at least one hundred workers. Kill them all and then count them. We must secure this ship. I will prepare for the arrival of the next icebreaker and gas carrier. Go! Good hunting. Remember Grozny,' he instructed.

Opening the interior bridge door and stepping forwards, the first assaulter met a crewman making his way up the stairs. The man's mouth opened in astonishment just as the Chechen fired his weapon into the surprised face.

Dasha closed the distance to the wayward gas carrier as it steamed unguided towards the ice. He was not sure what he was going to do about it. The plan called for the capture of the carrier. Rafted up alongside the *Boris Gakkel*, the carrier would ensure the scene looked normal when ships approached from the mainland. There was no way he was going to be able to stop the carrier impacting the ice now. He would have to sink it. With only two remaining anti-ship missiles he did not intend on wasting one on a partly loaded ship.

'Mikhail, take the wheel,' called Dasha as the man walked back into the armoured bridge. Nodding, Mikhail took over and Dasha moved to pick up the satellite telephone. Punching in the codewords for a successful mission, he sent a text message to Talhig and Sheikh.

'How will we sink the carrier?' asked Dasha, walking back to stand next to Mikhail. The ship grew larger in the bridge windows.

'I suggest we fire the cannon to hit below the waterline along the stern. There'll be no gas tanks there. We should be safe from exploding the cargo, I think,' ventured Mikhail.

'We have no other options. Make it so. Fire when you are ready,' ordered Dasha and retook the wheel. The helmsman was sitting uncomfortably in the engineer's chair attending to his bleeding forearm.

Mikhail walked down to the firing console and lay the cannon's targeting onto the gas carrier's stern. He programmed the shot placements he wanted, pausing a second to check his calculations before initiating the firing sequence.

Rumbling in their mounting, the twin 30-millimetre cannons spun and elevated slightly to achieve the programmed range. They rapidly fired off the 20 shells Mikhail had ordered; the firing computer adjusted the cannons slightly as it walked the shells along the stern. Water plumed into the air as each shell slammed into the thin metal of the gas carrier's hull. The metal was torn open and the ocean rushed in. The wind ripped away the smoke from the cannons and revealed the gas carrier already settling deeper into the water. White smoke replaced the black of diesel coming out of its exhaust and the giant propeller began to slow.

'Target the lifeboat,' ordered Dasha. He saw men running up the stairs towards it. The lifeboat mounted to the rear of the bridge. Without a word, Mikhail fired three more shells. The heavy rounds stripped away the lifeboat.

'Well done,' said Dasha as he watched the carrier come to a stop, its engine destroyed.

Slowly, the ship started to sink deeper in the water. The trip to the bottom of the sea would take several hours. Those sailors who had survived the attack would not last long in the frigid waters, even if they managed to escape the confines of the hull.

Dasha wheeled the cutter around to head back to the *Boris Gakkel.* The first phase of the mission to bring the fight to the Russian Bear was complete.

Talhig

Talhig had been trying to snatch a few hours' sleep when a violently shaking on his shoulder roused him. The guard he had placed on his room urged him to wake up.

'What? What is it?' Talhig hissed as he struggled to the surface from his deep sleep. Snapping his eyes open in the gloom, he focused on the dim shape of the guard. His hand was emitting a soft blue glow.

'Message for you, from someone called Dasha. We just received the transmission, but its time stamped eight hours ago. You need to read this,' urged the guard. He forced the mobile telephone closer to Talhig's face. The blue light reflected off his deep facial scars.

'Okay, okay,' replied Talhig batting away the telephone so he could sit up. Glancing at his watch, he noted it was just coming up to 4pm. Taking the offered handset, he focused on the screen, reading the words quickly. A deep frown furrowed his forehead. Talhig gritted his teeth in annoyance. Looking up at the guard he held his finger to his lips to silence any questions. Nodding, the guard stepped back and waited quietly.

So, it's begun. Too early but there's no helping that, thought Talhig.

Time for action.

'Call the men to arms and meet me in the dining room. The time for caution has passed. Our attack's moved forward,' ordered Talhig.

'Sir.' The guard spun on his heels and rushed from the room.

Talhig tapped a message into the telephone's screen, pressed send and waited. Almost immediately the handset vibrated with a reply. Talhig's smile broadened as he read it. He levered himself off the bed and took a moment to look down over the juddah he wore. For the glory of Chechnya, he would no longer hide.

He grabbed the juddah by the collar and lifted it away from his body. As the juddah slid away it revealed the green multi-cam uniform worn by most of the ex-Soviet states. Talhig strode confidently to the door and drew a deep, proud breath. He threw open the door and marched to the dining room. As he passed men in the corridors, they gave a low roar of loyalty and approval. Talhig could feel their excitement. It matched his own.

Talhig found the room full of his freedom fighters for Chechnya. Loyal and unwavering. He thrust himself confidently through the door. Talhig climbed up onto a table and surveyed each man. They watched him intently.

'Cut the power to the building. Blind the Russian dogs,' he demanded.

Two men ran from the room to carry out his order. A minute later the compound plunged into darkness. In the dining room, battery-operated lamps were switched on and brought a soft, calm glow to the room.

'Phase one of our mission to fight the Russian Bear is a success. You were not to know but another team have already taken the fight to the Russians. Though compromised our fighters kept true to the cause and were victorious. That team secured an installation near the gas platform we will be assaulting. They have sunk three ships and captured a gas production ship. Phase two, our glorious phase, is to commence. I have contacted the helicopters. They're lifting off with our equipment and will be here in thirty minutes. The Russians will know something is happening. We must keep them at bay until the helicopters arrive to collect us. If Allah is with us, my men, the Russians will be slow to react. As soon as the helicopters are on the ground, gear up and get ready for a fight. We go to glory, Allahu Akbar!' shouted Talhig, pumping his right fist into the air. He revelled in the moment.

The men returned the chant and erupted in cheers. The excitement they had been hiding since setting foot in Russia roared from their throats.

'Let's get ready,' said Talhig as he stepped down from the table and strode from the room. He headed outside, and dialled Sheikh's number. He waited patiently for the connection.

'Da?' answered Sheikh quietly.

'Phase one is complete. Phase two is moving ahead. The men are ready. We're ready. Glory to Mother Chechnya,' said Talhig. Pride strained in his words.

'Glory to you and your men, Talhig. The Russian Bear will be on its knees soon. I've faith that you will succeed. Do not forget Grozny. Allahu Akbar,' replied Sheikh and terminated the call.

Georgiy

Georgiy breezed through the control room. He was on his way to the office to tackle hours of reporting. He was beginning to feel the tedium of his duty, fatigued from the lack of action and stimulation. The Chechens were doing just what they said they would. Their movements did not fit with the warning he had received. The fact that they all wore military style boots meant nothing.

Yawning, Georgiy noticed that the screens showing the hidden CCTVs were blank. A shrill whine of background feedback signalled the loss of the microphones.

'What's happening?' he asked Georgiy. He looked at Private Lazarov, his personal radio operator. 'Is there a problem with our equipment?'

'No, sir. I was just coming to get you. Everything's working fine here. The compound has lost power,' supplied Lazarov abruptly.

'They could be making their play. Did anything happen before the power went out?'

'Da. The cleric removed his juddah to reveal a uniform of some kind. The light was very dim. It's already getting dark outside. He gathered the Chechens in the dining room. Then we lost everything. I think they cut the power. They know we've been monitoring them.'

'I think you might be right.'

Staring at the blank screens for a moment, Georgiy mulled over the possibilities. There was one course of action available to him.

'Stand the Alpha team to. Be ready to depart for the compound in fifteen minutes. Is the Orion still on station?' asked Georgiy, referencing the RPV assigned to assist with keeping the Chechens under surveillance.

'We have a one-hour coverage gap which is thirty minutes old, sir. The Orion assigned developed an issue and returned to base. The replacement should be on station shortly,' replied Lazarov.

'It is what it is. Stand the men to, Laz. I'll meet them out front. You stay here and relay the RPV feed to me when it comes online. Advise headquarters. Pass on my intentions to confront the Chechens,' instructed Georgiy as he strode from the room to grab his gear.

Lazarov sounded a quiet alarm to bring the Alpha team into action.

In the corridors, Georgiy could hear raised voices and rushing movement as the special forces teams quickly organised themselves for the possibility of combat.

Alexi

Alexi dove for his console. He was hyperalert since his interaction with the suspicious *Stenka 18* contact. The head of Plyos security had instructed Alexi to keep a close eye on the northern platforms. Huffing quietly to himself, Alexi wondered what the man thought he did every shift. Monitoring the platforms was his primary role. Shaking off his frustration, he had spent those hours trying to isolate and lock on to the intermittent satellite radar contact which had to be *Stenka 18*.

Six hours earlier a burst of radio traffic had grabbed his attention – the words that erupted from his headset had chilled his heart. The production ship, *Boris Gakkel*, had initiated a distress call that suddenly cut off in a harsh burst of static. Scanning his screen, Alexi had seen the track for *Stenka 18* establish itself close to the *Boris Gakkel*. Missing from the surface picture were the targets for the two tugs. He could see the gas carrier *Isa Umarov*, which had been alongside the *Boris Gakkel*, heading away to the north. The gas carrier's signal disappeared from his screen two hours later.

Rolling ideas around in his head, Alexi had opened the emergency folder gathering dust in the console's top drawer. He took a moment to collect himself. He scanned through the list of procedures in the folder and found the one he wanted at the end. As if it were so unlikely to occur, someone had placed it last. He thumbed through the plastic-coated pages until he arrived at the procedure's title page. Nothing of use. Turning the page, a telephone number in large, bolded font leapt out at him. Underneath it, neatly written by hand was the instruction, 'call immediately, use phrase *Razbil Steklo*'.

Alexi knew the telephone number. He had to follow the process. Alexi nervously selected a telephone line and tapped the digits into his touchscreen communications console.

'Da,' had come the stern and aggressive answer.

'Chairman Umarov, this is Alexi Chirikov. I'm the duty controller in your oil and gas security section,' he had advised cautiously, instantly recognising the voice of the chairman of Plyos Energy, Khasan Umarov. Alexi had never met the man and by reputation it was better that way. Umarov had grown Plyos Energy from an idea to a global powerhouse in 15 years. He was a ruthless businessman.

'What do you want? I'm busy with an emergency. I'll call you when I can. Do not disturb me,' Umarov had grumbled. Alexi could feel Umarov's irritability.

Alexi had tried to call the chairman every 10 minutes for the next five hours, but always his telephone was engaged.

Reaching forward to dial again, Alexi saw an incoming line

light up on his console.

'Pylos Energy Control, Alexi,' he answered.

'What is it you want, Alexi? I've been busy,' replied Umarov. An unhurried tone had replaced his previous irritation.

'Sir, *Razbil Steklo*,' replied Alexi firmly. There was no time to gather all his courage. Alexi hoped he sounded professional. He had just used the emergency phrase for a major incident in the gas fields.

Alexi heard a sharp intact of air.

'Why haven't you called me?' shouted Umarov.

'I've been trying to call you every ten minutes for the last five hours, sir,'

'Where?' questioned Umarov, ignoring Alexi's explanation.

'The production ship, *Boris Gakkel*, serving the Shtokman gas field, sir.'

'No, no. You mean the Ispytaniye platform, don't you? What was your name?' asked Umarov, confusion in his voice.

'Ah, Alexi. No, sir. There's nothing happening at the Ispytaniye platform. I'm talking about the *Boris Gakkel*. I received a garbled mayday, then lost contact with the ship, five hours ago. The signals for the two supporting tugs and the *Isa Umarov* have also disappeared.' Alexi's voice was urgent.

'Could it be your equipment?'

'I don't see how, sir. I have no indication there's anything wrong with my end. Is there something wrong on the Ispytaniye platform?' questioned Alexi. He was confused.

'Have you been briefed yet?'

'On what, sir?'

'There's a terrorist attack planned for the Ispytaniye platform. That's what I have been busy with all day. Why aren't you part of this?' replied Umarov, anger rising in the voice.

'I'm not sure, sir. I have nothing in email and have received no calls today,' replied Alexi nervously. Someone was in trouble. He hoped it was not him.

'Keep an eye on Ispytaniye and the *Boris Gakkel*. I will investigate this. Stay at your console until I say you leave. Do not move. You're my man there from now. I'll have someone with you shortly. Is the *Boris Gakkel* sending emergency data?' asked Umarov.

'I've received nothing, sir,' replied Alexi.

'Force the connection. Find out what's going on,' ordered Umarov.

'Yes, sir.'

The call went dead in Alexi's ear.

Leaning back in his chair, Alexi watched his screens. Red flashing bars announced track loss and incursion warnings around the *Boris Gakkel*. Scrolling the mouse pointer across to highlight the target for the *Boris Gakkel*, he right clicked to open a menu and selected *emergency transmission – force* from the list.

Immediately, a data block appeared on a spare screen to his right. A stream of information on what was happening aboard the ship spewed across it. Scanning the data, Alexi could see the bridge was no longer operating. The production consoles appeared unmanned throughout the ship. Gas continued to flow from the Ispytaniye platform to the north, which was an automated process.

Unsure of what to do next Alexi rapidly typed up a short email, containing what he knew and sent it to Umarov. A few seconds later Umarov replied with a simple, 'stay at your station'.

Alexi fished around in the refrigerator for a can of Red Bull then returned to monitoring other platforms. His relief would arrive in two hours. Not that Alexi was going to make his date with the blonde tonight. He grabbed his mobile telephone off the console, then scrolled through to find the text she had sent him with her details. He tapped in his reason for not making the date and waited. The response was almost instantaneous. Alexi stared at the telephone uncertainly. The pretty blonde obviously had a mean streak. She was not happy with him. Shrugging, Alexi figured it might have been in his favour to miss this opportunity.

Alexi heard the sharp slamming bang of a car door outside the container. A few seconds later the container's door almost ripped off its hinges and four men rushed in.

'Secure everything. Secure your console!' shouted the first man to enter.

'It's always secured. Who are you?' asked Alexi. For a second, he had a vision of the men dragging him outside. The he would disappear for calling the chairman directly.

'Security. Keep working. We're here to assist you,' replied the man gruffly. He sat down in the chair next to Alexi. The security man scanned the screens. He was trying to make sense of the information and focused on the emergency data stream from the *Boris Gakkel.*

'Ah. Okay,' replied Alexi and turned his eyes forward. A second security man stayed in the room. The other two stepped back outside and took a position guarding the entry door. Alexi saw them pull small Tula Arms Plant SR-3 machine pistols from inside the folds of their jackets. He had a gel blaster in the same model. Alexi knew the guards would not be carrying toys.

Captain Brusilov

Brusilov looked out into the clear night sky as the last of the lines dropped away. Two tugs were in position to pull the gas carrier away from the berth. He hoped the weather would stay this way for the whole transit, though he knew the chances of it were low. He ordered slow ahead and the ship started to make way. Brusilov dismissed the tugs. The ship steadily headed for the harbour entrance and moved into the channel. At the end of the leads, he could see the icebreaker *Yamal* waiting patiently. After moving to the centre of the bridge, Brusilov lifted the radio handset clear of its bracket.

'Plyos Energy Control, this is the *Leonid Khabarov*, over,' he called, tapping his foot as he waited for a reply.

'*Leonid Khabarov*, Plyos Control, go ahead,' answered Alexi. He glanced at the security man.

'We've departed the berth and are heading outbound. I can see the *Yamal* waiting for us. ETA the *Boris Gakkel* a little less than 12 hours, over.'

'Roger. Stand by,' advised Alexi.

Alexi lifted the telephone to call his supervisor.

'What're you doing?' asked the security man.

'I must call my supervisor and return the *Leonid Khabarov* to the berth. We know something has happened on the *Boris Gakkel*. We can't send a gas carrier and icebreaker into harm's way,' replied Alexi.

'There have been no orders to stop shipping. Keep it going. This situation will resolve before they arrive on station,' countered the security man.

'I don't think that's right.'

'Do as you are ordered, Alexi,' stated the security man. He shifted his jacket to show a holstered Makarov 9-millimetre pistol. The threat was clear.

Shrugging, Alexi keyed his radio.

'*Leonid Khabarov*, Plyos Control, you're cleared to proceed. No reported issues or delays at the *Boris Gakkel.* Good watch, sir.'

'Thank you. *Leonid Khabarov*, out,' ended Brusilov. He gave the order for full ahead and contacted the *Yamal* to discuss their passage with her captain.

CHAPTER FOUR

Georgiy

Georgiy shrugged into his body armour and scanned down his front. He performed a quick mental check of his equipment. Satisfied, he pulled a MP-433 9-millimetre pistol from its holster on his belt and slid home a full magazine. Racking back the slide, he chambered a live round, checked the safety, and placed it back into the holster. He swung a 7.62-millimetre AK-15 around to his front, pulled back the cocking handle and let it hammer forwards. A round stripped out of the magazine and seated in the chamber. Georgiy had always preferred the stopping power of 7.62-millimetre rifles. He had insisted on the AK-15 variant of the new AK-12 as his personal weapon.

The early evening was already cold and getting darker by the minute. He never liked this time of year. Cold and dark were two of his least favourite things.

Georgiy shifted on his feet impatiently. He was just about to call out to his teams when they came hurrying out of the building's front door. Each man was combat ready. They moved with a measured professional pride and efficiency as they made for the vehicles. Georgiy counted them off. Yakov appeared in the doorway.

'Ready, sir,' he shouted and charged down the steps. He missed the second last one in his haste and ended up in a pile at Georgiy's feet. Laughter erupted from the other operators as they clambered into their vehicles and gunned the engines.

'Pick yourself up. You're in front of the men,' growled Georgiy, reaching down a hand to help his second in command to his feet.

'Fuck, fucking, fuck!' shouted Yakov as he sprung from the ground, ignoring the offered hand. He yanked open the driver's door to Georgiy's Patriot and threw himself into the seat. Yakov stowed his assault rifle and started the engine.

'Slow down, Yakov. We need to get there in one piece. If there's a fight I need to focus, be safe and look after the men. That's what a commander and leader does. Good decisions mean all of us come home,' coached Georgiy. He leaned on the frame of the door and looked at the other vehicles. He could see plumes of exhaust smoke rolling up behind the lead car. Each vehicle held the individual operators of the Alpha, Bravo and Charlie elements of the assault force.

Pride swelled in his chest. Georgiy felt the thrill of what he hoped was the adrenaline needed to join with the Chechens in combat. He still harboured a deep though well-hidden hatred for them. Georgiy had lost good men during the years of the Chechen civil war. Begrudgingly, he admired the Chechen tenacity and skill when it came to battle. He knew the next hour was going to be difficult. Not all his team would be breathing when this was over.

'Yad Five, this is Orel, radio check,' called Georgiy using his personal callsign. Command had issued the callsign Orel to Georgiy when he first entered the world of special forces. Yad was the root callsign for the unit.

'Orel, Yad Five, loud and clear. You have been authorised to proceed. Good hunting,' responded Lazarov. His unhappiness at being left out of the fight at the deserted control centre was obvious. There would be no action for him today and he envied his teammates.

'Roger,' answered Georgiy, feeling the man's frustration. He took a final look around before signalling for the vehicles to move out, then dropped into the passenger seat. He was sure he could hear the heavy beat of approaching helicopters bouncing off the mountains in the distance.

Talhig

'The helicopters are inbound! Team leaders get your men organised,' commanded Talhig as he marched outside. He had ordered the compound's power restored to assist with the helicopter landings in the gathering darkness. His men had isolated the CCTVs and microphones, disabling their power independently.

Looking around for his communications specialist, Talhig saw him hunched over a terminal, next to a small satellite dish. The satellite terminal packed into a small suitcase, easy to keep hidden from Russian eyes. Around Talhig, his assault troops organised themselves and prepared to receive the helicopters. A team of five men sprinted out onto the open ground beside the compound. Their task was to ensure the area was free of hazards before the helicopters landed.

'Commander,' acknowledged Corporal Mairbek Yeugenov, the unit's radio operator, as he looked up to see Talhig approaching.

'Mairbek, how long until the FSB drone is back on station?' questioned Talhig. Their Russian Bratva contacts had supplied Talhig with tracking information for all RPVs in the Russian arsenal. A small screen displayed the location of the incoming Orion as it flew towards them.

'Ten minutes, sir. We will be in range of its sensors just as the helicopters land. It'll be a tight window to get everyone equipped and loaded,' replied Mairbek.

'Da, it will be tight. There's a team on the last seventeen who will provide security. They will allow the men to pick up their equipment and begin loading. I would think that the FSB Alpha team are already on their way.'

'Do I need to make arrangements for the security team to be picked up?'

'No. Unfortunately their blood will spill far from Chechnya. I can't do anything about their sacrifice. They are giving their lives for the mission.'

'A good sacrifice, sir.'

'Da. A good way to die,' replied Talhig absently.

He could hear the inbound helicopters. The heavy thundering beat of the two Mi-26 heavy lift helicopters echoed off the mountains. Like the rhythm section of a song, the higher pitched rotors of the accompanying two Mi-17s kept the sound powering forwards. A smile spread across his face as he saw the lead Mi-26's navigation lights hugging the foothills. The machine's dull green paint made it invisible in the dim sky. On cue, the men securing the landing site activated a white light strobe to mark the centre of the field. Arranged around the edges were infra-red strobes. The pilots would be flying on night vision. The strobes were aids to help them locate the field among the lights of the town.

'Sir, the FSB Alpha team are on their way! They've just left their accommodation. Ten minutes and they will be here,' advised Mairbek excitedly. He had accessed a surveillance satellite which was slowly working its way through space above them.

'Let them come. I want the first Russian blood spilt on their own soil.'

Talhig walked to the front of the compound and strained to see in the rapidly failing dusk. He rued not having his night vision equipment. The approaching helicopters carried all the assault teams' specialised mission equipment.

Smuggled into Russia a month earlier, the helicopter crews staged at a small strategic landing area, 60 kilometres to the south of the town. An Mi-26 and one Mi-17 carried much of the equipment they would need for the assault and subsequent defence. The remaining two helicopters would carry the troops and remaining supplies.

'Raven flight, this is Falcon Bravo, over,' called Talhig into a handheld radio. He had secreted it below his juddah before revealing the deception.

'Falcon Bravo, Raven One,' replied the co-pilot of the first Mi-26.

'I have your visual. Call the landing site,' requested Talhig.

He could see the faint outlines of the other airframes in trail behind the first. They were frustratingly slow in their approach.

'We have the site. Five minutes out. Is the site secure?'

'For the next five minutes only. We'll have Russian special forces here shortly. You'll be landing into a hot zone. Raven Two, you're assigned to provide ground support until the security team has landed, over,' ordered Talhig.

'Roger. Ravens One, Three and Four will land. Raven Two will provide support,' replied the co-pilot. Answering clicks on the radio told him the other pilots had heard and acknowledged the orders.

'See you on the ground,' ended Talhig and clipped the radio back onto his belt.

Talhig paced around the compound setting up defences in anticipation of the Russian arrival. The feeling of defencelessness gnawed at his mind. If the Alpha team arrived before the helicopters it was going to be a close-run game. His men had nothing to fight back with other than their hands. Talhig did not intend on wasting his fine troops because he could not get at the weapons in time.

Satisfied with his quick assessment, Talhig jogged back to the side of the compound facing the landing site. The steady throb of rotors hammered against the town as the first Mi-26 flared for landing. It dropped onto the ground at the northern end of the site. He could see lights in people's homes close to the compound. Talhig smiled at the confusion they would be experiencing.

The second Mi-26, Raven 2, circled low over the compound. Talhig saw a door on each side rack open. A pair of GShG-7.62 rotary cannons ran out. The pilot put the helicopter into a defensive hover high above the compound and waited for the Russians to arrive.

Talhig could see the four large ferry tanks attached to the small winglet mounts either side of the fuselage. The aircraft would need to use the gas platform's refuelling facilities to reach the rendezvous with the freighter post mission. For those who survived, there would be months of torturous smuggling and evasion until they could once again stand on Chechen soil. Even then they would be immediately pressed into the new war Sheikh would trigger as soon as this mission was successful.

The men of the assault team were running across the space between the compound and the idling helicopters to gather their equipment. The clam shell doors of the last Mi-17 opened. The security detail rushed out, heading for the compound. They were heavily armed, ready for a fast, violent fight against the Russians.

Behind the rushing team, the loading doors of each helicopter opened. Loadmaster and flight engineers began pulling bins of weapons and equipment out for the assault force to access. The first freedom fighters to arrive equipped themselves and turned to help their comrades. The assault force knew their survival window was getting smaller with every extra second they took to gather their equipment.

'They're here, Commander!' Mairbek yelled to Talhig as he saw the lights of approaching vehicles.

Nodding in silent acknowledgement, Talhig raised his radio to his lips and looked up at the Mi-26 above him.

'Raven Two, engage the vehicles approaching the compound. Do a single run. Then land to load the troops. The security team will be in place by that time.'

'Engaging.' Came the curt reply.

A second later the shredding scream of the starboard rotary gun opening fire split the night. Expended brass casings rained down over the compound.

The security detail rushed past Talhig and sorted themselves into their positions.

A line of green tracer reached out and smashed into the last vehicle in the Alpha team's convoy, shredding it. The gunner continued to hammer the vehicle until it stopped and burst into flames. The remaining three vehicles of the convoy veered away into side streets to escape the onslaught.

The pilot lowered the Mi-26, slowly moving forwards to give

both of his gunners the opportunity to engage targets. As the helicopter flew along the street, the pilot could see the Russians disembarking their vehicles and heading for cover. With the Russians forcing their way into the surrounding buildings the only targets were the vehicles. Opening fire, both gunners destroyed the empty four-wheel drives in seconds. They walked their fire up and over the buildings the Russians had entered, peppering the walls, and smashing the windows. Lights flickered and blanked out.

Lifting the Mi-26 up and over the buildings, the pilot then turned and headed for the hive of activity at the landing site. He could see men milling and running around as they prepared to leave. Ten minutes and they would be gone.

Georgiy

Georgiy thrust his AK-15 out of the top floor window of the building which looked out over the mass of activity in the compound. Four helicopters, even as they idled, ripped the bare ground away and threw dust and debris into the dusk air. The Chechens were displaying white light as they geared up. Troops had started boarding the helicopters. It made it easier for the Alpha team to see what was happening, though it made the Chechens' actions more efficient. Georgiy figured the terrorists needed the added level of speed. The time for concealment was gone.

The fight was on.

Poking the barrel further out to find a target, Georgiy leaned forwards in the window frame. He moved just enough to see what was happening. Instantly, bullets hammered the outer walls around him as if someone had shone a spotlight on his position. The fire came from a team of men he had seen moving into position minutes before. Ducking back, Georgiy closed his eyes as the remaining glass in the window blew in and showered him.

'Fuck,' he cursed quietly. 'This is Orel, Bravo element, engage the men defending the compound. Charlie element snipers, commence engaging the helicopters,' he called over the radio. The Alpha element of his assault force had been in the vehicle shredded by the Mi-26's rotary cannons.

Georgiy could hear the panicked cries of civilians as they ran from the apartments around him. He wished them luck if they managed to get clear.

An answering volley of fire from his men crashed into the Chechen positions. Georgiy envisioned his men slowly working their way along the protective walls of the buildings to gain ground and position. Using the sound of their fire and movement, Georgiy kept track of his team as they made their way steadily forwards.

The whoosh of an RPG-9 erupted from the Chechen positions and the rocket slammed into the side of the building Georgiy took shelter in. The floor jumped beneath his feet and dust rained down from the ceiling. Taking the chance to look back out the window, Georgiy saw the Chechen who had unleashed the RPG standing up to fire another rocket. Snapping his rifle into his shoulder, Georgiy fired off five rounds. The Chechen dropped to the ground. A hand reached out from cover to retrieve the RPG. Georgiy fired a single round. It impacted the ground next to the hand. Hastily, its owner withdrew it.

'Charlie in position,' said Yakov over the radio. He sounded breathless. It was obvious he was excited. Yakov was in command of the sniper team who had forced their way to the top of the building opposite to Georgiy. Georgiy could see the muzzles of two Izhmash SV-98M sniper rifles, both chambered for .338 Lapua Magnum. Georgiy had every confidence they could take on the helicopters at the landing site.

'Engage,' ordered Georgiy.

A harsh gout of flame erupted from the muzzles of both rifles simultaneously. Georgiy saw two men fall to the ground as they ran up the ramp of the rearmost Mi-17.

'Target the helicopters, not the men. We can clean them up

later.'

Yakov answered him with two clicks on the radio.

Lifting a pair of Zenit LDB range finders to his eyes, Georgiy tried to observe the fall of shot from his snipers but was unable to see the impacts. He keyed his radio and stopped before he could utter a word. Three men were dragging a large case from one of the Mi-26s. Hurriedly flipping open the top, the men each pulled out what Georgiy was sure were RPG-32 Barkas. As the men threw the weapons onto their shoulders and sighted towards the assaulting team, Georgiy knew their target.

'Yakov! Get off the roof! Rockets inbound, get off the roof!' yelled Georgiy into the radio. He opened fire and sent a long futile burst towards the helicopters. He saw the flash of flame as the Chechens fired the Barkas towards their chosen target. Georgiy's burst of fire only succeeded in drawing the attention of the freedom fighters holding the line at the entrance to the compound. Dropping back away from the window, he stared in disbelief as two missiles impacted the opposite roof and exploded. A third missile roared past his window, continued down the street and exploded against the side of a small house. The front wall of the building collapsed, and the roof caved in, trapping the occupants.

Masonry and dust erupted into the air from the roof where

Charlie team had been and crashed down onto the street.

'Charlie element report,' called Georgiy.

Silence.

'Charlie element report!' called Georgiy again.

Silence.

'Charlie element!' yelled Georgiy.

Cursing, Georgiy surged off the floor, crossed to the door and jogged down the stairs to the ground level. The hammer of assault rifles was louder here. He could see the five members of Bravo element trading shots with the well concealed and protected Chechens.

The helicopters started to increase their power for take-off, and Georgiy knew his time was almost over.

'Yad Five, this is Orel,' he called over the radio.

'Go ahead, Orel,' answered Lazarov.

'Is the Orion on station?'

'Just arriving now, sir,' advised Lazarov. He had been watching the data block for the Orion come on station and start transmitting images of the battle. Lazarov shook his head as he saw for the first time the chaos which his comrades were engaged in. He could see the increasing blade count of the helicopters as they prepared to leave. The position of the Chechens protecting the compound was easy to discern by the muzzle flashes.

'Is it armed?'

'Da. Four laser guided Kh-thirty eights.'

'Target the helicopters.'

'The RPV will be in range to fire in a few minutes.'

'We don't have that much time!' cried Georgiy over the radio, frustration in his voice. 'Advise headquarters what's happening as well.'

'Already have, sir. They've informed me that they are dispatching fighters to assist. ETA thirty minutes. Reinforcing ground troops are also being organised. No ETA on them, over,' advised Lazarov.

'Give the launch command to the Orion controller as soon as it's in range,' instructed Georgiy.

Watching the battle unfolding in front of him, Georgiy knew the missiles would be too late to take out the helicopters. Already the last of the Chechens were climbing on board. The doors and ramps were closing.

'Orel, Yad Five, over.'

'Go ahead, Lazarov,' replied Georgiy.

'The Orion is in sensor range. I have a heat signature moving towards the rear door of the building you're in. The track is moving slowly along the alleyway. The heat trail behind leads back to the compound. I think you have a Chechen trying to flank you,' advised Lazarov urgently.

'On it,' said Georgiy. He turned to the nearest operator and tapped him on the shoulder. 'We have a contact moving along the rear of the building. I'll sort it out. Join up with the rest of Bravo and keep the Chechens busy. Missiles will be inbound as soon as the Orion is in range. Pass it on,' advised Georgiy. Nodding quickly, the operator rose into a crouch and jogged away to join the rest of the element.

Georgiy twisted on his heel and ran towards where he figured the back door of the building would be. Weapon up and ready for a fight, he made his way down the corridor. It opened into a small common room. To his front was a door which appeared to lead onto the alleyway.

'Where's the contact?' he requested from Lazarov as he came up to the door and tried the handle.

Locked.

'Moving past the door you are currently at. I have good tracking on you and Bravo element. I cannot see Alpha and Charlie elements though.'

'They're gone,' answered Georgiy curtly.

'Roger. The contact's on the other side of the door. Hold,' advised Lazarov. 'Now moving away, along the alleyway. Looks to be heading around the building towards the front. That door will bring you in behind them.'

'Okay. Keep me informed,' replied Georgiy. Stepping back, he took a moment to look at the door's lock. He crashed his right foot with all his momentum next to it. The door smashed open against the outside of the building; the sound lost among the stunning noise of the battle which raged behind him.

Peering cautiously out into the alley, Georgiy scanned the Chechen positions. He saw no movement and stepped down onto a concrete pathway. He walked quickly around to the corner of the building and glanced into the next alley. Three quarters of the way along the path was a man moving quietly and quickly. Silently hoisting his rifle to his shoulder, Georgiy sighted on the man's back and tightened his finger on the trigger.

As he peered through the sight, Georgiy knew there was something wrong with the man's outline. Even if he had been rugged up against the cold, with an equipment harness over the top, his shape would not have appeared so bulky.

Georgiy took in a sharp breath of cold air.

'Suicide bomber in the alleyway! Suicide bomber in the alleyway. Clear the building!' he screamed into the radio, hoping to warn his men.

Hearing Georgiy's urgent call the Chechen broke into a sprint, trying to make it to the Russian position at the front of the building. As the Chechen rounded the corner, Georgiy flicked his AK-15 to full auto and fired. The bullets streaked out and cut into the man's back, racing up to smash his head from his body. The body stumbled forwards uncertainly, then slowly began to fall around the corner. Georgiy paused.

The Chechen soldier's bomb vest detonated in a brilliant flash and ear-splitting explosion. The explosion surged into the bottom floor of the building and smashed into the Bravo element operators sheltering there. Flame and debris erupted across the street and into the alleyway. Thrown from his feet, Georgiy crashed into the unyielding wall of the adjacent building. As dust and debris dropped over him, Georgiy gathered his scattered mind. He rolled upright, weapon to his shoulder and ready to continue the fight. His head hurt. His vision was slightly blurred.

Staggering forwards, he arrived at what used to be the corner of the building. The entire front of the structure sagged towards the ground. The three closest buildings were in the process of collapsing in sympathy. Georgiy could see that the last men of his team were gone. He was the only one left to take the fight to the Chechens.

Dragging up his courage, Georgiy leapt into the shattered remains of the building. Without looking down he hurried over the torn bodies of his men. He took a position where he could see the Chechen position and the landing site.

As the first of the Mi-26s rose into the air, Georgiy knew it was over. In quick succession the rest of the helicopters lifted from the ground. They followed the lead Mi-26 as it gained speed and hugged the ground, quickly lost in the early evening sky. The only evidence that the helicopters had been there was the distant beat of receding rotors. Dust and debris swirled around the compound and blew down the street.

'Yad Five, the helicopters have escaped. Pass it on to the Air Force to chase them down. Reassign the missiles to the defences in front of the compound. I'm the only surviving member of the team. Everyone else is dead. I will finish this,' instructed Georgiy.

'Roger, stand by. Launching in ten seconds.'

Georgiy cursed and slammed his gloved fist into the windowsill next to him. Only 30 seconds more and he could have taken out the helicopters.

'Incoming. Take cover!' Georgiy yelled instinctively without acknowledging he was the only survivor. He fired off the rest of his rifle's magazine and dropped below the line of the window.

After their suicide brother detonated his rig, the Chechens had continued firing for a moment longer and then ceased. Georgiy could imagine the Chechens wondering what was happening and whether they had succeeded in killing the enemy.

They will find out soon, thought Georgiy.

Four massive explosions roared into the night from the Chechen positions. Debris, bodies, and dirt arced into the air as the Kh-38s slammed into their targets.

Georgiy vaulted through the window. He flicked the empty

magazine on his rifle into his dump pouch. He landed on the debris littered street, then charged down the road, slamming home a fresh magazine as he went. He drew his weapon to his shoulder, ready to engage any survivors. A man rushed from the smashed and sagging doorway opposite. Instinctively, Georgiy spun towards the threat and sighted on the man.

'Georgiy, it's Yakov! It's me, Yakov!' shouted the man as he put his hands up and skidded to a halt.

Georgiy threw him a questioning glance, noting the blood which covered his second-in-command's face.

'I heard your call and ran. The others could not get up fast enough. The men are dead,' said Yakov glumly.

'I'm glad you survived. Everyone else is dead. Avenge our comrades, Yakov,' responded Georgiy encouragingly. 'Let's get in the fight.'

The Chechen position was quiet. Flames burned brightly where parts of the compound had caught fire.

Georgiy stalked up to the first body, nudged the man with his foot and passed over him. The freedom fighter was missing his legs. There was no fight left in him. Entering the defensive line, Georgiy looked along it and saw only dead fighters.

He jumped in fright and spun around at the sound of gunfire. Yakov had shot the last survivor, just as he was rising to engage them.

'We need to secure the compound,' ordered Georgiy. Without a word, Yakov rushed forwards and entered the building, looking for the targets.

Returning a few minutes later, Yakov walked up to Georgiy.

'They're gone. What the fuck just happened?' enquired Yakov breathing heavily. He had never shot anyone before. He would remember the Chechen's triumphant and determined face until the day he passed on from this life.

'We lost the first round,' replied Georgiy, absently wiping a line of blood from his face. He was not sure whose it was, but it felt like his own. He slid a mobile telephone out of his cargo pants and dialled his commander, surveying the destruction as he waited for the call to connect. He tucked the pain of losing his men neatly into the back of his head for the moment.

Alexi

Pylos Security

Alexi inwardly groaned as he glanced nervously across at the stern-faced security man who was his constant shadow. He was tired and starting to feel the stress of the situation. No-one was listening to him. The men on the *Boris Gakkel* needed help: the ship had probably been highjacked. Thirty minutes earlier his relief had come on duty, called in hours before he was meant to start work.

Lev Tereshkov had entered the room wide eyed and worried. Security guards had escorted him inside. At least the Plyos security men had decided one of their number was enough in the cramped control room. The other three moved out to guard the front door and deserted carpark.

Full of questions that Alexi had no answers for, Tereshkov had taken a seat and logged onto the spare terminal. Alexi gave him his handover briefing and the three men settled into the cramped space designed for no more than two.

Alexi jumped as the desk telephone started ringing. He never had to use that handset; normally calls rang through his radio console. Only two entities used that telephone number. The Federal Security Service and Chief Intelligence Office had a direct line to the control centre.

'Plyos control centre, Alexi speaking,' he announced.

'Major Constantin Chernenko, I'm the FSB controller for the Murmansk sector.'

'Yes, Major Chernenko, how can I help you?' Alexi asked. He felt the weight of fatigue on his shoulders. For a moment he felt depressed and exhausted.

'We have a situation.'

'I am across the issue on the *Boris Gakkel*, sir. Plyos Chairman Umarov is aware.'

'Who is *Boris Gakkel*?' queried Chernenko.

'Not who, sir, what. It's our production ship which services the Shtokman gas field. We believe it's hijacked,' said Alexi. The security man frowned deeply at him. Alexi mouthed FSB and got a curt nod in return.

'I know nothing of this. Is it confirmed?'

'No. We lost coverage of its support vessels, and the ship is sending a discreet emergency feed.'

'That issue is currently not what I'm calling you for. Who's with you?' asked Chernenko. His voice was gruff and tired. He had been trying to work his way through another quiet shift when it seemed that Chechens were suddenly running amok in the region.

'I have Lev Tereshkov, the night controller, and four security men from Plyos Energy. They are here to secure the centre,' replied Alexi quickly.

'Who's that you are talking to? What do they want?' questioned the Plyos security man urgently next to Alexi. He had rethought his first reaction. As the conversation continued, he did not like the fact that Alexi was freely giving out sensitive information.

'Hold on, Major,' said Alexi into the telephone and turned to the security man. 'It's the FSB controller of Murmansk, Major Chernenko. Is that okay?'

'Yes. Continue,' replied the security man.

'Who's that? Who's questioning me?' asked Chernenko irritably. There was a crushing headache brewing behind his eyes.

'Just the company security man. He's here to ensure I don't tell anyone what's going on. He said it's okay to talk to you though, Major,' replied Alexi smugly as he eyeballed the security man.

'Security? He's nothing. Good. I will have a man with you soon. The FSB is taking the lead on the response. We will secure our borders against these Chechen terrorists.'

'Terrorists?' asked Alexi. Inwardly he groaned at the thought of more people crowding into the small space.

'Has no-one told you?' snapped Chernenko. He felt like he was talking to a child. Civilians were always difficult to deal with in stressful situations.

'My chairman advised that there was going to be an attack on one of our gas platforms.'

'It's those damned Chechens. There's intelligence that a main force of terrorists staged at the town of Kirovsk have left the area in helicopters. They're heading for your Ispytaniye platform.'

'Helicopters, you said. I will see if I can find them,' responded Alexi leaning forwards to scan the screens.

'How can you track them?' asked Chernenko suspiciously. His own sensor operators had been unable to find any targets in the area around Kirovsk.

'I have access to satellite radar feeds and other sensors to track ships moving around the oil and gas fields. Helicopters fly between those platforms. It's our job to keep an eye on things,' replied Alexi unhappily.

Alexi reached for his can of Red Bull and lifted it to his lips. Empty. Cursing silently, he motioned for Tereshkov to get him a fresh one from the refrigerator. Nodding absently, Tereshkov pushed past the security man and pulled a can from the refrigerator. He opened it and handed it to Alexi. Nodding his thanks, Alexi took the can and drained half of it.

Alexi typed in the name of the town Chernenko had mentioned, slewing his main working screen to look inland. Seeing no targets, he called down a plotting tool from his desktop and calculated the most direct route from Kirovsk to the Ispytaniye platform. Immediately, a line formed on the screen and stretched up to the platform. Scrolling slowly, Alexi drifted the display offshore and followed the line. As he moved the screen, Alexi picked up four radar contacts 100 kilometres off the coast. They were following exactly along the path he had plotted.

'I have four contacts passing the one-hundred-kilometre mark from the coast. They are on course for the Ispytaniye platform. ETA to the platform is two hours, maybe more. The weather's terrible in the area. There's a storm hammering the northern gas fields.'

'I have no contacts on my screens,' responded Chernenko a frustrated tone in his voice. He looked over the shoulders of his two sensor operators. Their screens continued to show no targets in that area.

'Plyos buys the best equipment and sensors to protect its assets, Major. Maybe the FSB needs to invest in some?' A sense of happiness filled Alexi's chest as he took the chance to have a stab at Chernenko and the FSB. He'd tried to join the organisation before taking up his position with Plyos. The recruiters were scathing and uninterested in him. Alexi had never discovered why.

'Enough. I will have a man with you in twenty minutes. What are the current positions of the helicopters?' requested Chernenko. He had not missed Alexi's jab.

Alexi sighed and passed the information on to Chernenko. Without responding, Chernenko disconnected the call.

'Well, he was a nice guy,' said Alexi to himself quietly as he sat back in his chair. On the screen in front of him the contacts for the four helicopters disappeared. 'They're gone!'

'The targets?' asked Tereshkov.

'Yes.'

'If they are close to the ocean, we will lose them in the sea clutter. I would hate to be the men on those helicopters.'

FSB Northern Operational Command

Murmansk

Admiral Unkovsky, Commander Northern Sector, scowled over his coffee at Major Chernenko.

'What's the situation?' he demanded. His gravelly voice, carved from years of chain smoking and heavy drinking, was losing its power. Unkovsky had risen to his current position through networking, not competence.

'Plyos Energy are tracking the helicopters. I have the positions. They're concerned that one of their ships has been highjacked,' replied Chernenko.

'What ship? I saw nothing about a ship in the briefing.' Unkovsky's eyes narrowed.

'The controller believes there's a problem with the production ship which services the Shtokman gas field. It's transmitting an emergency signal.'

'Dismiss it. Concentrate on the confirmed information. The worried words of a civilian are not solid intelligence,' ended Unkovsky casually.

Both men sat at a small table in a meeting area next to the sensor operator's room. Unkovsky shifted in his chair uncomfortably and gazed at Chernenko. He could feel his ability to cope with the situation drifting away. Tasking the icebreaker *Aysberg* to steam for the gas fields to ascertain what was happening was one thing. But this situation was developing into something completely different. Unkovsky knew he needed to end it quickly. Deep down, he felt ill equipped to deal with it for any length of time.

'I've arranged for Naval Aviation to send jets to shoot down the helicopters. Pass the coordinates to the operations centre at Olenegorsk Air Base,' instructed Unkovsky.

Chernenko nodded and dialled the number for the base's operations room on his mobile telephone. He passed the instructions to the duty flight controller. As he ended the call Unkovsky's mobile started ringing. The Admiral's face reddened with anger when he saw the caller's ID.

'Da!' answered Unkovsky sternly. He listened for a moment, his face growing redder. 'Nyet, FSB will handle this! The President has ordered it. The President! Have respect. It's our area. We will handle it with assistance only. I thank our friends in the GRU. But I do not need more than information from you. Nothing more. Nyet, I'll maintain control of this situation. FSB's the lead here. No-one else!'

Mashing a fat thumb on the cancel button, Unkovsky ended the call and tossed the handset onto the table. He looked up at the nervous face of Chernenko.

'Fucking GRU, the navy, the government! They all want to

get in on this. The army even wanted to take over. The fucking army! What do they know about things? Chernenko, FSB will maintain command and control of this operation. We'll be the ones to take the glory when the situation resolves.'

'Yes, sir,' replied Chernenko cautiously.

'I want an Alpha team enroute to Shtokman field and the Ispytaniye platform. If the GRU's intelligence is correct, this is going to be a major incident. We need to be on top of it, Chernenko, not at the bottom of the heap. It's FSB's sole glory after this mess finishes. Get the best commander and a team assembled and airborne.'

'Major Georgiy Urvantsev is the best man for the job. He was in command of the team that was in contact with the Chechens at Kirovsk,' supplied Chernenko confidently. He had known Urvantsev since they had been in the academy together as young fresh-faced cadets. Urvantsev had streamed into combat operations while Chernenko had stayed safely behind a desk. Both men were successful in their own way.

'I know him. A good man. Did they take any casualties?' asked Unkovsky.

'Only Urvantsev, his second-in-command and a radio operator survived the battle, sir. They were a small team. The Chechens had more firepower and a degree of surprise,' supplied Chernenko.

'Recover Urvantsev and his men from Kirovsk. Assemble another team and get them on their way. I want our surveillance aircraft to do a run over Shtokman field and the Ispytaniye platform. I want to know what's going on.'

Nodding, Chernenko tapped the numbers into his telephone to connect with the small aviation element the FSB had at their disposal in Murmansk. He tasked a helicopter to collect Urvantsev.

Olenegorsk Air Base

92 kilometres south of Murmansk

Rolling onto the threshold of the long main runway, two Mikoyan MIG-31BMs of the Russian Navy 458th IAP unit lined up for take-off. Dim runway lights streamed either side of the cracked concrete surface. They gave each pilot an adequate guide to maintaining the centre line.

Lieutenant Christophe Litke settled into his hard ejection seat and finished the final flight control checks. The operations officer had allocated him callsign 'Jeda One Five' for the mission. He scanned around the cramped cockpit of his fighter. Satisfied, Litke advanced the throttles of the two massive Soloviev D-30F6 turbofan engines slightly and applied the brakes. In the seat behind him sat Lieutenant Rudolf Novikov, his weapons sensor operator. The two men had teamed up three years previously and were a well-oiled and effective crew. Outside of the cockpit they were firm friends and spent many hours drinking and chasing after the women of Murmansk.

'Good to go, Rudi?' asked Litke. Litke had never used his friend's full name.

'Ready,' replied Rudi as he adjusted his sensors for a high-speed take-off.

Both fighters scrambled to intercept the terrorist helicopters following the short battle in Kirovsk. Although too big and cumbersome for the task, the MIG-31BMs were the only aircraft standing on alert.

Litke held the brakes for a moment and did a final control check. He smoothly moved the throttles forwards slightly. He released the brakes and pushed the stiff throttles into afterburner. Immediately, he felt the satisfying thump and rumble through the airframe as long twin flames roared from behind the jet. Rapidly accelerating down the runway, Litke reached V1 in seconds and V2 20 seconds after he had started rolling.

Roaring into the evening sky, Litke pulled the nose of the MIG-31BM high to gain altitude. He wanted to give his wingman enough room to manoeuvre. Pulling back slightly on the throttles, Litke dropped the engines out of afterburner. The rumble and shaking of the airframe settled. Building speed, Litke guided his bullish and aggressively styled fighter towards the last known position of the Chechen helicopters.

Talhig

150 kilometres from the Russian mainland

Rain and ocean spray slammed into the Mi-26's windscreen and the wipers struggled to cope with the onslaught. Wind hammered against the fuselage and the massive helicopter slewed from side to side with each gust. Tightening his seat belt, Talhig looked past the pilots and into the night. Since leaving Kirovsk, it had been like a violent and uncomfortable roller-coaster ride as the pilots guided the airframe over terrain and ocean. They managed to maintain as little height as possible. The higher the helicopters flew the easier Russian radar could track them.

Minutes earlier an alarm had flared on the dash between the two pilots. A radar was tracking the helicopters. Deftly working through menus, the pilot isolated it to a space-based radar system. A short radio call to the three helicopters struggling in the conditions behind had brought all to just 50 metres above the cold and unforgiving ocean. The pilots intended on hiding their airframes among the sea clutter to confuse the Russian radar operators.

Talhig marvelled at the skill and professionalism of the pilots. They sat in their seats, working the controls like machines. Cross-talking constantly, the two men functioned like a single entity. Talhig felt safe and proud to be in the hands of men like these.

The mission would succeed, because how could it fail?

Talhig turned to look back into the unlit interior of the Mi-26. He could barely make out the dim shapes of his soldiers seated along the sides of the fuselage. A long pile of crated equipment and weapons occupied the centre line of the helicopter to sustain their coming fight. While Talhig could not see his people well, he could smell their vomit. He felt a surge of pity but steeled himself at the thought. In just two hours these same troops would be heading down the ramp to storm the platform and wipe it clean of the enemy. He trusted that his soldiers – his brothers and sisters – would achieve their assigned tasks.

Twisting to stare back through the windscreen, Talhig wondered if he would see a fish arc past. A low altitude alarm had started blaring as soon as the pilots dropped towards the ocean. Isolating the alarm, the pilots had continued their descent. A bright warning light continued to blink furiously, vainly trying to get someone's attention.

Jeda One Five

MIG-31BM

'Novater Control, this is Jeda One Five, over,' called Litke over the radio. Sweat was pouring down his face and pooling in his mask. His helmet felt like it was trying to slide off his slick scalp. Litke could not seem to get his breathing under control. Even with five years of flying experience in the harsh north of Russia, he was finding it hard to cope. The conditions he found himself in were atrocious. The heavy MIG-31BM wallowed, pitched, and climbed as if the machine had developed a mind of its own.

Litke, one hour into the search for the helicopters, was beginning to feel the fatigue of constantly correcting the wayward fighter.

Behind him, Rudi tossed around in his seat, his eyes unable to hold focus on the MIG's sensors. Rudi was using the powerful Phazotron Zaslon radar in the nose of the aircraft to try to scan the clutter and chaos of the ocean 500 metres below. The passive electronically scanned array radar allowed Rudi to search for targets out to 400 kilometres. More than enough to detect the helicopters. On the chance he did manage to locate them he would lock the targets with his Baget 55-06 computer. At his disposal were four Vympel R-33E air-to-air missiles to make the kill. The helicopters would be no more. The trick was finding them in the chaos of the ocean. Rudi was sure the helicopters would be hugging the surface. As the weather tried to tear the aircraft from the sky, he was sure he could hear the R-33E missiles vibrating against their hardpoints under the fuselage.

'Go ahead, Jeda One Five,' responded the radio operator in the air command centre on the Servornomorsk-3 airbase. Control of the naval flight transferred to the Air Force base to enable better coordination and control of the search.

'We're over the last reported location of the helicopters. No sighting, I say again, no sighting on radar,' grunted Litke as the fighter suddenly thrust upwards, driving him hard into the pan of the seat.

'What are the weather conditions, Jeda One Five?'

'Zero visibility. Significant up and down drafts. Very dangerous conditions, Novater Control.'

'Roger. Stand by,' advised the radio operator and leaned back to look at his supervisor, who asked for their fuel status. 'Say your fuel, Jeda One Five.'

'We have ten thousand kilograms remaining,' replied Litke. It was a reasonable guess. He could not quite read the virtual gauges displayed on the screen in front of him.

'Return to base, Jeda One Five. We are sending other aircraft to take over the search.'

'What is their ETD?' enquired Litke.

'Forty-five minutes.'

'Novater Control, this is Jeda One Five, we are returning to base. Estimated time of arrival is ninety minutes,' said Litke. He checked in with his wingman. The relief in the pilot's voice was palpable.

'Let's go home, Rudi,' said Litke over the intercom.

'No arguments from me.'

Damien

Damien's slumbering mind fired wearily and listened to the furious hammering noise which had started seconds earlier. His consciousness swam up to understand the noise. Then the sound was gone. Again, the hammering started. Damien's face crunched and creased with annoyance as he struggled to remain asleep.

Damien heard the door to his cabin unlock and swing open.

Instantly, he snapped his eyes open. His mind came fully awake and alert. His body tensed for action. Damien could see a man outlined against the light coming in through the open doorway. Another man, the sound of his heavy work boots thumping on the deck, walked quickly towards where he lay. That figure lay a light hand on Damien's shoulder and called out to him in urgent Russian.

Exploding into action, Damien snaked his left arm up and

around the outstretched arm of the man bending over him. He latched onto his assailant's shoulder, forcing himself up and off the bed. Using his momentum, Damien sent the surprised and unprepared man wheeling backwards. With a grunt the man crashed to the floor, landing on his rump. The man tried to roll away from Damien, who, like a crazed person, roared at him in panicked anger.

Damien charged forwards.

He grabbed the man's hair and yanked it back, forcing him to his knees. Whimpering in stunned fear, the man tried to wrestle free. Damien countered every move and expertly held him in place. He dropped his right knee into the man's back, pulled back on his head and put pressure on the man's spine. Dimly, Damien could hear frantic shouting from the doorway. Ignoring the second threat, Damien continued to control the man on the floor. Sliding his left arm down, Damien curled it around the man's throat and squeezed, throttling him. Gasping and struggling, the man tried to free himself. His arms waved helplessly in the air as he tried to grab at Damien.

Suddenly, the cabin filled with blinding light as the man at the door flipped a switch. Damien dropped his eyes and waited for them to adjust. The man in his grasp wore the same uniform he did.

Damien's head hurt. It was like he had had a heavy night of

drinking. Confusion stirred in the back of his mind. Something did not seem right.

Who was this man? he wondered.

'Stop! Australian! Stop! You're killing him!' yelled the figure in the doorway. The man in Damien's clutches had started to go limp.

Snapping his head up to fix the man in his sights, Damien recognised the driller from the shift before his.

What is he doing in here?

'Stop!' the driller shouted again and moved closer.

Blinking rapidly, Damien looked down and, in the light, realised the man in his hands was the drill hand from the same shift. Confusion hammered in his head.

'What? What do you want?' croaked Damien, his throat drawing closed.

'You're late for shift!' yelled the driller. He moved to within a pace of Damien. He looked at the pain and fear on his comrade's face. Damien's muscular left arm still crushed his throat. The driller saw that Damien wore only a pair of shorts. His body was hard and covered with scars. A tattoo which looked like a constellation covered his back.

'Oh,' replied Damien. He dropped his arm from under the drill hand's chin and stood up. Like a switch, Damien could turn his aggression on and off.

Damien helped the drill hand to his feet, patted him down and checked his throat for injury.

'You'll be fine. A bit sore, but you'll be fine. I'm sorry, my friend. You startled me,' apologised Damien.

Nodding, the drill hand turned for freedom and rushed from the room, taking the driller with him.

Damien hurriedly pulled on his heavy work clothes. He eyed the shower, but knew he had no time. As he moved to leave, he paused, returned to the table near the bed and retrieved his Gerber Gator folding knife.

PLYOS ENERGY HEADQUARTERS

ARCHANGELSK
EMERGENCY MEETING

Slightly dishevelled because of the late notice of the meeting, four men sat across from Chairman Khasan Umarov. They eyed him carefully. Umarov was the exact opposite of his men. He had taken the time to shave and carefully dress in a dark suit. He had time while he waited for his driver to arrive with his grey Mercedes GLE AMG63 SUV. His life centred around efficiency. Umarov presented a strong professional image no matter the hour or crisis which was unfolding, as did his security chief, Yuri Andropov, who sat off to one side. He dressed as he always did, in black cargo pants, boots and a grey shirt.

Though the crisis before them was like nothing they had experienced before, there was no need to present poorly. Umarov nodded to each of his men. Without a second thought, he decided to cut their bonus for the year. That way they would remember to be presentable at all meetings in the future.

'Gentlemen. We have a crisis unfolding, the likes of which we've never experienced. I'm informed this morning that the FSB have discovered a terrorist group targeting one of our facilities. I have received an update. The terrorists are right now heading in helicopters for the Ispytaniye platform in the Shtokman field. They intend on taking it over and destroying my property to shame our country. Our glorious Navy and Air Force are unable to find them. Our own control centre had contact briefly, but the terrorists have disappeared. I can only hope that the Chechens crashed into the ocean. But I doubt it. They have a tenacity to survive and fight which many could learn from.'

He paused for effect.

'There's another unconfirmed issue. It could be that the *Boris Gakkel* is under threat. Our control centre has initiated an emergency data stream. It shows five people onboard out of the normal one hundred worker complement. There is also an intermittent, small contact close by. Nothing confirmed. We don't know if they're linked,' briefed Umarov.

Pausing again, Umarov fixed each man with an unflinching stare. He was unimpressed by the panic growing on their faces.

'Those, gentlemen, are side factors here. The loss of the Ispytaniye platform would cripple and destroy this company. Plyos Energy will not survive. Nor will it get the chance to rebrand. It will be the end,' lectured Umarov. He held the group in the palm of his hand with his well-polished oratory skills. Umarov received high praise as a speaker in difficult political circles.

'There's severe weather over Ispytaniye currently, sir. How could helicopters land? We have grounded ours. How could these Chechens hope to land safely and then conduct an assault in an Arctic storm?' questioned Yuri. He was a man bold enough to engage Umarov critically.

'That, Yuri, is something we do not quite know. But what I do know is that the Chechens will carry this through. I'm not interested in their political struggles against Russia. We have interests in Chechnya. I do not see why we have become a target. But, Yuri, more to the point what can we do about it?' pressured Umarov. He had faith in his security chief after many years of loyal and productive service. Umarov hoped Yuri had a solution.

'Do you want shipping stopped to the *Boris Gakkel*? I show a gas carrier inbound with its icebreaker.' Yuri was looking at a small tablet in his hand.

'Do not stop any shipping. We must continue to operate. What's happening on the Gakkel is unconfirmed. No, we must continue production,' ordered Umarov flatly.

Yuri nodded in reply and took a deep breath.

'How do you want this resolved?' asked Yuri pointedly.

'Ispytaniye cleared of terrorists and kept intact. The FSB is organising an assault force to intercept the terrorists. If there's a problem on the *Boris Gakkel* the military can attend to it. If it sinks, we have little to worry about, other than some pollution and lost productivity. Another production ship can take its place in a few days,' stated Umarov, ignoring the seemingly expendable lives of the production crew.

'I know of an organisation which may be able to assist. They will be able to react faster than our military forces,' replied Yuri carefully. 'If you authorise the expenditure, sir. They have helped us in the past.'

'I'm not aware of this. What help have we received from outside before?' said Umarov, surprise in his voice. He prided himself on knowing exactly what happened in his company.

'That, sir, is why I would use them again. Very discreet, very capable, and professional. They'll clean up the Chechens on Ispytaniye as if they never existed.'

'Chechen fighters are not peasants, Yuri. They fight for country and belief. The two drivers of men which are hard to put down. As Mother Russia has found to her bloodied fists over the years,' responded Umarov dramatically.

'I can call and make the request,' continued Yuri.

'Call,' replied Umarov, abruptly reaching for the latte he had served himself in a tall glass cup. Umarov took a sip and smiled.

Turning to his manager of platforms, Serge Semenov, Umarov regarded him for a moment. He took in the man's concerned face.

Replaceable, thought Umarov.

'Have you advised Ispytaniye and Nevzgody platforms?' he asked pointedly.

'I'm waiting on your word,' said Semenov nervously. He felt he had made a mistake with the chairman, but he could not work out what it could possibly be. There was something amiss in their exchange.

'Advise them. Ispytaniye is the target. Get them ready for the assault. Tell Nevzgody out of courtesy to assist their sister platform if needed. Order both platforms to continue working. We will not stop production for some misguided Chechens,' instructed Umarov.

'Yes, sir,' replied Semenov. He stood and hurried for the door, heading down the stairs to the security control room to pass on the chairman's clear orders.

Yuri waited patiently for the meeting to finish, then quietly excused himself and went into the next room. He pulled the doors closed behind him, fished out his mobile telephone and scrolled through the contacts until he had the one he wanted. He pressed dial and waited.

'Hello, Mad Hatta Bar,' answered a woman in a brusque, thick Yorkshire accent. Yuri winced at the rough and uneven edge to the woman's voice. Music and conversation sounded loudly in the background.

'Can I speak to Mister Thompson please,' asked Yuri, trying to inject a light tone into his voice to disguise the importance of the call. He had no idea who this woman was. She had answered the telephone on the three occasions he had called for assistance.

'Of course, you can, darling. Nice to hear your voice again, Yuri,' flirted the woman. 'Just you hold the line, handsome. I'll connect you. Bye for now.'

Yuri stared in disbelief at the handset. He had never mentioned his name before and always used different telephones. Suspicion rose in his throat. Before he could take his thoughts any further, Mister Thompson came on the line.

'Mister Andropov, a true pleasure to hear from you,' said the man Yuri knew as Mister Thompson. The hint of a South African accent hung on his words.

'I would appreciate your help with some trouble we're having.

If you're willing?' asked Yuri.

'Yes, I have heard. Your situation is difficult. Give me the full details as you know them,' requested Mister Thompson.

Yuri was again surprised at the speed and depth of Mister Thompson's intelligence network. Without pausing, Yuri passed on what he knew about the coming assault.

'Are you able to assist? Discreetly and completely? No witnesses, no evidence,' said Yuri.

'Same as the last three operations? Of course, Mister Andropov. The Taipan Organisation accepts the contract. I have a team who've just completed a mission in Norway. They have the right skills for this operation. Due to the difficulty and conditions, I will need to place an additional fee on top of the normal costs. Is this acceptable?' asked Mister Thompson quietly.

'It is.'

'Good. I'll dispatch the team as soon as they're ready. On station tomorrow morning at the latest.'

'Very good. Thank you, Mister Thompson.'

'Always a pleasure, Mister Andropov. Good day.'

The connection went dead in Yuri's ear. He opened the doors and strode back into the room. Umarov looked at him expectantly.

'It's organised. They will be on Ispytaniye by tomorrow morning at the latest,' said Yuri gravely.

'Very good. I hope they're as good as you say,' said Umarov, fixing Yuri with a stern gaze.

Yuri did not miss the dangerous tone in the man's voice.

Don Murphy

SVALBARD
NORWEGIAN ARCHIPELAGO

'Well done, lads, good mission,' said Don as he welcomed the Taipan 21 team back to the small house he had rented as the base of operations in Longyearbyen. The three men looked at him, smiled and walked through the door into the warmth of the house. Each man dressed against the cold in heavy coats which hid their armour and HK MP-7A2 submachine guns. Thickly lines of fatigue and dirt covered their faces.

Sitting at the only table in the room was a recent Taipan recruit. Ex-USAF Senior Master Sergeant Noah Williams nodded to the men. Following the final mission of Taipan 16 in Afghanistan, Don had argued he needed to add a combat controller who was joint terminal attack control qualified to assist the teams. Noah had supported him in the final stages of the disastrous Taipan 16 mission. Don had spent a year encouraging Noah to join the organisation. Noah had rapidly become the asset Taipan needed on the modern battlefield. The highly specialised skills of a JTAC-qualified combat controller allowed Don to protect and monitor his teams with greater precision.

Don lined up three shots of Blanton's Original single barrel whiskey for his men and one each for himself and Noah. Following a well-worn ritual, the men gathered, looked each other in the eye, nodded and shot the whiskey. Each man gently placed the glasses back onto the table.

'Debrief in fifteen. Cleaned up,' ordered Don. He watched the Taipan 21 team drop their gear in the living room. Don would police it for them as the men headed for the bedrooms at the rear of the house. 'Not a bad job,' said Don to himself.

'It went well, Don. That RPV you procured for me performed perfectly,' said Noah. He had used an Elbit Hermes 450 RPV to maintain communications and a high bandwidth full motion video link with the team as they worked through their mission. The added intelligence the platform gave them had made the difference.

'The Israelis build top shelf equipment. Especially drones,' replied Don.

Don dug out the remaining ammunition from the team's chest rigs and placed it into large canvas bags. He cleared the MP-7s, wiped them down and dropped each into a dedicated hard plastic case. To the casual observer, the weapons and armour would look nothing more than a traveller's luggage on a trip to Svalbard.

Don's mobile telephone started ringing.

He crossed to the table where he had left it. In the background, he heard showers starting. Don drew his favourite 10-millimetre Heckler and Koch P30 pistol from the Platatac BattleTech holster on his hip and placed it next to the telephone. The end of a mission was when a team in the wild were the most vulnerable. It was his responsibility to keep them safe.

Don checked the number on the screen. Unlocking the telephone, he engaged an encryption application to secure the call.

'Murphy,' he answered formally.

'How did the job go?' requested his handler. The man's soft South African accent seemed stronger today.

'No issues. The team's cleaning up now. We leave tomorrow,' replied Don. His handler, Mister Thompson, was a hard man and charged with running the Taipan Organisation.

'Are they tasked?'

'Negative. No jobs for the next two weeks. They're going to take leave and go home,' said Don shifting on his feet. He had expected his handler to call, but the quick shift in conversation told him another operation was in the offing.

'Cancel it. I have a new mission for Taipan Two One. Are they fresh? It will be difficult.'

'Fresh enough after some sleep. They're not a bad team. A bit on the rough side but starting to shape up.'

'You need to let go, Don,' stressed Mister Thompson. 'There've been five teams since Taipan One Six. You need to move on. One Six were good but they weren't good enough for the mission which destroyed them.'

'Yes, sir,' answered Don sullenly.

He had never fully recovered from the loss of two members of Taipan 16 in Afghanistan two years earlier. Damien Hunter had been the only survivor. Don's favourite operator. No man had come close to his level of ability or professionalism since. In the last two years, Don had formed five teams. Two had disappeared on operations and another slaughtered the moment they arrived in location. Taipan 20 had been retired early due to injuries. Taipan 21 was the new team of three and were cutting their teeth on routine missions.

'I've sent you the operational details. There's a charter flight on its way to collect you.'

Don's email tone pinged in his ear.

'I'll make sure we're on it,' replied Don.

'Scan the briefing notes for me. Especially the location. It requires a high-risk insertion,' instructed Mister Thompson.

Opening the email, Don skimmed the contents.

'Hmmm. Going to be difficult. It's a hard place. We'll need additional support when we get to Russia. We're not welcome there,' responded Don. His heart skipped a beat when he saw the objective, but not for the reason Mister Thompson might have thought.

'I've set up a safehouse in Murmansk for you to operate out of. A nice place this time. No-one will know you're in the country. Our friends in the FSB will see to that. The client will also see to your protection. Their chairman is a powerful businessman and well connected. Taipan Two One will fly direct from Norway to the objective.'

'I'll work out the details with them on the flight out of here.'

'Do we have any assets in the area that I may not be aware of?' asked Mister Thompson. He had detected a subtle change in Don's tone. The two men had worked together for the last 15 years. Mister Thompson knew Don's every move.

'Not an asset. A person, yes, but he won't help us,' replied Don.

'Who?'

'Damien Hunter.'

'What's Chainsaw doing there? The last information the Organisation had was that he had become drug-fucked and burnt out. I thought he might even be dead,' replied Mister Thompson callously.

'He works on one of the northern Arctic exploratory oil and gas platforms in the Shtokman gas field. I arranged for him to get the job to try and straighten him out. Fate seems to be bringing him back to us. Damien's on the sister rig to the one that the

Chechens are reportedly heading for.'

'Chainsaw clouds your mind, Don. Taipan will not allow it to happen again. Understand?' stressed Mister Thompson.

'I am aware, sir.'

'In your assessment, would Chainsaw be available for the operation if required? Is he capable of assisting if we need additional support on the ground? He was a top operator in his day. Though I'm not so sure now.'

'It's reported that his mental state is poor. Nightmares and irrational action. But he's drug and alcohol free. I don't think he's in any state to help. Even if he was, I don't think Damien is too fond of our organisation these days. Not after Afghanistan.'

'Get Taipan Two One mobile and in the air. Brief them on Chainsaw. If they encounter him, Damien is to take part in the mission or they eliminate him. Do you understand?' instructed Mister Thompson, ignoring Don's last comment.

'Yes, sir.'

Damien

Rushing up the last stairway to the drilling floor, Damien noticed there were fewer workers around than normal. His interest piqued immediately; the rig was quieter. Less noise normally meant something had broken, but this felt different.

He approached the hatch which would let him out onto the floor. Through the window set in the door he could see the drill working through the last few pipe lengths.

Immediately, he was on guard and scanning his surroundings. Before he opened the hatch, he replayed in his head the passage up to the doghouse. Damien was sure something was amiss. The mess room had been empty. He had heard the ringing of running boots in a stairwell. There had been an almost total absence of workers along the way.

Frowning, Damien opened the hatch and was immediately assaulted by noise and wind. The steel decking was slick and icy. Pulling his thermal face wrap higher under his eyes, Damien heard a continuous string of curses from the toolpusher. He berated Damien for being late.

Not everything was different, thought Damien as he pulled his heavy gloves on and went to work.

Fedor

Fedor cursed and berated his superiors for sending him out into the storm. He struggled against the wind as he moved across the helicopter flight deck. His face stung from the beating Damien had delivered. The plaster holding his nose straight was wet and frozen. Under his arm he carried a combined strobe and radio homing unit for the incoming helicopters to lock onto.

Peering through the driving sleet, Fedor looked at the two company helicopters. They sat at the northern end of the massive landing deck. The far end of the pad provided a natural lee from the wind and provided a measure of protection for the machines. Neither helicopter was meant to be there. Both should have left by 6pm to conduct a crew transfer to the Ispytaniye platform. He was meant to have been on one of those aircraft. The weather had shut down flight operations. Fedor was too wary of his superiors to have told them.

Crabbing against the wind, Fedor made his way along the deck until he reached the tail of the AgustaWestland AW189 helicopter. He placed the unit onto the slick deck. Fedor liked the Agusta. It was a comfortable and practical helicopter. The Kamov 32S beside it was a totally different aircraft. He hated it.

Fedor activated the unit's magnetic clamps to secure it to the deck. He flicked the single switch mounted on the otherwise bare front panel. He cringed back as an ultra-bright white light strobe started flashing on top. He knew it flashed alternatively in infra-red as well as transmitting a homing signal. Nervous that someone would see the bright flashing light, Fedor looked around. The upper superstructure was empty.

Fedor had stayed in his cabin between shifts as he waited for the appointed time to make his way up to the flight deck.

He had purposely maintained his distance and broken contact with everyone in the last five hours. Fedor could not afford any interruptions or delays to his mission. His superiors had no tolerance of failure. Unknowingly, Fedor had cut himself off from a vital piece of information. He could have used the information to warn his superiors of the compromise of the Chechen operation. The company had advised the platform boss 30 minutes earlier of the attack on the Ispytaniye platform. Security had decided to react and were working out what to do to assist their sister platform. All of which Fedor was ignorant.

He stood up and started heading back along the deck, trying to keep his feet. If he fell now, no-one would find him for hours. Glancing down onto a section of the drill floor, Fedor saw Damien working. Fedor's eyes filled with hate. He paused to stare at the top of Damien's helmeted head.

As soon as the Chechens landed and took the platform, Hunter would be his to play with. The Australian was going to be his prey for a while. Fedor felt a surge of excitement at the thought of it. Seeming to sense Fedor's hate, Damien turned to look up at him. Damien held his stare for a long moment and returned to work.

As Fedor rushed off the deck, he wondered how the man had known he was there.

Talhig

'We have the beacon, sir,' called the pilot of Raven 1 over the intercom.

'Excellent. Excellent. How long?' asked Talhig.

'We are approximately ten minutes out. I can't see the platform yet. By the beacon, Ispytaniye is meant to be directly in front of us. Our navigation must be slightly off with the storm. I expected that Ispytaniye was further to the north,' supplied the pilot. He would be grateful to drop the aircraft on the deck and get some rest. Both pilots were at the end of their physical endurance. Exhaustion was biting deeply into their ability to fly.

'Advise the other callsigns. Prepare for the assault landing as planned. Our aircraft with the two Mi-17s on the landing deck and the other Mi-26 on the ice next to the platform,' replied Talhig.

Talhig stood and gained his feet on the deck. He treaded carefully down the gyrating fuselage.

'Ten minutes! Get ready. Ten minutes!' he shouted and slapped each soldier on the shoulder to encourage them. Each man looked him in the eyes and gave a curt nod.

Stopping in front of Asma and her small team of fighters,

Talhig dropped low to her ear.

'You and your girls are with me, Asma. I want you as my right hand throughout the assault,' he ordered. Asma nodded and tucked her thick black hair beneath an American made advanced combat helmet. She cocked her PP-19 Vityaz 9-millimetre submachine gun. Talhig could not hear the orders she barked at her soldiers. The helicopter was deafening.

Making his way up the fuselage, Talhig quietly thanked the Russian Bear for making such a rugged and survivable aircraft. Lesser helicopters would have broken apart and dashed into the sea in lighter conditions than those that currently battered the airframe.

'Can you see the platform?' asked Talhig as he arrived to stand behind the pilots. He strained his eyes to look through the sleet and dark sky. He was sure he could make out the glow of lights in front of them.

'Yes, sir. We picked it up visually only now. The main platform lighting plays out over the surrounding ice. Easy to see now. The infra-red signal on the unit has failed. The white light strobe and homing beacon are active. No problems with landing as planned,' stated the pilot confidently. 'Wheels down in two minutes. The platform's radar has energised and is scanning us. In this clutter it will be amazing if they can discern us at all. The closer we get the stronger paint they'll get.'

'It doesn't matter. Nothing can stop us landing. They don't have weapons to fight back with. Unless they can turn their radar into a weapon, we are very safe.'

CHAPTER FIVE

Nevzgody Platform

Security control room

'Dimitri, there're airborne contacts heading for us!' yelled Khabib Nurmagomedov as he concentrated on his radar console. Khabib was one of four radar/radio operators on the platform. His time in the Russian Air Force had placed him well for the transition to employment in the oil and gas industry. Advised of the security threat to the Ispytaniye platform, Khabib had been relieved that they were not the target. His radar screen was now telling him something different.

'Not Ispytaniye? They're meant to be heading to Ispytaniye. That's what control told us.'

Security Supervisor Dimitri Navalny stared at the radar screen disbelievingly.

'The targets look like they're on approach for our landing

deck. Not Ispytaniye. I estimate they will be landing in two minutes. They're coming here!'

'Sound the general alarm and enact the threat procedure,' instructed Dimitri.

'What procedure?' questioned Khabib. There was no threat procedure.

'Invent one.'

Turning from the radar screen, Dimitri picked up a desk telephone and called the Plyos security control room.

'Plyos Security, Alexi,' came a tired and worn voice.

'Alexi, this is Dimitri Navalny on the Nevzgody platform.'

'Da, Dimitri. Are you prepared in case you need to assist Ispytaniye?' asked Alexi.

'The Chechens are coming here. Not Ispytaniye!' yelled Dimitri into the handset.

'You're safe, Dimitri. They're going to Ispytaniye. That's the information we have,' corrected Alexi. The man on the other end of the telephone sounded very excitable.

'No. We have radar contacts heading this way. ETA one minute!' shouted Dimitri.

'Are you sure?' queried Alexi.

Dimitri had placed the call on speaker. In the background, Alexi could hear the wailing of the platform's emergency siren. On Alexi's own console an alarm sounded. A red circle around the Nevzgody platform started flashing red. Alexi silenced the alarm and enlarged the tracking window. He saw four airborne targets heading for Nevzgody.

'Yes. What do we do?' begged Dimitri.

'Lock everything down, Dimitri. Lock yourself in. Don't let them into the facility,' stressed Alexi.

'That's impossible,' stated Dimitri. He could secure most of the facility but not everywhere.

Yuri Andropov came through the door and stood behind Alexi. Tapping him lightly on the shoulder, Yuri indicated for him to hand over his headset.

'Dimitri, this is Plyos Security Chief Yuri Andropov. I instruct you to go out and make sure it's the Chechens who're on the helicopters. Do you understand?' advised Yuri.

Dimitri looked around the control room in disbelief.

Who the fuck did Andropov think he was!

'Did you hear me?' asked Yuri.

'Yes, sir. I'm not going out there,' spluttered Dimitri. His face grew pale and sweat beaded on his forehead.

'You will, Dimitri, or you will not have a job as soon as you hang up this telephone. Go outside. Make sure of the identity of the people on the helicopters. I want to know where the threat is,' ordered Yuri. His face was glowing red with anger. Alexi could feel the heat rising from the man.

'Yes, sir,' relented Dimitri. He sullenly dropped the telephone into its cradle.

'What did they say?' asked Khabib.

'I'm ordered to go out and see who's on the helicopters. Turn off the fucking alarm. It's giving me a headache,' replied Dimitri as he grabbed his heavy weather coat and left the room. His head hung low as he stepped outside and into the battering storm. Dimitri was sure he could hear the approaching helicopters. He wondered if this was the last thing he was going to do on this earth.

Damien

As soon as the general alarm started sounding, Damien stepped back from the pipe he was seating and looked up at the toolpusher for direction. The man was rapidly talking into his radio. The toolpusher waved his arms angrily at the men in the control room opposite. A loud Russian voice roared out of the loudspeakers ordering everyone to evacuate the deck and make their way into the accommodation spaces. Ominously, there was a direct order to secure all doors after passing through them.

To Damien the platform felt stable. There was no list. No feeling that it was sinking. No fire alarms were sounding. This was something different. He was immediately on guard. Instantly, he felt his years of combat experience click into place. The hair was standing up on the back of his neck. Something unpleasant was about to happen.

The men in the drill control room had commenced the process to slow the drill and stop it. Damien calmly walked towards the doghouse. He had no intention of becoming trapped in the accommodation spaces, but he would vacate the drilling floor. As he moved, he was sure he could hear the approaching sound of helicopters. Cocking his head and slowing his pace, Damien turned to look up at the helicopter deck.

A brilliant light was strobing against the sleet which hammered at the hard metal deck. Damien recognised it immediately. It was the same intensity he had used to guide aircraft and helicopters onto targets as a combat controller and during his time with Taipan. The figure he had seen moving on the helicopter deck earlier must have set it.

Suddenly, pushed to one side Damien reeled as the toolpusher and driller rushed past. They were heading for the doghouse. The door banged open and they passed through. Neither paused to secure it. The rest of the drill crew followed. Damien was alone on the floor. Glancing though the control room windows, he saw it was devoid of the team already. Very much alone, Damien felt a wave of calm professionalism settle over his mind.

He felt on mission.

Damien looked up into the storm as the sound of approaching helicopters grew louder. The nose of a Mi-26 heavy-lift helicopter appeared cautiously through the gloom. It edged slowly forwards.

Damien jogged for the doghouse door. As he stepped through, he paused to look back. The noise of rotors was deafening as the blunt nose of a Mi-17 seemed to force its way past the Mi-26 and set up for landing.

Decision made, Damien stepped into the doghouse and headed for his cabin for a quick stop.

Talhig

As the Mi-26 flared for landing Talhig could just make out the other Mi-26, Raven 2, making for the ice floe next to the platform. The glow of the platform's powerful floodlights reflected off the aircraft as it ducked and wallowed. The drafts caused by the winds eddying around the platform's structure made the pilot's work difficult.

The pilot of Raven 2 struggled for control, lost it, regained it, and lost it again. His airframe was carrying the heaviest load. With the autopilot unable to cope with the conditions, it had been a horrible machine to hand fly for the last four hours. Trying to regain the hover, he called out to the co-pilot for height and tried to keep the helicopter level. There was no margin for error. A stall warning suddenly blared. The pilot saw the altimeter rapidly unwinding. They were heading, uncontrolled, for the ice.

The aircraft lost the cushion of air under the massive rotor disk. The helicopter plummeted like a stone. Pulling on as much power as he could, the pilot tried to flare into some form of controlled crash. The weight of the massive machine was against him.

The Mi-26 smashed into the ice, pancaked on its belly for a second, then bounced into the air. Pulled over by the weight of its two ZMKB Progress D-136 turboshaft engines, the aircraft tilted to the right and caught its blades on the ice. Exploding pieces of ice and rotors flew in all directions. Shrapnel hammered deadly holes in the fuselage. The Mi-26 flailed against the ground, beating itself to pieces. As the helicopter slid across the ice the fuselage broke in two places – just behind the cockpit and in front of the tail boom. The cockpit continued its journey, scooting over the ice and crashing into the large foot which anchored the platform to the ocean floor. Bouncing off, the cockpit dropped into a gap in the ice and disappeared into the ocean.

The main body of the Mi-26 slowed to a halt and began disgorging men and equipment out onto the ice in a fan of pain and destruction. Above, the surviving helicopters were making their final approach.

'Raven Two is down!' yelled Talhig above the noise of the helicopter as the pilots pulled power to flare towards the landing pad.

'There're helicopters on the deck!' grunted the pilot as he twisted on more power to arrest their rate of descent.

'Fuck. They aren't meant to be here! They're meant to have finished a crew transfer and headed back to the Nevzgody platform,' called Talhig. He braced for what was sure to be a rough landing. There was still room on the pad for the Mi-26 and maybe one Mi-17, but not the planned two. 'Call off Raven Four. Have them land on the ice. We will use the cranes to lift the men aboard,' ordered Talhig from where he hung onto the backs of the pilot seats.

As he gave the order, he saw what had to be Raven 3's nose pass below the Mi-26. It was making for the landing pad. The Mi-26 was mushing towards the smaller helicopter. Talhig held his breath, sensing the impact. The pilot of Raven 3, oblivious to death hovering metres above him, focused on landing his aircraft. He wanted to get out of the storm.

Raven 3 was carrying too much forward speed, however, and the wheels skidded forwards when they touched the steel deck. Dropping the collective to stall the rotors, the pilots tried desperately to slow the landing. Rocketing forwards, buffeted by the wind coming off the superstructure, Raven 3 ploughed into the Agusta. In a split second both aircraft crushed together. Flame erupted, instantly consuming both airframes. Still carrying too much speed, what remained of Raven 3, its crew and troops tore the Agusta off its securing mounts. Both helicopters plunged over the edge and onto the ice below. A massive fireball soared into the air. The raging Arctic wind blew it south.

'Raven Three's down,' called Raven 1's pilot.

'Get us on the deck, now!' shouted Talhig. Mishaps were common during operations, but he had never suffered a 50 per cent loss before firing a single shot.

Without answering, the pilots eased the large helicopter forwards. They were edging towards the far end of the pad which Raven 3 had cleared for them. Gently feeling for the deck, and drifting steadily forwards, the pilots expertly placed the Mi-26 exactly where they intended.

The boxy shape of the Kamov KA-32S sat, rocking gently in the rotor wash 5 metres away. Raven 3 had missed the strobe light as it crashed. The white light flashed off the pale faces of the pilots, giving them a ghostly machine-like appearance. Behind them, Raven 4 squeezed into the tight space behind.

Talhig sprung up and headed down the fuselage as the pilots shut down the helicopter. Both men breathed a sigh of relief.

Talhig ordered the rear ramp lowered. He yanked open the door in the starboard side of the fuselage before a crewman could do it for him. After dropping down the stairs, Talhig was immediately assaulted by sleet and wind. Grimacing, he stepped down onto the icy deck and paused to look around. The platform's brilliant lights were blinding. As Talhig's eyes adjusted he saw a man working his way up a set of stairs towards him.

Talhig started crossing over, figuring it must be their contact.

'Who are you?' shouted Dimitri nervously against the storm. He had seen the first helicopter crash. It had taken all his courage to continue up the stairs. The man standing in the storm, dressed in dark aggressive clothing, looked like a soldier. A bitter fear was filling Dimitri's chest.

'Friends. Who are you?' responded Talhig. He was not so sure this was the person they were to link up with. The man wore a heavy jacket with security patches on it. Their contact was a worker.

'I am Dimitri Navalny, head of security for the platform. What're you doing here? Who are you?' responded Dimitri uncertainly. He eyed the man's combat uniform and weapons. He knew in his heart that a Chechen terrorist stood before him. A hard lump formed in his throat. Dimitri felt sick.

Talhig regarded Dimitri for a moment. This man was not who he had been expecting. He pulled a KBP P-96M 9-millimetre pistol from a holster in the centre of his chest rig and pointed it between Dimitri's terrified eyes. He pulled the trigger. Dimitri's lifeless body fell backwards and tumbled down the stairs.

'Unload and move out!' Talhig yelled through the storm. His soldiers were already moving down the rear ramps of the helicopters. Laying an arm on each side of the stair's railing, Talhig dropped his weight and slid to the bottom. He stepped over Dimitri's body and continued towards a hatch he knew led to the control room. He had spent hours poring over the plans for the platform and felt he knew it intimately.

Behind Talhig, his soldiers were pulling open hatches which led into the superstructure and pouring inside. The sound of shooting began to echo throughout the platform.

Damien

Moving quickly to his cabin, Damien looked up and down the deserted corridor. As he ducked inside, he heard the unmistakable sound of automatic weapons fire. Damien flipped the flimsy door lock into place. He knew he had only minutes to react. Whoever had launched the attack would start kicking in cabin doors looking for anyone dumb enough hide. Better to die on your feet than cowering under a bed.

Never on your knees, thought Damien recalling Taipan's motto.

It had been a long time since those thoughts had burned so brightly in his pain-ravaged mind.

He spotted his hardcover copy of Matthew Reilly's *Ice Station* and flipped it open. Hidden in a hollowed-out section was a 9-millimetre HK USP Compact pistol. Etched into the black paint of the slide was a stylised bone. He dropped out the pistol and checked that it still contained a full magazine.

He dropped it into a pants pocket.

Slipping off his heavy work boots, Damien pulled on his comfortable pair of black MACV-1s. In his small ensuite, he retrieved three full magazines for the USP from a hidden compartment in the bottom of his toiletry bag.

Passing the full-length mirror mounted on the back of the ensuite door, Damien paused and looked at himself. If he had a chest rig on, he would have thought he was back working for Taipan. Suddenly, he held his body straight. The ghosts in the fog of his mind receded. Every muscle in his body felt taut and ready for action. Damien could feel the thrill of combat descending over him. He readily accepted the exhilarating feeling.

His head was clear.

Damien felt alive for the first time in years. The prospect of joining in combat had reinvigorated him.

Padding quietly to the door he unlocked it, drew the pistol, and listened carefully. The corridor sounded quiet. Cracking the door, he looked carefully down the corridor and saw no movement. Stepping back, he looked along the line of door hinges to get an obstructed view of the passage hidden behind the door's bulk. From what he could see he was alone. Satisfied, he stepped out.

Damien turned left and headed deeper into the rig.

Fedor

Fedor stood over the mangled corpse of Khabib Nurmagomedov. He looked around the blood-splattered control room. He was not sure if he was doing the right thing. His orders were to place the beacon, meet the Chechen leader and escort him. Fedor had changed the plan slightly. On impulse he had secured the control room. Khabib had been surprised to see him burst in brandishing a crowbar. The radar operator had tried to escape out the opposite door.

Leaping after him, Fedor had delivered a blow to the back of Khabib's head. The man had slumped, stunned, to the ground. Not wanting him to regain consciousness, Fedor bludgeoned Khabib's head to a bloody pulp.

Breathing heavily, Fedor stepped away from the corpse, dropped the crowbar and waited.

A few minutes later the external door to the room slowly

opened and the muzzle of an assault rifle poked through.

'Don't shoot! It's me, Fedor Davydov. I'm your contact! Don't shoot!' he yelled nervously.

The door slammed back on itself. A woman dressed in a combat uniform, armour and looking every bit a killer walked in. Behind her came the man he was expecting. The Chechen leader.

'Fedor?' Talhig asked. Asma kept her weapon pointed at Fedor's chest. Talhig took in the body lying on the ground. The blood covering the walls was testament to the ferocity of the attack. He figured this had to be their contact. The man's face appeared bruised and beaten.

'Yes, yes that's me. Fedor, yes!' he stammered. Fedor felt like he was making a fool of himself the way he was talking but could not help it.

'Good, I'm Talhig, this is Asma. You have secured the room I see. Well done.'

'Welcome to Plyos Energy's Nevzgody platform. A gift from my superiors to their Chechen friends,' said Fedor with a flourish and enthusiasm he hoped would impress Talhig.

'Nevzgody?' queried Talhig quietly, fixing Fedor with a vicious gaze. He stepped passed Asma and stared at Fedor coldly.

'Yes,' answered Fedor, a nervous tremor in his voice.

'Not Ispytaniye?'

'No. Nevzgody,' repeated Fedor. He was quickly growing unsure of himself.

'You're supposed to be on Ispytaniye. We're supposed to be on the Ispytaniye platform!' roared Talhig.

'I couldn't get there. They cancelled the flights. I did my best. I did what I could,' stammered Fedor. He felt a wave of annoyance at the way Talhig was reacting. Fedor was the man on this platform. Talhig needed to respect that.

'So, we're on the platform that's still drilling?' replied Talhig, disbelief edging into his voice. The magnitude of the disaster was starting to dawn on him.

'Yes, but it's due to cut over to gas production in a week's time,' supplied Fedor.

'Are you connected to the pipeline yet?'

Behind Talhig, Asma shifted into Fedor's view to get a better angle on the man. Fedor was sweating profusely and giving off the cloying stench of fear. She could see he carried no weapons.

'Three pipes, with two connected. The last one will hook up soon and then pumping to the production ship starts. I don't understand you. What's the problem?'

'Ispytaniye was our goal. We needed a working, pumping platform for the mission to be successful. You have not supplied that to us. You have guided us to a platform that does not pump gas!' exploded Talhig spittle flying from his mouth.

'This is good enough!' yelled Fedor in return. He moved towards Talhig. Fedor's anger and growing embarrassment boiled over. He continued to close on the Chechen commander. Before he took another pace, Asma appeared in front of him, a gentle smile on her lips. Fedor noted how attractive she was. He was immediately distracted.

'Get rid of him, Asma,' said Talhig casually. Finished with Fedor, he called for his communications specialist over the radio. He had to advise Sheikh of the change in mission.

'No!' shouted Fedor as Asma whipped a wickedly curved hawk bill Karambit knife across the front of his neck. With his throat opened to the air, Fedor struggled to breathe. He thrust his hands up to close the gap. As he fell to his knees, Asma slammed the blade between his ribs and punctured his heart. Fedor died. Forgotten before he hit the ground.

'Supervise the laying of the explosives and get a team onto the ice. Sort out the mess from Raven Two. I want our anti-air online as soon as possible. Find my communicator, he's not answering the radio. I need to contact Sheikh.'

Without a word, Asma stepped over Fedor's body and stalked quickly from the room. She seemed to be almost gliding effortlessly over the deck as she walked. Talhig still found her distracting.

Taking in the bank of closed-circuit camera displays

against the far wall, Talhig surveyed his prey. He could see his soldiers methodically hunting their way through the platform slaughtering every worker they came across. A team were working at the cargo crane to lower 10 men down to the ice. There may be survivors from the crashed Mi-26. Talhig needed the cargo it carried. The men were a bitter loss, but it was the missiles that the helicopter carried that he wanted most.

Suddenly, the CCTV screens went blank.

Frowning, Talhig breathed in the clogging smell of blood and found he had no stomach for it anymore.

Nikolay

Cursing for the hundredth time, Nikolay pounded his fist into the centre console and shook his head.

'How could we have lost the port engine again, Chief!'

Nikolay was rapidly starting to lose patience with the *Aysberg*. The ship was tired in every respect. He was growing to hate his new command. Maybe he should have taken a shore posting like his father had advised him to. It had never occurred to Nikolay before that even his father had lost faith in him.

'There's nothing I can do, Captain. I repair one thing, something else fails,' answered the chief engineer. He was growing as frustrated as his captain. The port engine refused to work for more than a few hours at a time.

'Okay. Okay. Keep working. To relieve the strain on the starboard engine, we will maintain ten knots,'

'Da.'

'Keep me informed,' ordered Nikolay.

'Da.'

Striding to the starboard side of the bridge, Nikolay stared out into the night. The 24 hours of twilight at this latitude remained hidden behind heavy clouds. Storm cells ripped and tore at the ocean's surface. It had been more comfortable near the ice floes. As they changed course and entered open water, the conditions had worsened. Nikolay had complete faith in the might of the Russian shipyard which had built the icebreaker. The ship's poor maintenance was what shook his continued confidence.

The *Aysberg* was starting to show signs that it was not as happy to be back in its designed role as it once had been. The ship was taking on water through poorly repaired hatch covers in the foredeck. The pumps were effectively clearing it. Nikolay did not like taking on any water. The toilets had stopped working. The electricity to the galley had failed hours earlier and there was no way to restore it. The cook was only able to produce cold coffee and sandwiches. The steady thump and rumble of waves striking the old steel of the hull worried Nikolay the most. All it would take was a weak point to open the hull to the sea and it would be all over. Nikolay doubted they would even have time to don their survival suits before slipping below the surface.

'Distance to the ice pack?' he requested from his third officer for the tenth time in the last two hours. The man was tired. Constantly working at keeping his captain informed was a full-time job. *Feeding the beast*, as he liked to think of it. The first officer was supervising the engine repairs. The second officer was trying to find a solution to fix the compromised forward hatches.

'Eighty miles, sir. We will pass within ten miles of the *Boris Gakkel*. No other contacts in the area. I have calculated our drift and set. We're making very little progress. I calculate our speed through the water as five knots. The ocean's not our friend today, Captain,' replied the third officer. He was exhausted, physically, and mentally. He was unable to sleep in the current conditions. He knew better than to ask to rest. The captain did not look tired.

'I guess we keep plodding along until we get there,' replied Nikolay quietly.

Damien

Before turning the corner near the mess room, Damien stopped and listened. He was trying to detect anything out of the ordinary. Satisfied, he slid around into the corridor. Outside the mess room doors, someone had staked a pile of bodies. Damien recognised a few faces. The blank eyes of the mess assistant who had shown him a meagre kindness stared at him. His life extinguished. The air was thick with the smell of blood and gore. The polished floor slicked with its mess.

Padding forwards with his pistol up, Damian was ready to engage any target which presented. He continued down the length of the corridor, stepping around the bodies. He glanced into the mess room. Chaos. Overturned tables were full of bullet holes, and the floor was slippery with blood. Damien grimaced to himself at the image. Triggered by the thick clogging scent of the blood, memories of past battles drifted like ghosts through his mind.

Tucking away the weakness, Damien stalked further down the passageway. He had decided to head for the cargo-loading area on the opposite side of the platform. It was near the large crane which lifted cargo off the ice. He could easily access the outside stairways to the flight deck from there. Damien's goal was the emergency communications console mounted on the bulkhead inside the flight operations room.

Damien had scoped out every point of communications, escape and egress he could locate within a few days of arriving on the platform. He had mapped the facility extensively. He did not want to deal with who he would have to call when he made it to the communications panel. Damien figured he would work it out on the way. There was time.

A cabin door snapped open to Damien's right. A large man dressed in a combat uniform walked out into the corridor. Blood and sweat covered his face. The man was breathing heavily.

Turning to engage him, Damien investigated the room. It was a sea of blood and brutalised human flesh. The man had been at work on four workers who he had trapped in the room's tight confines.

Grunting in surprise the man lifted his rifle. Realising he had no time to open fire, he dropped it and thumbed a combat knife from his harness. Planting his feet, the man smiled cruelly. He held up a finger to his lips and motioned Damien forwards.

Frowning in amusement, Damien slid the pistol into a pants pocket. He drew out the short blade Gerber Gator and unfolded it slowly. The Chechen chuckled when he saw what Damien was bringing to the fight. Russians had forged hatred in this man. He thought Damien was one of his enemies. Easy meat like the workers in the cabin.

Damien looked deep into the man's eyes and saw a person devoid of compassion. Stepping aggressively into Damien, the Chechen tried to end the fight quickly with an open frontal assault. Laughing softly, Damien slipped to the left. The Chechen stopped and regarded him for a moment. He saw no fear in the man facing him. The laughter was unsettling. The Chechen recognised that he may have picked someone who had combat experience. Gritting his teeth, he dropped his shoulders and took a knife-fighting stance. His left arm was out to the side and his right held the knife centred with his body.

Maintaining a look of complete disinterest, Damien surveyed the man's stance and his first movements. There was some skill there. He needed to end this quickly. It was only a matter of time before someone else came along.

Again, the Chechen stepped into Damien, slashing the air with his knife. Fixing the man's eyes with his own, Damien came up onto the balls of his feet and lunged forwards. He curled his right arm around the man's fighting arm, feeling the knife slice the fabric of his heavy work shirt as it passed under his armpit. Before the man could react, Damien slid his arm further along to his back, gripped the rear of his helmet harness and spun him around. With the soldier's back to his front, Damien rammed his knife into the side of the man's neck. Blood fountained out. The Chechen struggled like a fish on a hook. Grunting and trying to call out, the man found his throat blocked by steel. Damien sawed through the cartilage of the Chechen's throat. The man continued to fight furiously to the last of his strength.

Dropping the dead man to the ground, Damien eyed his

equipment and uniform. Russian issue, but the man was something else. Regular Russian forces did not carry out this type of operation.

Terrorists, mercenary or soldier?

Damien wiped his blade on the back of the soldier's thick winter jacket, folded it and slid it back into a pocket. Squatting next to the lifeless body, Damien started to unsling the soldier's rifle. He tugged at the fasteners of the chest rig. Whoever was assaulting the platform had killed innocents. That was something Damien could not live with.

Damien decided he would go hunting.

The sound of voices and booted feet suddenly sounded further down the corridor. Gritting his teeth in annoyance, Damien knew he had no time to strip the body of the weapons and the gear he needed to get into the fight.

He dragged the soldier's heavy body through the open cabin door, dropped it to the deck and pushed the door closed with his right foot. Grabbing the body by the arms he moved deeper into the gore and blood-splashed space. He shook his head at the cruelty the man had visited in the room; Damien was glad he had ended his life.

Damien tossed the body into the ensuite and closed the door, then turned to survey the pile of sliced and tortured bodies. The sound of approaching footsteps grew louder. Dropping to the floor, he burrowed among the bodies and waited. Blood dripped over his face and soaked his clothes. Calmly pushing the feelings of disgust away, he breathed deeply and maintained his composure. This was not the first time he had hidden among bodies.

Outside, the sound of boots and conversation came level with the door and passed by without pausing. He waited a few seconds before sliding out from his hiding place. In the ensuite he stripped the dead soldier of his equipment. He could hear cabin doors opening and closing along the corridor. The attackers had to be conducting a search and destroy mission to clear out any remaining workers.

Cursing softly, Damien shook his head and moved to the cabin door. He cracked it open slightly. Thirty metres away, four men were working in teams of two, searching through the cabins and office spaces.

He waited for both teams to head into a cabin each, then pushed the door open and stepped into the passageway. Pulling his pistol free, he jogged in the opposite direction.

A shout from behind echoed in Damien's ears. He launched into a sprint towards an intersection in the corridor. A voice shouted in what sounded to Damien like Chechen for him to halt.

Damien dropped to the deck as the men opened fire, sliding

on his right side, and aiming to swing around into the next passageway. Bullets hammered into the walls above him. Pieces of cheap laminate showered down around him. He twisted his head to protect his eyes.

Driving his hand along the wall where the two passageways intersected, he shifted his direction and slid around the edge. Bullets impacted along the deck behind him. He crashed into the far wall, then levered himself upright. He moved back into the cover the corner afforded him. When he peered around the edge slightly to investigate the corridor, he saw the four men moving towards him. As they passed through the piles of bodies, the man in the lead slipped on the blood-soaked floor and crashed heavily to the deck.

The others paused to help him to his feet. Damien stepped out, raised his pistol, and fired a neat single head shot into each of the standing men. As they dropped to the ground the man squirming in the blood tried to get his rifle into the fight. Damien placed a bullet between his eyes. The crashing boom of the pistol echoed loudly against the walls.

Damien edged towards the still bodies. He had to collect their gear and work out who these people were. He was three steps clear of the junction when the hatch at the far end of the corridor opened and a team streamed in, weapons up and looking for the source of the firing. Cursing again, Damien doubled back and disappeared down the passageway. He had to get himself some firepower.

Behind him the sound of shouting and boots striking the deck echoed as the team took up pursuit.

Talhig

'I have a line open, sir,' advised Corporal Mairbek Yeugenov. He had set up his communications equipment on the table below the CCTV monitors. He could not work out why the CCTV monitors had gone blank. The system was functioning, just not displaying. He would have to deal with that later. There were more important things to accomplish first. Mairbek had hacked into the nearest of two Canadian Polar communications and weather satellites to give Talhig his line to Sheikh.

'Thank you. Get those cameras back online, please,' responded Talhig as he walked across the room. Moments earlier there had been a sudden rise in the ferocity of automatic weapons fire which had been rumbling spasmodically through platform. Asma had called in that 10 workers had barricaded themselves in a meeting room and attacked a fire team with knives and chairs. All were dead.

Talhig took the offered handset, and he dialled Sheikh's

secure telephone number.

'Talhig, my friend, what news do you have for me?' responded Sheikh without a greeting. His voice sounded tight and unhappy.

'The mission is not going to plan, Sheikh. There are many difficulties here. Our contact on the platform guided us to the wrong location. We're not on the Ispytaniye platform. Instead, we are on Nevzgody. The contact's incompetence cost him his life. The platform's all but secured, Sheikh.'

'Are you able to leave a small force on Nevzgody and relocate to Ispytaniye?' asked Sheikh.

'Negative, sir. There's a storm hammering the area. We barely made it to this platform.'

'Regardless, you have secured a Russian platform in the Arctic against overwhelming odds. Well done to you and your men! Casualties?' asked Sheikh quickly. To Talhig he did not sound interested. Something was distracting Sheikh.

'We lost one helicopter with fifteen soldiers when it crashed into the platform. One Mi-Twenty-Six crashed on the ice. The pilots died along with five men. Conditions are atrocious. It's worse than we planned for. There's a team currently on the ice setting up the anti-air. Another team is moving through the platform rigging the explosives.'

'Good, good, Talhig. I am sorry for your losses. The glory of

Chechnya will sing their names in time.'

'Yes, sir,' responded Talhig uncertainly. *What was Sheikh talking about?*

'Dasha has achieved his mission successfully,' stated Sheikh.

'I'm aware. Early, but successful all the same. He'll need to hold station until we're ready for the next phase,' returned Talhig.

'Da. There has been a development, my old friend. There's a problem.'

'Yes?'

'Talhig, the Russians have compromised the mission. They have the entire battle plan. Russian army units are massing in response throughout Chechnya. I'm forced to postpone the uprising planned with our brother freedom fighters,' said Sheikh gravely.

'How? We maintained complete secrecy.'

'The GRU had a spy in our very midst, Talhig. A filthy Russian pig was taking our hospitality and money. He was sending everything we planned directly to his handlers. We caught the man last night. One of the communications men. He had access to everything. Everything, Talhig. Except for Dasha's mission. It's with the grace of Allah that we kept that mission only to ourselves. I have the pig traitor here, in the room with me,' relayed Sheikh bitterly.

'What about us?' asked Talhig, quite sure what the answer was going to be.

'You're to continue the mission. There will be more focus on you now though, brother. It'll be difficult for any of you to escape and return home. Very difficult.'

'Yes?' Talhig could not believe what he was hearing. It sounded like his men and women were never to return home.

'You're to sacrifice your own lives for the glory of Allah and Chechnya if need be. You will be martyrs, talked about and praised. History will record your names,' insisted Sheikh, suddenly enthusiastic.

'These are good, loyal soldiers, Sheikh,' said Talhig, disbelief in his voice.

'And their sacrifice will be rewarded by Allah,' countered Sheikh. He had picked up Talhig's tone.

'I'll not waste their lives. What about our pick-up? Is it still available?'

'You will do as ordered. By me. But Talhig, because you care for your people, I will grant you the option to escape to the freighter. Destroy the platform first. Dasha has completed the first steps in the mission. He will destroy the production ship before you carry out your orders. I want an environmental disaster to bring the Russian Bear to its knees. You know that's the plan. You will carry out the details. If you escape and return home, then I will praise you. If you do not, I will still praise you, my old friend.'

'Yes, Sheikh. We will succeed.'

'I knew I could rely on you, Talhig. Before you go. I want you to hear something,' said Sheikh. He crossed the floor of his office.

Sheikh looked down at the pulped face of the GRU spy where he lay on the floor. The man had finally given his identity as Captain Boris Godunov, not Private Mahmud Isaev as everyone knew him. Two of Sheikh's expert interrogators had encouraged as much from the man as they could. Now he barely clung to life. Gritting his teeth with the anger which surged up his throat, Sheikh pulled his Makarov 9-millimetre pistol from its holster. He pointed it into the face of the spy. The traitor. Sheikh pulled the trigger and kept pulling until the magazine ran dry. 'Did you hear, Talhig? I dispatched the traitor myself. With my own hands.'

'I heard.'

'Remember Grozny,' said Sheikh as he disconnected the call.

The words sounded hollow to Talhig as he handed the handset back to Mairbek, who knew better than to engage with his commander.

'Not a word of this conversation leaves the room, Mairbek. The mission continues.'

Dasha

The shrill ringing of the satellite telephone caught Dasha's attention as he eased the cutter up against the hull of the *Boris Gakkel.* Dasha planned to ride in the lee of the large ship to escape the worst of the weather coming from the west. Throttling down the engines, he listened to the telephone ring. He ignored it. He concentrated on positioning himself so the crew could secure the boat's lines to the ship. Dasha had arrived next to a shell door let into the hull used to move cargo from smaller ships into the bowels of the massive vessel.

The telephone stopped ringing.

Dasha watched the crewman up forward take the line tossed to him. A shout through the open port door of the bridge announced the stern line taken up. Cutting the throttles to idle, Dasha allowed the lines to tighten. The missile cutter thumped against the fenders of the landing dock where it jutted 2 metres out from the hull.

'Mikhail, turn off the jammer. Find someone to help you repair the damaged missile container. We're going to need it,' directed Dasha. With a curt nod Mikhail shut down the jamming equipment, then climbed up the short stairs from the firing room. He headed out onto the deck.

The telephone started ringing again.

Dasha crossed to the receiver and picked it up.

'Da?' he answered. He absently watched the final securing of the cutter through the small windows of the armoured bridge.

'Dasha?'

'Da,' he replied nervously, he recognised the voice.

'It is Sheikh Taimieov, your commander. Why didn't you answer when I called?'

'I was securing the cutter alongside the production ship, sir. I could not leave the wheel,' replied Dasha. His voice trembled slightly. Of all the telephone calls to pass off, he had to pass off his commander. With his helmsman injured, Dasha had taken over all manoeuvring of the cutter.

'I'm changing your orders. Is everything secure?' asked Sheikh pointedly.

'Yes, sir. We have sunk two tugs and the gas carrier. The boarding team have secured the production ship. I'm waiting on orders from General Chechenskiy to initiate the next phase. I've not heard from him yet.'

'And you won't. The mission has changed. Your task is to rig the production ship immediately for destruction. I order you to blow up the *Boris Gakkel* as soon possible.'

'Sir, we aren't carrying explosives. It was never in our plan to place charges. My orders were to stand off, await destruction of the gas platform and then attack the *Boris Gakkel* with the last of our missiles to finish the job.'

'I'm aware of what your orders were, Dasha. I'm changing them. Are you arguing with me?' asked Sheikh, a dangerous tone creeping into his voice.

'Nyet. I will carry out the new orders, sir. Once I have recovered my men from the production ship I will stand off and send the last of the missiles against it.'

'If you survive the explosion, steam for the mainland. Hand over the cutter to the same men you collected it from. They'll be waiting. Is that clear?' ordered Sheikh.

'Crystal, sir.'

'Good. I want the *Boris Gakkel* destroyed. If the deaths of your men require that to happen, then so be it. You're to sacrifice yourself and your men for the glory of Chechnya if the need arises.'

'Da,' answered Dasha. He immediately picked up the underlying meaning of what his commander was saying. Getting back to the coast was not an option, regardless. Taking a deep breath, Dasha felt the weight of his own approaching death.

'Allahu Akbar,' forced Sheikh.

'Allahu Akbar,' replied Dasha and placed the receiver back into its cradle.

Walking slowly to the centre of the bridge, he paused, collected his thoughts. Decisions made, Dasha began issuing the orders that would speed up their final moments.

Damien

Uncurling himself from on top of a heating duct, Damien softly slid to the floor. He stood against the wall, waiting, listening. He had scooted up onto the duct as a group of men opened the outer door of the corridor he had been moving down. Damien considered his observations of the men he took at first to be soldiers. They had the air of well-trained and motivated terrorists.

As he waited in his hide, Damien watched teams working methodically through the corridors. They were hauling anyone they found into the open, killing them and moving on. A secondary team of three men would follow slowly and collect the bodies on a cart. Once it was full, they wheeled it away to wherever they stored the dead.

Their professionalism worried Damien. Terrorists, even well-trained ones, were not up to the level of these men. They were something different and would be harder to take out. He had not seen them moving in less than twos. He witnessed a tight team of five female fighters moving quickly down the corridor heading for the far section of the platform. At their head was an attractive woman. By the blood he had seen splashed across her front, a stone-cold killer. Listening intently to their conversation as they passed beneath him, Damien confirmed that they were Chechen. He knew there was going to be more trouble. Chechens were effective killers.

A steady stream of Chechens had jogged underneath him. They carried what looked like boxes of explosives. The teams were heading in both directions. Their actions and movements were precise. These men knew exactly where they were going. Working quickly, they had laid charges every 5 metres. They connected a tie line up to the ceiling and spliced it into what looked to Damien to be the platform's own fibre optic network.

Damien had pondered what that could mean as he watched them work. In 10 minutes, they had cleared the space, their deadly packages left behind.

So, the Chechens are going to blow the platform.

Listening to the silence, Damien eased around the corner of a connecting passageway and weighed up his options. The number of Chechens who had made a beeline for the crane and cargo area had ruled out sanctuary in that direction. There was still the option of heading to the helicopter operations room. That was where he had been aiming to go. The Chechens, not by design, continued to cut across his route, slowing him down. By the way they were slaughtering everyone, they had no plans for holding hostages. As Damien pondered his next step, he heard the heavy thud of boots in the main corridor.

Damien eased himself slightly around the corner to allow his right eye to focus down the corridor. Hurrying towards him was a lone Chechen, a harassed and unhappy look on his face. The man looked like he was late to his own funeral. In his right hand he held a small black hard plastic case. The Chechen was not wearing armour.

Perfect, thought Damien as he slid the folding knife from his pocket and readied himself.

As the Chechen came level with Damien, the man detected movement in his left eye and spun towards the threat, lifting his AK-74M.

Before the man could react, Damien plunged the knife into his chest. He clamped his right hand over the man's open mouth. The hard plastic case fell from the Chechen's grasp. A muffled cry of pain and fear hammered against the inside of Damien's hand. Using the momentum, he had generated, Damien lifted the squirming, choking man off his feet. He jammed the Chechen up against the closed door of a cabin.

Leaving the knife embedded, Damien felt for the cabin's handle, found it unlocked and pushed it down. The door sprang inwards. They both tumbled into the dark space. It took Damien a second to realise that the man was dead. They were alone. The room had blood splashed up the wall behind the oversized single bed and spread through the covers. Someone had been surprised while they slept and dispatched in here.

Rolling the soldier onto his side, Damien inspected his shoulder patches and saw the symbol of a Wolf. He worked through the man's pockets and found his identity card, *Corporal Tapa Tchermoeff*. A Chechen by his identification. The card confirmed Damien's suspicion.

Blood stained the front of Tchermoeff's combat uniform. Grimacing, Damien hoped the dark green colour of the camouflage pattern would hide it well enough to the casual observer.

He reached out into the corridor and retrieved the fallen plastic case. It was light in his hand.

After locking the cabin door, Damien stripped Tchermoeff of his clothes and equipment. Leaving his MACV-1 boots on, he dressed in under a minute. The uniform was an almost perfect fit. He looked the part. Adjusting the equipment harness to fit his larger, more muscled chest, Damien checked its contents. Aside from full magazines for the AK-74M and a fighting knife, the man was carrying a bayonet and a single water bottle. There was no food. A kilogram of what looked like plastic explosive bulged in a pouch.

Interesting.

Tucking his HK pistol into an empty pouch on the harness, Damien inspected the AK. He found it well cared for and carefully cleaned. Tchermoeff had been proud of his weapon. Now it was in the hands of someone he would consider an enemy. Racking back the cocking handle, Damien saw a round in the chamber. He clicked down the safety lever to single shot. Every shot he fired had to count.

Pausing, Damien breathed in deeply. He felt the heroin high of combat surging through his body. Realising how much he missed it, he smiled happily. He felt relaxed and at ease with himself.

Did I make the wrong decision to leave Taipan? he wondered.

He was empty and ruined after the last mission in Afghanistan, but he could have recovered. He could have kept going. Pushing those thoughts to the back of his mind, Damien directed himself back on mission. It was the number of terrorists he had to kill in the future that he was unsure of. But there would be killing.

Damien cast his eyes over the case lying next to Tchermoeff's body. He picked it up and carried it over to a table hard up against the far side of the room. Flicking open the heavy catches, he pushed up the stiff lid and looked inside.

Shaking his head, Damien was not sure his luck would keep holding. The case contained a laser ordnance initiator sitting on top of what looked like spare detonators. Laser initiators were not common on the battlefield. They required a delicate fibre optic cable to carry the detonation signal from the controller. Pursing his lips, Damien was sure he had happened on an important piece of the Chechen plans.

Connecting dots that were not there before, Damien looked up. He saw a fibre optic cable running through a fireproof gland above the door. The cable carried the platform's internal computer systems, CCTV, and the internet to each cabin. It allowed workers to keep in contact with families, but also to perform off duty work. That was what the Chechens had been wiring their explosive charges into.

Damien now knew what the laser initiator was for.

Talhig

'Sir, we have reports of an armed Russian attacking our men!' shouted Mairbek at Talhig.

'What? How can that be?'

'There are reports that teams are starting to find the bodies of our soldiers across the platform.'

'Get Asma on the radio,' instructed Talhig. He should have expected some bravery from the Russians. There had to be combat veterans among the crew.

'No answer. It could be the metal of the platform inhibiting the transmission, sir,' advised Mairbek, looking up from his equipment. The mass of metal that made up the Nevzgody platform was perfect for defeating ice, but it also interfered with radio communications.

'Do a net-wide call. Warn everyone that there's at least one Russian fighting back. I want everyone on alert. I want the Russian hunted down and killed. It shouldn't take too long,' instructed Talhig.

Frowning at the new complication, Talhig added it to his list of things to work out. He had decided that as soon as the charges were ready, he would evacuate the assault team. The original plan had called for them to hold the platform for up to 72 hours. That parameter was gone with Sheikh's orders to destroy the platform as soon as possible. Talhig knew the freighter scheduled to take them on board would be in position in a few hours' time. He saw no point waiting.

They would be gone before dawn.

Georgiy

OLENEGORSK AIR BASE

Georgiy glanced at his watch and saw that it had just passed 11pm. His stomach was growling with hunger. He stood with

Yakov inside a large hangar on the naval reconnaissance base. They watched as a single Mi-26 fitted with long range fuel tanks landed on the hard stand to their front. A short distance away crouched Private Lazarov, his radio operator. Lazarov was fussing with a man-portable radio pack.

'I gather we're taking that to the platform?' queried Yakov, apprehensively.

'Looks that way. Come on. The new team are on board,' said Georgiy. He pushed the pain of losing his own men hours earlier to one side of his mind. Best dealt with later. The grief would bite deeply into him when time allowed. Right now, satisfying his hunger was a higher priority.

Still dressed in their blood and dirt-stained uniforms, Yakov, Georgiy and Lazarov strode to the back of the Mi-26. The massive helicopter's rotor blades slowed to idle. The ramp was beginning to lower as a refuelling truck came to a halt along the left side. A crewman opened the side door, lowered a short stair, and stepped out to greet the refuelling operator.

Georgiy waited for the ramp to touch the concrete. He stepped aboard, peering into the dimly lit interior at the 15 FSB Alpha operators. The men were in winter camouflage and sat quietly on either side of a pile of equipment secured to the centre line of the fuselage. The silent operators took in the three newcomers' dishevelled and dirty appearance. They knew who was walking towards them.

'I am Major Georgiy Urvantsev. This is my second-in-command, Lieutenant Yakov Davydov and my radio operator, Private Fydor Lazarov. I know you have received a briefing on what occurred between my last team and a force of Chechen terrorists. We know they've changed their target at the last minute. They have taken the gas platform Nevzgody, not their original target. Why this occurred is unknown. Our mission is to retake that platform. We will be up against a professional and dedicated combat force and the weather. An Arctic storm has been moving through that area for the last twenty-four hours. There's a good chance some of us will die today. But we will die protecting Russia from the Chechen scourge. Questions?' asked Georgiy.

The Alpha team looked passively at him.

'Very good. Relax while the crew refuel. Yakov, see to the men. Find out if there's anything to eat. Laz, relax,' said Georgiy. He walked through the fuselage and up to the flight deck. He held a quick discussion with the pilots. They appeared competent and confident to take on the coming weather. It comforted Georgiy. The task ahead was close to impossible. The Chechens had managed it. So could his team.

Moving back into the fuselage, Georgiy acknowledged the men of the team who he knew. He took a seat near the open ramp. Looking out at the floodlit hardstand he was glad it was not raining. It was cold enough without being wet.

'Fastest thing I could get for you, sir,' said Yakov. He dropped into the seat next to Georgiy. Yakov pushed a cold tin of beef Kasha with a plastic spoon sticking out of it into Georgiy's hand. He reached over and dropped another can into Lazarov's lap. Recognising it instantly, Lazarov nodded his thanks and gave him a thin smile. The strong smell of the meat permeated the fuselage.

'Thank you. I think,' replied Georgiy. He started pushing the food into his mouth.

'How is it?' Yakov grinned. He had eaten plenty of beef Kasha during his time in the military.

'It will not kill me. I hope,' replied Georgiy, smiling wryly. He chuckled to himself. The noise of refuelling filled the fuselage. Georgiy settled down to wait the 45 minutes it would take to top off the fuel tanks. Then the next phase could commence. His mind clouded with the grim reality of the mission. Plans and counterplans filled his mind.

The operator nearest to Georgiy stood up. He opened a large plastic case and pulled out three winter camouflage jackets. Silently, he handed one each to Georgiy, Yakov and Lazarov. Nodding their thanks, the men shrugged into the jackets and settled in to wait.

Asma

'Where's Corporal Tchermoeff with the laser initiator? I need to run the test,' called Asma as she turned to look around. Two long wisps of hair hung out from under her helmet. The wind whipped them into a whirl around her face. Asma concentrated on completing the fibre optic junction which connected the lower explosive charges with the ones coming down from the upper superstructure. The decision to use the platform's own fibre optic network to flow the detonation command was a stroke of genius as far as Asma was concerned. She had not looked forward to running kilometres of detonation cord. Her soldiers had taken less than two hours to lay the charges and connect them to the fibre network. She was proud of them.

Asma looked over the railing and down at the hive of activity below. She stood next to the large crane used to move stores off the ice. The noise of the crane working cargo lost to the wind as soldiers hauled up equipment. Floodlights mounted along the perimeter of the third level brightly lit the ice out to 200 metres around the platform.

Four large boxes containing KB Mashinostroveniya manufactured 9k333 Verba surface-to-air defence missiles lifted smoothly off the ice and headed aloft. The boxes would join the other eight stacked in the cargo laydown area behind her. In the next 30 minutes they would move to strategic points on the platform. From there they would engage any air threat that may materialise. Asma was confident the weather would keep any snooping Russian aircraft from sneaking in too close. Her main concern centred on the fact that they had two less helicopters to escape this forsaken place.

'He was coming. Tapa called in on the radio five minutes ago. He should be here by now,' reported Sergeant Belita Okueva. Her use of Corporal Tchermoeff's first name told Asma that there was more to the relationship than professional soldiering. Smiling softly, Asma nodded and turned to look at her second-in-command.

'Go and find him, Belita. I need to conduct the test before we head to the control room and set up the initiator for the commander.'

'Okay,' replied Belita. She slung an AK-74M over her back and headed inside. Belita felt a sudden relaxation course through her body. She was free of the wind which tore at everything in the exposed cargo area. She broke into a slow jog down the passageway.

Looking down over the railing, Asma could make out the shattered remains of the Mi-26. Drag marks in the snow led to where the missile teams were setting up the salvaged equipment.

She could see the dim shapes of the two modified High Precision System 9M337 Sosna-R surface-to-air missile defence systems. Normally vehicle mounted, the redesigned Sosna-R systems fitted easily into a Mi-26, mounted on a cut-down gun carriage. It took six men to manoeuvre each one into position. The Sosna-R gave them protection out to 10 kilometres. Anything that managed to get closer than that would encounter the Verbas. They were lethal within three.

The door behind Asma crashed open. Belita erupted from the warm interior. Her face strained with anger.

'He's dead. Murdered!' yelled Belita. Gripping her rifle, Belita wanted someone to kill in revenge.

'What?' answered Asma, not sure of what Belita had said. Her words had come out in a rush and the wind carried them away. She stared at her second intently.

'Tapa's dead. I found him in a cabin. He's dead,' cried Belita moving closer to Asma to yell into her ear.

'Show me.'

Leaving the cargo operations to a private, Asma and Belita entered the platform. Asma allowed Belita to lead as they jogged down the corridor. If there was a person still alive on the platform capable of killing one of her men, best it was Belita who encountered them first. Halfway down the corridor, Belita paused at an open cabin door and pointed inside.

Stepping through, Asma pulled her pistol from its holster and swept the room. Lying in the centre of the cabin, in his underwear, was Corporal Tchermoeff. Blood pooled around him. His face was pale with death.

'The blood on the wall is not his,' offered Asma. She knelt next to the corpse and inspected Tchermoeff. She could see where a knife had entered his chest. Perfectly placed to hit his heart and stop it. Whoever attacked Tchermoeff had either been very skilled or lucky to make the placement.

'His uniform and equipment are gone. Someone stripped him and left him like a piece of meat. I noticed the cabin door was slightly ajar and looked in. The initiator's not here,' supplied Belita pointing to its empty box. She forced away the tears that formed in her eyes. She refocused them on vicious revenge. She was going to tear the flesh from the bones of the person who did this.

'Secure Tchermoeff's body and organise the girls. I'm going to see the commander. Then we're going hunting,' ordered Asma. She stood up and hurried from the cabin.

Damien

Damien padded carefully along the passageway which led to the main engine and maintenance rooms embedded low in the platform's structure. He was guessing there would be less activity in these sections. As he worked his way down the ladders and passageways, Damien had worked on a plan, though it was not a good one.

He had the Chechen's initiator, which gave him leverage. It was time to go on the offensive. First, he had a call to make. Damien knew he could access, via a long climb through the emergency escape tunnels, the helicopter flight deck. The tunnels originated in the maintenance rooms, on the lower levels.

Damien stopped at the hatch which led onto the central maintenance room. He stopped and listened at the door. Hearing no sound from inside or behind, he cracked the hatch and pulled it open slowly. White LED strips lit the interior in a blazing light. The brightness enabled a perfect working environment for technicians who serviced the equipment. Stepping through, Damien pulled the door closed and surveyed the cramped room. Benches with dismantled equipment lined the walls. Bolted to the floor along the centre line of the space were large tool cabinets.

Damien walked towards the ever-present table and chairs assigned to the technicians so they could have breaks. The men drank copious amounts of tea and coffee which made up most of their true workday. Damien could feel the weight of the laser initiator as it thumped gently against his leg, secure in a cargo pocket on his pants. He had stripped the initiator from its bulky protective case and pocketed it, along with the detonators. Stopping, he reached out and picked up a mug of what looked like white tea. He felt the sides. Cold. The Chechens had taken the platform over two hours earlier. There seemed to be no-one else here. Glancing around the table, he saw an open packet of sweet honey Pryaniki biscuits on the far edge of the table. Half of the contents were missing.

Feeling the growl of hunger stir in his stomach, Damien plucked a biscuit from the packet. Enjoying the delicious flavour, he looked around and up to the roof for the emergency escape hatch he knew would be there. He found it closed in the far corner of the roof. The hatch would open upwards. In its corner position, the hatch enabled men to locate it in smoke and darkness. A ladder bolted to the wall led up to the hatch. Damien strode across to it.

Damien heard the hatch to the room start to undog. He swallowed the last of the biscuit. Spinning, he levelled the AK and took a sight picture. The door swung open slowly. The door opened wider. The back of a man appeared. He was looking out into the passageway and retreating into the room. The man slipped through and closed the hatch. Leaning against it he let out an audible sigh of relief. Damien was sure he heard the choking cough of a sob.

The man turned. He leaned his back against the door. His eyes screwed shut. As he opened them, the man focused on the muzzle of the assault rifle pointed at him. A quiet, amused face stared at him.

Damien immediately recognised the toolpusher but continued to hold the rifle on him. Smiling, Damien shook his head. He put an index finger to his lips to indicate silence. The toolpusher looked like he was about to faint away. He slid down the door slightly. His legs sagging out from under him.

Damien lowered the rifle, walked over to the table, and picked up the mug of tea and biscuits. He took them over to the toolpusher, still slumped against the door, and offered both to the man. Taking them uncertainly, the toolpusher gulped down the tea and had eaten two biscuits before Damien could have eaten a quarter of one.

'Sapasibo, sapasibo, Damien,' said the toolpusher, nodding his head in thanks.

'What're you doing here?' asked Damien in his distinctly Polish-accented Russian. He squatted down to look the man in the eyes.

'Hiding. What are you doing here? I think they're Chechens. They will slaughter us. We need to call the army.'

'Da, they're Chechens. They have killed, I suspect, everyone but us.'

'What will we do?'

'Survive, Evade, Resist and Escape,' replied Damien, quoting the mantra of every combat survival school in the world. Damien had been through most of them and their associated interrogation programs. He had enjoyed the experiences, especially the United States Air Force cold weather training in Alaska. Damien would be happy to retire one day to a cabin near an Alaskan lake with no-one else around. He would be comfortable there.

'I don't understand,' said the toolpusher.

'Then maybe it's not for you,' replied Damien, smiling. He was amazed this overweight and belligerent man had lasted so long.

'Can you use that?' asked the toolpusher, pointing at the assault rifle. 'Why are you dressed like them? Are you one of them?'

'I can, I'm not and I was trying to blend in before you turned up. I'm not what I seem. My background is different to yours,' replied Damien. He fixed a deadpan gaze on the frightened man. He knew the toolpusher would be dead weight.

'How can we survive this? We must escape.'

'Can you fit through the escape hatch in the roof?' asked Damien.

'I think so.'

'That's where we're going, mate,' instructed Damien and

stood up. He slung the AK over his back. He walked over to the ladder, took the first rung, and looked back. The toolpusher was hauling himself slowly off the deck.

Talhig

Asma burst into the control room. Talhig rounded towards her pulling his pistol from its holster.

'Why aren't you answering your radio?' demanded Talhig, slipping the pistol back home.

'No-one has called me,' replied Asma, looking confused. She pulled out her R-187P1 Azaret combat radio, looked at the screen and jammed her index finger on the press to talk. Immediately, a squeal of feedback sounded through Mairbek's communications gear. 'My radio works.'

'We have an armed Russian loose on the platform. He's been killing my men.'

'Six so far. I have already gathered my team to go hunting. I'll get him. We have a problem though,' replied Asma.

'Da?'

'The laser initiator is gone. Corporal Tchermoeff was carrying it. Ambushed and murdered. Whoever it was took his equipment, uniform, and the initiator. Along with the remaining detonators. I think it is the Russian who has been killing our men,' supplied

Asma gravely.

'I agree, it could be the same man. He might be security. He looks like we do now. I want that initiator back, Asma. Do not return until you have it and have killed the Russian. Ensure it's done. Now! The mission timings have moved forwards. As soon as the last of the explosives are set, the timer goes on and we evacuate to the freighter,' ordered Talhig. He gestured for Asma to exit the room.

'Is there anything I need to know?' asked Asma. She could see the pained expression on Talhig's face. There was something behind the mission parameter change.

'Mairbek already knows. Asma, the mission's compromised. The Russians know we're here. Sheikh has postponed the uprising indefinitely. Our orders are to blow the platform, escape as best we can to our pick-up. Then find our own way home. There'll be little assistance from Chechnya. We must look after ourselves.'

Asma gritted her teeth in frustration and stared at him.

'I know, I know. But now we look after ourselves. I intend on surviving this. Pick a team to remain behind to operate the missile systems. They will cover our escape and give their lives to the cause.'

'I will. There's a team on the ice now. They will be the ones to stay.'

'Very good. Asma, search the platform. Kill the Russian and

get the initiator back, those are my orders. Then we can get out of here.'

Without replying, Asma made for the door, issuing instructions to her team over the radio as she went.

Damien

Damien moved lightly and quickly up the escape tunnel ladder. He occasionally looked down to see the toolpusher's struggling bulk. The man's belly kept snagging on the ladder's rungs. He was puffing like a steam engine. It had taken almost 45 minutes to pass through the midpoint of the platform. Damien glanced at his watch and saw that the hands were just moving through midnight.

A round hatch appeared in the dimly lit tunnel ahead of them. Reaching up, Damien slowly undogged the hatch and pushed it carefully clear. The hatch opened on the deck of another maintenance space. Damien smiled at the deserted room.

Satisfied no-one was in the room, Damien pushed back the hatch and stepped up onto the deck. Damien walked over to the entry door and consulted the platform map mounted next to it. Orientating himself, he found they had arrived on deck 5. The same one he had killed the Chechens on, near the mess room.

Grimacing, Damien had no intention of staying here any longer than he needed to. Behind him, the toolpusher slowly appeared in the hatch opening. He struggled to pull his bulk free. With some effort he managed to slide through. The toolpusher rolled onto the deck, heaving enormous lungfuls of air into his straining body.

'Are you okay to keep going?' asked Damien as he crossed to stand over the man.

'Da, da. I'm okay. I need a moment to catch my breath.'

'One minute. Then we're leaving.'

'That's all I need,' replied the toolpusher. He was trying to inject bravery into his voice. Inside, he thought his straining heart was going to explode. His mind continued to cloud with panic.

'We need to go out that door, along the corridor to the hatch which leads outside. I'm thinking we should go outside and climb up to the flight deck. It might be safer for us and quicker for you. No more tunnels. It's midnight already. I can't be sure that the Chechens haven't worked out another way to blow the platform.'

'Blow it up?'

'Da,' replied Damien simply.

'We must escape,' stammered the toolpusher.

'That's part of the plan. Time to go outside.'

'Outside? I'm not going out there.'

'You can stay here if you like,' pointed out Damien.

'Nyet. I will come,' replied the toolpusher in a high panicky voice.

'Thought so. We need jackets,' said Damien. The Chechen uniform he was wearing came with a battle jacket, but it would not last long on the exposed outside deck. The toolpusher wore a light over shirt.

'Where are we?' asked the toolpusher.

'Deck five,' supplied Damien.

'There will be spare jackets near the exit hatch.'

'Good. Your minute's up. Let's go,' said Damien. He crossed to the hatch and cracked it open. The corridor was clear. The mess room with its pile of bodies hidden from view by the curve of the platform. Damien knew it could only be 50 metres away. The absence of soldiers and noise on the rig was worrying. Damien had expected more activity. They had to be looking for him by now. The longer he had the laser initiator the harder they would search for it.

Pulling the hatch open, Damien stepped through into the corridor. The toolpusher followed close behind. As one they hurried down the passageway. Arriving at the hatch which would let them outside, Damien pulled two heavy jackets off their pegs and handed one over to the toolpusher. Both men shrugged into them and immediately felt the building warmth the jackets provided.

Damien yanked open the hatch and stepped onto the walkway, feeling exposed. He was immediately assaulted by the surging wind which roared around the superstructure. It tugged at the jacket and lashed his face with sleet. A muffled curse from beside him told Damien the toolpusher had exited the warmth of the platform's interior as well.

Asma

'No reported sightings, Asma,' said Belita as she walked along the deck seven corridor towards her commander.

'No surprise. This place is a maze. A man could hide here for a long time if they know their way around. The Russian must know it well.'

'A veteran, do you think?'

'Da. A skilled one too. I think he knows what the initiator is for. There's no fear in this one.'

'The charges can't be detonated another way?' asked Belita.

'Manually. I planned for the initiator to do the work. Manually, we cannot explode enough to destroy the platform,' replied Asma, a frustrated tone to her voice.

'Then we need to find him.'

'Does each deck have a search team?' asked Asma. She had ordered it to be so.

'A team of two on each deck is currently searching. There aren't enough for larger teams. The rest of the platform appears to be secure,' supplied Belita.

'All they need time to do is make a radio call or fire their weapons and we'll know where to look,' responded Asma.

'Orders?' asked Belita, her eyes shining with excitement.

'Keep searching. The plan has changed. The timeline's brought forward. We will need to recover the initiator soon. Belita, understand when I say we need to be away from here as soon as we can,' stressed Asma.

Georgiy

TWO HOURS OUT

Battered by the wind, the Mi-26 carrying the Alpha team wallowed and pitched as the pilots fought to keep it in the air. Georgiy had worked with the team during the last hour to hammer out a plan to infiltrate the platform and neutralise the Chechen force. He did not feel confident in survival or success, but it was his job to lead these men into combat and do what they could to control the situation. The weight of leadership on a tough mission crowded Georgiy's mind as he refined the plan with his men.

Georgiy had received a satellite telephone call from Admiral Unkovsky 30 minutes earlier. He admiral informed him of the compromise and execution of the GRU intelligence source in the Itt Stag group. The last report received from the operative had contained two details Georgiy needed to know. The Chechen team on the Nevzgody platform would rig it with explosives. There was a possibility the terrorists would suicide themselves instead of trying to make for a small freighter linked to their escape plan. Additionally, there may be another, undetected group of Itt Stag fighters. A ship called the *Boris Gakkel* was transmitting distress information, though the situation remained unconfirmed.

He briefed the team that they would be assaulting a platform rigged to explode, regardless of the outcome. The Chechens would attempt to escape. Georgiy hoped this was not going to be a one-way trip.

Damien

Damien eased his way up a steep grated walkway. He turned to look for the toolpusher. The man puffed and lagged. The pair had managed to climb only one more deck. The toolpusher was unaccustomed to physical activity. Damien quietly hoped the man would have a heart attack, so he could get on quickly with the plan. Waiting again for his companion, Damien made the next level to the gangway platform. He braced himself against the wind. Sleet hammered against the superstructure around him and stung his face.

Damien peered through the storm to the ice floe below. He saw the unmistakable outlines of two missile batteries and a crashed helicopter. Men moved slowly around in the open as they finished setting up the equipment. He shook his head at the new threat; he would need some time to refine his plan. He waited for the toolpusher, thinking. He was unable to ascertain what type of missiles the Chechens had assembled, but he would guess that they were anti-air. If he could not take out the Chechens, he might have to make an escape in one of the company helicopters. The anti-air meant he would have to hug the ocean when he lifted off. Damien knew his chances of survival had just dropped down a rung.

Looking down at the toolpusher, Damien willed him to hurry. He gritted his teeth, about to open his mouth to shout some encouragement. The hatch in front of the toolpusher crashed open and slammed against the superstructure. Out of the opening rushed four heavily armed Chechens.

Staggering back, the toolpusher held up his hands. Damien was sure the man was whimpering for his life. Without pausing the lead soldier stepped forward, drew a pistol, and shot the toolpusher in the forehead. Crashing to the walkway, the toolpusher's body wobbled like jelly as death settled over it. The soldiers swarmed over the body, stripping away the toolpusher's jacket to search him. The one who had shot him stood over the searchers, watching their work.

Damien knew what they were looking for.

After a few seconds of searching, the soldiers stood up. Damien could see the animated discussion. He watched them impassively. He wanted to know who these Chechens were. To test them.

Turning slowly, the soldier who shot the toolpusher looked up and saw Damien. The Chechen fixed on his eyes, snapped up a short sub-machine gun and opened fire.

Ducking, Damien lifted his AK and aimed back down the line of fire. Before he could finger the trigger, the soldier deftly stepped out of sight and back inside. Two of the Chechens forced their way up the gangway towards Damien. Moving with efficient and effective fire and movement, the pair quickly closed the distance. Damien pulled back slightly and sheltered in the protective lee of a turn in the superstructure.

Taking a knee, Damien drifted his head and weapon out from cover. He sighted on the lead soldier and fired off three rounds. The soldier dropped to the deck. The second soldier let fly a long burst of automatic fire which drove Damien back into cover.

Sensing that the soldier was changing magazines, Damien stepped from cover and immediately saw his error. The soldier had sprinted the last 20 metres and was on top of him. The soldier wore a dark-green helmet, face wrapped against the cold. Dark eyes shone out above the wrap.

The soldier's AK-74M swung up in a vicious arc aimed at Damien's unprotected head. Blocking the strike with his rifle, Damien drove his right knee into the soldier's crutch. Coming off the deck and slightly into the air the soldier grunted. Pain flashed briefly in their eyes.

The kick would have dropped any man. Catching sight of the person's eyes again, Damien realised his mistake. This Chechen was a woman. The blow would have hurt and hurt badly but did not have the same effect.

I'm for it now, he thought.

Chechen women were skilled and ruthless fighters.

Dancing forwards, the Chechen fighter stepped inside Damien's space and delivered a shattering punch to his face. Turning slightly saved Damien from a smashed jaw. The punch skidded across his face and into his shoulder. Pain flared. Before he could react, the fighter slapped the AK from his hands. She tried to ram the barrel of hers into Damien's stomach, but

Damien deflected the rifle away, trying to control the fight. As the rifle's muzzle slid past his hip the Chechen pulled the trigger. A withering burst of fire roared against his leg. Damien felt bullets tugging at the sides of his trousers as they passed through the fabric searching for his unprotected legs.

Driving his fists into the front of the woman's body armour, Damien shoved with all his strength. He forced her backwards, staggering. As he stepped forwards, he heard a soft clunk. The laser initiator had fallen clear of a bullet-riddled pocket and landed on the walkway.

Damien drew his pistol and fired.

The fighter held up her AK defensively, shuddering as the rifle took the impact of Damien's bullet. Tossing the damaged weapon aside, she rushed Damien as she pulled her own pistol free. The woman was trying to get inside his fighting space. Recognising what she was doing Damien stepped back, snapped the pistol up and fired a single round into her face. It crumpled under the impact of the bullet. The Chechen fighter's legs sagged, and her body dropped to the deck.

Looking past the dead soldier, Damien saw the remaining Chechens charging towards him. As their comrade dropped to the deck, they opened fire.

Bullets crashing around him, Damien pulled open the entry hatch for deck 8 and leapt inside. As he slammed the door shut, he realised he had left the rifle behind along with the laser initiator. Unable to do anything about it, he disregarded the failure and sprinted down the corridor.

Talhig

'Inbound aircraft,' called Mairbek. He turned to look at Talhig, who stood staring out of the window at the flight deck. Sleet hammered against the thick glass.

'How many?' responded Talhig as he walked over to look at the radar display.

'Two. A transport by the look of its return and maybe one escorting fighter. Their tracks are intermittent. This storm is making it difficult for the scanner. They're only a few minutes away.'

'That will be the FSB surveillance plane, I think. Ready the missile batteries,' ordered Talhig.

Jeda One Five

MIG-31BM

'Keep a close eye on the fuel, Rudi. It'll be close at this rate,' ordered Lieutenant Christophe Litke. His second mission of the day was turning into a worse situation than the first. Litke was escorting the vulnerable FSB IL-76MD-90A surveillance aircraft to the highjacked Nevzgody platform. The flight had already overflown the production ship *Boris Gakkel.*

The heavy MIG-31BM felt like it was going to fall out of the sky as it wallowed and shook behind the slow and pondering IL-76. Gritting his teeth, Litke worked the throttles and controls to keep a tight visual on the lumbering transport. With visibility less than 100 metres, it was taking all his skill and experience to maintain position.

'I am, my friend. I want to get back alive. There'll be a tanker waiting for us one hundred and fifty kilometres from base. Can't miss that, Litke. Or we will be in the ocean. The platform's radar is emitting. If there's anyone alive, they will have seen us by now,' said Rudi from the rear seat. The two windows he had to look out of were streaming with water. The dark thick clouds in the twilight sky surrounding the jet were almost invisible to him. All Rudi had where his sensors and instruments to keep him in touch with the outside world.

The run over the *Boris Gakkel* had been uneventful and confirmed nothing. There was a vessel tucked against the hull of the production ship. It did not answer the hailing from the communicator on board the IL-76. Litke had conducted a low pass but received no response.

They were now on their final run to the Nevzgody platform.

'Jeda One Five, Volga Three Two, over,' called the communicator on the FSB IL-76.

'Go ahead, Volga Three Two,' answered Litke.

'One minute to the platform. We will enter an orbit and conduct observations. We have five hours of fuel remaining.'

'Acknowledged. I have two hours remaining. I will need to make the tanker before we land, over.'

'Roger. Entering orbit in thirty seconds.'

Litke looked across at the IL-76 and saw it pass over the faint fuzzy lights of the platform. To keep in touch with the facility, they would need to orbit no higher than 500 metres. Even then Litke knew that only electronic sensors could penetrate the storm with any certainty. Electronic eyes would give them an indication of the Chechen activity. Gently following the IL-76, Litke entered a lazy orbit and watched his fuel dwindling.

ICE FLOE MISSILE BATTERY

Maintaining electronic silence, Warrant Officer Makhmud Esambayev ordered his missile operators to track the incoming aircraft using the platform's radar feed. Taking cues on the radio from Mairbek in the control room, they had enough data in the firing computer for the two High Precision System 9M337 Sosna-R missile batteries to fire when needed.

The 9K333 Verba missile operators ranged around the platform. They were having trouble picking up the transport and fighter.

'Ready on the batteries,' called Esambayev over the radio. 'Energise!'

As one, the two operators enabled the radar scanner for each battery and started emitting energy. Instantly, they picked out the two targets and moved from track to lock in a split second.

'Fire!' yelled Esambayev.

Four large Sosna-R missiles roared out of their launchers.

Jeda One Five

Settling in for a stressful jockeying of the controls to keep in a stable orbit with the IL-76, Litke had lost sight of the platform in the murk and gloom below. He was sure he could just make out a faint glow of reflected light from the long finger of burning excess gas.

A screaming alert sounded in his helmet and Litke jolted out of concentration. The MIG-31BM snapped over onto its port wing. In his fright at hearing the missile alert tone he inadvertently snatched the controls over.

'Missile launch! Immediate starboard turn. Descend now. Extend, extend!' shouted Rudi into the intercom as his head whipped over to the right with Litke's turn. Without waiting for Litke to react, he activated the active and passive jamming emitters embedded in the tail and along the spine of the aircraft. Chaff and flares streamed from ports along the side of the fuselage.

Jamming the throttles into afterburner, Litke felt the shuddering boot of the additional power. The aircraft surged into the storm as he snapped the aircraft over into a hard descending starboard turn.

'Volga Three Two, Jeda One Five. Missile launch, missile launch!' warned Litke as he grunted against the G-force of the turn.

'We will pass clear on the tail of the transport,' instructed Rudi as he narrowed the attack on his threat receiver. 'One missile has us, Litke. Three for the transport. They're in trouble.'

Litke saw three streams of flame flash past his canopy. He took a deep breath and held it against the mounting pressure. The missiles were actively tracking the IL-76. A split second later a massive fireball erupted, lighting the clouds a brilliant orange.

'The transport's gone! Reverse course and stop descent. Level out at fifty metres,' instructed Rudi.

'Roger,' answered Litke. In the back of his mind, he knew they were never going to make the tanker. The afterburner was consuming fuel at an alarming rate. He levelled the MIG-31BM's wings, pulled back on the control stick and snapped the heavy fighter into a port turn.

'Missile has lost track. It's going to pass below us. Well done. Let's get out of here,' called Rudi.

'Where's the platform?' asked Litke. He had lost his situational awareness in the dark. There was no way he was going to crash the aircraft, but he did not know where he exactly was.

'The turn has brought us on course to pass very close to it,' supplied Rudi.

'Great,' responded Litke.

Makhmud Esambayev

Makhmud heard the explosion of the IL-76 before his operators announced it. The murky flash of light in the night sky almost half a kilometre away had signalled its demise. The roaring of the escort fighter's afterburners told Makhmud they were still in the fight. Turning towards the rumbling noise, Makhmud could not believe his eyes. Rushing towards them not more than 50 metres above the ice floe was a massive fighter.

A MIG-31, Makhmud thought.

The bright blue-orange of its afterburners licked and snapped at the air behind it.

'Verba operators get ready!' he shouted into his radio. The fighter was going to streak right over the top of them.

Jeda One Five

Keeping the nose of the fighter as close as he dared to the ice, Litke peered through the sleet and ice haze hammering the armoured windscreen. He saw the massive form of the Nevzgody platform and the great flame it emitted as it burned off excess gas. Shifting his gaze, Litke saw dark shapes on the ice floe in the glow of the platform's lights.

That must be the missile battery.

He blinked sweat out of his eyes.

'Target front, going guns,' he called over the intercom. An answering double click came from Rudi. Litke sighted on what looked to be the wreckage of a large helicopter.

With seconds to aim and fire, Litke crushed the trigger closed on his control stick. The Gryazev-Shipunov GSh-6-23M rotary cannon thundered below his feet. Pressing gently on the left rudder pedal he skidded the fighter. Litke fanned the fat 23-millimetre cannon shells across the ice.

He saw satisfying plumes of snow and ice erupting into the air as the shells impacted among the missile batteries and helicopter wreckage. A large, brilliant explosion roared into the air as a shell hit one of the Sosna-R batteries. A missile cooked off and screamed unguided into the storm. The rocket motor drove the missile in an arc over the platform and it disappeared.

As they flashed over the remains of the battery, Litke caught sight of men with shoulder-launched missiles tracking him from the lower deck of the platform. Like machines, the men turned with the MIG-31 as it rushed past them.

'Missile launch! Three missiles inbound,' shouted Rudi, just as the warning alert sounded in Litke's helmet again. 'Stay low and extend! Give her all she has!'

Without answering, Litke pushed the nose of the massive fighter lower and skimmed across the top of the ice floe. He was heading for the open ocean 10 nautical miles away. The ocean would give him somewhere to hide electronically among the clutter and jumble of the waves.

'I'm making for the ocean!' he yelled.

'Not going to make it. Impact in two seconds. Prepare to eject,' called Rudi. He was already tucking his backside deeper into the seat. The ejection seat would blast him into the storm. He could hear flares and chaff automatically ejected into the fighter's wake as the computer tried to confuse the missiles and save the crew.

'Fuck that,' responded Litke.

Glancing at his airspeed, Litke saw it was approaching Mach One.

Carrying too much speed, he thought.

Dropping the nose to dip the aircraft, Litke pulled back as hard as he could on the control stick. Rushing up into the sky, he tried to execute a high yo-yo manoeuvre to clear the missiles. As the fighter rapidly climbed into the sky it slowly rolled onto its back. Overstress alarms sounded. The aircraft was close to exceeding its structural limits. Confident in the men who had built his magnificent fighter, Litke kept the control stick back. He yanked the throttles to idle.

The fighter entered a tight loop, rapidly losing headway.

Two of the Verba missiles continued along the fighter's original course and impacted the open sea in the distance. The third stayed with the aircraft and followed unremittingly.

Litke rolled out of the loop and slammed the throttles back into afterburner.

'One missile's still with us, Litke. Brace for impact. Now!' informed Rudi. He could see nothing from the rear seat but was sure he could feel the missile's breath on their necks as it tried to cleave them from the sky.

Sensing its target starting to slow and flatten its loop, the missile's proximity radar calculated it had entered the kill envelope and detonated. A mass of shrapnel spread out in a deadly cloud and crashed into the MIG-31BM.

Litke felt a rapid series of impacts along the fighter's fuselage and alarms started sounding. His eardrums stretched and popped as shrapnel punched through the canopy and depressurised the cabin. A roaring slipstream of frigid air rushed through the cockpit behind him. It caught in his helmet and wobbled it from side to side, blurring his vision.

Lights flashed on the instrument panel. There was an immediate loss of power from the starboard engine. The massive fighter yawed and strained under the asymmetric thrust. He closed the throttle for the dying starboard engine and pulled the port engine out of afterburner. Ignoring the alerts and blinking lights, Litke could still feel life in the aircraft. He took stock of what control he had. The fighter constantly wanted to turn into the dead engine. By the reduced effectiveness of the controls Litke figured he had lost the starboard rudder fin as well. The rudder pedals slapped against his feet. Unable to look behind to assess the damage, Litke was at the mercy of the aircraft's surviving sensors and the feel he had as an experienced pilot.

'Rudi, you, okay?' he grunted over the intercom.

Silence.

'Rudi!' Litke yelled. He tried to turn in his seat to look behind into the rear cockpit, but secured by his harness there was no way for him to move. Staring into the mirror mounted on the port side of the canopy frame he saw a juddering image of his friend, head slumped on his chest. He could just make out a large hole in the fuselage near Rudi which opened to the sky. The fighter jerked around as Litke fought to control it, throwing his friend from side to side.

'Mayday, Mayday, Mayday, Novater Control, Jeda One Five. We've suffered damaged by missiles launched at us from Nevzgody platform. Volga Two Three's lost. I have severe damaged and am escaping the area,' called Litke.

'Jeda One Five, Novater Control, acknowledged. Despatching aircraft to assist. We're tracking you,' came the wooden, almost mechanical reply of the controller.

Taipan 21

Droning at 30,000 feet, the United States Coastguard Lockheed WC-130J Hercules ploughed steadily through the tops of the storm. The crew had diverted hours earlier from a routine weather collection flight to collect passengers. Having had just enough time to refuel, take on their guests and equipment the Hercules had immediately departed for the Arctic. Nearing their target at 1am, the crew were tired.

The Taipan 21 team members moved confidently around in the cargo area of the aircraft sorting their equipment. The three men helped each other into parachutes and helmets. Strapping TMC PHT HALO masks to their faces, the men checked the oxygen supply they would need for their high-altitude low opening jump.

Enroute, the target had changed to Ispytaniye's sister platform, Nevzgody.

Jason Hertzog locked his mask into place and tested the oxygen flow. Checking his watch, Jason saw they had five minutes to run until they would be over the drop site. His other team members, George Botha, and Alan Slovo made up the Taipan 21 team. All had been in the South African National Defence Force, 5th Special Forces Regiment. They had all been proud members of the Recces when the Taipan Organisation had come knocking. It was rare to have a fully South African–crewed Taipan team. It harked back to the first days of the Taipan Organisation's missions in the Congo and Rhodesia. The three were developing a reputation for their ruthless efficacy in executing any mission assigned to them.

The dim white lights in the cargo hold changed to red and the two loadmasters stood up and locked on their tethers. The Taipan 21 operators disconnected from the aircraft's oxygen supply and plugged into their individual bottles.

Opening slowly, the rear ramp of the Hercules dropped away to show the dark twilight sky. Thick angry clouds were below them. Faces hidden behind oxygen masks; the loadmasters stood either side of the ramp. Both held up a hand and crossed their middle fingers behind the index.

Thirty seconds.

Nodding, Jason called the team to action and the three men ran through their final checks. They shuffled towards the ramp. Maintaining their momentum, the team looked at the loadmasters and saw a thumbs-up. Walking carefully off the ramp, Taipan 21 dropped into the angry Arctic storm.

CHAPTER SIX

Asma

Slamming her left fist against the body of her submachine gun, Asma cursed and kicked out at the wall opposite. She stalked in a circle, barely able to contain her anger. A blazing hatred burned in her for the Russian who had escaped them. The man had slaughtered two of her girls. Women she had fought with for years. Good women, good fighters, her girls. Her face flushed bright red with anger.

Belita gave her commander space, equally feeling the tragic loss of true friendships forged in combat. Stepping back as Asma rounded to look her deep in the eyes, Belita waited for her next orders.

'This man is going to die slowly, at my hands. I want him alive. I want to cut off his balls and stuff them down his throat.

He's going to suffer. I want him found! Keep him alive,' ordered Asma.

'I think I know where he's going,' ventured Belita.

Something about the man had intrigued her as she watched him fight on the stairs. There was more to this one than merely a combat veteran. The Russian had not tried to flee until the odds were well against him. And then only after he had taken down two good fighters. Belita figured he was special forces trained. Each time the Russian broke from cover he had been heading up the platform. If he was one to hide, he would have gone deep into the structure, but he was not. He was following a plan.

'Where?' asked Asma.

'He's either heading to the control room to call for help or he's heading to the flight deck,' replied Belita. She had felt confident in her theory before verbalising it. Now she was not so sure.

'I understand the control room, but not the flight deck. Why? Is this Russian an effective killer and a helicopter pilot? Is he some sort of superman?' chastised Asma. She felt the keen edge of her words and watched Belita wince at the scorn.

'It was only a theory, Asma.' Belita cowered. Her heart sank and she felt stupid.

'Even if the Russian could fly a helicopter, the storm will stop him taking off. It would take a person with great skill and luck to even attempt it. No, I think he's going for the control room.'

'He would surely know we would have taken that first, Asma. It's basic battlefield doctrine to disrupt, take and hold an enemy's communications.'

'Correct. Then maybe he has no plan and is just heading up, hoping to outdistance us. He must have seen the explosives. The Russian will want to be off the platform, as we will. How though?'

'There is only the crane to the ice or the flight deck. There are no other ways out of this place,' pointed out Belita.

'Detail a team to guard the crane. We'll secure the flight deck and the control room,' ordered Asma. 'Belita, bring our girls back inside. I don't want them left out there.'

Belita nodded and disappeared outside. Two minutes later she was back without the bodies of her fallen comrades. A triumphant look on her face.

'Asma! He dropped the initiator. We have it!' Belita exclaimed, holding up the device for Asma to see.

'Ha. He's no superman. Give it to me,' instructed Asma, returning Belita's wide grin. 'Get the girls' bodies and then carry out my orders.'

Belita nodded and returned to the storm.

After Belita closed the hatch, Asma keyed her radio.

'Talhig, Asma.'

'Go ahead, Asma,' replied Talhig. It seemed he was almost sitting on the radio he had answered so quickly.

'I have lost two fighters and killed one Russian. He did not have the initiator. There was a second man. He killed two of my girls,' relayed Asma. Even as she spoke her throat caught on the image of her slaughtered fighters.

'You need to recover the initiator, Asma,' countered Talhig, annoyance in his voice. The loss of Asma's team members was not important.

'Talhig, I have it. The man dropped it. I will bring it to you.'

'You always amaze me, Asma. You're my right hand. Quickly, get the initiator to the control room and then we can be away. The missile teams have shot down one aircraft and damaged another. The pressure is increasing.'

'I believe the Russian is trying to get off the platform. There are only two ways. The flight deck or the crane. Belita has detailed a guard to the crane. We're going to secure the control room and flight deck. I'll see you in a few minutes.'

'Good. I will see you soon,' finished Talhig.

Asma turned to look up and down the corridor and drew in a deep breath. She held it, and then let it out in an explosive burst.

Jogging away, she headed for the stairs which would carry her higher.

Taipan 21

Jason turned into the howling wind and expertly skidded his parachute onto a short final. The ice rushed up to meet him and his Rocky Blizzard Stalker boots gently made contact. He slid forwards. Dumping the air from the canopy, Jason waited for a moment longer as his momentum slowed. He slapped a hand onto the quick release wheel for the harness. Still full of the storm's wind the unrestrained parachute stripped away from his body and disappeared behind him. Sliding to a graceful halt, Jason turned and watched his teammates perform the same manoeuvre and pull up within 20 metres of him.

Stripping off their helmets and jump gear, the three members of Taipan 21 stood in their winter camouflage uniforms. The team carried enough gear to complete a fast and dirty kill mission. None of them thought the odds were particularly steep. Their intel had the terrorist force at 50.

Good odds to earn their pay.

Hefting their silenced 5.56-millimetre Vektor R5 carbines, the team joined up. Each carried a Bastelle Tactical Air Initiated Launcher grappling system in protective bags on their backs.

'We're three hundred metres from the platform. Ignore the missile teams on the ice. Don advised that there's another team tasked to deal with them,' ordered Jason. He pulled a thick woollen beanie down low over his forehead. An EXIO winter warmer protected his face. It hid the plume of his breath. As he spoke, the team worked on fitting crampons to their boots to allow them to traverse the terrain ahead.

The team moved out over the ice.

Guided by the glow of the platform there was no need to don their night vision. They closed the distance in less than 20 minutes and then skirted the easily observed missile batteries. They used the cover of the storm driven sleet and snow. Blackened and scarred ice marked where missile exhaust had scorched patches in the snow.

'Someone else has had a go at the missile teams,' pointed out Botha as they arrived at the base of the platform. He indicated the twisted wreckage of a surface-to-air missile battery which lay ruined off to one side of the detachment. Scattered bodies surrounded the scrap metal. As the team slipped off their crampons, Botha readied his launcher and searched for a good place to aim it.

'No idea who that could've been,' replied Jason. He regarded the destruction thoughtfully.

'Give the boss a call. We're about to initiate,' advised Slovo as he followed Botha's lead and prepared his launcher. He had selected a spot to the right of a large crane he could see jutting out into the sky. He saw no sign of movement.

Jason grunted in reply.

'Watchtower, Mamba, over,' called Jason into his L3Harris Falcon III AN/PRC 152A radio. High above them in the clear air above the storm circled Taipan's RPV. It would relay communications to Don, who was operating out of Murmansk. The wind tugged at his heavy combat smock. Jason felt warm and safe inside it.

'Go ahead, Mamba,' replied Don. Beside him Noah sat watching the feeds from the RPV. He frowned at the complete white-out the screens displayed. Jason never failed to annoy Don by refusing to use his Taipan-issued callsign, opting for his Recce callsign instead, *Mamba*.

'We've made the platform. Just about to commence scaling the outside. Storm's intense. There are indications that someone has attacked the missile batteries, over.'

'The FSB lost a surveillance aircraft not long ago. Their escorting MIG took out one battery. The fighter is damaged and limping away from the area at this time,' supplied Don.

'Roger. We'll be comms dark as soon as we enter the superstructure. Too much metal for even Noah to hear and see what we're doing,' said Jason. He chuckled at the thought of Noah straining to keep tabs on them.

'Good luck. Report in when the mission's complete.'

'Confirm, what's left of the missile teams are to be handled by someone else?' requested Jason. He was happy to take out the Chechens on the ice before they entered the platform. The more kills he made the better.

'Affirm. There's an FSB Alpha team inbound. By our tracking, their helicopter is fifteen minutes behind you. Keep ahead of them. You're not to contact the Alpha team. Ensure you conduct your exfil before they get inside the platform,' stressed Don.

'Roger, out,' replied Jason.

Nodding to Botha and Slovo, Jason raised his launcher, sighted on the railing 100 metres above and pulled the trigger. Botha and Slovo followed suit. With a soft plopping noise, the launchers fired the grappling hook towards their target. Thin rope streamed out behind the hooks. The wind drove it against the rounded side of the platform. All three hooks arrived on target and locked on the handrail.

'Let's go,' ordered Jason. Without waiting he triggered the retrieve lever. The launcher began quickly raising him through the air. Shrugging the carbine off his shoulder, Jason flicked off the safety.

Moving at 5 metres per second, Jason rushed through the frigid air and was at the handrail in the blink of an eye. As he arrived, he stared at five Chechens who were waiting quietly, their weapons trained on him. From the way the men held them, the Chechens knew how to use them.

Before they could open fire, Jason flicked the retrieve lever back down and he dropped out of sight. Automatic fire erupted over his head and bullets tore out into the night. Jason halted a few metres below the crane. He saw that Botha and Slovo had already paused. They were waiting for him to clear the way.

Letting his rifle fall to his side, Jason plucked two Rheinmetall Denel Munitions M26 grenades from his chest rig. Wasting no time, he pulled the pins and tossed them over his head and onto the platform near the crane.

Lifting his rifle up, he sighted on the handrail. He heard yelling and a face looked over the edge behind the muzzle of an AK. Jason fired two rounds into the Chechen's face and the man dropped out of sight.

A split second later the grenades detonated with a muffled whump. The roar of the storm hid the sound of the explosions. Thin smoke drifted up, ripped away by the wind. Jason moved the launcher lever to retrieve. He again rose to the platform's handrail.

The grenades had done their job. The men who had tried to kill him were torn and twisted by the fine shrapnel from the M26s. Vaulting the rail, he disconnected himself from the rope and secured the area for the arrival of Botha and Slovo.

Casting aside their launchers, the team cracked open the hatch leading into the platform and filtered inside.

Damien

Slipping into an office on deck 10, Damien took a moment to pause. He rolled the encounter with the female fighters through his mind and cursed the loss of the initiator. As the memory replayed, Damien became more convinced that they had been actively hunting him. No surprise. If their commanders were smart enough, they would not take too long to work out where he was heading. There were only two options: the flight deck or the control room. If the Chechens had taken the control room, as he would have, then he assumed they had access to the CCTV monitors. It would be easy enough to observe his movements and isolate him. Damien wondered why they were not being more proactive in using them.

Weighing up his options, he decided to double back on his trail and try to throw off any pursuit. For the last 10 minutes he had ducked and weaved around roving groups of Chechens as they searched for him. It had been easy to evade the teams. Damien was confident he could successfully keep out of their clutches if he had enough time. With the platform rigged with explosives, and the laser initiator surely back in their hands, Damien's time to take the fight directly to the Chechens dwindled.

Damien slipped out of the office and back into the corridor. He headed to the closest hatch which led to the outside and passed through it. Taking the time to carefully scan around him, Damien found himself alone in the storm. The beast of a system seemed to have eased slightly.

Catching a distant sound on the wind, Damien was sure he could hear the beat of rotors. Turning his head slowly from side to side, he tried to isolate the sound. His ears caught it, lost it, caught it, and lost it to the wind again.

Might have company soon.

It would be no surprise if the Russians had launched a mission to retake the platform. As soon as the platform moved to alert status the mainland would have known. The team that attempted it would have to be at the top of their game. If Damien knew anything about Russian special forces, it was that they did not take prisoners. Nor did they distinguish between a Chechen and a friendly dressed as one.

Damien moved in a slow smooth trot down the ladders and gangways, headed back down the platform. His discarded AK and the initiator from the earlier contact were gone. Retrieved by the Chechens. Continuing down he halted over the toolpusher's body, stripped of his clothes and lying cold and naked on the hard grated walkway. The toolpusher's fat bloated body was full of bullet holes. Streams of blood had frozen around the openings rent in his skin. The man's excess fat pushed through the holes in the grate like a cake sagging through a wire frame.

Why did the Chechens strip him? wondered Damien. He cracked open the hatch and looked inside.

Finding the corridor free, Damien retraced his steps to the escape tunnel and took it down towards the mess deck level.

Asma

Asma threw the door to the control room open and burst into the room. She fixed Talhig with a fiery look.

'This Russian's killed my girls,' she growled at him.

'I know. But, Asma, focus on the mission. We have lost one of the anti-air batteries. War comes with casualties. The initiator, please. That's our task. Losing people is part of this war against the Bear,' soothed Talhig.

He crossed to her and held out his hand for the device. He could see the rage and anger seething through her face and body. Talhig felt a surge of affection and desire for her. This was how she had been when he had first met and fought with her years earlier. It was this that had attracted them to each other.

'Don't give me that rubbish. And don't look at me like that,' fired back Asma as she handed him the initiator. She had seen and recognised the glint in Talhig's eyes.

'Mairbek, connect the device and run the test. I want the system ready to fire as soon as possible,' responded Talhig. They were back on mission. A wide happy grin split his face.

Mairbek stood up from his console, crossed to Talhig and plucked the initiator out of his grasp. He immediately set to work.

'We should task an additional team to stay behind to ensure the platform's protected while we make our escape. A sacrifice, but one worth making. Their glory will be for Allah,' pointed out Asma.

Talhig regarded her for a moment. Asma was no lover of Islam. It had inhibited her life and forced her to grow into the woman who stood before him. Asma's mention of Allah was for effect only and the ears which may be listening.

'Very well. One to each of the main levels where the fibre junctions are for the explosives. If there's a problem, they can detonate their individual levels. Asma, delegate five loyal, dedicated men to remain behind. We will be leaving in an hour, no later. Make it so,' instructed Talhig.

Asma turned and stalked out of the room. Talhig watched her go.

'Mairbek, advise the pilots of the plan. I want the men split evenly between the helicopters,' ordered Talhig.

The pilots and the crew of the two helicopters had stayed out in the storm. The flight engineers performed checks and maintenance as best they could. The loadmasters had connected the aircraft to the platform's aviation fuel tanks and had been pumping it into their parched steeds.

'Where are we going?' asked Mairbek.

'To link up with the freighter. According to the plan, it'll be on station by now. I don't care if we're early. They can take us on regardless.'

As Talhig looked around the room for inspiration, he saw the CCTV monitors spring into life.

'You got them going?'

'Took me a while to force a reboot of the system.'

'Good,' replied Talhig and scanned the screens. He could see his men patrolling the platform. Talhig caught sight of Asma moving swiftly down a corridor. He settled down to see if he could spot the Russian.

Nikolay

Frustrated and unhappy, Nikolay looked at the track on the Transas ECDIS and could not believe his life had taken such a poor turn. The port engine of the *Aysberg* had completely failed and the engineers had no way to fix it. The icebreaker needed to head to a shipyard for repairs. FSB Maritime headquarters, however, felt it best to keep the crippled and floundering vessel out in the Arctic storm. Nikolay continued to guide the stricken ship for the edge of the ice pack closest to the highjacked gas platform.

Nikolay heard the satellite telephone start ringing on the bulkhead behind him. Crossing quickly over the rolling deck of the bridge, he lifted the receiver.

'Da?' he enquired.

'Nikolay, Admiral Unkovsky. I have new orders for you.'

'Admiral. Where would you like us to go?' Nikolay tried to hide the annoyance in his tone.

'Is your ship in good order?' enquired Unkovsky. He was sure he could hear stress in Nikolay's voice.

'We have lost the port engine entirely, Admiral. The engineers cannot fix it. We must head to a shipyard. I'm maintaining course to intercept the ice pack, in accordance with your earlier instructions.'

'You will not be supporting that operation anymore. You are to steam with all available speed to the following position,' ordered Unkovsky. Passing the coordinates to Nikolay, he could hear the man quietly repeating the numbers to himself.

'What's at that position, sir? I think that's open ocean,' Nikolay asked curiously.

'You are correct. The Chechens damaged a naval aviation fighter aircraft. That course will place you along the aircraft's line of travel. Retrieve the crew if they ditch. The men will not survive in the water. How long will it take for you to get there?' requested Unkovsky.

'It's not far from here. Without the port engine and with the current sea conditions. I estimate we can be on station in an hour, maybe less,' calculated Nikolay.

'Set the course. If you pick the crew up, you're to continue east and take them to the Trefoil army base in the Franz Josef Archipelago. The crew will go to the hospital there. I'll have the pilot instructed to close the distance to you as quickly as he can.'

'Da. What about the platform?'

'That situation is in hand. Be on station as soon as possible to recover the aircrew if they need your help. That is all,' stated Unkovsky then terminated the call.

Nikolay shrugged and replaced the receiver. It seemed that his first voyage on the *Aysberg* was going to be one where they wandered aimlessly from point to point in the Arctic Ocean at the whims of Admiral Unkovsky. All the while pounded by the weather.

Jeda One Five

Litke was being shaken violently in his ejection seat as the fighter tried to tear itself apart. Rumbling vibrations rippled through the airframe. Every emergency light rapidly blinked at him from the instrument panel. Fighting the controls, Litke had managed to limp the aircraft clear of the Chechen missile teams and out over the ocean but unable to gain altitude, the fighter skimmed 50 metres over the cold and unforgiving water. Saltwater and sleet hammered against the windscreen.

The aircraft had lost its primary flight systems and was barely staying in the air on the secondary. As the fighter yawed through the air, Litke knew that all it would take was the failure of one more system and the jet would pitch into the ocean. Both he and Rudi lost forever. Litke had had to slow down to stop a continuous banging and thumping noise that was sounding from the rear of the fuselage.

It must be loud, thought Litke. He was able to hear it over the roaring slipstream rushing past him as air sucked through the large hole in the aft cockpit.

Glancing in the mirrors to see how Rudi was doing, Litke saw that the slipstream had jammed the man's head hard up against the right side of the cockpit. There was no sign of life.

'Jeda One Five, Novater Control.' The voice of the land base controller burst inside Litke's helmet. The controller had been silent for the last few minutes.

'Jeda One Five,' gasped Litke. He was shivering from the cold. Fatigue bit into his movements as he battled the fighter's damaged controls. The effort to speak and fly surprised him. He thought he had a reasonably efficient rhythm going.

'Jeda One Five, Novater Control. The navy has diverted a ship to come to your assistance. If you require it. What's your status?' requested the controller calmly.

'The aircraft feels like it's coming apart. I don't think it will stay in the air much longer,' replied Litke quickly. He hoped the controller did not hear the desperation creeping into his voice.

'Are you able to turn to heading one nine zero to intercept the ship?' asked the controller as he studied his long-range radar display.

'Wilco. How far away is the ship?'

'At your current speed, you will close the distance in ten minutes. They're steaming towards you with all the speed they can apply. You can eject over the vessel. They will pick you up. Has your weapons systems operator regained consciousness?'

'Negative, Novater Control. I cannot confirm his status. I am turning on to heading one nine zero. Advise the ship we're coming,' replied Litke his breath raged with the frigid air he was breathing.

'Roger. Good luck,' responded the controller.

Good luck. They were going to need more than that. Maybe he needed to start praying to some God to save them.

Too late now.

Skidding the jet as flat as he could onto the new heading, he tapped the port engine's throttle forwards slightly to close the distance quicker.

Instantly, the thumping and hammering started again from the aft section of the fuselage. Shaking his head and gritting his teeth, Litke closed the throttle back to its original position. The thumping ceased but the hammering did not.

Suddenly, there was a roaring bang from behind the aft cockpit and a sharp jolt hammered through the airframe.

Litke felt the aircraft slew away to starboard. His helmet thumped against the left side of the canopy. Reacting quickly, he pulled the control stick over to the left and jammed his foot deeper into the right rudder. The aircraft bucked and wallowed but continued its slewing turn. Litke immediately realised whatever he had disturbed by increasing power had come away. The jet was entering its final death roll.

'Rudi! Prepare for ejection! Prepare for ejection!' yelled Litke over the intercom. He was unable to see his friend through the violently shaking mirrors.

Ahead, he made out the dull lights of the ship he hoped would be quick enough to rescue them.

'Rudi. Eject, eject, eject!' commanded Litke.

The fighter snapped over onto its starboard wing and the

nose dropped towards the ocean. Accelerating into its final dive, the aircraft started to come apart.

Grabbing at the ejection handles, Litke yanked them up. The canopy exploded away. Rain and wind crashed into his face. Litke realised he had forgotten to lower his face screen as the Zvezda K-36D seat he sat on fired.

The seat hammered him out into the storm.

Ejected horizontal to the rapidly approaching ocean, the seat self-righted and accelerated him higher into the sky, then separated automatically. A small drogue chute appeared above him. As the seat fell way, the main parachute opened. Litke yanked to a stop as the canopy filled with stormy air. He bounced and swayed in the parachute harness.

Catching sight of his stricken aircraft, Litke saw there were large holes in the fuselage. Fuel streamed away into the air. The missile's shrapnel had stripped away the thin metal skin protecting the starboard engine, exposing it. The massive fighter was in its last throes.

The aft cockpit's canopy blew away suddenly and Rudi roared free of the aircraft. Litke lost sight of his friend among the low clouds.

The thunder of his fighter impacting the ocean reached Litke as he realised the ocean was rushing up towards him. Hammering desperately at the round harness of the parachute release, he managed to activate it just as his legs contacted the water.

As he slid below the surface his whole body shuddered violently. The frigid water closed over him.

Litke pulled down on the tabs to inflate his lifejacket. He felt the rapid inflation and then he was heading back to the surface. Breaking through, he entered a world of lashing water and dark waves. He rode up the side of a large wave, saw the approaching ship and dropped back into the trough. His strobe was active. He hoped it was enough for the crew to see him. A crippling numbness was already grabbing hold of his legs.

Cresting the next wave, he saw the ship had stopped and was lowering a smaller boat. As Litke dropped again, he hoped they would pick up Rudi first. His friend needed help more than he did.

Taipan 21

Engaging the last Chechen soldier to their front, Jason dropped the man to the ground with two supressed shots and moved forwards. Passing over the bodies of three soldiers who had been moving towards the crane and loading area, the Taipan 21 team commenced clearing each cabin and room as they pressed forward.

Taipan's intelligence had reported that no more than 50 Chechens comprised the assault force. Jason and his men were oblivious to the 20 who had already died in the helicopter crashes and by Damien's hand. Less the six they had already killed, the team had much less work to do than they assumed. Their brief was for a complete clearance of the platform. No prisoners and no bodies. A clean-up crew would follow once it was secure and remove all trace that anything had happened. Plyos Energy had been very specific. They wanted no-one to know there was a disruption to production which would affect their share price and profits.

Weapon up, Jason secured their front and slowly stepped down the corridor as Botha and Slovo worked through the cabins.

'Jas, look in here, brother,' called Botha as he stepped clear of the door.

'Jeez, what the hell happened?' asked Jason as he investigated the room Botha was indicating. A pile of bodies was in the centre of the room. Three more were on the bed in various states of mutilation. Blood splashed across the walls and floor.

'Mix of bodies here, mate. I see Chechen as well as workers. It's their morgue. What sick fuck carved those poor bastards up?' continued Jason.

'Could be in the pile. I count five Chechens. That makes eleven taken out. I guess the guys on the rig put up a fight, killed a couple, then the others got their revenge. Horrible way to go,' breathed Botha. He had seen plenty of death and murder in his time. He did not condone torture for pleasure. That was beyond him.

'Less for us to take on. I saw at least five men still operating the surviving anti-air battery. So, we could have a little over thirty on here to take care of. I think those are good odds, boys.'

'Not very fair on them,' pointed out Slovo.

'Let's get going,' ordered Jason as he unstowed the tube for his Camelbak and took a quick sip of water.

Moving off, they worked their way to the mess room and looked in. The mass of blood and upturned tables told the story of what had happened. The corridor was slick with blood trails. It was like they had stepped into a slaughterhouse.

As Jason turned out of the room and moved forward again, he caught sight of a Chechen turning the corner. The man stopped, watched them intently for a second and disappeared back around the corner.

'Get him, boys.'

Damien

Rolling back around the corner away from the men he had seen in the corridor, Damien shook his head in frustration.

This passageway seemed to be the most popular on the entire platform. Every time he wanted to use it a group of Chechens had the same idea.

Hearing the soft sound of charging boots, Damien readied himself for a fight. He replayed what he had seen in his mind. The men dressed in winter camouflage uniforms. They were also not carrying AKs. They were holding South African–made supressed assault rifles. There was another player on the rig.

Damien tucked close to the wall and tensed his body. Waiting patiently, he was counting on the men believing that he had retreated at the sight of them. He lay in wait for the first man to carefully edge his way around. Damien saw the muzzle of an assault rifle slide forwards. The top of a man's head slowly moved into view.

Before the man had time to see him, Damien dived forward, and slid his right arm around the back of the man's head in a tight and unforgiving lock. Struggling and using every trick he knew, the man tried to throw Damien off.

Damien dragged him quickly around the corner away from his support, smashing his forehead in the man's nose just as he was drawing a knife to stab down into Damien's legs.

Suddenly, the man went limp in his arms and dragged Damien to his knees. Kicking out, Damien stopped his fall. He pulled the man up in front of him. Hedging his bets, Damien figured this was a mercenary team sent by the company. They should have orders to kill the Chechens but save any workers. Damien glanced down, reminded that he wore the uniform of a Chechen.

The man stirred faintly in his arms. From around the corner came the close, slow approach of boots. The man in Damien's arms had not been faking; he was truly stunned.

'Who are you?' demanded Damien in Russian.

No response.

'Who are you?' asked Damien, this time in English.

'Fuck off,' came a grumbling reply.

'You're the fucked one here, mate. South African, by the accent. You lot a clean-up crew sent by the company?'

'You're going to die. Yeah, we're from the fucking company.'

'I'm not Chechen. I'm only dressed like one. I work for the company.'

'Australian or New Zealander?' asked the man.

'Australian.'

'Victor Alpha Eight Delta,' said the man quietly; he knew whose muscular arm was chocking him.

'You boys Taipan?' asked Damien. He loosened his grip and turned the man to face him. VA8D was one of the standard recognition phrases used by the teams to identify assets and each other.

'Taipan Two One. You Chainsaw?'

'That's not my name. How did you know I was here?'

'We all know who you are, Chainsaw. I'm not fucking impressed by the bullshit. I'm Slovo. Botha and Jas are around the corner.' He snorted through his damaged nose. He blinked away pain and fixed Damien with a deadly stare.

'Call them in,' responded Damien. He had not heard his callsign used for the last two years. His hackles came up as soon as Slovo had used it in place of his name.

'Jas, Botha, it's all good I've found Chainsaw. Come forward,' called Slovo. He stepped away from Damien, picked up his rifle and straightened his uniform. Blood dribbled from his nose. He wiped it away. Taking a deep breath, Slovo fixed Damien with a cold stare.

Two men cautiously moved around the corner and faced Damien.

'Fucking hell. The legendary Chainsaw really is here. I recognise you, mate. Fucking lost your team. Fucking abandoned them I heard,' shot Botha. He spat a thick glob of phlegm at Damien's feet.

'You don't know much. I'm Damien. Chainsaw is my callsign,' he replied, bristling.

Jason walked up to Damien and eyed him carefully.

'Yeah, whatever. I'm Jason, this is Botha and you have already met Slovo. You dumb bastard, Slovo. How the hell did he get around you? Are you going to assist with the clearance, Chainsaw?' asked Jason.

'Damien. No. I don't do that work anymore. The Chechens have rigged the platform with explosives. I had their initiator but lost it in the fight. I was looking for some more firepower and then I was going to retrieve it. Won't be long before they realise you boys are here. CCTV,' replied Damien. He pointed up at a camera set into the passage's ceiling.

'Weak cunt. Get on the mission. Get on the gas with us. We'll show you how killing's done,' said Slovo, squaring his shoulders and glaring at Damien.

'I've done enough killing, Slovo.'

'You taken any out?' asked Jason, ignoring the smouldering anger of his teammate.

'Five. Two were female fighters,' replied Damien. 'We can't stay here and compare kill counts. The Chechens have roving patrols searching for me. I'm assuming the CCTV will be of great help to them.'

'We go when I say so. How many of the bastards left do you think?' asked Jason, moving to assert his authority.

'At least one of their helicopters crashed on landing so that would have taken out quite a few. I don't know how many were meant to make the assault.'

'Fifty,' said Botha.

'At a guess there could be twenty or so left,' said Damien. He eyed the Taipan team and had no respect for them. Taipan must be scraping the bottom of the barrel to hire these three.

'We're going to secure the control room and flight deck, then work our way down using the CCTV to pick off the survivors. Another crew are taking out the missile teams on the ice. I'd expect them to assault this place when they've finished. This job needs doing and us departed before then. A clean-up crew will arrive after that to sort the bodies and any witnesses.'

'Plyos is paying for the full treatment. Egress plan?' asked Damien.

'Why the fuck do you want to know that, brother?' asked Slovo angrily.

'Because it's going to be better than the one I had planned. I think Taipan would be unhappy if you left me here. You knew I was here. So, they know I'm here,' replied Damien.

'You're fucking history. Old garbage they dumped. You aren't fucking coming with us,' said Botha aggressively.

'We take him. He's right. They'll want him,' said Jason quietly. He was watching Damien closely. Regardless of what Botha and Slovo said, Chainsaw was still a polished-looking killer. The way Damien held himself and the confidence he exuded told Jason all he needed to know.

'Fucksake,' pushed Botha.

'Enough, Botha. The decision's made. Chainsaw, you can come with us, only if you help with the clearance. Egress is via one of the helicopters on the flight deck. We use it to head for our pick-up. Doesn't matter which aircraft we take. Botha and Slovo can fly anything. You keep this in mind, though, Chainsaw. Snap your fingers, snap your neck, mate. You fuck us, we fuck you. Clear?'

'Deal,' said Damien, a light smile on his face. Jason's display of dominance was mildly amusing. He had already weighed his options. He knew he did not have anything more attractive to choose from. This team would kill him without batting an eyelid. Damien decided to cut them away as soon as he could after he had retrieved the initiator. There was no way he was going to let the Chechens destroy the pristine environment for their own gain.

'Move out,' ordered Jason.

'Who's your handler?' asked Damien.

'You know him. It's Don,' said Jason.

'How is he?' asked Damien, a soft edge to his voice.

'Still holding on to memories of you and fucking Taipan One Six. The legendary team of recent times in the organisation. Don has had a few teams since. Now Two One has arrived and we will be the new legends,' replied Jason arrogantly.

The four men moved off down the corridor.

Georgiy

Turning into the wind, the pilot fought to bring the Mi-26 into a hover for landing. Ten metres from the ground the air cushion drifted out from under the massive rotors, sending the aircraft dropping with a crushing thump onto the ice. Captured by the wind, the rotors pivoted the aircraft's nose high into the air. The tail rotor span perilously close to the ice. Immediately, the crew cut the power and started shutting down the aircraft. As the rotors slowed, the nose dropped, and the helicopter sat level on the ground. It rocked from side to side as the wind hammered against it.

The internal auxiliary power unit started screaming to keep the systems powered and warm in the Arctic temperatures.

Picking himself up off the helicopter's deck, Georgiy cursed his stupidity for climbing out of his seat just prior to landing. He had wanted to get a look at the terrain through the small portholes let into the fuselage. The 15 men of the Alpha team regarded him quietly. Yakov smiled sympathetically. Shaking his head, Georgiy ordered the rear ramp lowered.

Each man of the Alpha team sported his own preference in equipment and weapons. Georgiy maintained his AK-15. Yakov had swapped his AK-12 out for a Izhmash 5.54-millimetre AN-

94 assault rifle. Over his back he slung a 12-gauge Saiga-12K 030 tactical shotgun for the close work he expected to encounter once they managed to breach the platform.

Hugging the icy terrain for the last 50 kilometres to keep below the platform's radar had been a test of endurance for the pilots. Both were slumped with fatigue in their seats. Landing 500 metres from the platform and their first target – the missile crews – the Alpha team rose as one from their seats and readied their equipment. All slipped on crampons to deal with the icy conditions outside.

'Let's go,' ordered Georgiy. He stepped down the ramp and onto the ice. His crampons bit into the slippery surface. He moved out, looking for any sign that they had not escaped detection. He could just make out the platform through the gloom and sleet. The bright flame of the excess gas burn was going to be a guiding beacon as they approached.

Georgiy had received intelligence during the flight that another team hired by Pylos Energy would already be on the ground and assaulting the platform. Georgiy's first task was to clean up the missile crews and only then move to secure the platform. The other team should have departed by then. It was Georgiy's job to clean up any leftover Chechens and secure the area for the arrival of additional forces. Missing from the brief was who Plyos Energy had hired.

Jogging forwards, the team covered the distance to their target quickly. Georgiy pulled the men to a halt 50 metres out from the Chechens manning the missiles. He could see a wrecked battery and five men walking around, maintaining, and inspecting the surviving launcher. With no cover, the Chechens found themselves fully exposed to the storm. Their heads hung low as they tried to shield themselves from the onslaught.

'Go,' called Georgiy into his radio and crept forwards.

The Alpha team sniper dropped three of the five men before the sound of his Izhmash SV-98D rifle chambered for the powerful .338 Lapua Magnum cartridge echoed across the ice. Georgiy shot the only Chechen to react to the gunfire. The man had managed to unsling his rifle before Georgiy killed him. The final Chechen attempted to run towards the platform.

Eager for action, the men of the Alpha team all opened fire at once. A hail of bullets cut down the man before he had covered 5 metres towards the dubious safety of the rig.

'Secure the site. Disable the missiles. Advise command we've accomplished the first goal. No casualties,' ordered Georgiy. He walked forward and looked over the Sosna-R launcher. It was ready to engage any airborne targets which might present.

'Command's advised. Orders are to proceed to the platform. The other team have not finished their clearance yet. We're to use caution during the assault,' advised Lazarov.

'Thank you, Laz. That's where we were going anyway. Do we have air support? Can we at least get a drone over us?' asked Georgiy. Lazarov typed the request into the Sagittarius terminal strapped to his left forearm.

'Negative, sir. No support.'

'It's just us and whoever this other team is then,' said Georgiy, looking up at the platform.

'Missiles and the launcher are neutralised, sir,' advised Yakov as he struggled against the wind towards Georgiy. The gale snatched most of his words away. Georgiy could guess what he had missed. Their first objective had been easy. The Chechens had not stationed guards to protect themselves. Georgiy figured they did not expect to be around long enough to attract attention.

Their mistake was the Alpha team's win.

'Thank you, Yakov. Lead the team to the platform. You can take the next objective,' said Georgiy. He looked at the face of his Vostok watch and saw it was just past 2am. He felt none of the fatigue normal for the time.

'Sir.' Yakov's chest swelled with pride and ambition. Sprinting away, he called the men together and explained the next phase. Georgiy followed along behind, keeping an eye on his lieutenant's actions.

Below the massive crane jutting out from the platform, Yakov paused and examined the three black ropes which hung down from the railing high above. A small pile of discarded crampons lay abandoned on the ice.

'I'm guessing this is how the other team got up,' he called to Georgiy.

'I agree. We use them too,' instructed Georgiy.

The operators removed their crampons and tossed them onto the pile.

'Up you go,' called Yakov and pointed to the three closest operators. Instantly, they moved forwards, took the ropes in their hands, and started climbing. Behind them the rest of the team turned their weapons up to cover them.

Georgiy was glad Yakov had not chosen to go first. He would make a good commander in time.

Talhig

Staring intently at the CCTV monitors, Talhig tried to work out who the men were who worked methodically along the corridors. The way they moved called them out as professionals. There had been three initially, then a fourth man had joined them. That additional man had to be the Russian who had been killing his soldiers and stole the initiator. Then lost it.

Was he a company security man, here all along in case this happened?

'Who are you?' he said quietly to himself.

'I don't know, but they're clearing our men out of every place they find them. We have lost another ten men already,' responded Mairbek as he heard the quiet words from his general. Mairbek had been issuing warnings and orders to steer reinforcements against the assault, but it was all in vain. The men of the assaulting force moved and engaged each group of soldiers with ruthless efficiency. No prisoners. Mairbek hammered his fist against the table each time he saw one of his wounded comrades executed.

'This is senseless slaughter. Allocate the task to kill these men to Asma. Recall all but the demolition protection team. I want this room secured. We'll leave in the helicopters as soon as we can,' ordered Talhig.

'Sir,' responded Mairbek and issued the orders. Pausing, Mairbek stared at the bank of cameras. 'There's another group of men climbing up to the loading deck. There's no answer from the missile teams.'

Gunfire echoed through the platform below Talhig's feet.

'This can only mean that the Russians have landed a Spetznaz force on the ice. This force must be the advance party of an assault on the platform. How many of our men remain?'

'Fifteen have answered the radio. They are regrouping for the retreat to us,' said Mairbek gravely.

Who are they? Talhig thought.

He watched a running battle between the first team of assaulters and two of his soldiers. His men were trying to disengage and retreat towards the control room. The men were giving a good account of themselves.

Jumping slightly as the satellite telephone started ringing, Mairbek plucked it off the receiver, listened and handed it to Talhig.

'Da?' he answered.

'How's the operation going, Talhig?' asked Sheikh. His voice sounded distant and disengaged.

'The Russians have started assaulting the platform, Sheikh. How they arrived we don't know, but they are here now. I have fifteen men left,' supplied Talhig. He felt the weight and sorrow of his words.

'I know. Our intelligence assets advised me an hour ago. The FSB dispatched an Alpha team to retake the platform.'

Why did his leader not warn him?

Talhig gripped the telephone and stared hard at the night through the windows. By the bright lights of the flight deck, he could see the helicopter crews pulling away the refuelling hoses.

'There's another team here. The Alpha team is behind them,' said Talhig flatly.

'I know nothing of that, Talhig. A helicopter would have landed the Alpha team fifteen minutes ago.'

'The men who are working through the platform, killing my soldiers, have been here for the last thirty minutes,' responded Talhig, confusion echoing in his voice.

'Impossible. It's the Alpha team. Talhig, your orders have changed. We cannot afford to wait any longer. You're to blow the platform immediately. I have ordered Dasha to initiate the final part of his plan. We will wait no longer,' ordered Sheikh.

'I can't right now, Sheikh. A Russian worker stole the laser initiator which sets off the charges. I have retrieved it, but we need to run the final set-up tests. I believe the Russian is ex-military. He's very skilled. The bastard has killed my men. I have soldiers stationed at the fibre optic junctions. They will set off a local command on the top five floors in the event the main initiator fails. I need more time before I can set the system up.'

The receiver was silent. Then Talhig could hear Sheikh's harsh angry breathing.

'Make sure you achieve your mission, Talhig,' replied Sheikh through gritted teeth. Sheikh and the Itt Stag movement needed a win for their cause.

'I will achieve my task, Sheikh. There's no doubt in my mind. Is the cargo ship in place? Now that the Russians have arrived, we need to make our escape,' asked Talhig.

'Wait,' instructed Sheikh.

Talhig glanced at the monitors and watched his men fighting

for their lives. Their action had stalled the assault team's advance. His soldiers' sacrifice would mean that others might live.

'Talhig?'

'Go ahead, sir,' replied Talhig formally.

'Delayed due to the weather. I have arranged for a refuelling point on Rudolf Island in the Franz Josef Archipelago for you. The ship will be rerouted to wait off the island. You can fly out to it. The island is four hours flight time from the platform. Can you make it?'

'We will. There's a Russian base to the south of Rudolf Island, though,' pointed out Talhig.

'I'm aware. Our Russian Mafia friends assure me that there is a supply of aviation fuel at a small airfield which services the island. Expeditions to the north or researchers occasionally use it. No-one is there currently. I will ensure you and your valiant men survive, Talhig. Ensure you leave a rear guard behind to kill as many of the Russians as possible. You must ensure the demolition proceeds uninterrupted. You're all valuable to the cause. Allahu Akbar.'

'Yes, Sheikh. I remember Grozny,' replied Talhig automatically.

I have not forgotten my home, he thought to himself sourly.

The tone in Sheikh's voice did not fill him with confidence. Without anywhere else to go, he would lead his fighters to Rudolf Island and hope that the ship would be there.

Taipan 21

'Persistent little pricks,' grunted Botha quietly to himself as he edged slowly forwards along the deck. Crawling closer to the two Chechens who were hampering their advance, he had decided enough was enough. It was time to finish them. Neither soldier had seen him creeping up behind them, his stealthy approach masked by gunfire and grenade explosions.

A few minutes earlier, Botha had stripped out of his equipment and slipped into a heating duct barely large enough to accommodate his bulk. He'd worked his way to the rear of the Chechens, then dropped down into an empty corridor 50 metres beyond their position. Botha had swiftly moved down the deserted corridor towards his prey. Cursing the continuous corners in the round platform, Botha had used the noise of the battle to guide him.

Like a snake stalking its next meal, Botha slid quickly over the deck towards the soldiers. He had left behind his rifle and carried only a long Bauchop Persian fighting knife and a Vektor SP-1 pistol. He left the pistol in its holster; Botha was going to make his kills with the knife. He had chosen to crawl towards the Chechens to make it that much harder.

Stalking to within a few metres of the distracted men, Botha rose and gripped the nearest man's helmet. He yanked the Chechen's head back, jamming the knife deep into the soldier's exposed throat. He yanked out the blade and dropped the gagging man to the ground, then slashed at the next Chechen. Dancing forwards, Botha flashed the blade past the eyes of the shocked man. He smashed it through a gap in the man's armour and pierced his heart. Both Chechens lay lifeless on the deck.

Despite pulling viciously on the knife, he couldn't remove it from the Chechen's chest. Locked among the ribs. Without missing a beat, Botha drew his pistol and forced it against the side of the soldier's head. He pulled the trigger. Botha heard the roar of the pistol and watched the soldier's head explode against the wall. Frustration at losing his knife drove his actions.

Silence echoed through the corridor.

Jason jogged up to the captured position and looked silently at Botha's blood-covered face and uniform.

'You're the man, Botha.' Slovo grinned as he walked past, slapping him on the shoulder.

'That's how you kill, Chainsaw. You kill men with your hands. My hands killed these little men,' shouted Botha beating his chest like a gorilla.

Damien regarded him for a second.

'I've killed men with my hands before, Botha. It's not new to combat,' pointed out Damien. He walked behind Jason. Damien had procured a fallen AK-74M and dropped the muzzle as he neared the blood-splattered Botha.

Botha spat on the ground and turned as Slovo handed him his armour and rifle. Shrugging into his comfortable rig, Botha gripped his weapon. He checked to make sure there was a round in the chamber and looked towards the stairs leading to the next level. A large 7 adorned the wall, with an arrow pointing up. Four more levels and they would be in position to make a break for the flight deck.

'Grenade!' shouted Damien as he dropped to the deck behind the bodies of the Chechens. Jason dropped as soon as he heard the shout. Damien had seen an arm appear from a cabin near the stairs and lob the grenade.

Rolling towards them along the deck was a Russian RGN hand grenade. Botha and Slovo reversed course and dove backwards. The grenade caught them and exploded.

The grenade's explosion peppered Botha and Slovo with shrapnel. Both men howled in pain. The blast stripped Botha's armour away from his body. His rifle smashed. Slovo's legs were a mass of bleeding flesh. He crashed to the deck yelling for Jason to grab him and pull him clear.

Flipping painfully onto his back, Botha looked back down the passageway and saw three figures appear. Drawing his pistol, he sighted on the first one. Before he could get a shot off, the leading figure fired a short burst of automatic fire. Nine-millimetre bullets tore into Botha's hand and smashed it into a bloody and broken pulp. Howling with anger, he pulled out his knife and struggled to rise. Ignoring him, the three soldiers swiftly moved past and shot Slovo in the back of his right arm when he tried to bring up his rifle.

'Go!' shouted Jason as he leapt up and sprinted past Damien, who was already coming to his feet. Both men ran to the nearest outer hatch, pulled it open and disappeared outside. As Damien passed through, bullets hammered against the door.

Fuck, I'm sick of running, he thought as he dogged the hatch closed and followed Jason into the storm.

'Hey!' yelled Damien against the wind.

Jason continued to move away from him along the walkway. He was heading towards a set of stairs leading to the next level.

'Hey!' repeated Damien.

Jason slowed and turned to face him.

'What?'

'You left Botha and Slovo behind. They aren't dead,' said Damien.

'They know the deal. Wounded men in a place like this don't walk out. Botha and Slovo would have done the same to me.'

'That's not the Taipan way. My team would never have done what you just did,' said Damien.

'Your team is dead, Damien. Dead. There was no-one to rescue them. Dead men are just dead men.'

'Fuck you!' yelled Damien and swiped the butt of his rifle up in an arc towards Jason's face.

'Calm down!' countered Jason as he moved to one side and easily deflected Damien's swing.

'Don't talk about my team again. We didn't operate like you.'

'Yeah, well. It's worked for us,' said Jason, holding up his hands in mock surrender.

'Taipan teams are meant to look after each other. That's what makes them strong and effective.'

'My team, Two One, wasn't like that. Where we come from, South Africa, it's a brutal place. You become that way after a time.'

Shaking his head, Damien pushed past and headed to the stairs.

Behind him, Jason took a sight picture on Damien's back and considered pulling the trigger.

'We're fucked anyway. Botha and Slovo could fly helicopters, but I can't,' pointed out Jason, lowering his rifle as he saw Damien turning.

'I can fly one,' Damien answered bluntly and fixed Jason with a dangerous gaze. 'You point a rifle at me again and it will be the last time.'

'Fair enough, brother.' Jason shrugged.

Asma

Botha gritted his teeth and looked up at the beautiful woman who stood impassively above him.

'Do it. You fucking Chechen bitch. Fucking finish it!' he shouted, spraying bloody spittle over the legs of Asma's uniform.

Asma glanced down at the man's blood and spit on her uniform. Grimacing, she reversed her PP-19 Vityaz and crashed its butt into Botha's mouth, smashing his front teeth.

Choking on broken teeth, Botha opened his bloody mouth and cried out in pain. His body bucked involuntarily. He tried to maintain focus. Pain arced and swelled through his face. Locking eyes with the woman, he poured as much hate into them as he could to intimidate her.

Chuckling, Asma looked at the other man they had captured. This one would bleed out if they did not stop the steady flow of blood from his torn legs. Impassively, Asma padded over and smashed the butt of her submachine gun into the man's ripped and exposed legs. He jerked away desperately and cried out in heavily accented English. Her girls laughed at him. Slovo looked up into their faces and knew they would be the last people he would ever see.

'Who are you?' she asked Slovo in slow heavy English.

'Can't even speak, you fucking bitch,' shouted Botha from where he lay in a steadily expanding pool of his and Slovo's blood.

Ignoring him, Asma looked at Slovo.

'You will die. I can help you. Who are you?'

'Fuck off,' responded Slovo. His voice was shaking. He thought he sounded scared. Slovo frowned at his own fear. He did not recall feeling it before. Though he had seen it on many faces in the past.

Nodding, Asma stood up and walked a few paces down the corridor to look at the two dead Chechen soldiers.

'Talhig, it's Asma,' she called over the radio.

'Da?'

'I have caught two of the intruders. They speak English with a heavy accent. I don't recognise it. They're not Russian. What do you want to do with them?'

'I can see you on the camera. The other two have escaped outside. I don't know where they are. The cameras out there aren't working,' said Talhig.

'I'll get them. What do you want to do with these men? By the looks of their equipment, I think they are mercenaries. It could be as you said, Talhig. The company may have sent them.'

'I have a report that an Alpha team has commenced an assault on the platform.'

'These men are not Alpha. They're mercenaries,' replied Asma.

'Dispose of them. As you see fit, but be quick. The Alpha team will be nearing you shortly. As soon as you finish, you and your girls are to return to the control room. The initiator has passed its tests and the charges are ready. The five men remaining behind have called in at the junctions. They're prepared. We are leaving, Asma.'

'Where to?' she asked curiously.

'I will tell you when you get here. Ten minutes, Asma. If you are not here, I will leave you behind,' stressed Talhig.

'My girls and I will be there in less. We just need to ensure these men do not know anything that we may find useful,' said Asma as she turned and grinned down at Botha. His wide and bloodshot eyes had taken on an aggressive, insane look. Botha's mouth opened as he tried to breathe. Asma could see the jagged stubs of his teeth.

'Don't take too long. You're needed here,' ended Talhig. He did not envy the men Asma had captured. Talhig had seen the pain and suffering she was capable of inflicting if the mood took her. By the tone in Asma's voice, that mood had taken her.

Sliding out her wickedly curved hawk billed Karambit knife, Asma marched over to where Botha lay.

Botha's screams echoed along the corridor. Slovo's followed quickly as the three Chechen fighters took to both men in vengeance for their lost comrades.

Damien

Damien rapidly led the way along the walkways and stairs which led higher into the platform. He passed over the empty drilling floor with Jason close behind.

'Which helicopter can you fly, Chainsaw?' asked Jason. He had decided that Damien was worth keeping around until they made it to the pick-up point. If only for his flying ability. After the famous Chainsaw's usefulness expired it was a bullet in the head and into the ocean for him.

'I can fly either, but I'll take the Kamov. I like that one. It's easy to fly and rugged. Exactly what we need,' replied Damien. He was still unsure about Jason's motives. The mission remained uncompleted, but Jason had already initiated the egress phase and had left two men behind. Don would have been ashamed of this team if he knew.

'Do you have comms with Don?'

'No,' replied Jason simply.

'No drone to relay?' pushed Damien.

'No. No assets available,' lied Jason. He knew very well that Noah was monitoring the mission with the RPV which turned lazy circles high above them.

'How did you infiltrate?' asked Damien as he climbed the last ladder to the flight deck. He halted and peered through the sleet at the windows of the control room. Through them he could see a man pacing around.

'Jumped in. Hell of a ride and great fun,' stated Jason proudly. He still felt the thrill of dropping through the storm clouds and making a successful landing. It reinforced the bulletproof image he had of himself.

'Interesting.'

'Yeah, yeah, brother. Enough talk. What now?' replied Jason shortly.

'The Kamov's forward on the deck and should be near the Agusta. I scoped them out when I first arrived here. Always have an escape plan. But first I have one last thing to do.'

'No, Chainsaw. The mission's a bust. It's time to leave,' stressed Jason hardening his eyes.

'Only take a few minutes,' pushed Damien.

'What?'

'I'm just going to duck into the control room and get that laser initiator. That's where they will have set it up. Perfect access to the fibre optic network.'

'Just fucking leave, it brother. Leave these fanatics to their slaughter.'

'It's not the Chechens, it's the damage to the environment. Look around, Jason. This place is pristine.'

'All I see is ice and fucking snow. If it was that pristine the world would have stopped this platform from existing. No, Chainsaw. No-one gives a fuck about this place.'

'Wait here if you like. Keep the stairs to the flight deck clear until I get back.'

'Your funeral,' ended Jason as he turned away to survey stairs.

Talhig

'Are you ready to leave, Mairbek? Abandon the equipment. The explosion will take care of it,' stated Talhig as he paced up and down the floor of the control room. His mind was keen and excited. They were so close to completing the mission.

'A few minutes, sir,' responded Mairbek. He was closing the lids on his satellite terminal and HF radio. He reached for his AK-74M and straightened up.

Damien

Gripping the handle to the control room door, Damien paused and looked through the window set in the centre. A Chechen was standing up from a table and the other had stopped packing equipment and was looking around. Damien could see the laser initiator in the centre of a table. Running from it was a thin bundle of fibre optic cable which snaked towards the floor. Damien drew in a deep breath.

Twisting the door's handle, Damien threw it open and charged into the room, bringing up his AK. He shot the man rising from the table with a single shot to the side of the head. Lifeless, the man dropped onto the table, scattering the equipment onto the floor, then fell with a heavy thud to the deck.

As Damien reversed his aim and sought out the second target, he saw the other Chechen raising a pistol. Dropping into a crouch, Damien spun towards the threat. Before he could bring his rifle to bare, Damien saw a bright flash of flame from the outstretched pistol. He instantly felt the bullet impact the receiver of the AK, smashing from his hands. The rifle skittered over the deck and came to rest next to the dead Chechen.

Rolling forwards, Damien ducked under the stream of bullets the Chechen was pumping at him. As the man paused to adjust his aim, Damien stood up and rushed towards him.

Talhig had jumped in fright as he saw the armed man burst into the control room and kill Mairbek. Reacting quickly, he had drawn his pistol, but the newcomer was lightning fast. Bullets fired from his pistol ricocheted around the room. Talhig watched the man roll upright and come at him, drawing a fighting knife as he approached.

Pulling the purposeful knife from his chest rig, Damien lunged at his opponent. Bending with the force of the onslaught Talhig stepped back and dropped the empty magazine from his pistol. He was slower than Damien's onslaught as he tried to fish a fresh magazine from a pouch.

Gripping the front of Talhig's armour, Damien aimed the knife at his neck and drove it down viciously. Seeing Damien's flanks exposed, Talhig dropped the pistol and drove both of his fists into Damien's sides. Talhig leaned away from the descending knife. Air exploded from Damien's lungs and the knife careered off the shoulder strap of Talhig's chest rig. Talhig slammed a fist into Damien's left hand. The knife flew from his grasp.

Recovering himself instantly, Damien drew in a large breath, adopted a fighting stance, and launched at Talhig. His fists a blur, he landed four heavy blows to Talhig's exposed face. His nose broke under the onslaught and Talhig's eyes pricked with involuntary tears. Stunned by the speed and ferocity of the assault the Chechen felt his knees sag.

To finish the job, Damien dropped his left elbow down into Talhig's broken nose and drove him to the deck. Groaning in pain, Talhig stayed down. He knew that Asma would not be far away.

Stepping away, Damien bumped up against the table with the initiator. He grasped it, quickly disconnected the fibre optic cable from the device's top and dropped it into a pouch on his rig. Eyeing the fallen Chechen where he lay watching him, Damien's eyes hardened. He walked over and picked up the dropped combat knife. He slid it back into its sheath. Damien regarded the man before him. He was sure this had to be the commander of the Chechen force.

Slipping free the Gerber Gator knife from his pants pocket, Damien levered the blade out and stepped forwards, intent on finishing the job. He stood over Talhig, taking another moment to stare at the man's scarred and damaged face. Cocking his head, Damien heard the heavy strike of boots on the stairs leading to the room. He cursed softly and folded the blade.

Stooping down, he retrieved his ruined AK and disappeared out the door.

As the door closed behind him, Damien span around to jam the rifle through the handle and did his best to lock it in place to give more time for their escape.

Asma

Asma charged up the internal stairs to the control room, quickening her pace as the sound of gunfire echoed from the room. When she reached the inner door she slowly opened it. She took in Talhig lying on the floor and Mairbek's unmoving body near his equipment. The dead body of the radar operator and Fedor lay against the far wall, stacked there by Mairbek. She rushed into the room and squatted next to Talhig.

'The Russian has taken the initiator again! Get him,' choked out Talhig as he tried to breathe through his shattered nose. Warm blood coursed down his face and dropped onto the deck behind him.

Shaking her head, Asma made for the door, tugged on the handle, and found it jammed.

Talhig pulled himself into a sitting position as Asma's remaining three girls arrived. Gritting his teeth, Talhig placed his hands either side of his nose, drew in a ragged breath and forced them together. A shattering pain filled his face. A brilliant white light seemed to blanket his eyes. Feeling along the line of cartilage, he was satisfied his nose was as set as it was ever going to be. He gained his feet, watching Asma struggling with the door.

Damien

'Got it,' called Damien as he rushed up to Jason, indicating for him to head for the stairs.

'Did you have company?'

'Not long and they'll be through that door. Then we're buggered.'

'Yes, we will be. Can you clear the Chechen helicopters when you take off?' asked Jason.

As he edged out to look over the flight deck, Jason could see the massive Mi-26 taking up over half of the available space. The Mi-17 to its rear had its tail boom hanging out over the edge. There was some room up forward. Jason could only see one Plyos Energy helicopter there.

'The Agusta should be to the left of the Kamov,' replied Damien as he joined Jason.

'What does the Agusta look like?' Jason asked.

'Sleek tail, boxy fuselage, slim nose, why?'

'Well, mate. It's not there,' pointed out Jason and nodded with his head to indicate where he was looking.

Frowning, Damien followed Jason's directions. His eyes landed on the empty space next to the Kamov. The Kamov KA-32S, with its distinctive coaxial rotors, boxy fuselage, and twin tails, made it immediately recognisable. The twin main rotors gave the aircraft an excellent power-to-weight ratio, and high cargo and ordnance lift capacity, for its size.

'Not sure where it is. Gives us some more room to take off. I can pull the Kamov back a little more into the Agusta's space. I'll need you to cover me while I get the engines warmed for flight. The fellas in the control room are going to be very angry when they make it through that door.'

'It's in my best interests to do that, Chainsaw. How're you going to move a helicopter?'

'It's on wheels,' responded Damien. He threw Jason a baleful look.

'How long do you need?'

'Five minutes. The electronics will be on ground power. Just need to start the engines, warm them to minimum and we're off. You need to find me at least five minutes. Do what you need to.'

'Sounds easy enough,' replied Jason, shrugging. 'Let's get on with it.'

'Your assigned mission isn't finished yet, Jason,' said Damien.

'Sometimes they aren't. It's the nature of the beast,' replied Jason absently. He had no interest in talking to Damien further.

'As I said, times have changed in Taipan.'

'No, they haven't. Taipan One Six just got the easy missions. Don's little favourites,' spat Jason. He was trying to get a rise out of Damien. Some form of conflict.

'Like I said, it must be different now.'

As he moved cautiously along the walkway, Damien kept a close eye on the control room. The Chechens inside were moving around a lot but did not seem to be making any progress to dislodge the rifle from behind the handle. Damien made the wide steps to the flight deck and glanced behind him. Jason was coming out of the shadows, weapon up.

Taking the first three steps in a crouch, Damien paused and looked at the control room. He saw no change. He eased his head over the edge of the deck.

The surface was slick with sleet and rain. The wind whipped across the steel, spraying water and the reek of aviation fuel into the air. The Mi-26 and Mi-17 rocked gently on their undercarriages. Damien saw no sign of crews. He would have to pass close to the cockpit of the Mi-26 as he made for the Kamov.

Taking a second longer than Jason liked, Damien rose and took the last five steps. His boots landed softly on the flight deck. He looked around carefully, then ducked over to the side of the Mi-26. Jason scooted up behind him and arrived with his back to the cold metal of the helicopter's fuselage. Jason's eyes were half closed against the wind. Uncovered parts of his face were bright red and raw.

Jason watched Damien move casually around the nose of the Mi-26 and start towards the Kamov. Damien walked as if he belonged on the flight deck. Damien was fully exposed as he made the halfway point. Anyone who might happen to look in his direction would spot the intruder immediately. Grimacing, Jason looked around. His sixth sense was telling him they were not alone.

Rolling his scan back to stare at Damien, Jason picked up movement in the Mi-26's cockpit. A face appeared, disappeared, and then reappeared. The glass frosted over where the man's excited breath blasted against it. Lifting his supressed rifle, Jason took a sight picture and pulled the trigger. The light sound of the gun firing disappeared with the wind. Entering exactly where Jason had aimed, the bullets smashed through the plexiglass and carried away the man's head. Blood splashed across the inside of the cockpit.

Jogging around to the front of the helicopter, Jason looked in to see another man staring at him. He was trying to push the body of his comrade off himself and escape the cockpit. Jason calmly hefted his rifle into his shoulder and fired three rapid shots into the space. The first two missed though they starred the plexiglass. The third found the man's throat and hammered him back into his seat. Jason fancied he could hear the gurgling sound as the Chechen slowly died. Smiling happily, Jason walked backwards, securing their rear.

Damien pulled the chocks free from around the Kamov's wheels and snapped his head up at the sound of the suppressed rifle firing. Damien tossed the last chock away. He saw Jason taking out the two men in the Mi-26's cockpit. He yanked open the right-hand cockpit door of the Kamov, reached in and released the park brake. Free, the wheels rolled easily back the few metres Damien needed. He reset the brake, then settled into the pilot's seat and began surveying the instruments to refamiliarise himself with the controls. It had been a long time since he had flown a Russian helicopter.

Commencing the prestart check, Damien opted for an abbreviated engine start. A feature he had always loved about Russian equipment. There was never really a need to fully complete a checklist before heading into the air. Above him the shrill whine of the two Isotov TV3-117V turboshaft engines sounded loudly across the flight deck. Watching the engine temperatures slowly climb towards their minimum operating limits, Damien engaged the rotors. They began to turn slowly above his head.

Out the door, Damien could see Jason kneeling on the deck. He appeared to be firing at someone. The rifle kicked in his shoulder as Jason fired controlled bursts back down the flight deck.

Jason sensed eyes on him. He looked up and mouthed for Damien to hurry up. A thump sounded through the aircraft as something hit the rear. It sounded like someone had thrown a handful of stones at the fuselage. Damien knew they were taking fire.

He wasn't going to wait for the engines to reach their minimum operating temperature. He twisted the throttle on the collective gently and found the engines responsive, if a little sluggish.

Good enough. He hammered his gloved fist on the plexiglass window set in the door to catch Jason's attention and motioned him to get on board.

Reacting immediately, Jason let off a full burst of automatic fire, leapt to his feet and sprinted around the nose of the Kamov, using the aircraft as cover. He pulled open the opposite door and leapt into the cockpit.

'Strap in. It's going to be hairy,' stated Damien as he finished buckling his own harness.

'Fucking hairy. You should have been outside, mate. There are quite a few Chechens in those damned helicopters.'

'Well, at least you'll be a bit closer to finishing the mission then,' ribbed Damien. He applied more power and the Kamov came light on its wheels.

'Get us the fuck out of here,' yelled Jason.

'Right then,' stated Damien. Applying more power, he lifted the little helicopter free of the deck. The Kamov drifted back towards the Mi-26. He needed a few more metres to clear the superstructure arching over them. The sound of small arms fire peppering the fuselage sounded loud in their ears.

'Fuck. Hurry up!' shouted Jason as he finished strapping himself in. He felt vulnerable and exposed with only thin plexiglass and aluminium to protect him.

Ignoring his panicky passenger, Damien deftly pedal-turned

the Kamov to the left and pulled more power. Bullets continued to hammer against the aircraft as he gained enough height to lift over the Mi-26. Looking past Jason, Damien saw that the soldiers in the control room had managed to open the door. As they poured onto the deck the Chechens began firing at them. He was sure he could see long black hair streaming out behind one of them. As they passed the Mi-17, Damien saw the crew watching him and firing pistols at the Kamov.

Shaking his head, Damien dumped the collective and dropped the little helicopter over the edge of the flight deck and into space. He needed to get out of the range of the surface-to-air missiles as soon as he could.

'Fuck!' shouted Jason as he pushed his hands instinctively against the helicopter's roof to steady himself, his stomach trying to free itself from his body.

'Nervous flier,' said Damien with a chuckle. He pulled the boxy helicopter up short of the ice and sped away from the platform. Warning lights were blinking on the instrument panel and the controls felt sluggish.

The buggers have hit a few vitals, thought Damien.

'Head to Rudolf Island. That's the Taipan pick-up point. It's a four-hour flight-time away. We'll arrive well within the window for collection. Scheduled for eighteen hundred this evening,' instructed Jason.

'Position?' asked Damien.

Jason pulled a notebook out of his chest rig and thumbed through the pages. He worked out their current location. Jason gave Damien a course to steer and slumped back in his seat.

'Let's hope the old girl keeps together long enough to get us there,' said Damien. He turned onto the heading Jason had given him. Already the storm was trying to make life hard. Sleet and snow hammered against the windscreen. The wipers were struggling to cope.

'Just have to call home,' said Jason quietly. He pulled a Harris Flacon III PRC/AN-152A free of its pouch. He checked to ensure that radio was on the correct channel. Reaching up to his left ear, he pushed in an earphone, wriggling it to make sure it seated correctly. He did not want Damien to hear Don's voice.

'Thought you had no comms?'

'Can't give away everything, brother,' chuckled Jason. 'Watchtower, Mamba, over.'

'Go for Watchtower.'

'Mission's a bust. I have linked up with, Chainsaw. We're heading for the pick-up point. The mission is uncompleted. Botha and Slovo are dead,' relayed Jason.

'Mamba, return to the platform and finish your mission,' instructed Don. His voice sounded tinny and jarring in Jason's ear.

'Negative. We have left the platform and are inbound for the pick-up. Make sure the aircraft is there. As scheduled, to collect us,' continued Jason.

'Mamba, I note your failure to complete the mission. Consider your employment terminated,' replied Don firmly. He would not tolerate Taipan 21's failure.

'And the pick-up?'

'If Chainsaw is there, we'll collect both of you. If he isn't, then no pick-up. You know the rules of play. Our RPV is going off station. You will have no comms until the pick-up aircraft arrives.'

'Roger. We'll both be at the airfield, out,' ended Jason and pulled the earphone free.

'All good?' queried Damien.

'Right as rain, mate. Right as rain. Fly on.'

Georgiy

'Seems we're late to the party,' said Yakov quietly as he walked down the corridor from the cargo area.

In front of him, Alpha operators were methodically checking cabins and splitting up into their assigned search teams and moving off.

'Looks like it,' replied Georgiy. He walked beside Yakov and eyed the bodies littering the deck. The team had been surprised to see the bodies near the crane. The corridor leading from it seemed to have been the scene of much of the action. By the blood and bodies strewn around, it had been fast and violent. Bullet and shrapnel holes pockmarked the walls.

'Search teams commence clearing the platform deck by deck. Charlie team, format on myself and the major. We're heading for the control room. I will run the operation from there. Take prisoners where you can. Headquarters will want someone to interrogate. If you can find anyone alive,' instructed Yakov as he stared at the scene before him.

'Good,' said Georgiy, pleased. 'Let's get going.'

'Helicopter?' asked Yakov quizzically. He could feel faint vibrations through his feet as if a helicopter was on the deck and firing up.

'Could be. That means they are making ready for their escape. Time to get up there.' Georgiy broke into a non-tactical jog. He had had enough of these Chechens. He wanted it finished.

Moving quickly down corridors and along stairs, Yakov followed the map displayed on the Sagittarius tablet strapped to his left arm. They found every turn deserted. The signs of combat were evident. The contractor team had launched a successful mission against the Chechens.

On deck 7, Georgiy found the evidence he needed for who had caused the carnage. Yakov stooped down to examine the mutilated bodies tossed to one side of the corridor. Near them were the bodies of two Chechens who had been manning an improvised defensive position.

'How big was the contractor team?' asked Yakov.

'I wasn't told,' replied Georgiy.

'Well, this is what's left of two of them. I'd say the Chechens captured them. And then carved them up. Horrible way to die.'

'I think the Chechens would argue that point with you, Yakov. Their men are lying over there dead. Most likely killed by these men. They would feel most justified.'

'Are you praising them, sir?' asked Yakov, a hard tone in his voice.

'No, Yakov. I just understand,' replied Georgiy with a weary tone. 'Let's go.'

'Four more decks,' said Yakov and motioned the men of Charlie team forward.

Georgiy rushed up the stairs to the level below the control room. Stepping into the corridor, he was surprised to see a Chechen standing with his arms raised to a box mounted in the ceiling. Hearing Charlie team storming up the stairs, the man dropped his arms and raised his AK. Before the Chechen could react, Yakov drove him to the deck with three 12-gauge slugs from his Saiga tactical shotgun.

Arriving at the hatch which led into the control room, the lead operator of Charlie team slowly stretched up. He peered through the small porthole set into the door. After taking in the scene, he dropped back down and scooted over to Georgiy.

'Deserted, sir. I can see bodies.'

'A quiet breach, please,' ordered Yakov. He slung the shotgun over his back and shouldered his AN-94, ready to take on any Chechen who might be hiding in the room.

Slowly cracking open the hatch, the first man slipped through. Silence followed the breach. The operator pulled the door open for the others.

In the room, Georgiy saw the bodies and blood splattered the walls. Broken electronics littered the floor where it had been torn from consoles. He looked up through the windows and saw a Chechen running up the last steps to the flight deck.

Rushing to the windows, Georgiy saw the blades starting to turn on a Mi-26 and the Mi-17 behind it. Chechens were rushing up the ramps of both aircraft and disappearing inside. What looked to be a security team were guarding the top of the stairs.

'They're escaping!' yelled Georgiy.

He yanked open the door and ran outside alone.

Talhig

'Learn!' bellowed Talhig at the co-pilot of the Mi-17 where he sat in the cockpit of the Mi-26, among the blood and gore of his comrades. Frigid air roared in through holes in the windscreen. The pilot shuddered.

Talhig had immediately ordered the flight crew of the Mi-17 to separate when he had discovered the Mi-26 pilots were dead. One pilot would fly each. Pulling rank, the pilot of the Mi-17 had delegated the duty to the co-pilot. That man now sat unhappily in front of Talhig trying to explain that he did not have a rating for the massive and complex helicopter. Nor had he ever stepped foot on the flight deck of one.

'Da,' was all the pilot could think to say. The loadmaster and flight engineer had managed to get the engines started a few minutes earlier. They were slowly coming up to operating temperature. The Mi-17's engines were already operational and the last of the freedom fighters were climbing on board.

Gunfire echoed over the flight deck.

Talhig moved down to the ramp and looked across towards the control room. Five men were moving quickly from the door and engaging the rear guard. He could make out the muzzle flashes of the assaulting group and that they wore white camouflage smocks, but little else. Gunfire echoed inside the platform as well. His plan to bring glory to Itt Stag was rapidly collapsing.

'Asma! Contact!' yelled Talhig.

Asma and the three surviving women of her team surged out of their seats and jogged down the ramp to immediately engage the enemy. The last man in the assaulting group slumped to the ground, lifeless. Returning the favour, the Russians cut down two of the Chechen soldiers forming the rear guard. Their bodies tumbled down the stairs.

Lobbing grenades, Asma moved forwards and dropped another of the soldiers attacking them. Through the control room windows she saw more men in white smocks flooding into the room. Reversing her course, Asma ducked back into the helicopter.

'There're more coming from inside the platform. It must be the Alpha team. We need to lift off!' shouted Asma above the noise of the helicopter's engines. The rotors had started to turn faster.

'Are the men assigned to the manual detonation still at their positions?' asked Talhig. He had unslung his AK-12. He was ready to kill someone. Nothing had gone to plan on this mission. He was feeling the weight of an approaching defeat. With the second loss of the laser initiator, he had to rely on his brave soldiers who would suicide themselves for the cause. But from the sound of gunfire inside the platform, he figured he had his answer. This was a disaster.

'They're not answering their radios. We need to leave,' urged Asma. The sound of bullets hitting the fuselage echoed around them. Asma looked back out at the battle. She saw Belita's body buck and twist as Russian bullets cut her down, crashing to the flight deck alongside the other women of her crew. A sudden sadness gripped her mind. She turned it into hate. Her girls were all gone.

'Get on the cannon!' yelled Talhig at the loadmaster who ran past him towards the ramp. He had been on his way from the cockpit to start his pre-flight checks. Arresting his movement, the loadmaster reversed course without a word and stepped behind the starboard GShG-7.62-millimetre cannon. He readied it for action.

Talhig charged up to the flight deck, looked the nervous pilot in the eyes and slammed a fist down hard on top of his helmet.

'Get us in the fucking air. Now! Or I will shoot you!' he roared, his face bloody red. Talhig felt his heart thumping rapidly in his chest. Blood throbbed through his damaged nose. He felt tired and energised all at the same time.

Stopping the pre-flight checks he had been trying to complete, the pilot called the Mi-17 and advised them to take off. As the Mi-17 lifted away and into the storm, the frame of the Mi-26 rumbled with the roar of the rotary cannon. The loadmaster sprayed the area in front of the control room. Pulling power on the collective, the pilot saw no warning lights on the instrument panel. The Mi-26 came light on its wheels. Checking left and right as best he could, the pilot cleared himself for a rapid departure.

Asma ducked back inside as the massive helicopter's rotors beat viciously at the air. The rear guard were all dead. No-one was alive on the platform that she cared about. The flight engineer rushed past her to the ramp and pulled the lever to raise it. Turning the helicopter slowly, the pilot tried to give the loadmaster on the rotary canon as much opportunity to engage as he could, all the while working out how to keep the beast of a helicopter in the air.

Feeling the Mi-26 start sinking back to the deck, the pilot applied as much power as he could. He heard a warning siren start sounding and backed off slightly, arresting the helicopter's descent. The pilot backed slowly off the platform. The hammering of the canon shook the airframe. The noise and lack of experience distracted the pilot. He let it drift too far back and clipped the tail rotor on a derrick. The aircraft bucked. Cursing, he felt the pedals battering against his feet. The tail rotor was damaged.

Talhig glared out at the empty deck where the Kamov had

been. He knew the Russian who had again taken the laser initiator had suddenly become a pilot and escaped them.

What kind of man was he?

Thrown from his feet by the pilot's clumsy flying, Talhig's head slammed into the deck. Asma grabbed him and hauled him over into a seat. Dazed, Talhig looked at her uncertainly. Ignoring him, Asma locked his seatbelt into place and lay his head against her shoulder.

The pilot steadied the Mi-26, moved forwards, and turned out towards the sea. He dropped the massive helicopter off the flight deck. The rotary cannon fell silent as the turn obscured the loadmaster's targets. Stepping across the walkway to the port cannon, the loadmaster charged it and tried to swing it along the length of the aircraft to engage. Unable to get enough angle the loadmaster opened fire regardless. A long tongue of flame stretched out form the cannon. Thousands of bullets hammered across the flight deck.

Heading unsteadily into the storm, the pilot of the Mi-26 tried to find the Mi-17 in the murk.

Georgiy

Georgiy found himself in a cauldron of bullets and smashing metal. He had been lucky enough to duck behind a piece of solid metal fencing when he had seen the rotary cannon run out of the Mi-26's fuselage. What followed was truly devastating. Thousands of 7.62-millimetre rounds hosed the 20 metres of deck the Alpha team moved across. Men ceased to exist. Georgiy's ears hurt. His head felt like a giant was pounding on it. Yakov squeezed in beside him, taking up his own share of the precious cover.

Behind him, the operators who had moved up from the interior to engage the Chechens slammed the hatch shut. They sheltered as best they could in the shredded control room.

Suddenly, the hammering stopped. The heavy thumping beat of rotor blades increased. Georgiy heard a crunching noise, then the rotors started to move away. Chancing a look, he peered over the fencing. The Mi-17 was gone, and he could just make out the tail of the Mi-26 as it disappeared into the storm. The port cannon of the Mi-26 opened fire; its heavy weight of lead hammered high into the superstructure. As the helicopter disappeared into the stormy sky the bullets drifted off and away from the platform.

Wiping water and sweat from his face, Georgiy slowly stood up and surveyed the destruction around him.

Spent brass cases littered the ground, the blood and ruined bodies of his men mixed among the brass. The bodies of Chechens covered the stairs and fight deck.

Taking a depth breath, Georgiy stepped forward.

'Yakov, see to the men. I want this area secured. Make sure there are no terrorists left alive.'

Without a word Yakov yanked open the damaged hatch to the control room and started bellowing orders.

Stalking towards the flight deck, Georgiy was glad for his years of combat experience. The clogging stink of blood was thick in the air. He made his way carefully up the stairs to the flight deck, nudging each body with a boot. When no man responded, he ascended. Georgiy stood uncertainly on the slick metal deck. Looking around, he tried to take in everything that had happened. He narrowed his eyes against the sleet and wind.

Scanning across the thousands of brass cases that had fallen from the Mi-26's cannon he saw piles of discarded equipment. The Chechens had left everything behind they no longer needed.

Turning slowly, Georgiy analysed what the Chechens had been hoping to achieve. They had left the platform rigged with explosives. He had seen the charges as they cleared the facility. None had detonated. Chechens would never leave a job undone unless forced to. Something had gone badly wrong for the terrorists. Normally, they sacrificed themselves rather than retreat. Confused by the waste of an opportunity and unable to understand why he had not been vaporised, Georgiy walked to the centre of the flight deck. He looked carefully around himself. He felt suddenly tired.

Hearing the ring of boots behind him, he turned to see Yakov walking quickly towards him.

'The whole platform's rigged with explosives. We can't find how they were going to initiate it. Sophisticated layout. Wired into the platform's optic fibre network, but again there seems to be no way to set it off. There were five terrorists left behind. All dispatched. They appeared to be in place to detonate the charges manually. This is a strange set-up. I feel like I'm missing something,' said Yakov. The skin around his eyes showing above a face wrap was black with soot and gun smoke.

'I don't think the Chechens' mission went to plan. I wonder where they think they are going to go?' considered Georgiy, turning to look out into the storm.

Dasha

Dasha recovered the last of his crew from the *Boris Gakkel*. He gunned the engines and pulled away from the production ship's bulk. He planned to head away at least 20 nautical miles to launch the last two Termit missiles and then head for the mainland. The tone Sheikh Taimieov had used during their conversation did not support his plan. Dasha agonised over what he was supposed to do. He and his crew remained dedicated to the cause. As a crew they would follow any given or implied order. Dasha felt their great leader had implied he was to sacrifice himself, his crew, and the cutter to the cause.

'Dasha! Inbound contacts,' called Mikhail. He was manning the sensor suite in the compartment at the rear of the bridge.

'Sea or air?' asked Dasha as he steered the cutter out into open water.

'Surface contact. Large vessels.'

'Who are they?'

'I don't have that information. Look on the AIS,' prompted Mikhail.

Shaking his head, Dasha glanced down at the display. He frowned, not sure if he was reading it right.

'Who is it, Dasha? The return doesn't look like a warship,' called Mikhail.

'You're not going to believe this, Mikhail. By the AIS the contacts are the icebreaker *Yamal* and the gas carrier *Leonid Khabarov*, 10 miles out. I don't understand. Surely their company knows we have taken over the production ship?'

'Do we target them, Dasha? They can't know we are here.'

'The *Leonid Khabarov*'s not loaded. Mikhail, I have an idea. We'll find glory in my plan.'

CHAPTER SEVEN

The Leonid Khabarov

Peeling away to the east, the icebreaker *Yamal* followed a familiar track. The ice had thinned in the last few days since Brusilov had left the *Boris Gakkel.* He really had no need for the nuclear-powered icebreaker, but he appreciated the additional work it took away from his ship's hull. Picking up a pair of binoculars from the sill below the bridge windows, he focused on the production ship. It was just appearing over the murky horizon. Sea mist and haze stirred up by the storm to the north obscured his view. Regardless, he felt uneasy.

'Hail the *Boris Gakkel.* I still cannot see our tugs. They're not on radar or AIS,' ordered Brusilov of his first officer. As they approached the production ship the bridge team had noticed a complete lack of radio traffic. The Transas ECDIS showed no targets other than the *Boris Gakkel* in the area. Brusilov checked with the master of the *Yamal.* They had the same surface picture.

'*Boris Gakkel*, this is the *Leonid Khabarov*,' called the first officer. He looked at the ECDIS and saw no change in targets. Only the production ship and the *Yamal* were visible.

'*Leonid Khabarov*, this is the *Boris Gakkel*, good day,' came a stiff reply.

Brusilov turned to look at the first officer. He did not recognise the voice. It did not have the easy, practised, and bored flow of the normal operations staff on the ship.

'Ask where the tugs are,' instructed Brusilov.

The first officer nodded. 'This is the *Khabarov.* We do not show any AIS targets in the area other than yourself and the *Yamal.* We have received no calls from the tugs to discuss berthing. Can you advise?'

Silence.

'*Gakkel*, did you copy?' called the first officer.

Silence.

'*Boris Gakkel*, this is the *Leonid Khabarov*.'

'Go ahead,' said the same stiff voice.

'Did you copy my last?'

'Da. The other carrier broke away in a heavy squall which came through earlier. The tugs are attending to her and getting a tow underway. They may be outside your AIS range,' supplied the suddenly cool and oily voice.

'We have no contacts. Advise berthing arrangements.'

'Continue your approach. Hold station two cables from the ship and wait for the tugs to finish their work. They will attend to you.'

Quickly crossing the bridge floor, Brusilov snatched the radio out of the first officer's hand and pushed him angrily aside.

'We will not be able to hold station in these conditions. Who am I talking to?' he demanded.

'Continue your approach, *Leonid Khabarov*. The *Yamal* can assist you.'

'The *Yamal* is an icebreaker, you idiot. Not a tug. Who am I talking to?'

'Continue your approach,' came the now quiet voice.

'The man's an idiot,' said Brusilov. Shaking his head, he changed to the channel for Plyos Energy Control.

'Plyos Energy Control, this is the *Leonid Khabarov*.'

'*Leonid Khabarov*, good morning, this is Plyos Control, go ahead,' came Alexi's tired reply.

'We have an unusual situation here.'

'Go ahead.'

Brusilov looked at the receiver for a second and wondered what was going on. Everyone he had spoken to in the last few minutes seemed slightly off. After relaying his observations to the Plyos Energy controller, he paused.

'Get the glasses on the *Gakkel*. I want you to tell me if you see anything out of place. Call the *Yamal*. Get them to do the same,' Brusilov ordered.

Brusilov watched his first officer make the radio call and pick up the binoculars.

'*Leonid Khabarov*, this is Plyos Control. Chairman Umarov has advised that you are to close with the *Boris Gakkel*. Report your observations. We believe there has been an incident and need your on-scene assessment.'

'What's going on? Is there any danger to my ship?'

'Negative. Proceed as directed, Captain.'

'I will proceed how I see fit. Something is not right with all of this,' he replied.

'Captain!' yelled the first officer.

'I am talking to Plyos, wait,' reprimanded Brusilov.

'Captain!' yelled the first officer again.

Huffing, Brusilov dropped the handset. He decided he had had enough of talking to these people. He paced over to stand next to his first officer. The man was looking through binoculars at the *Boris Gakkel*.

'What is it?'

'There's another ship there. Near the bow,' supplied the first officer.

'One of the tugs?'

'No, sir. It's a warship. An Osa II missile cutter. I served on one for my military service.'

'Show me,' responded Brusilov. He took the binoculars from the first officer. He had not known the man served his mandatory service with the navy. It certainly did not show in his work ethic.

Brusilov lifted the binoculars to his eyes, adjusted them and focused on the bow of the production ship. Frowning, he watched a small dull grey cutter slowly clearing the bow and moving into open water.

Suddenly, the stern of the missile cutter dropped deeper into the water as it put on a burst of speed. Thick exhaust smoke poured from its side-mounted exhausts.

Dasha

'Fire, Mikhail!' yelled Dasha over the roar of the cutter's engines. He had ordered full power and the vessel surged ahead through the waves.

'Ten seconds,' replied Mikhail from his console where he intently watched the targeting computer.

Dasha held a course that would split the empty water between the gas carrier and icebreaker.

'Firing!' yelled Mikhail and pressed the button to launch the port rear Termit anti-ship missile.

An ear-splitting roar drowned the cutter as the missile ejected from its container and thrust into the air. Clearing the cutter's bow, the main rocket motor ignited and the missile streaked away on its short journey to the gas carrier.

It covered the distance in seconds, impacted midships and exploded. A brilliant flash of light erupted from between the third and fourth Moss tanks. The centre of the ship reared up into the air, driving the bow and stern deep into the ocean. As the middle of the ship fell back, its spine sheared. The *Leonid Khabarov* cleaved in two. The bow swung away from the rest of the ship, then fire suddenly rushed forwards, engulfing it.

Dasha could see the automatic fire suppression systems of the carrier trying to extinguish the flames. In seconds the bow section started to disappear beneath the surface. Driven by the still-functioning engines, the stern containing the bridge surged forwards. Water smashed through damaged hatches and bulkheads. The shattered ship twisted to port, then listed into an unrecoverable roll. The *Leonid Kharkov* slipped below the surface to follow the bow to the ocean floor.

A cheer sounded throughout the missile cutter.

'Engage the icebreaker,' ordered Dasha. He spun the cutter's wheel to head directly for it. He was purposely putting as much distance as he could between himself and the *Boris Gakkel.*

'Engaging,' called Mikhail. He triggered off the twin 30-millimetre guns mounted on the forward deck. The cutter rumbled as the cannon quickly fired 500 rounds at the icebreaker. Flashes, sparks, and debris erupted from the icebreaker's superstructure as the shells impacted along the length of the ship.

Slewing the cutter around, Dasha pointed its bow at the *Boris Gakkel.*

'Mikhail, fire the last missile. Allahu Akbar!' he cried and gritted his teeth. Dasha planted his feet and stood as straight as he could. Pride swelled in his chest.

'Firing,' Mikhail replied and launched the final Termit missile.

Streaking out of its container the missile gained almost no height as it hugged the ocean's surface.

Dasha jammed the throttles to the stops and reversed the wheel. Gathering speed quickly, the cutter streaked away from the scene.

The Termit's 454-kilogram warhead slammed into the side of the *Boris Gakkel* and detonated.

Through the rear windows of the bridge, Dasha saw the missile strike the ship. Saw it punch inside and explode. The ship jumped as if bitten. The gas contained in the *Boris Gakkel* ignited like a nuclear explosion.

Dasha watched the expanding fireball rushing across the water towards them and willed the little cutter to go faster. The shockwave engulfed the *Yamal* in seconds, smashing the sturdy icebreaker deep beneath the surface. The expanding explosion hunted down Dasha and his crew. A wall of fire pounded and hammered the missile cutter into submission as it passed by.

Starting to dissipate its energy the fireball died away.

The ocean steamed and boiled.

Alexi

PLYOS ENERGY CONTROL

Rubbing his tired, red eyes, Alexi was regretting how many cans of Red Bull he had consumed. His body felt raw and edgy after nearly 24 hours in the seat. The security guard and FSB man would not allow either of the controllers to leave the room. They had resorted to urinating in the single small rubbish bin. The putrid smell of ammonia clogged the close air of the room. Alexi felt like vomiting.

Intently watching the tracks for the *Boris Gakkel*, the *Yamal* and the *Leonid Khabarov*, Alexi saw them converge.

But when his screen refreshed the tracks suddenly vanished.

'They're gone!' shouted Alexi, too loudly in the enclosed space. Beside him their jailers jumped with fright.

'What?' asked Yerofey Novikoff, the night controller. Yerofey had joined Alexi a few hours earlier.

'The tracks for *Gakkel*, *Yamal* and Khabarov dropped off the screen,' spluttered Alexi. Quickly running a diagnostic tool, he found his equipment functional.

'Sensor issue?' queried Yerofey, staring at his own screens.

'Just checked. All good. What's happened?' asked Alexi, more to himself.

'Get the chairman on the telephone,' ordered the security guard.

Damien

'Can't you silence that fucking siren!' yelled Jason. He looked angrily across at Damien. They had been in the air less than 30 minutes.

The instrument panel of the Kamov was full of blinking lights he did not understand. A random siren had been sounding since take-off. It was getting on Jason's nerves. The helicopter was bouncing around everywhere. The unrelenting motion tossed Jason unmercifully about in his seat and harness. Beside him Damien's face was calm. His brow creased with concentration. Damien's arms and legs worked the controls in a continuous cycle as he battled the stormy air.

Damaged by small arms fire the Kamov was slowly dying as its fluids leaked out. Both engines were damaged. They drove the rotors in an uneven rhythm which shook the fuselage. The fact the Kamov was still flying at all was a testament to the strength the Russian manufacturers had built into the machine.

'I can barely see the instrument panel with all this jerking around, mate. I don't know what that siren is trying to tell me,' replied Damien coolly. The vibrations of the helicopter made his voice sound like he was in a Looney Tunes cartoon.

'It's fucking doing my head in,' Jason pointed out. He looked out through the side windows of the cockpit. Sleet hammered against the plexiglass. He could not wait to be back on the beach in Durban, soaking up rays and pretty women.

Jason suddenly felt weightless, stripped of his thoughts. He snapped his eyes forward. The helicopter looked like it was dropping away from him. His legs rose off the floor. He felt his body strain against the seat harness.

Damien tried to catch the helicopter as it dropped into a pocket of unstable wind shear, but lost the initial battle. He let the aircraft fall, trying to build up forward airspeed. He caught a glimpse of the ocean streaking up towards them, then pulled as much power as he dared. Another siren started to cry its shrill tone at them.

'Come on. Get your nose up,' said Damien quietly. Jason turned slowly to look at him. Dust and debris were rising around them.

Finding the pitch and angle he needed to save them, Damien bottomed out their dive and clawed the aircraft back into the sky. The crest of a wave slapped against the windscreen and the nose threatened to plunge into the sea. Keeping pressure on the controls, Damien climbed away from the ocean and back into the turbulent sky.

'A bit close that time,' he said. Damien's breathing had increased slightly.

'Fucking think so?' yelled Jason, firing back.

Chancing a quick glance at the Taipan 21 operator, Damien saw vomit staining the front of Jason's uniform. Its stench was starting to fill the cockpit. An amused smile played across Damien's lips.

'Weak stomach?' he asked.

'No, I, fucking, do, not. Can you just fly this piece of shit and get us safely on the ground,' replied Jason. He wiped the excess vomit off himself and shook it onto the cockpit floor.

'You'll hurt her feelings, Jason. Talk to her nicely and the old girl will get us to Rudolf Island.'

'How long?' groaned Jason.

'No idea. I'm just flying the course you set me as best I can. At a guess, three or so more hours of this and we should be there,' estimated Damien.

Shaking his head angrily, Jason was silently thankful that Damien appeared to be a skilled pilot. He doubted Botha or Slovo would have saved them from that dive or been able to keep them in the air even this long. For a moment he thought of his two teammates. Sniffing in annoyance with himself, he forced their images out of his mind. He focused on the sleet hitting the windscreen. The screech of the wipers was starting to get on his nerves as well.

Georgiy

'What the hell was that?' yelled Yakov into the wind. He stared out into the storm.

'Explosion of some kind. What's out that way?' asked Georgiy.

'A gas production ship,' said Yakov.

'Do you think the Chechens flew out there and blew the ship up?' replied Georgiy.

'Maybe, sir. I have no idea,' replied Yakov.

Seconds earlier the clouds had lit up and a rumbling explosion travelled across the ice and water, impacting the superstructure. The deck had wobbled and jumped slightly as the shockwave passed through. Not enough, though, for Yakov and Georgiy to lose their footing on the slick deck.

Georgiy's satellite telephone started ringing. Plucking it free of its pouch on his chest rig, he extended the antennae and answered the call. Yakov watched expectantly. He was amazed that there was satellite reception with all the cloud cover. Listening intently, Georgiy ended the call.

'Gather the men. New orders. We're leaving,' stated Georgiy. He turned and started walked through the chaos and destruction towards the control room.

'Where are we going?' asked Yakov.

'The navy is tracking the Chechens. Their course has them heading east of here and slightly south. The only land within flight distance is the Franz Josef Archipelago. We're to recover to the Mi-26 and take off in that direction. Headquarters will update us in the air.'

'What about that explosion? Did they say what it was?' asked Yakov.

'There was a second terrorist team. They took out the production facility along with five ships. No-one was sure there was another team, it was unconfirmed. I guess we know better now. Itt Stag has achieved one of its objectives. Just not the primary one.'

'At least we're still in the fight. Do we leave a party to secure the platform?'

'No. Plyos Energy and headquarters are sending teams to

clean up and get production back underway,' supplied Georgiy.

Without continuing the conversation, Yakov went about gathering the surviving Alpha operators and organising them to depart.

Ten minutes later the men were moving back across the ice towards the Mi-26. Georgiy could see its rotors turning as the pilots warmed the aircraft for flight. He had received another satellite call as he strode over the ice. Confirmation that the Chechens were heading for Rudolf Island. Well outside the range of the Alpha team helicopter's remaining fuel.

Welcoming the team inside, the crewmen guided the operators to their seats and helped them strap in. The flight engineer walked along handing out steaming cups of tea and soup. Nodding their thanks, the Alpha team gulped them down then moved to replenish their ammunition and check equipment. There was still another fight in the offing.

Georgiy took only tea and walked up to the flight deck.

'We'll need to refuel somewhere to make those islands, sir,' replied the pilot, Captain Konstantin Semyonov. His co-pilot, Lieutenant Aleksandr Kovalevsky, rechecked the fuel calculations and came up with the same result. The Mi-26 would run out of fuel and fall from the sky an hour before seeing land.

'Wait,' instructed Georgiy. He walked back out on to the ice.

He pulled out the satellite telephone. He relayed the issue to the FSB special operations room located in Murmansk, and received a solution almost immediately. Ending the call, he jogged back up to the flight deck.

'There's a solution. An FSB icebreaker called the *Aysberg* is enroute with engine problems to the army base at Trefoil. They have a helicopter deck. We'll land on it and take enough fuel to continue,' supplied Georgiy.

'Is the deck big enough to take this aircraft?' queried Semyonov.

'No,' replied Georgiy simply. They had no other options.

'Guess we'll work it out on arrival,' said Kovalevsky and returned to the last of the pre-flight checks.

Five minutes later the massive helicopter was lifting into the sky and heading east.

Nikolay

Walking quickly down to the ship's infirmary, Nikolay nodded reassurance to worried-looking crew on the way. The Arctic was unforgiving. Their captain's reputation and the state of the ship did not help.

Not pausing to knock, Nikolay pushed open the door to the infirmary and strode into the space. Summoning all his authority, he crossed to the bedside of the pilot they had rescued. The ship's medic and assistant quickly moved to one side to allow the captain space beside the bed.

'How is he?' Nikolay asked. He stared down at the stressed and unhappy face of the pilot. The man's face was red and rubbed raw.

'Lieutenant Litke will be fine, Captain. He has some frostbite to his fingers and mild hypothermia from immersion, but will recover,' supplied the medic. He would have been happier if a doctor had been on board for the mission. One had not been available on departure. It was up to him to keep the men safe.

'Good, good. Is he awake?'

'He is. Not very talkative yet.'

Nodding, Nikolay regarded the airman.

'Lieutenant Litke, I am Nikolay Voronoi. Captain of the FSB icebreaker *Aysberg*. Can you hear me?'

'Yes,' replied Litke softly. The stress of the ejection into the frigid Arctic water seemed to have addled his mind. Litke could not think straight. His back and knees hurt.

'You're safe now. Our passage is to the Trefoil army base in the Franz Josef Archipelago. You'll be hospitalised there. Then we will head to a shipyard for repairs. You will be my guest for a few hours.'

'Thank you. Where's Rudi?' asked Litke. His neck hurt from the ejection. Litke could not turn to look for his friend.

'I'm sorry. We only found you. The conditions were very poor. The search could not continue any longer,' replied Nikolay quietly. This was why the man looked so stressed. He was worried about his crewman.

'Rudi is my friend,' said Litke glumly and tears welled in his bloodshot eyes.

'Again, I am sorry. I'll come by and see you later. My men will take care of your needs,' ended Nikolay. He patted Litke on the shoulder gently, glanced at the medic and headed back to the bridge.

'Captain, the Admiral is on the telephone for you,' advised the first officer as Nikolay arrived on the bridge. Nodding, he took the offered receiver.

'Captain Voronoi,' he said formally. He had no love for the Admiral, and he was growing tired of rushing around the ocean. They needed to sail for a shipyard.

'You have a change of orders. Again,' advised Admiral Unkovsky flatly. He was growing more and more unhappy with how things were panning out for his career. This event was not turning into the glory-ladened bounty he thought it would.

'Where to now, Admiral?' replied Nikolay, barely disguising his annoyance.

'It's confirmed. The Chechens have destroyed the Plyos Energy ship *Boris Gakkel* and several others. An Alpha team has secured the Nevzgody gas platform. The Chechens have escaped, Nikolay. Intelligence has them heading to Rudolf Island. To the north of your current destination.'

'What do you want me to do, sir?' asked Nikolay. He looked absently out at the weather. He noted the storm starting to dissipate, but the waves were still large, and the icebreaker rolled uncomfortably.

'An Alpha team is on its way to you via helicopter. They need to refuel and will be with you in less than an hour.'

'I'll make all preparations to receive them. Is it just fuel they require?'

'Da. You're to make for Templitz Bay on Rudolf Island immediately. I do not have any other assets in that area. I want this to be an FSB operation from start to finish. After you arrive on station at Rudolf Island you will support the Alpha team when they have defeated the terrorists,' said Unkovsky.

'I understand, Admiral. Do you have anything more for me?' asked Nikolay.

'Nyet. Carry out your orders. I will be in contact,' replied Unkovsky.

'Very well, Admiral,' said Nikolay as he hung the receiver onto its hook.

Turning, he saw the first officer looking expectantly.

'Ready the helicopter deck for refuelling operations. We're going to have visitors. I have a new course for you to steer,' instructed Nikolay.

Chairman Khasan Umarov

PLYOS ENERGY BOARDROOM

Looking down at the screen of his mobile telephone, Umarov saw it was the security controller. Taking a deep breath, he answered the call.

'Da?' he asked gruffly.

'Sir, Alexi Chirikov, duty controller. We have lost all three tracks for the *Boris Gakkel*, *Yamal* and the *Leonid Kharkov*,' said Alexi, his voice tired and worn.

'I am aware, Alexi.'

'Ah. Sir, how did you find out? It just happened. Do you know what's going on?'

'It's a disaster,' replied Umarov. He ignored Alexi's questions. As the chairman of Plyos energy he had many informants to keep him in power. An FSB source advised him as soon as the Chechens had launched their attack on his ships. Umarov's brain struggled to comprehend the damage to his company's reputation. Umarov would need to work hard to keep Plyos Energy alive.

'What about the Nevzgody platform?' asked Alexi.

'Secured. The FSB have saved it for us, with some external help. But it's safe. There were no survivors among our crews unfortunately. Alexi, finish your shift and go home,' sighed Umarov and ended the call.

Damien

Unable to see land, Damien looked at the fuel gauges. Only about 30 minutes of fuel remained. A rueful look played over his face. The last three hours of flying had stretched his physical limits. The receding storm had allowed for additional visibility, but it was not helping them currently. A dark, murky twilight dawn was slowly replacing the night.

The Kamov continued to shudder and shake around them. Fifteen minutes earlier the hydraulic system had failed, forcing Damien to fly the wounded beast manually. His arms ached. His stomach was full of muscle spasms as he worked his core. Jason had been silent for the last 30 minutes.

'You okay?' asked Damien.

'Fine. Get us on the ground,' shot back Jason. He was in no mood for talk.

'How long until the pick-up is scheduled?'

'A bit less than twelve hours,' replied Jason looking at his antique Rolex Submariner watch. Passed down to him from his father, the watch was the only thing he had left to remind him of the man who had hardly been in his life. The South African Army of the 1960s and 1970s had seen to that.

'Where's this island of yours?' asked Damien, scanning his surrounds.

'In the north of the chain. There's a Russian Army base at Trefoil in the south. We are not going anywhere near there.' Jason ripped open a pouch and pulled out a dark-green Garmin Oregon 700 GPS unit. 'Let's see if this works.'

'You had a GPS the whole time?' queried Damien, shaking his head.

'They don't work so well up here. You know that, brother. This bit of kit takes wide area augmentation system feeds as well. Might be able to get a fix,' replied Jason.

He turned the unit on, waited for it to boot and watched as several satellite contacts appeared on the screen. The GPS unit worked to lock on to enough satellites to get a fix.

'Well, what do you know? I have our position. Rudolf Island is thirty minutes away. Turn a few degrees to the left and we'll pick it up,' advised Jason.

'Lucky. We only have around thirty minutes of fuel left.'

'Keep us in the air. I will make sure you get a seat on the aircraft out.'

'Aircraft?'

'The island has a short airstrip. Taipan are sending an Antonov twenty-four to pick us up.'

'I guess there are spare seats now,' said Damien.

'Certainly are. Botha and Slovo might not be too happy you're taking one up though. But then I'd say they are very dead by now. Their opinion doesn't matter anymore. And I told Don you would be on the aircraft.'

Drifting the Kamov the few degrees to the left indicated by Jason, Damien hoped the fuel gauges had some leeway built into them.

Talhig

Talhig brooded. He ran through the operational plan from start to present. He could not make out what had gone so wrong. Ambitious it had been, but the mission felt achievable. The loss of the laser initiator had been a blow, but that should not have meant the failure of the mission. Talhig knew the teams left behind on the platform had failed. They had felt no explosions as they flew away towards Rudolf Island. Talhig had the uncomfortable feeling Sheikh had hung them out to dry. There would be no pick-up or refuelling for them on the island.

Talhig had thought Sheikh a friend.

Maybe, thought Talhig, *it was only me who felt the friendship.*

'Sixty minutes,' called Asma as she sat down next to Talhig. She had been up in the cockpit talking to the pilot. They had another three hours of fuel and time up their sleeve. Having grown used to the controls of the large Mi-26, the pilot looked less nervous. But the Arctic wind blasting through the holes in the windscreen had nearly frozen him to the core.

A kilometre behind flew the Mi-17 with the other half of the surviving Chechen freedom fighters in its belly. It had two hours of fuel remaining. The pilot had found the going much harder in the medium-sized helicopter compared to the Mi-26. He was tiring rapidly, and with no co-pilot to help, was reaching the limits of his endurance. Like the flight through the storm to the Nevzgody platform it was a severe test of man and machine. The pilot was starting to think he would break before the helicopter did.

'Thank you,' replied Talhig, a touch of sadness ringing his voice.

'Are you okay?' asked Asma, placing a gentle hand on his forearm.

'This mission has been a failure. We have failed. We have not given glory to Chechnya,' said Talhig, a deep sigh falling from his mouth. He had no idea Dasha had been successful in carrying out his attack.

'No, but not all our missions have been glorious. We have suffered many failures and successes over the years. This is just one of them. It's time to move on. Home to Chechnya. Regroup and reorganise for the next operation,' encouraged Asma. Talhig and Asma may have gone their separate ways years earlier, but she still held warm feelings for him. Talhig was kind and professional. He was everything she desired in a man, but the war against the Bear came first. She looked at his puffy, scarred face and the slight skew of his broken nose. He was still a strong man. Asma would remain by his side.

'I think Sheikh has abandoned us.'

'How?'

'I feel it. The last telephone call was dismissive. I don't think he has organised anything to help us. I believe we're on our own.'

'Then we will ensure as many of our soldiers return home as possible,' said Asma, lifting herself proudly in the seat.

'What if Chechnya is no longer safe for us? All we will do is remind Sheikh of the failure. What could have been. We were unable to bring him victory. There will be a price to pay for that, Asma. You know how it will need paying.'

Asma considered him for a long moment.

'Then we break away. Form our own group. The fight against the Russians must continue,' she said.

'Aren't you tired of the killing yet? I am,' stressed Talhig, grabbing her hand and holding it tightly. 'I love my Chechnya, but I am weary of war.'

'When the Russian Bear leaves our land, I will be tired of the killing.'

'I thought that way once. This operation has changed my mind. My men are only ten strong now. Your girls are all gone.'

'They can be replaced,' urged Asma, returning the grip he had on her hand.

'Yes, with more lambs to the slaughter. Minced by the war machine. I am losing faith, Asma,' said Talhig quietly.

'The troops need a strong leader. You were that leader, Talhig. Cry your tears when we have regained our own soil. Right now, you're the one in charge. You must collect yourself and lead. I want you to lead, Talhig,' said Asma. The deep lines on his strong scarred face made Talhig look like he had aged 20 years.

'For you, Asma. If it comes to it, it will always be you and me,' replied Talhig. He stood up in the dim interior of the helicopter. The twilight of the Arctic was hard on his eyes. If it were not for his watch, he would have no idea if it were day or night.

'Sixty minutes and we will be among our friends and heading for home!' he shouted to the five soldiers who shared the massive cargo area with him. 'Remember Grozny!'

Grozny! came the collective shout from the tired freedom fighters. Talhig felt a surge of pride and love for his people. He inwardly hoped it was going to be enough to get them home to Chechnya and whatever fate awaited them.

Damien

'We're on fumes,' announced Damien. He was looking at the two red flashing lights next to the fuel gauges. The Kamov still felt like it had life left in it. Damien knew that there were no facts backing up the hope.

'Do you see the airstrip?' called Jason pointing across the cockpit at the straight dark line which streaked for a short distance through the white expanse.

'Got it.'

'Templitz Bay is where we need to hole up until the relief arrives. There are old huts there.'

'I see it. Is there anyone on the island?' asked Damien.

'Deserted between visits.'

'Someone left the lights on then,' said Damien. He stabbed his left index finger towards the dark shapes of the small buildings set back from the water of the bay. Lights were shining dimly through the haze.

'Have to sort that when we get there, brother. I'm not aware of anyone. It's too early for Taipan to be here. We have a few hundred metres to cover from the airstrip to the buildings. The jog will keep us warm,' joked Jason.

Damien nodded and concentrated on guiding the dying Kamov onto a short final for landing. He studied the island as they drew closer. Jagged and rugged terrain dominated the island. Snow and ice completely obscured the ground. As Templitz Bay drew closer, Damien could see the rocky shoreline. It sloped gently up to the foothills of a low mountain range. The island looked cold, unforgiving, and hostile.

'On final,' called Damien, though he was not sure that Jason would understand.

Easing the Kamov down towards the airstrip, Damien paused for a second. He was sure he felt the controls grow suddenly loose and sluggish. Frowning, he continued the descent.

A loud bang sounded from above them. The Kamov lost power as the right engine succumbed to its wounds and disintegrated.

'Hang on!' shouted Damien. He heard a sharp intake of air from Jason followed by a short curse.

The helicopter dropped rapidly towards the ground, nothing left to give.

Damien hauled back on the collective and wound on the throttle as far as it would go, the left engine rewarding him by flaming out and spooling down. Its fuel exhausted. Dumping the collective to flatten the blades, Damien tried to autorotate without the speed or height he needed.

They crashed heavily onto the southern end of the airstrip, the Kamov bouncing into the air, tipping over and slamming into the ground on its left side. Splintering, the twin main rotors disintegrated and fired out deadly shards of carbon fibre in all directions.

Damien and Jason tossed around violently in their seats, hanging on as the Kamov's rotors flailed against the ground, beating themselves to death. A grinding, shearing noise filled the cabin as the rotor mast broke away and spun across the airstrip. The helicopter stopped moving and came to rest in a cloud of fine grey dust and snow.

Breathing in slowly, Damien looked down at Jason, wedged against the left door. The South African scowled back up at him.

'Not the best landing, I admit, but we can walk away from it. Guess that's something,' said Damien lightly. He threw open the right door, unbuckled his harness and started climbing out. Jason did not answer him.

Damien stood next to the wrecked Kamov, gave it a pat and thanked the tough machine for getting them this far. Straightening his gear, he found he had four full magazines left for the AK-74M which he had dragged out of the cockpit. His USP was still in a pouch on the front of his chest rig. There were two magazines left for it.

Jason appeared through the cockpit door, climbed out and

stood next to Damien. His look of contempt at Damien's landing skills had not changed. Both men shivered in the biting wind which swept over the terrain. There were no trees or structures other than the ones lining Templitz Bay a short distance away. The dull light of a new day drifted over the mountains.

'Shall we?' asked Damien.

Shaking his head, Jason stepped off and led the way. Damien noted the Taipan operator had his primary weapon up and ready to engage. Jason was not as sure of his situation as he wanted to appear.

Georgiy

Standing between the two pilots, Georgiy watched as they lined up with the stern of the *Aysberg*. The icebreaker had turned into the wind to help the helicopter land safely. As they approached, Georgiy calculated the size of their helicopter versus the landing deck. One was smaller than the other. The Mi-26 would not fit.

'Going to be tight,' breathed Semyonov absently as he carefully and lightly adjusted the controls. He focused all his remaining attention on the sailor standing on the rolling flight deck. The sailor was waving a pair of lit red torches, trying to guide the massive helicopter onto the small space.

'*Aysberg*, this is Taymyr Three Nine, FSB helicopter on your stern. I can see the guide, call your speed,' requested Semyonov.

'Taymyr Three Nine, our speed is six knots. You're cleared to approach and land. The deck is ready for you,' advised Nikolay. He watched the massive helicopter slowly losing height and feeling its way forwards. There was no margin for error. He hoped the pilots had enough experience and skill to make the landing.

'Six knots, roger. Commencing approach. We will land well forward on the deck. Advise us if the rotors are too close to any of the superstructure,' called Semyonov. He could see that the flight deck on the icebreaker cut like a well into the superstructure of the ship. Which meant it should be free of any hazards.

Georgiy gripped the back of the flight crew's seats and stood his ground. He wanted to watch the landing and be on his feet if it went wrong. Though he had already noted he had no hope of escaping from inside the beast if anything did go wrong. The last thing he would experience would be frigid water clutching at his heart.

Drifting to the left, Semyonov crabbed the Mi-26 sideways slightly to line up with the guide who was trying to keep his feet on the pitching deck. Easing down and forward Semyonov was working the controls continuously as he stayed one step ahead of the moving ship, the air, and the want of the massive helicopter to drop out of the sky.

Arriving a few metres above the stern, the Mi-26 glided towards its landing spot as the deck rolled beneath it.

'I'll be dropping us the last metre. Going to be a bit rough and bouncy until she settles,' called Semyonov. Beside him, Kovalevsky was calling out heights and engine temperatures. They had 45 minutes of fuel remaining.

As he drifted the aircraft above the deck, Semyonov concentrated on the edge of the massive rotor disk which stretched out ahead of them.

'Baranova? How are we looking?' called Kovalevsky to the loadmaster, who stretched as far as he could from the port hand door in the forward fuselage.

'Main gear is over the deck. Tail is out over the stern. No obstructions. You're clear to land, sir,' advised Warrant Officer Joseph Baranova. Even with his heavy flight gear and no skin exposed to the Arctic temperatures, he felt deeply cold as he hung out of the fuselage.

'Thank you. Here we go.'

Semyonov chopped the collective and the massive helicopter dropped to the deck. Impacting off-angle, the Mi-26 tipped to the right and bounced into the air. Semyonov reduced the power to the rotors as he tried to arrest the bouncing roll. He dropped the nose onto the deck to stabilise the pitching motion. He forced the collective down to its stops to flatten the rotors.

Dropping back onto the slick deck, the helicopter bounced lightly from side to side before settling. The machine matched the motion of the ship. Rolling the throttle closed, Semyonov shook his head happily at the successful landing.

'Start shutting down,' he called to Kovalevsky.

'APU on. Starting the checklist.'

'Baranova, get out there and secure us to the deck. Prepare for refuelling,' advised Semyonov over the intercom. He could see the ship's crew moving quickly over the deck towards his parched helicopter with hoses.

'Well done. I'm going to see the captain,' said Georgiy and thankfully climbed down into the fuselage. Passing Yakov, he called him to his feet and told him where they were going. The surviving operators would stay on board, keeping as warm as they could. The flight engineer was already preparing more tea to hand out.

'Take me to the captain,' instructed Georgiy to the first sailor he encountered. The man nodded and spoke into a handheld radio. Another sailor hurried over to collect them.

He led the way off the flight deck and into the accommodation spaces, along stairs and passageways to the bridge. Georgiy's head was still trying to map the route when they suddenly arrived at the door. The brightly lit interior of the ship was dazzling after the dim gloom of the helicopter.

Stepping onto the bridge, the sailor indicated the captain, who stood stiffly as he intently watched the refuelling operations.

'Captain,' called Georgiy as he walked up to the man.

'Da?' challenged Nikolay, turning towards the unfamiliar voice on his bridge.

'I am Major Georgiy Urvantsev. This is Lieutenant Yakov Davydov, my second. We are FSB. I'm in command of the Alpha team and the current operation.'

'I am Captain Nikolay Voronoi, Master of the *Aysberg*. Welcome, welcome. Call me Nikolay,' he replied. He turned to his third officer. 'Tea.' The harassed man nodded quickly and rushed from the bridge. Nikolay took in the look of the two operators standing proudly in front of him. Grime and blood covered their white combat smocks and uniforms.

'Thank you for the fuel. Your help is much appreciated. Do you have any further information for me?'

'Did you know that the Chechens have been successful in sinking five of Plyos Energy's ships to the south of the Nevzgody platform?'

'Da. We were on the Nevzgody platform and saw the explosion.'

'From the Nevzgody platform?' asked Nikolay, amazed they had seen the explosion from that distance.

'It was enormous. I guess the gas in the production ship

ignited. Were you briefed on the rest of my mission?'

'Nyet. Just to be in this position. You would land and I would give you fuel. Then I am to steam for Templitz Bay at Rudolf Island. That is all.'

'The Chechens who escaped the platform are flying to Rudolf Island. They are trying to make their escape. Intelligence intercepted a satellite call from the leader of the Itt Stag group rerouting their rescue ship to that island.'

'Not a friendly place. I was, for a short time, stationed at the army base in the south of those islands. It was an unpleasant time,' said Nikolay reminiscing.

'Well, there will be no rescue for them. Another team captured the freighter five hours steam south of here. The crew needed some encouragement to give up their part of the plan. There's no hope for the Chechens. I don't think they know. My team's tasked to eliminate the last of them.'

'Prisoners?' asked Nikolay.

'No.'

'So it is, then. I will be in position in Templitz Bay in case you need support. Refuelling will take another fifteen minutes. Then you can be on your way. Can I do anything more for you?' asked Nikolay. The third officer arrived with hot sweet tea and passed the mugs around. Nikolay's was handed to him in a fine China cup with a wide mouth.

'Nyet. Thank you again. I'll head back to my men. As soon as we have enough fuel we'll depart,' said Georgiy, drawing deeply on the mug of tea and scalding the roof of his mouth.

'My pleasure,' replied Nikolay and turned to watch the activity on the flight deck.

Nodding, Georgiy and Yakov drank down their tea and handed the mugs to the third officer, expressing their thanks. They linked up with the same sailor, who guided the pair back to the flight deck.

'Not the life for me,' said Yakov as they walked up the helicopter's rear ramp.

'Only for a specific type of person. I like my boots on the ground as often as possible,' replied Georgiy.

Damien

Damien and Jason jogged along the heavy gravel track which led from the airstrip to the huts they could see over the featureless terrain of the island. Moving quickly, they chewed up the distance. Their breath plumed out into the air behind them. Neither showed any sign of fatigue from the hours of combat. Both had their rifles tucked tight to their chests. Damien moved lightly over the rocks, like he was barely touching the ground. Beside him Jason ran heavily, crunching the rocks with his boots.

They neared the three buildings which were set back from the quiet waters of Templitz Bay. The debris of past polar expeditions began to stick up from the snow which cloaked everything. Damien recognised a large rusting boiler from the steam era. The broken and rotting remains of long boats piled up near the wall of the largest building. It looked older than the other two.

'Let's check out the one with the lights on. There must be someone here. The last report I received, the island appeared deserted,' said Jason as he pointed to the building he wanted to investigate.

The shoreline around the bay was free of snow where the tide moved in and out. Light grey rocks littered the bay, flat and weathered by the extreme conditions. In the distance, small icebergs floated by. The bay was free of ice, along with its approaches. Warmer water welled up from the shallow floor of the ocean, which made the island a perfect staging post for Arctic expeditions.

'Yep,' replied Damien and slowed to a walk. Lifting his rifle to his shoulder, he scanned the terrain looking for anything out of place. Nothing piqued Damien's senses. He was not sure who was here, but he did not get the feeling that they would be a threat.

'Stop dragging your boots,' stated Jason, shaking his head. He felt the urge to needle Damien. He had not failed to notice how effortless Damien moved over the gravel.

'Just taking in the scene.'

'Look at the place. It's a rubbish dump sitting in ice and snow. Horrible.'

'It's got a charm to it,' replied Damien as they moved towards the building.

As they drew closer, Damien was sure he could hear laughing and the sound of soft music playing.

Interesting, he thought.

Signalling a halt, Jason quickly circled the small building. Moisture clouded the windows. The harsh conditions had bleached the wooden walls a dull grey.

'No back door. There's a generator running in a shed against the far wall,' whispered Jason as he returned to Damien's side.

'Through the front door, then. Don't kill anyone,' instructed Damien, a deeply serious tone to his voice.

'I won't if there isn't the need to,' replied Jason. He stepped away and over to the door. He signalled for Damien to enter. Nodding, Damien positioned himself at the door and felt for the handle. Finding it unlocked he twisted it slowly until the lock's tongue slid out of the jam.

Damien glanced at Jason and received a nodded okay.

Throwing open the door, Damien charged into the room with Jason behind him. Damien pulled up short when he saw the scene before him. He smiled.

The room was warm and lit by yellowed electric lights, revealing a group of five people. Most held wine glasses paused in front of their mouths at the intrusion. They looked at Damien and Jason, open-mouthed and surprised. The music issuing from a small stereo in the middle of the table was from a different era. Damien was sure the female artist was singing in French. A large plate of food dominated the table the group sat around. A mix of empty and partially full red wine bottles scattered over its surface.

No-one moved.

'Morning. A bit early for a drink, isn't it?' said Damien in English.

The group continued to stare at them.

'Bonjour,' repeated Damien in French, hedging his bets.

A man stood up from the far head of the table, moved around the silent group and walked over to Damien.

'I speak English. We're having breakfast and celebrating. Who are you?' he asked with a thick French accent.

'Who are you?' countered Jason, making sure the man could see his rifle.

'I am Paul Gaugin. I'm the leader of this expedition. Who, gentlemen, are you?' he asked. Paul had taken in the blood-stained combat uniforms worn by the intruders. Both had hard professional eyes. If he had to guess, experienced and skilled killers, but not Russian.

'I'm Damien Hunter, and this is Jason. We just need a place to rest while we wait for our ride. We don't want any trouble,' responded Damien. He dropped his rifle to his side and extended his right hand. Suspiciously, Paul extended his and shook Damien's.

'Guess we're all friends now, Paul. Who are your people and what expedition are you on? We have some time to talk,' said Damien, injecting a calm, friendly tone into his voice.

'You will all stay in here until we leave. No exceptions,' stated Jason before Paul could speak. Jason pushed forwards and walked up to the table. 'We're in charge. You do as we say,' he continued in a slow voice as if he were speaking to children. He brandished his rifle to enforce his point. Plucking a glass of wine from the fingers of the woman seated closest to the door, he lifted it to his lips and drained it. 'Not bad,' he stated. He picked up a chunk of soft yellow cheese, stuffed it in his mouth and nodded his thanks.

Damien looked at Paul and silently expressed his apologies.

'Damien, yes?' confirmed Paul. He could tell who he should be talking to. By the other man's accent, he was South African. Paul had always found them an overly harsh people in his dealings. Jason was reinforcing that point.

'Correct.'

'The two women closest to you are Carla Deneuve and Marion Cotillard. The men across from them are Gabriel Rodin and Maurice Lavigne. The quiet one at the back on the couch is Grace Heroux, my lead excavator,' introduced Paul.

Damien looked around the table and settled his gaze on Grace. She held his eyes without a hint of fear. Grace tipped her half-full wine glass at him and nodded. Damien smiled warmly back at her. Seeing his reaction, she turned her head away and looked at the fire burning in a heath against the far wall.

'Excavator?' queried Damien.

'We're on an archaeological mission to uncover the secrets of past polar expeditions which have used this bay. This is our first week here. There have been many discoveries already. We are celebrating a successful week. It's harsh, but a history-rich place,' explained Paul. Damien detected a swell of excitement and pleasure in the man's voice. This was something he obviously loved.

'Archaeologists?' said Jason, turning around and shaking his head. 'Past is past, mate. Nothing to learn from it and nothing of interest hides in the dirt. Fucking archaeologists. Another fucking time-wasting pursuit.' Jason plucked a red apple from the table and tossed it to Damien.

Talhig

Swooping low over Rudolf Island the Mi-26 and Mi-17 carrying the freedom fighters executed short finals and lined up to land. Talhig looked out of the window beside him and stared at the wrecked Kamov helicopter at the southern end of the airstrip. It whipped out of view as the pilot pedal turned the massive helicopter to the right and dropped to the ground. The Mi-26 bounced a few times, then came to a stop. The pilot started shutting the machine down. As the rear ramp started lowering, the Mi-17 came into view, landing just ahead of the wrecked Kamov.

Snow and grit fountained into the air and thrashed the inside of the helicopter. Shielding his eyes, Talhig slipped out of his seat belt, picked up his rifle and walked down the ramp. Asma followed on his heels. Skirting the Mi-17 as it shut down, the pair walked over to the wrecked Kamov. Talhig stopped beside it, silently regarding the scene.

Slipping a satellite telephone from his coat pocket, Talhig waited for a lock and dialled Sheikh's number. Waiting, he gazed around the island and grimaced. Rudolf Island was an inhospitable and hard place. After 15 rings, he disconnected the call.

'No-one is here, Talhig,' pointed out Asma.

'Someone is. I recognise this helicopter. Don't you?' he asked. Talhig could see Plyos Energy written along the side of the machine.

The Russian with his laser initiator is here somewhere, he thought.

'I meant the refuelling crew. Where are they?'

'Maybe delayed. We will be taking on fuel here and then flying out to the ship. I will try Sheikh again.' He dialled the number and waited. Sheikh did not answer and Talhig again cancelled the call.

'Have we been abandoned?' asked Asma.

'I think we have been, Asma. I think we have,' replied Talhig unhappily.

Abruptly, the telephone started ringing.

'Da?' answered Talhig.

'Talhig! Where are you?' asked Sheikh, his voice full of concern.

'Rudolf Island, where you told us to go. There is no-one here, Sheikh,' said Talhig quietly. He stared at the snow and ice in front of him. He pictured Sheikh in his warm safe headquarters sipping on an ever-present cup of coffee.

'The Russians captured the ship I sent to get you, Talhig. The Russians are all over us now. We can't operate outside our own borders. The Bear has clamped down quicker than I thought possible. We have more than one spy among us, I suspect. I will root them out and kill them all,' preached Sheikh, his voice high with stress and anger.

'Could our new Mafia friends have sold us out?' asked Talhig, considering the options.

'They would never betray the trust.'

'We only paid them in money, Sheikh. That was all the trust they had in us. We paid our bill.'

'Enough, Talhig. I don't want to hear that kind of talk. What news do you have for me?'

'Have you abandoned us, Sheikh?' asked Talhig pointedly. Asma snapped her head up to look at him. Such a boldly open question was not something she had heard from Talhig before. Worry creased her brow.

'Talhig, my old friend, how could you think such a thing of me? I have tried to rescue you and my loyal freedom fighters. But at every turn the Russians are an obstacle,' stressed Sheikh. He could hear dejection in Talhig's voice. The man was folding under the pressure just as he had feared. It was time to truly turn off the tap and abandon the mission. Talhig and his assault force were now on their own, Sheikh decided.

'How will you help us, then?' asked Talhig.

'I have no resources left to assist you. Take on as much fuel as you can and construct a plan. You, Talhig, will need to find glory in the last embers of the mission. The glory of Chechnya requires your sacrifice.'

'Yes, I remember Chechnya, Sheikh. I remember my country very well and the wars which have raged and destroyed her beauty. I love my country,' replied Talhig.

'Find a way to have your name in the history books. I cannot help you anymore.'

'What of the second phase of the mission? Were our brothers assaulting the production ship successful?'

'They were, but wasted. The Russians have already reported in the media that we are terrorists. Their propaganda machine is deflecting the anger of the international community towards us. They have named me as the orchestrator. A larger price is now on my head. Our heads. The Russian Bear will survive this. We needed the gas platform destroyed. You failed the cause, Talhig. You have failed me and our country,' said Sheikh accusingly, his voice lacking any emotion.

'We landed on the wrong platform, remember? Doomed from the start.'

'Find a way to redeem yourself, Talhig. Do not return to Chechnya. There're no friends here for you,' said Sheikh coolly as he ended the call.

Talhig slowly lowered the telephone and dropped it into his pocket.

'Well?' asked Asma.

'We're abandoned. There's no-one coming,' said Talhig, looking at the ground. His heart filled with grief.

'What did he say?' pushed Asma. She could not believe their commander would have left them to die.

'Our glorious commander reports the second team has been successful in their mission to destroy the gas production ship. Their mission kept from all but me and Sheikh. The Russians have countered our moves and turned the blame on to Chechnya and Itt Stag. We're now called terrorists.'

'What do we do?'

'Sheikh has ordered me to find a way to redeem our failure. He blames me.'

'But you're not to blame for this, Talhig. What are your orders?' questioned Asma squaring her shoulders. She was determined to support him.

Talhig stared at the wrecked Kamov. The aircraft had landed hard. The belly was crushed and the machine was lying on its left side. The violence of the crash was evident from the damage to the fuselage.

'This was the helicopter which escaped from the platform. This carried the Russian who stole the initiator and ruined the mission. He's responsible for all of this!' spat Talhig. Anger rose in his throat. His exposed face grew red.

'Then we kill him. There's nowhere to hide on this island.

The three buildings we flew over are the only places to go. I will strip the lungs from his body for you and cut off his balls for my girls,' encouraged Asma. She had seen the fire reignite in Talhig's eyes and sought to fan it.

'Asma, we will take back the initiator,' said Talhig, a fanatical gleam creeping into his eyes.

'Just give the order and I will go hunting.'

'I want to be the one to retrieve it from his dead body. Then we will return to the Nevzgody platform. Our men will fight their way in. We will detonate the charges. I will turn this into a victory for Chechnya.'

'It'll mean our deaths,' said Asma excitedly, the thrill of more combat in her heart.

'In war, sacrifice happens every second of every battle. Combat is sacrifice. Even if you live. I'll redeem myself. My death will be for the glory of Chechnya. Our home.'

'I will see that you are redeemed, Talhig.'

'Set the two pilots to guard the helicopters and commence refuelling. You're with me. The rest are to fan out and flank the buildings. The Russian must be inside one of them. We start with the one showing light,' ordered Talhig quickly.

Asma jogged over to the gathered soldiers and began allocating tasks.

Talhig turned to look at the buildings, focusing on the one he could see faint murky light shining from. He intended to avenge his damaged pride today.

Damien

'We have company,' said Damien as he ducked back inside the building. Hearing the heavy beat of approaching helicopters, he'd slipped outside to watch the Mi-26 and Mi-17 come into land near the crashed Kamov. Using a pair of compact Levenhuk Atom binoculars he had found in the chest rig he scanned the troops deplaning. He watched a pair inspecting the wreck. They did not look like a Taipan pick-up team.

He took out a hard plastic water bottle, unscrewed the cap and took a cautious sip. Satisfied, he drained the container. His first drink in hours.

'Our pick-up?' asked Jason.

'Unless they look Russian and are flying helicopters?

'The pick-up aircraft is a fixed wing. They would be Russian, though,' supplied Jason.

'I don't think it's our lift, mate,' said Damien.

'What's going on?' asked Paul, walking up to Jason.

'I think the bullet is about to hit the bone,' stated Damien, looking around the room.

Without a word, Jason planted his right hand firmly on Paul's chest and pushed him roughly to the floor. Jason held up a silencing finger to his lips and stared hard at him.

'No need for that, Jason. Paul, the men we're waiting for have not shown up. But others have. I don't know who they are or why they're here. What day is your pick-up and how?' requested Damien politely.

'Next week, Wednesday. By aeroplane,' said Paul as he picked himself up off the floor. Straightening his shirt, he avoided looking at Jason. Paul had decided the man was dangerous, maybe unhinged. The one calling himself Damien seemed the most adjusted and professional of the two. Paul was going to try to align himself to the sanest of their captors.

'Then we can safely say those soldiers are not here for either of us. Could have followed us here from the platform. Paul, get your people into some cover. It's going to get messy. Jason, get ready for a fight,' said Damien.

The archaeologists stared around uncertainly.

'I'm always ready,' quipped Jason. He moved over to a window facing the airstrip and cleaned away a small circle of fogging and peered out. 'They've moved into an assault line. Two teams, five men apiece. They're flanking the building. A team of two are coming straight down the road. They'll be here in less than a minute. Snap your fingers, snap your neck, Chainsaw. Remember?' said Jason as a hard gleam shifted into his eyes.

Damien regarded Jason coolly for a moment. 'I remember, mate. Shall we?'

Talhig

Seeing movement in a window of the building with the lights showing, Talhig lifted his rifle and let a long, frustrated burst of automatic fire ripple forward. Bullets struck the soft walls. The onslaught tore chunks out of the wood and smashed the window.

Talhig heard an approaching helicopter and turned to look out to the south. In the near distance, he could see the bulk of a Mi-26 rapidly closing on the island. It could only be from the army base at Trefoil. Talhig felt a deep surge of anger rolling up his throat.

Seeing the opening of combat, the rest of his assault team took shots at the building. A soldier on the left flank dropped into the snow, sighted an RPD 7.62-millimetre light machine gun, and opened fire. Bullets peppered and ripped through the buildings. Windows smashed. The lights went out.

CHAPTER EIGHT

Georgiy

Georgiy could see the scene unfolding as they approached the short airstrip. From where he stood between the pilots, the helicopters on the airstrip were easily visible as were the men fanned out on the ground and attacking one of the buildings.

'Who are they shooting at?' queried Semyonov.

'I have no idea,' replied Georgiy. Again, he felt like he was missing some vital parts of the puzzle. 'Land from the east. Give us some distance from the troops on the ground. They must be the Chechens.'

'Roger. Can you see the two men near the helicopters? They just dropped what look like refuelling hoses. They're pointing weapons at us!' yelled Kovalevsky, lowering a set of binoculars as he spoke.

'I'll sort that out,' replied Georgiy and walked out of the cockpit. 'Private Tereshkova, I have a job for you!' he shouted back along the fuselage.

Tereshkova, the team sniper, unbuckled himself and jumped eagerly to his feet.

'Do you see the two men beside the Chechen helicopters?' Georgiy asked as he pulled open the right-hand side door. A blast of frigid air rushed into the interior of the helicopter. The rest of the operators cringed away from it. The ride from the platform had been cold and miserable enough without Georgiy opening doors in the fuselage.

'I see them,' responded Tereshkova.

'Take them out,' ordered Georgiy.

Without a word, Tereshkova turned and walked quickly back to his seat. Pulling his beloved Izhmash SV-98D sniper rifle from its protective case, he checked to ensure it held a full magazine. He walked back to the open doorway.

'Tell the pilot to hold here, please,' asked Tereshkova politely. Georgiy relayed his request.

Shouldering the rifle, Tereshkova judged the windage and declination and adjusted the scope. Taking a breath, he released half of it and drifted the crosshairs onto the first man. He squeezed the trigger. The noise of the massive rotors above them drowned out the report of the rifle. The Chechen dropped to the ground. Adjusting his aim slightly to pick up the second soldier, Tereshkova paused. He had expected the man to run for cover, but he held his ground. Tereshkova saw flame erupt from the end of the Chechen's rifle as he opened fire at the approaching helicopter. Breathing in again, Tereshkova fired. The second Chechen folded onto himself and slumped dead onto the frozen ground.

'Good job,' praised Georgiy. He walked back to the flight deck to supervise the landing. Nodding, Tereshkova walked back to his seat and slid his precious rifle back into its case, smiling to himself. He was pleased with his shooting.

Semyonov guided the Mi-26 into a slot forward of the Chechen aircraft. As soon as the wheels touched the ground the rear ramp dropped down. The Alpha team rushed out and secured the airstrip. The sound of automatic gunfire roared across the air.

Frowning, Georgiy boldly walked into the open and surveyed the one-sided battle going on less than 500 metres away. Establishing that none of the shooting was coming in their direction, Georgiy saw he had a window of time to launch a short sharp offensive.

'Yakov,' called Georgiy, looking around for his second. He spotted him inspecting the Kamov.

'Sir?'

'Two teams. Match the Chechens' flanks and work your way

in. I will take Laz and go directly down the road. No prisoners. Those are our orders.'

'I remember,' replied Yakov. He moved off to split the team into two assault teams.

'Laz?' called Georgiy.

'At your elbow, sir,' replied Lazarov.

'As always,' said Georgiy, chuckling. Lazarov had made a habit of appearing close by him in the field. The man was the perfect radio operator to have in combat. Georgiy valued Lazarov's professional fearlessness and his skills. Lazarov had stood many times by his side when bullets had been kicking up around them and explosions ruffled their hair. The man was truly unshakeable.

'Do you want me to shoot them all?' asked Tereshkova, interrupting Georgiy as he walked over. He was eager to be in the fight.

'Not this time. We will join in combat with them. The men need to stretch their legs. Provide us with support from here,' said Georgiy.

Silent and unhappily, Tereshkova began to walk away.

'Tereshkova, I'm sorry. I was too harsh. Set up an observation position and shoot as many as you like. Leave enough for the rest of the men, though. They will be unhappy if you do not,' advised Georgiy.

With a light step, Tereshkova waved his acknowledgement

behind his head and scaled the short fuel tower on the eastern side of the airstrip. Quickly settling himself, Tereshkova sighted on a Chechen at the rear of the force who was hammering away at the building with an RPD. Tereshkova fired and drove the man into the rocks.

'An Orion RPV is overhead, sir,' advised Lazarov. He had flicked away the cover of his Sagittarius tablet. Full motion video was streaming down from the RPV. Lazarov twisted the tablet so Georgiy could see it.

'Will it link us to headquarters?' asked Georgiy.

'The Orion is relay capable. I'll see what I can do. What do you want to send?'

'Advise them we have cornered the Chechens and are moving in to finish it,' said Georgiy flatly.

Without acknowledging, Lazarov opened the channel to connect to the FSB operations room in Murmansk. Finding the connection successful he typed Georgiy's instructions and pressed send. A reply came back seconds later.

'Headquarters acknowledge. You're authorised to proceed. The army is sending reinforcements from their base at Trefoil. ETA is one hour,' relayed Lazarov.

'It'll be all over by then. Let's go. The boys can't have all the fun, Laz,' ordered Georgiy. He jogged to the far side of the airstrip. Lifting his AK-15 to his shoulder, he advanced down the road. The heavy gravel of the track was slick and wet beneath his boots. Georgiy was glad they had left the storm out to sea. All they had to contend with now was the haze coming off the ocean.

Lazarov followed him carrying his 5.45-millimetre Nikonov AN-94 at port arms in front of him. Lazarov found that the delayed recoil feature of the assault rifle suited his shooting style. He just hoped he would get to do some shooting this time.

Damien

The inside of the building was a whirl of wood splinters, bullets, and ages-old dust. Ripping the insulation from the wall panels, the fusillade of bullets fired by the Chechens was slowly destroying the 80-year-old building. Broken wine glasses and bottles littered the table and floor. Red wine flowed across the surfaces and mixed with the blood flooding out from four of the French archaeologists. The bodies of Paul, Maurice, Carla, and Marion lay scattered and broken around the room. None of them had heeded Damien's command to get down on the floor. They had paid the ultimate price.

Damien looked around the room, shielding his eyes from the debris. He saw Grace slowly crawling over to him. Her brunette hair had come adrift from its ponytail, her pretty face splattered with what could have been either blood or wine. Grace's determined and unphased look attracted Damien's attention. She maintained a deep calm. The opposite of her comrade Gabriel Rodin, who was crying out in terror and rolling around the floor in panic. Jason was sliding through the debris littering the floor towards Gabriel. Damien figured he might be going to use the incoming fire as an opportunity to silence the strange thin scream coming from the Frenchman.

Jason reached Gabriel and delivered a half power punch to the side of the man's jaw. Stunned for a moment, he stared with wide eyes at Jason. Damien was not sure what was happening inside Gabriel's mind, but it could not be clear or coherent thought.

A light thump sounded against the wall beside Damien.

'Grenade!' he yelled and rolled away towards Grace. She froze and stared at him, uncertain of what to do. Colliding with her, Damien shielded her body as the grenade detonated on the other side of the wall. The building foundations shook with the small explosion.

'Little pricks are closing in, Chainsaw. If they can lob grenades at us, they aren't too far away. Time to move!' shouted Jason over the chaos.

'Only one way out,' replied Damien. He looked into Grace's eyes and saw for the first time that they were a pale blue-grey colour. It was like she was wearing contact lenses. Damien had never seen eyes like them before.

'If they're still heading down from the airstrip, we should be able to go out the door and left along the bay,' said Jason.

'Where can we go after that, Grace?' asked Damien. The archaeologist had been here for the last week. He assumed she would know where to go.

'We have a small boat next to the jetty at the southern end of the bay. Could we use that to get away?' supplied Grace in English. Her voice was clear in the din of the onslaught. Damien was immediately taken by her smoky French accent.

'If it's the only option we have it's the one that we're going to take. Nowhere else we can shelter that way?' asked Damien urgently.

'No. It's just open bay behind here. We use this as our common room and for eating. The sleeping accommodation is in the large shed,' replied Grace. She took a second to look at the man pressed tightly against her. She felt a flush of excitement at the heat that was pouring from his body. Grace saw kindness and concern in his eyes.

Who is this man? she thought.

'Jason, we break out to the left and make for a jetty. Grace says there's a boat we can use to head out into the bay,' relayed Damien.

'I don't like those odds. The Chechens will cut us down in the open,' said Jason doubt in his words.

'Other ideas?'

'None. Fuck, let's do it. I'll take the fucking cry baby. You take her. Fucking typical, Chainsaw,' called Jason, an exasperated tone in his voice.

Jason gripped Gabriel by the shirt collar and hauled him to his knees. He dragged the man to his feet, and pushed him in the centre of the back, guiding him to the door just as it burst inwards and slammed against the wall. Two freedom fighters stood in the opening, weapons pointed into the dim interior.

Thrusting Gabriel out of the way, Jason tried to raise his rifle just as the first Chechen opened fire. A short burst of 5.45-millimetre bullets slammed into the front of his chest rig, knocking Jason backwards.

Snapping up his AK and rolling onto his back, Damien dropped the second soldier with a single shot to the head. The man's body tumbled out into the Arctic morning. Damien rolled his right hand on the foregrip slightly and aligned the sights with the other Chechen, whose eyes were adjusting to the gloom. Outside, the gunfire had slacked to allow the assault on the building to go ahead.

Damien fired three rounds; the first missed as the Chechen spotted him and dodged away. The second and third shots caught the soldier in the throat and right shoulder. Crashing to the ground, the man died in a gurgling, horrific mess of blood and spittle.

Grace stared at the quivering, dying soldier, then turned to look at Damien. He calmly grabbed at her hand and dragged her upright.

Jason rolled onto his right side and groaned.

'Fucking shot me. The fucking vark. Vark prick!' groaned Jason through gritted teeth.

'You okay?' asked Damien as he moved forwards with Grace in tow.

'Yeah, yeah, these weak cunts can't kill me. The armour took the brunt for me. Fucking hurts. Fucking winded me.'

'Get in the fight, Jason,'

'Yeah, yeah fuck off, Chainsaw,' replied Jason. He moved to his hands and knees and focused on the door.

Gabriel lay curled up in a ball beside him.

Jason took a shaky knee to guard the front door, which was still open. Outside there was no movement or incoming fire. The Chechens were waiting to see if the gunfire in the building had ended the battle. Pushing Grace gently in the back, Damien guided her into a position behind Jason and pulled her into a crouch.

'Stop pushing me,' said Grace. Damien looked at her uncertainly and saw the fire of annoyance in her eyes.

'Keep up or we'll leave you behind.'

'How about you keep up with me. I can run faster than you with all that gear you have on,' countered Grace.

Damien chuckled. He slipped his HK USP pistol from its pouch and handed it to Grace.

'Can you shoot?' asked Damien.

'I can. My father and I used to shoot clay pigeons together before he died. Shotguns. I haven't fired a pistol before,' responded Grace as Damien handed her the side arm.

He plucked the two remaining magazines clear of their pouches and dropped them into her hand. From the body of the dead Chechen he pulled a worn and scratched Makarov 9-millimetre pistol out of the man's chest rig and plucked three full magazines from their pouches. He turned to face Grace as he stuffed the magazines and pistol into his rig.

'Okay. It's easy if you've seen at least one action movie. The magazine goes in here. Pull the slide back like this, safety down. Those are the sights. Fire until the slide locks back. Press this button to eject the magazine, put a fresh one in. You can either depress this lever to chamber the first round or pull back the slide slightly. It'll go forwards. Keep firing. Kill everything you point it at,' instructed Damien quickly. He watched Grace's intelligent eyes carefully following his rapid instructions.

'Yes, so simple,' she replied, a sarcastic look on her face.

'The hard part will be squeezing the trigger with someone in front of the muzzle,' replied Jason, scorn in his voice.

'It will be,' replied Grace quietly, her mind full of the responsibility she had in her hand.

'Put this on,' said Jason reaching up and pulling a parka down from a peg which held the archaeology team's extreme weather gear. He handed Grace the thick jacket to put over her fleece one. After pulling it on, she crawled over and pulled a pair of insulated boots from a rack and slipped them on.

'Where's my gun?' queried Gabriel.

'You don't get one, dickhead. Run, rabbit, run,' laughed Jason. 'Get ready. We're leaving.'

'You're mad. I'm not waiting!' yelled Gabriel. He stood and bolted through the open door. He had covered less than 5 metres before a burst of fire cut him down. Crashing into the rocks, Gabriel rolled onto his stomach and tried to crawl back to the building.

'That's our opening,' called Jason. He ran, crouched over, to the door, quickly looked out and rolled through, turning sharply left.

'Go,' said Damien. He stepped over the soldier's body and out the door. He could see Jason sprinting towards the jetty 100 metres away. Damien heard the crunch of rocks behind him as Grace followed.

Letting out an exasperated cry, Gabriel struggled to drag his shattered and dying body over the cold rocks and back into the warmth of the building. A single shot rang out and his head kicked back. The Frenchman dropped lifeless onto the hard rocks.

A confusion of gunfire erupted behind Damien as he sprinted out from the cover of the building. Glancing over his shoulder, he saw another group of soldiers fighting the rearmost Chechens. Confusion reigned on the battlefield. The Chechens turned to engage the unexpected threat.

As he ran Damien spotted a ship slowly navigating its way into the bay. By the look it was an old Russian icebreaker. A davit swung out from the superstructure and the crew lowered a large rigid inflatable boat towards the water. Damien was hoping the ship was Russian and not here to rescue the Chechens.

Their boots thumped on the dock as the three ran for the French boat Grace had told them about. The occasional shot careered in their direction. Fully occupied now, the Chechens tried to survive the coming assault from the newcomers. Jason bent down and started releasing the lines which held the boat to the jetty. The water of the bay was flat and calm. Jason could see the bottom through the clear and pristine water.

'Start the engine, Chainsaw,' ordered Jason as he moved to let go the forward line.

Damien dropped into the boat, twisted the key in the ignition and tried to fire the engine. The starter ground away. The twin outboards refused to fire.

'Turn the fuel on!' yelled Grace from the jetty.

Nodding, Damien found the fuel lever and engaged the flow. He smiled as the two engines roared into life. Idling roughly, the engines tried to find some warmth as they came up to operating temperature.

'Look out!' yelled Jason. He was looking back along the jetty from where he worked to free the last line.

The thunder of boots echoed over the jetty as a Chechen ran along the boards. The man's right arm flapped uselessly at his side. Blood streamed down from a shoulder wound. The man's face clenched with determination. In his left hand, he held a grenade. The man was intent on sacrificing himself.

Without thinking, Grace snapped up her pistol and fired into the soldier's chest. Rocked, the man kept coming, his armour absorbing the blow. Adjusting her aim, Grace fired off the rest of the magazine. Bullets careered around the soldier. Grace walked the rounds up across his armour and into his face. It melted away under the onslaught. Still running, the soldier's lifeless body toppled over the jetty's edge and into the water.

A few seconds later there was a muffled thump. Water erupted into the air as the grenade exploded.

'That was close,' said Jason as he freed the last line.

'Wasn't that hard,' said Grace to Damien as she jumped down into the boat. She hoped her statement was enough to mask her horror at killing someone. She dropped out the empty magazine and loaded a fresh one.

'Get on, Jason. We'll head out to that ship and hope it's a friendly.'

'Yep,' replied Jason. He straightened and made to jump into the boat. A single rifle shot hammered his body. Blood fountained from his throat. Jason involuntarily jammed his hand against the opening in his neck. He gurgled uncertainly, then staggered and dropped onto the boat, bouncing off the inflated sides before falling into the water. He floundered weakly for a few seconds and went limp. Blood spread around his body as it bumped against the piles of the jetty.

With a quick glance at the dead operator, Damien gunned the engines and roared out into the bay.

Talhig

'Good shot,' praised Talhig from where he lay next to the large building.

'No doubt, Talhig,' responded Asma coolly. She lay the Dragunov SVDS 7.62-millimetre sniper rifle on the rocks beside her. Taking up her PP-19 Vityaz, Asma looked across at him.

'I'm not letting them escape. I want that initiator. The two of us will go back to the platform and destroy it,' he said, fixing the rapidly departing boat with his eyes.

'Then we need our own boat,' replied Asma. She would follow Talhig to the end of the earth, but she felt his obsession with the Russian was a faltering fantasy. There was no way, even if they recovered the initiator, that they would make it back to the platform. It would be swarming with Russians by now. It would be a glorious suicide mission, but a wasted one. Asma was never open to wasting her life. She knew their pilots had to be dead. The team of soldiers attacking them were professional and at the top of their game. There was no-one left to fly a helicopter for them.

'There's a launch coming towards the shore from that ship. I have a feeling the man with my initiator is heading there in that other boat,' stated Talhig. He watched the rapidly approaching RIB. Sailors dressed in light combat gear crammed the boat. He could see shotguns and the odd AK among the mix. 'Kill them as soon as they get ashore, and we'll take their ride.'

Nikolay

The navigation into Templitz Bay had been an easy test of the icebreaker's integrity. Small ice floes had blocked the entrance, but the old ship effortlessly pushed its way through. Turning the *Aysberg* into the head of the bay, Nikolay watched the unfolding battle between the Alpha team and the Chechens. He could already see that the tide had turned against the terrorists. The Alpha operators were rapidly closing in on the perimeter defence, pushing the Chechens among the three buildings.

Ordering one of the boats lowered, Nikolay had delegated his first officer to organise a party of sailors to assist the Alpha team. There was no lack of volunteers. They had taken all the small arms that the ship had on board. There was no body armour among their stores, only equipment harnesses. The icebreaker was kitted to undertake the boarding of fishing vessels, not to battle heavily armed terrorists.

Watching the ship's RIB head towards shore, Nikolay saw an approaching boat and focused his binoculars on it. A uniformed man stood at the wheel. There appeared to be a woman standing behind him. She was waving frantically at the ship's RIB as it passed 50 metres from them. Nikolay saw his first officer ignore the woman and continue to drive the RIB towards the intense battle.

Nikolay was aware that there was a French archaeology team on the island. He gathered the woman was one of them. The man, another story.

'Prepare to receive a launch at the boarding door,' ordered

Nikolay turning to his third officer. 'What weapons do we have left?'

'One pistol, Captain,' the third officer responded.

'Take it. I don't know who these people are.'

Georgiy

Georgiy slapped a fresh magazine into his rifle and slung it over his back. He pulled a field dressing free of a pouch. His men worked methodically through the Chechen lines. Lazarov had taken a bullet through his right bicep. The wound was raw and ugly. Shivering, Lazarov gritted his teeth, grunting as Georgiy rolled on some pressure to slow the blood streaming from his arm. He kept his AN-94 trained towards the front in case any Chechens chose that moment to attack them.

'You'll live, Laz,' stated Georgiy, and tied off the dressing. He slapped the man encouragingly on the shoulder.

Dropping his AK-15 back across his chest, Georgiy took in the scene before him.

The bodies of fallen operators mixed with those of the Chechens. He could see only two muzzle flashes coming from the Chechen positions. The surviving eight operators of his team had boxed the enemy in and were working closer to their positions. Georgiy could imagine the desperation and anger the two surviving Chechens must be feeling. Their world was just about to end.

'Let's go,' ordered Georgiy as he stood and dragged Lazarov to his feet. 'You good?'

'I'm in the fight. Lead the way,' replied Lazarov. His pale pain-racked face told a different story.

Moving swiftly down the road to link up with his men, Georgiy watched as three grenades arced out through the air. The grenades, lobbed high, landed among the last two Chechens, and detonated.

Abruptly, the battle ceased. A strange silence descended over the island.

The Alpha team jogged forwards and started clearing the buildings. Georgiy saw the *Aysberg* in the bay and its RIB arriving to touch the shore on the far side of the large shed. In the distance he could hear the beat of the approaching army helicopters.

Too late, thought Georgiy, feeling a swell of pride at the fast, brutal work his men had undertaken. He was unsure where the boat heading towards the *Aysberg* fitted in.

Talhig

As the noise of the explosions died away, Talhig and Asma watched the approaching RIB. They were both sheltering on the opposite side of the large shed from where the Russians had picked off the last of his soldiers. Talhig had tucked away any feelings he might have had for the men he had lost over the last 48 hours. His mind focused on the man who had ruined the entire operation. In his blindness, Talhig did not acknowledge that there was no-one left other than himself and Asma to take the fight to the Russians.

The RIB bumped against the shore. Two men leapt out to steady it for their comrades. The sailors looked nervous and unsure of their weapons. Most fiddled with their equipment harnesses. One man was hurriedly feeding shells into a shotgun he had forgotten to load on the ship.

'When you're ready,' said Talhig quietly.

Asma stood up and rushed towards the RIB. Taken by surprise, the sailors watched her running form and stared, unsure of who she was. The sailor who had been loading his shotgun twigged, gave a shout of alarm, and raised his weapon. Asma calmly sprayed the sailors in the RIB with automatic fire. Nine-millimetre rounds cleaved into the inexperienced men, who started toppling over the sides of the RIB.

The two sailors on the beach turned and drew their pistols. Talhig shot both as he moved forwards behind Asma.

Asma placed a foot onto the bow and stepped aboard, smoothly slid her Grach pistol free of its holster, and shot each remaining sailor in the head. She positioned herself behind the console, gripping the wheel and throttles. Talhig pushed the RIB away from the shore and leapt aboard. He started tossing bodies into the water as Asma reversed the RIB. Twisting the wheel, Asma spun the boat free of the shore and out to sea.

Talhig stayed low at the bow, his eyes fixed on the other launch, which was pulling alongside the ship. Behind them, Alpha operators ran around the side of the shed and started firing at the retreating RIB. Asma extended her arm behind her without looking back, clutched her submachine gun tightly and let a long burst of automatic fire fly in their wake.

Gathering speed, the RIB rocketed towards the ship.

Damien

Damien bumped the boat up against the two fenders a crewman had dropped over the side of the narrow dock. The dock folded out from the starboard shell door. He chopped the throttles while Grace threw over the lines.

'Who are you?' called the officer in Russian. He held a shaky pistol on them.

'I'm Damien, this is Grace. Permission to come aboard,' replied Damien quickly in Russian, a disarming tone to his voice. He was warily watching the wavering pistol as it moved uncertainly between himself and Grace.

'Where did you come from?'

'The island,' said Damien. He indicated where they had come from with a hook of his thumb over his shoulder.

'Are you Chechen?' asked the officer.

'No, Australian. I had to change my clothes into these. Grace is French. Can we come on board, please?' asked Damien. The sailor tending the lines had finished securing them and had stepped back.

The third officer was trying to process the blood-splattered and dirty clothing of the two people standing in the small boat. He chewed his lip uncertainly.

'Ah, yes,' replied the officer uncertainly. The man's mind was whirling. He had no experience to rely on, to work out what he should do. A nagging thought knocked against the back of his head that he should ask the captain before letting the people on board.

'Thank you,' said Damien happily and indicated for Grace to step onto the dock.

'Leave your weapons behind,' ordered the officer.

'I don't have any,' replied Grace holding her hands up and fixing the young man with a dazzling smile. She had tucked Damien's USP into a large inside pocket of the parka she wore.

'Okay. You leave your rifle and pistol in the boat.'

'As you say, chief,' said Damien. He dropped the AK and pistol into the bottom of the RIB. He kept the fighting knife firmly strapped to the front of his chest rig and his Gerber Gator folding knife hidden in his pants pocket. Damien hoped the officer would not see either as a threat.

Joining Grace on the dock, Damien smiled at the officer and indicated that they should all go inside. Over his shoulder Damien saw a RIB cutting through the still water of the bay and rushing towards them.

The third officer pushed open the final door to the bridge and stepped through, indicating for Damien and Grace to follow. Nodding, Damien turned lightly and put his left hand on Grace's side and guided her through first. He smiled at her quizzical look. Grace walked onto the bridge and was immediately impressed by its retro look. She was sure the Russians had dug the consoles and equipment out of a museum and installed them on the ship. She saw a man looking out of the windows towards the shoreline through binoculars. Three lookouts stood at their posts and a man with a bruised and battered face sat in a chair across from her.

'Captain, these are the people who came aboard,' introduced the third officer nervously.

'Who gave permission for them to come on board my ship?' asked Nikolay predictably. He lowered the binoculars and turned to face the newcomers. Immediately, he took in the blood-covered ripped and torn clothes they wore. His heart softened at the sight of the woman, her hair a frizzled mess and her eyes dancing with an excited light. Nikolay was immediately attracted to her.

'We didn't give him much choice, sorry. Just needed to get off that island and somewhere safe for a while. I'm Damien and this is Grace.' Damien introduced them in Russian, speaking for the third officer.

'You speak our language, but you're not Russian. That's a Polish accent,' replied Nikolay coolly. Shifting his eyes from Grace, he focused on Damien. He found hard, intelligent blue-grey eyes fixed on his own. Blood, dirt, and stubble lined the man's face. Nikolay guessed that beneath the battered combat uniform was a strongly muscled frame. Damien carried himself proudly. Nikolay was sure he was standing in the presence of a man who could kill him before he even saw the first move.

'Australian. Grace is French. Do you speak English? Grace does not speak Russian,' asked Damien. He assumed by the blank look on her face that she did not understand a word they were speaking.

'Yes,' replied Nikolay, chopping to heavily accented English. He had not spoken the language since his time on destroyers in the Pacific.

'I was on the Nevzgody platform when the Chechens attacked. I escaped here and found Grace and her archaeological colleagues. The Chechens attacked us, and unfortunately, killed the archaeological team. Grace is the only one to survive,' replied Damien. He felt it best to leave out that he had not been alone in his escape. His background was unimportant.

'How did you escape?' asked Nikolay. He was intrigued by the oil worker dressed in a combat uniform. There were questions he would want answered soon.

'I took a helicopter,' said Damien simply, hoping not to engage any further scrutiny.

'You flew a helicopter here?' Nikolay looked around the bridge to where Lieutenant Litke sat. 'Is this possible?'

'It is if this man has expert skills to fly one. What type of helicopter?' asked Litke. His face hurt. His fingertips were showing the first black colour of frostbite. Litke was depressed and unhappy at the loss of Rudi. He knew his friend would be dead by now even if he had survived the impact of the missile's warhead, but the thought of him drifting alone and injured in the frigid ocean was more than he could bear. Blinking away the tears which began to form in his eyes, Litke waited for the answer.

'A Kamov. Rugged beast. Unfortunately, I crashed it when I landed. I was out of fuel. Lucky to get here,' answered Damien quickly, fixing the man with a charming smile.

'It's possible, Captain. I have flown a Kamov. You have great skill as a pilot, Damien,' praised Litke.

'One of my many talents. Who am I speaking with?' asked Damien. He had taken in the man's battered appearance. He was not part of the ship's crew.

'It has not been a very normal few days for us. I have forgotten my manners. I am Captain Nikolay Voronoi, master of the FSB icebreaking patrol ship *Aysberg*. You have already met my third officer. My first is ashore with our RIB. My second is in the engine room overseeing repairs. Our port engine has shut down. This man is Lieutenant Christophe Litke, pilot of an MIG shot down by the Chechens. He was lucky that we were in the area to rescue him. Litke is recovering well from his injuries,' replied Nikolay.

'What do I call you?' asked Grace.

Damien had firmly decided that he was not going to call the Russian *Captain*. Damien had left acknowledging rank behind as soon as he discharged from the Royal Australian Air Force.

'You may call me Nikolay, young lady,' he replied blushing. Grace's accent was intoxicating. Blinking slowly, Nikolay regained his composure.

'FSB?' reconfirmed Damien. He watched Nikolay carefully; this man could cause him problems.

'Da. Northern Sector command, based in Murmansk. I was on a patrol of the Shtokman gas field when the Chechens launched their attacks.'

'Attacks?' asked Damien.

'You would not know. The Chechens blew up a gas production ship, two gas carriers, two tugs and an icebreaker.'

'The *Boris Gakkel*?' asked Damien.

'Da.'

'That was the production ship we were about to hook up to. I worked the drill floor. There was only a day of drilling left. Then the rig would have moved to full production.'

'It's gone now. Along with the crews. I believe there were no survivors found on the Nevzgody platform. Rescue ships are closing on the area as we speak. I will not be joining them. The *Aysberg* is an old ship. She needs to call in to a yard to repair the port engine.'

Turning to one of the lookouts, Nikolay called out to him in Russian. The man rushed from the bridge.

'I have asked for tea and food to be brought up for you,' informed Nikolay.

'Thank you, Nikolay,' replied Grace. She had removed her extreme weather parka. The temperature on the bridge was just a little too cold for her fleece jacket but too hot for the parka. Hoping no-one noticed, she moved the pistol from the parka to her fleece jacket pocket. Grace did not trust what was happening around her. She felt she could trust Damien, but the Russians were as unpredictable as they were officious.

'I've not eaten in a while. I'd love a coffee. If you have any,' stated Damien hopefully. He walked over to shake Nikolay's hand. Both men held the shake firmly for a few seconds, nodded and released their hold.

'Captain, our boat is approaching,' called the starboard lookout.

'How many on board?' asked Nikolay, switching back to Russian.

'Two,' supplied the lookout. He locked his binoculars on to the speeding RIB as it passed around the *Aysberg*'s bow.

'Did they advise the reason for returning?' asked Nikolay. He was unsure why the RIB had re-joined the ship. His orders to his first officer had been to assist the Alpha team.

'Nyet.'

'Could be transporting wounded. Advise sickbay to prepare to receive possible injured from the island,' instructed Nikolay sternly.

Without a word the lookout picked up his radio and made the call to sickbay.

Catching the eye of his now relaxed third officer, Nikolay ordered him to return to the shell door dock and receive the RIB and whoever was on board.

'There's an FSB Alpha team on the island taking the fight to the last of the Chechens. I don't know why everyone has decided to come to this forsaken island. I served to the south of here and it was a miserable time,' said Nikolay to Damien, switching back to English.

Talhig

'Take out the crew, Talhig,' said Asma quietly as she guided the RIB around to the dock. Slowing down, the RIB cut smoothly through the calm water and coasted forwards. On the dock stood a sailor ready to take their lines. A second man rushed out of the shell door when they were a few metres out. Asma passed her submachine behind her back and dropped it into Talhig's outstretched hand.

'Who are you? Where's our boat crew?' asked the third officer. He was puffing from his jog through the ship. In his mind, his training screamed at him not to run. He could justify a jog given the situation. He took in the two people approaching in the ship's RIB, and instantly knew something was wrong. They watched him with hard, cruel eyes. Both dressed in dirty combat uniforms. The woman at the helm looked every inch a killer. When the two people did not answer him, he cleared his throat. He pushed as much authority into his tone as he could muster.

'Stop. Are you from the Alpha team?' he asked, aware that his voice lacked the authoritative power he had been aiming for. Beside him, the sailor moved forward to take the RIB's lines. The third officer reached out to stop him.

Standing up, Talhig raised the submachine gun, sighted on the two men, and opened fire. The sound of the gunfire echoed loudly against the hull. Both men jumped in surprise as bullets tore into their unprotected bodies. They dropped to the deck.

'Get the lines,' instructed Asma as she bumped the RIB lightly against the dock.

Talhig leapt out of the boat, dragging the stern line with him. After securing it he walked quickly forward, retrieved the bow line, and wrapped it expertly around the deck cleat. Taking up the slack, Talhig pulled the RIB's starboard side against the flat face of the dock.

Asma cut the engines and climbed out. She glanced at the boat Damien and Grace had used to escape the island. She put out her hand and nodded towards the submachine gun which Talhig held. Smiling, he passed it over. Asma dropped out the magazine and slid in a fresh one. She placed the half full one back into a pouch and secured its flap.

'Let's get out of the cold and find that Russian. I want us on our way in thirty minutes,' commanded Talhig.

Looking around, Asma had no idea how her leader was

hoping to achieve his order. The only option was to return to the island and take a helicopter. There were surely none of their pilots left alive to fly them. The RIB would not make it and this icebreaker had to have a competent crew on board to make the transit. Neither Talhig or herself had the skills or experience to undertake the voyage. But she held her tongue, and moved to the shell door to look inside.

The space was clean and filled with ropes and bins of equipment. Asma spotted a hatch in the opposite bulkhead. She crossed quickly to grip the handle just as it twisted in her hand. The door opened and a worried looking sailor rushed through. He pulled up short as he saw Talhig pointing a pistol at him. He tried to turn around, but felt Asma's submachine gun press against his neck. With nowhere to go he stopped and waited to see if he was going to die.

'Can you take us to the bridge?' asked Talhig.

'Yes,' stammered the man.

'Lead the way,' ordered Talhig.

'I can't take you there. The captain has not authorised it.'

'See this?' asked Talhig, indicating the pistol.

'Da.'

'This is the approval. Lead the way,' growled Talhig.

Nodding, the sailor turned. His eyes grew wide when he saw Asma slide her cruel Karambit knife from its sheath. She spun him around to face back through the open door and pushed the knife against his back.

'Walk,' she breathed in his ear.

Stepping over the threshold, the sailor began to guide them down the passageway. Heavy frames painted a cream colour contrasted with the dark green flooring. The interior reeked of diesel and oil. Asma was sure she could smell the rust that bubbled under the paint.

This ship is old, she thought to herself.

A cabin door opened ahead of the trio and a sailor stepped out absently. He looked up the passageway and then down to where the three walked quickly towards him. Opening his mouth to speak the crewman closed it with an audible clunk when he saw Asma push her submachine gun forward. Firing off a quick burst that took the man in the chest, Asma smiled happily.

The sailor jerked in Asma's grip, trying to turn from the body of his comrade as she pushed him up the passageway.

'Keep going,' she demanded and pushed the knife deeper against his back. The tip pushed through his overalls and pricked the man's skin. Flinching defensively, the sailor continued forwards, stepping over the body. He turned his head in shock to look at the cream paint on the wall and hoped he would survive.

Georgiy

'They're all dead, Georgiy,' stated Yakov, standing near the shoreline, and looking out at the icebreaker. Georgiy was walking over towards him. Both men were tired and covered in dirt. The stress of the last few days etched deeply into Yakov's inexperienced face. Georgiy maintained a fresher, more alert look. He had years of combat experience to fall back on.

'The people in the hut?' he asked.

'An expedition of some kind. They never stood a chance. The Chechens cut the building to shreds.'

'I still don't know why the Chechens attacked them. Someone got away, though,' said Georgy, indicating the footprints heading towards the jetty.

'To the icebreaker?' queried Yakov.

'The only place for them to go.'

'Laz? Call the ship and find out if anyone escaped,' called Georgiy. Lazarov nodded from where he sat nursing his injured arm. Pulling his radio around to his front, he flipped open a notebook and looked for the icebreaker's working frequency.

Taking a deep, calming breath, Georgiy turned and surveyed the small battlefield. The eight surviving members of his team were working through the Chechen bodies looking for anything of intelligence value. The Chechens had fought and died bravely. Georgiy had never known a Chechen who was not fanatical, professional, and deadly when cornered. These men deserved to return home to their families. They had earned that right. Georgiy knew they never would. A mass at-sea burial and the evidence would disappear.

The closing sound of helicopters approaching informed Georgiy that the army were almost here. He was not looking forward to their hammer and anvil approach. His team had already neutralised the threat. Keyed up for action, the soldiers would find nothing for themselves to do.

'Was that gunfire?' asked Yakov, still staring at the ship.

'Sounded like it,' replied Georgiy.

'Look!' Yakov pointed into the water in front of the largest building. Dead men dressed in the uniform of the FSB marine branch floated against the shore.

'I don't think we killed all of the Chechens,' replied Georgiy. He regarded the icebreaker quietly. 'Find us a way to get to that ship.'

'Can only be by the helicopter. I don't see any boats,' relayed Yakov.

'Get it airborne. Semyonov can pick us up on the way,' ordered Georgiy. 'Laz, tell the ship they have company, and we are on our way. Send it.'

Nikolay

The muffled sound of gunfire echoed through the ship. Nikolay called his section heads and demanded to know what was happening. Not all departments answered.

'Lock down the engine room and the bridge. I think we have Chechens on board,' ordered Nikolay. When no-one moved, he noticed that he was the only officer on the bridge. The lookout he had sent for the tea and food had not returned. Shaking his head, Nikolay picked up the telephone and called the engine room. When his second officer answered, he issued his orders.

'Secure the bridge wing doors,' Nikolay called to the two lookouts as he made towards the main entrance door. Halfway there he heard the radio key. Spinning, he walked back to the main console, plucked the radio telephone out of its receiver, and took a deep breath.

'Station calling, this is the *Aysberg*,' he responded.

'*Aysberg,* this is Yad Zero Three. There may be terrorists on your vessel,' called Lazarov.

'They're already here! I can hear shooting,' replied Nikolay.

'Roger. We are spinning up our helicopter. We will be with you as soon as we can. Do you know how many are on board?'

'Nyet.' Nikolay shot back. They needed help now, not in the

10 minutes it was going to take the Alpha team to arrive and save the day.

'We're on our way. Secure yourself as best you can, out,' ended Lazarov.

'Do you have any weapons?' asked Damien. He had taken in their options. He did not think the bridge doors would stand up to a determined enemy.

'No. I sent them all with the shore party. My third officer had the last pistol, but he has not returned. I must assume he's dead as well.'

Georgiy

Grit, ice, and snow blasted Georgiy and his men as the Mi-26 hovered into position on the shoreline. The pilot held the massive machine out over the shallow water and delicately dropped the ramp onto the rocks. Without a word, Georgiy leapt on board to escape the onslaught, followed by his operators. Yakov brought up the rear. No-one bothered to take a seat. The trip was only going to be short.

Not waiting for the ramp to close, Semyonov pulled on power and the Mi-26 started to accelerate towards the *Aysberg*. He kept it low, swinging wide to allow enough time to enable him to line up with the small stern flight deck. Semyonov planned to disembark the team the same way he had picked them.

Behind the Mi-26, Russian Army Mi-17s appeared over the low rise of a glacier and turned onto final to land at the airstrip. Too late to be of any use other than to clean up the bodies.

Talhig

Moving up the last of the stairs to the bridge, Talhig looked past Asma and the Russian sailor at the closed door.

'Open it,' he ordered. Asma lifted her submachine gun. Talhig had his pistol at the ready. They had no idea what to expect once they entered the bridge. Talhig hoped by securing the bridge he could lock the ship down. Then Asma could hunt down the Russian and get the initiator back. At no time did Talhig think or believe his plan was flawed.

'I can't. It's locked. The door will only open when someone recognises you on the camera,' lied the sailor. Unless the captain knew there were enemy on board, the door would be unsecured.

Not believing him, Asma pushed the sailor up against the door and tried the handle. Finding it locked she stepped back and looked up at the camera. There was no indication someone was looking at her.

Talhig grunted unhappily and pressed the barrel of his pistol hard against the back the of the man's head. The sailor flinched at the hard metal circle crushing into the skin of his skull. His knees weakened and Asma had to hold him up.

'Open the door,' roared Talhig. 'Or I will kill him.'

The camera looked at them impassively.

'Open it!' yelled Talhig. Suddenly, he realised how deranged he sounded. There was a strained tone to his voice. He saw Asma register it.

The door remained closed.

'Step away, Asma,' he instructed.

Asma shoved the sailor up against the door. She took two paces backwards to stand behind Talhig. She pushed her fingers deep into her ears. The stairwell was narrow. The walls were metal. The noise of the gunshot was going to be deafening.

'Nyet!' screamed the Russian sailor and threw his arms up in a futile gesture.

Without blinking, Talhig pulled the trigger. The gunshot roared in the enclosed space and his ears rang with the concussion. The sailor dropped lifeless to the floor. Blood and flesh covered the door. Asma darted forwards and dragged the body clear.

'Breach the door!' ordered Talhig. He turned to walk back down the stairs.

Asma immediately ripped open a pouch and pulled out a small package of Semtex 10 plastic explosive. She ripped away the protective covering, then moulded the block of black explosive around the lock and handle. After driving in a chrome detonator, Asma unwound a short length of cord, connected it to the detonator and initiated it. She jogged down the flight of stairs to where Talhig was waiting patiently. Sheltering next to him, Asma counted down the seconds.

Five seconds later a heavy crump of noise and smoke rushed into the stairwell. Clearing their ears, Talhig and Asma rushed into the passageway. The blast had sheared away the door's lock and it swung inwards. They charged through.

Georgiy

Semyonov pedal-turned the Mi-26 to the right as he swept across the water. He kept the rear ramp lowered in anticipation of the swift disembarkation of the Alpha team. He lined up with the stern of the *Aysberg*, drifting the tail of the helicopter over the flight deck. Reacting to meterage calls from Baranova, he slowly backed up until the scraping of the ramp on the hard metal shuddered through the fuselage.

'Go!' yelled Georgiy as he stepped onto the deserted flight deck. Scanning the area, he found it deserted. No-one was waiting for them this time.

As the boots of the last operator touched the deck, the Mi-26 lifted clear and headed out to sea. Semyonov gained some height and then turned back towards the *Aysberg*. He engaged auto-hover, intent on holding station until the Mi-26 exhausted its fuel. The wash from the massive rotors ripped up the surface of the bay and sent small waves slapping against the *Aysberg*'s stern. Georgiy's orders were for Semyonov to loiter in case the team needed a quick extraction. He intended on waiting faithfully for his comrades.

Damien

The sudden explosion made Damien stagger. He dropped to the floor and rolled clear. The unexpected attack on the bridge had caught them all unaware. No-one had been watching the monitor which displayed the entrance CCTV. Debris rushed across the bridge. A piece of the door lock cleaved a path through the back of the sailor manning the port lookout position. Nikolay joined Damien on the deck. Grace fell to her knees and tried to clear her ears from the over-pressure. Litke remained in his seat, his eyes wide with in fright. He was suddenly back in the cockpit of his crippled MIG-31, trying to save Rudi. The starboard lookout turned slowly. His mouth hung open as he stared at the ruined door.

Damien's training kicked in and he quickly found his feet and stepped clear of the doorway. Two dark shapes rushed through the opening, weapons raised. The pair surveyed the bridge. Out of the small rear bridge windows, Damien saw a Mi-26 hovering menacingly 50 metres from the stern. What it was doing there he had no idea, but he hoped it had dropped Russian troops on board.

'Ostanovka!' yelled Asma. She swept the muzzle of her submachine gun over the people struggling to recover in front of her. The starboard lookout stepped forward uncertainly, confused. Asma lay the sights of her weapon over the man's chest and squeezed off a short burst. The man dropped to the ground.

Talhig stepped past her and dragged a man to his feet, staring hard into his face.

'Captain?' he yelled into Nikolay's face.

'Da,' responded Nikolay.

'Where's the Russian?' cried Talhig, spittle flying out. It landed on Nikolay's face. He tried to turn away from the wet spray.

'We're all Russian,' replied Nikolay. The Chechen's eyes were crazy and stressed. Nikolay was sure that the man who would end his life was staring directly at him.

'The one who came on board. Where is he!'

'Talhig! That's him,' yelled Asma. She had been scanning the bridge and fixed her eyes on a man slowly trying to outflank her. 'Stay where you are,' she instructed.

Talhig had not noticed Damien. He stared at the man who

had started moving around Asma. He recognised him instantly.

Damien stopped, nodded, and smiled coldly. He recognised both.

Pushing Nikolay away, Talhig grabbed Grace by her hair and hauled her off her feet and along the floor. A maniacal grin slid over Talhig's face. He jammed his pistol painfully into the right side of Grace's face.

'Give me the laser initiator. Give it to me! I have chased you across the ocean to get it. You have ruined my mission. Give me the initiator!' yelled Talhig. An unhinged tone powered through his words. He felt the edge of reality slipping away. A searing pain hammered through his chest. Ignoring it, Talhig pushed the pistol harder into Grace's skull.

'Let go of me!' shouted Grace in French. Asma frowned and turned to look at her briefly. She was going to enjoy killing this pretty one.

'Stay still, Grace. I'll handle this,' said Damien calmly in English. 'Who are you?' he asked switching to Russian.

'I am General Talhig Chechenskiy. This is Sergeant Asma Taisumov. We are soldiers of the Itt Stag. We are freedom fighters for our mother country, Chechnya. I recognise you. You were on the Nevzgody platform. You attacked me and took the initiator. My mission remains uncompleted until I get it back from you. Give it to me.'

'Terrorists, then? I can't say it's a pleasure to meet either of you. Your nose looks a little rough, mate. Can't say I'm sorry I broke it. I remember you, Asma. You're a killer. I took out some of your girls, though. Easy enough. I'm Damien Hunter.' Damien was goading them, and Asma flinched with anger and fixed him with a bloody stare.

Damien smiled back.

'I will shoot this woman,' replied Talhig.

'Why?' asked Damien.

Talhig blinked at him uncertainly. Roaring in annoyance, he kicked Grace away and grabbed Nikolay. Talhig was confused by Damien. The man showed no fear. Talhig had no intention of killing the woman. It was not in his makeup to slaughter innocent females. Russian men were a different story.

'This man I will kill,' said Talhig, trying to regain control of his voice. He thrust the barrel of his pistol into Nikolay's right eye. He turned to look at Damien. 'Russians do not mean anything to me. They have slaughtered and raped my people and my country for too long.'

Damien investigated Talhig's eyes and knew he was serious. Talhig's finger squeezed on the trigger.

'This laser initiator, you mean?' asked Damien. He quickly slid the small device from his chest rig and held it up. Talhig's finger pressure relaxed on the pistol's trigger.

Georgiy

Charging through the ship, Georgiy cursed at the lack of crew as he turned each corner. He had not paid enough attention last time they had called to the ship. Now he was unsure of their position inside the maze of passageways and stairwells. Leading with his AK-15, Georgiy jogged ahead of Lazarov and three of his operators. He had split Yakov off with the rest of the team to start searching the ship.

Suddenly, a set of boots appeared on the stairwell to their front and slowly made their way down. Halting, Georgiy waited silently to see who it was.

Cautiously, a Russian sailor moved nervously down the stairs. He had been in his cabin when the gunfire started. The eerie silence of the ship had reinforced his decision to stay hidden. He had only now ventured out to see what the problem was.

Stepping into view, Georgiy held his left index finger to his lips and gestured for the sailor to come to him. Halting, the sailor eyed the weapons and the dirty white camouflage uniforms of the four men in the passageway. The men looked like they were from another world. Only their eyes showed.

'We are FSB,' called Georgiy softly. 'Come to me.'

After hesitating for another second, the sailor scuttled over to

Georgiy. He checked the patch on his uniform, then looked at Georgiy expectantly.

'Where's the bridge?' asked Georgiy.

'You passed it. That last set of stairs takes you there. I heard gunfire,' replied the sailor. He was eying Georgiy's assault rifle.

'Chechen terrorists have boarded the ship. We're here to clear them out. Show us to the bridge. We need to see the captain and secure it.'

'Da. This way, I will take you,' replied the sailor. He pushed excitedly past the operators and guided them to the stairs.

Talhig

Talhig growled menacingly as he locked his eyes on the only person standing between him and the honourable completion of the mission. He stared at Damien's smiling face. Talhig roared in anger. He viciously pistol-whipped Nikolay along the side of his head and pushed the man away. Landing in Litke's lap, Nikolay's momentum carried both men off the seat and crashing to the floor. Talhig jammed his pistol into its holster, then yanked a Kizlyar Phoenix-1 tactical knife from his chest rig. The razor-sharp edge of the matt black blade caught the light from the bridge's ceiling and gleamed with harsh intent.

Talhig charged forwards, slashing the knife towards Damien.

Instinctively adopting a defensive stance, Damien dropped the initiator, picking his moment to dart out of the way.

As Talhig closed the distance, Damien lashed out his left hand in a controlled blow, catching Talhig on the right temple, causing him to stagger. Talhig used his momentum to carry him out of Damien's range and spun around. He recognised Damien as a skilled and deadly hand-to-hand combat operator.

'You're not a Russian oil worker,' growled Talhig. His breathing ragged and harsh. He was trying to control his anger. His broken nose hurt as he breathed. The pain in his chest continued to grow and a numbing sensation was pushing along his right arm.

Talhig realised he might be having a heart attack.

'Never said I was. You're in for a surprise,' replied Damien. He strutted in a circle around Talhig looking for an opening. Suddenly stopping, Damien slowly drew the KAMPO fighting knife from its sheath. He quickly glanced at the blade and noticed that the previous owner had spent all his time cleaning his rifle. The blade was rusty and pitted.

'Asma, do not interfere. Let this end how it ends,' ordered Talhig. He had seen Asma taking a sight picture on the back of Damien's head. She unhappily lowered her submachine gun just enough to comply with his orders.

Lowering his head slightly, Damien stopped smiling. A hardness fell over his face.

He stepped forwards, then darted to the right, aiming the point of the knife at the soft part of Talhig's armour. Rolling away from the blow, Talhig stabbed his blade forwards. Damien twisted away, driving his right fist into Talhig's mouth. A satisfying crunch rewarded him. Lurching back, Talhig spat a broken tooth onto the bridge floor. He grimaced at the pain. Years of command had dulled his fighting prowess. Talhig could see his own death in his opponent's eyes.

The pain in his chest seemed intent on draining his strength.

Letting out another roar, Talhig charged Damien. He ignored the quick flick of Damien's left hand which corrected his knife hold. Talhig drove forwards, feeling Damien's blade snag against the fabric of his armour. It slid off and punched deeply into his right shoulder. Pulling his shoulder down, Talhig trapped Damien's knife and twisted it out of his hands. They collided heavily, Talhig driving Damien off his feet and slamming him into the deck.

Damien slid over the floor before crashing against a steel console. The air rushed out of his lungs. Talhig's face was close to his. Damien could smell the man's sweat. Trying to roll out from under the Chechen, Damien twisted and kicked up with his knees. The heavy man smothered him.

Damien struggled to free his hands caught in Talhig's chest rig, and managed to yank both free. With all his strength he slammed the rolled knuckles of each hand under Talhig's armour into his unprotected flanks.

Roaring in pain, Talhig involuntarily jerked up and tried to pull away. Seeing his opening, Damien dropped his left hand to his pocket and slid out his Gerber Gator folding knife. He flicked the blade open and quickly punched it into Talhig's stomach. He repeatedly stabbed and twisted the knife. Thick blood covered Damien as it gushed from where he hacked open Talhig's body.

Crying out, Talhig blinked his eyes in panic. He slapped the blade from Damien's hand, wriggling to pull his pistol free.

A loud boom echoed through the bridge. Talhig's head snapped to the side. His skull exploded and rained gore across the console next to him. Damien violently shoved and pushed at the dead man's body, toppling him off.

'Nyet!' screamed Asma as she watched Talhig's body crash to the floor, lifeless. His legs kicked frantically. His arms shook for a few seconds as his body entered its death throes.

Spinning around, Asma raised her submachine gun, looking for the source of the gunshot.

Grace stood with her feet apart, a determined look on her face, pointing Damien's HK USP at Asma's head. A faint wisp of smoke rolled from its muzzle.

'Blayt!' screamed Asma.

'Drop your gun,' ordered Grace calmly in English.

Without pausing, Asma flicked the sights of her submachine gun slightly to the right and fired a single round. The pistol in Grace's hand exploded out of her grasp.

Clutching her bleeding fingers, her face drained of confidence and colour, Grace stared at Asma. Asma's beautiful face cracked open in a triumphant grin. Her eyes danced with the pleasure of killing.

'Ostanovka!' yelled a commanding voice from the back of the bridge.

Grace looked over Asma's shoulder to see a solid man dressed in a heavy winter camouflage smock and black trousers. Only his eyes showed above a black thermal face wrap. A black helmet topped his head. The man held an assault rifle pointed at Asma.

Clenching her teeth, Asma lowered her submachine gun to her side. As she turned, she plucked an RGN grenade from her chest rig and pulled the pin, smiling grimly. She looked down the barrel of the AK-15 in Georgiy's hands. She shook the grenade in her hand to give it emphasis. She was hedging her bets that the man holding the rifle would not risk killing everyone on the bridge if the grenade went off. With a kill radius of 4 metres, the grenade had just enough power to clear the bridge. It was the only grenade she had left.

Without hesitating, Georgiy shot Asma between the eyes. Her attractive face cracked open under the impact and the back of her head exploded, showering Grace in gore. As Asma's legs sagged out from underneath her the grenade dropped from her hands and rolled across the bridge floor.

Georgiy yelled a warning and dove out into the passageway.

Damien gained his feet and charged after the grenade, looking for somewhere to throw it.

The grenade rolled towards the tangled bodies of Nikolay and Litke, bumping to a stop against Litke's head. He turned to stare at the small grenade. Selflessly, he pushed Nikolay away and rolled onto the grenade.

'No!' yelled Damien as he changed his direction and headed behind a console.

A split second later the grenade exploded with a muffled whump. Litke's body absorbed the blast and bucked as the concussion passed through him. Damien sprinted from cover. He rolled Litke over to see a gaping hole in his chest. He did not need any more evidence to see that the man was dead.

Nikolay rolled onto his knees. He grabbed Litke's wrist, feeling for a pulse, but found nothing. He dropped Litke's arm and sat back on his hunches, his ears ringing. A blank look played across his face. Blood dribbled down the side of his head from the deep cut that Talhig's pistol had furrowed in it.

Damien leapt up and ran the few metres to Grace. She was shaking. Her eyes glazed. Pulling chunks of Asma's brain and skull from her hair, Damien tried to clean away the gore as best he could. He stopped; he was just smearing it deeper. He drew her in close to his chest, holding her tightly as the first quiet sobs started.

'Do not move!' yelled Georgiy in Russian. He stepped back into the bridge. Moving around him, three Alpha operators and Lazarov surged into the space, rapidly securing it.

'Good shooting,' praised Damien, looking up at him.

'Anyone with a weapon drop it to the floor,' ordered Georgiy. When no-one moved, he looked around at the blood and bodies scattered around the bridge.

Again, he felt he was late to the party.

Damien

Within an hour, the Alpha team had cleared the bridge of bodies. One of the surviving sailors was fighting a losing battle as he tried to sop up the blood from the deck. The sailor had succeeded in wiping down the consoles and bridge windows, then turned to tackle the most gruesome of the jobs.

Through the bridge windows were open ocean and small icebergs; the *Aysberg* had put to sea.

'Would it not be easier to transport Grace and Damien to the army base by helicopter?' asked Nikolay.

'The bodies from the battle are on the helicopters for processing. There will be no room,' pointed out Georgiy. He looked over at Grace and Damien. They sat next to each other on the floor near the rear bulkhead. Both exhausted. They had become inseparable as soon as the action finished.

'The French woman will go to her embassy. The Australian I am not so sure about. His identification does not check out. I'm not sure who he really is,' said Georgiy suspiciously. The identity Damien had supplied checked out as far as his employment with Plyos Energy. Then it became necessarily murky and indistinct. The mechanisms of government moved slowly. Georgiy knew he was not going to find an answer in time. The Australian Embassy in Moscow had been helpful to a point, then switched gears immediately to disrupt his enquiries.

'He's not a prisoner,' pointed out Nikolay. 'He saved my life.'

'I'm aware of that, Nikolay. He's not a prisoner as such. I think we have discovered someone the FSB will be very interested in talking to. Maybe even the GRU.'

'Gentlemen, we need to talk,' said Damien. He stood up and walked across to the two men. He had listened to the conversation. He was not happy with the direction it was taking.

'Sit down, Mister Hunter. We're discussing things,' ordered Georgiy. He raised a gloved hand to stop Damien's advance.

'I can see that. You're discussing my fate and I want some buy-in.'

'Sit back down or I will have you restrained,' replied Georgiy, the threat clear. He took a step forward.

'You look like a professional, Georgiy. I'm sure you recognise another operator,' said Damien. He hoped he could trigger some understanding and the kinship felt between operators of all countries.

Georgiy studied the way Damien carried himself. He saw the cool, professional, unhurried calm in his eyes. Georgiy could see the traits.

'Come forward,' Georgiy instructed. He waved Damien to them. He did not acknowledge that Damien had never stopped moving in the first place, ignoring his command.

'I'm happy for Grace to go to the French Embassy in Moscow as soon as arranged. But I'm not happy to enter mainland Russia. Shall we just say that I am not compatible with your country. Beautiful though it is.'

'In what way?' asked Nikolay. *Who was this man?*

'Let's just say that a previous employer has a competing organisation on the Russian side of the fence who do not like that competition. I've had a few trips to Russia to sort things out over the years. A meeting with your military apparatus is not something I want to engage with.'

'You're a mercenary?' asked Georgiy.

'A strong word. I prefer contractor. My preference in this situation is to disappear on my own before we berth,' replied Damien. He was feeling his way through the conversation. He had one last trump card he could us as a last resort. But he knew there would be a debt to pay.

'Out of the question. The FSB will want to talk to you, Damien,' said Georgiy stubbornly.

'I understand that, but I will not be stopped,' replied Damien. A hard, uncompromising edge was now in his voice.

'Wait, wait,' said Nikolay. 'Georgiy, is there any harm in letting Damien go his own way? I am comfortable with it. I can repay the debt I owe him.'

'Out of the question,' replied Georgiy.

Gritting his teeth, Damien realised he had to use his final lifeline.

'Nikolay, is your satellite telephone operating?' asked Damien quietly.

'Da.'

'I have a number you need to call. Ignore the strange name of the place that answers. Ask for Mister Thompson. Tell him Chainsaw requires a favour and relay our position. Give him Georgiy's name as well,' said Damien, slowly nodding his head at Nikolay to reinforce his words.

'You will make no telephone calls,' ordered Georgiy.

'I am the captain of this ship. I give the orders,' roared Nikolay defiantly, quickly putting Georgiy in his place. He lifted the satellite telephone out of its cradle. Damien called out the numbers he needed to input. As the telephone rang, Nikolay looked around the bridge. An hour ago, the place had been full of chaotic action.

Blinking in surprise, Nikolay looked at Damien, who smiled back reassuringly. In a second, he connected with Mister Thompson. Nikolay relayed the instructions Damien had given. Mister Thompson paused, chuckled, and advised Nikolay to have Georgiy stand by the telephone for an incoming call. Hanging up the receiver, Nikolay relayed Mister Thompson's order to Georgiy.

Georgiy shook his head in frustration. The telephone started ringing a minute later. Nikolay indicated for him to pick it up.

'Da? Major Georgiy Urvantsev.'

'Urvantsev, this is Admiral Vasily Unkovsky, Commander northern sector, FSB. You are under my authority currently, is that correct?'

'Da,' replied Georgiy uncertainly. He instantly recognised the Admiral's voice.

'You have a man with you, Damien Hunter?' asked Unkovsky gruffly.

'Da.'

'Georgiy, I'm ordering you to comply with all his requests. Captain Voronoi will transport him to a destination of his choice. He will leave when the time comes. No harm is to befall him. He's not a prisoner. He's a free man. Georgiy, Damien is a friend to the FSB. You will treat him as such,' ordered Unkovsky and ended the call.

'You have very powerful friends, Mister Hunter,' said Georgiy, dropping the receiver into its cradle.

Dasha

Dasha forced his tired eyes to stay open as he idled the missile cutter through a thick fog bank. Deep, numbing fatigue clouded his mind. It took all his concentration to maintain the course. Hammered and smashed by the massive explosion of the production ship the small cutter had tossed around in the ocean, rolling from beam end to beam end. The explosion had stripped the deck bare of the four Termit missile containers. All that remained was the twisted wreckage of their mounts. The forward twin 30-millimetre cannons canted off at a steep angle. They would not respond to any command. The stern guns had torn free and disappeared into the ocean. Most of the bridge instruments had failed along with the radar and communications systems.

The harsh metal interior of the cutter tossed the crew around like they were inside a washing machine. The only things that saved them all from death were the three Zvezda M503 radial diesel engines which had continued to operate. A continuous thumping vibration ran through the cutter – a bent propeller shaft.

During the hours the cutter had limped slowly towards the Russian mainland, the crew had tended to the injured and restored as many systems as possible. A flood had occurred in the engine room. It had taken hours to isolate and stop. The pumps effectively cleared the seawater from the space. Regardless, the engineers had worked in knee-deep water to keep the engines online. Damage control parties worked around them.

'Not long now, Mikhail,' encouraged Dasha. Mikhail was standing as a lookout on the bridge. He stared into the murk of the dark night.

'How can you be sure? We have no radar or navigation systems,' replied Mikhail. He did not turn to look at Dasha. Mikhail felt concerned that they were about to run aground, which would not have been unfavourable to Mikhail. He had had enough of this small cutter. There had been little time since achieving victory to savour it. Hour upon hour everyone worked at keeping the rust bucket afloat and operational. Mikhail was proud and honoured to be part of this crew of countrymen.

'I have faith in my navigation skills, Mikhail. We're going to arrive at the same point we departed. I assure you. We will hand over this hulk as per our orders. Then we will all go home,' smiled Dasha.

Even if his calculations were incorrect, he could not check or call for assistance anyway.

Nodding, Mikhail continued to strain his eyes to see through the thick fog. Ten minutes later he was sure he could see a line of shadow appearing along the bottom of the fog bank.

'I see land, Dasha. Directly ahead,' relayed Mikhail.

'Faith, Mikhail, is all you need. Inshallah,' replied Dasha and cut the throttles. The steady and comforting rumble of the engines died away. The slap of waves hitting the side of the hull was the only sound as the cutter sliced through the calm water. Allowing the boat to lose way, Dasha drifted close in shore. He picked up a pair of binoculars and scanned the faint shore. He saw no movement.

'Give them the signal,' ordered Dasha.

'Are you sure we're in the right place?' replied Mikhail, trying to recognise landmarks on the shore.

'See how the line of the shore drives up towards the point in the distance? We're back where we started,' supplied Dasha. He was quietly pleased he still had the skills of an exceptional navigator.

Nodding, Mikhail picked up a signalling lamp. He stepped out of the bridge, gained the deck, and walked to the bow. The cutter was starting to swing beam on to the shore. Dasha gave a nudge of throttle and port rudder to bring the cutter's head back towards the shore. Aiming the lamp at the shore, Mikhail counted off the sequence of on/off blinks of the light which would authenticate them to the shore party.

He received no reply.

Mikhail worked through the routine and waited.

No response.

Dropping the heavy lamp to his side, Mikhail rolled the light sequence through his mind to ensure he was using the agreed signal. His semaphore was rusty, but Mikhail was sure he was correct. He tried again.

No response.

Mikhail came back to the bridge with a dejected look on his face. He saw that Dasha wore the same look.

'There is no-one here, Dasha. They have abandoned us,' said Mikhail, glumly fixing his friend with a sad look.

Captain Brusilov

Struggling weakly in his survival suit, Brusilov could feel the steadily advancing tendrils of deathly cold seeping through his body. He had no recollection of how he came to be in the water or in a survival suit. He recalled being on the bridge, unhappy with his exchange with the *Boris Gakkel*. He saw a small warship pull around the production ship's bow. A missile cutter had no place being in the Arctic. Then there was an explosion and blackness. He had awakened as a wave slapped him in the face. Brusilov found himself floating on his back against a piece of wreckage. Someone had tied him off to it.

Fifteen hours in the frigid Arctic water had numbed his very being. Brusilov had thought the first waves of violent shivering had been traumatic. It was when the shivering had stopped that he knew he was in trouble. First to go was the feeling in his legs. It had disappeared with a feeling like water lightly running over his skin. His arms felt like lead. Brusilov had forgotten when he'd last felt sensation in them.

Water slapped against his face, adding to his irritation. He tried to shake it away, but more water rushed over him. Shaking his head harder, he found he could not clear the water from his face. He felt like he was going to drown. Suddenly, he felt the deep urge to live. To survive. Adrenaline surged through his numb, dying body. He tried to roll onto his front to escape the onslaught of water. He thought he heard a shout. Confused, he stopped moving and waited.

Another shout. A splash sounded near him.

Hungry arms enveloped him. Brusilov heard more words that he could not understand. He knew they were Russian. Brusilov's mind could not process them. For the first time he noticed a brilliant light shining down on him. Everything around him suddenly illuminated. He caught sight of someone floating near him on the other side of the wreckage. Concentrating hard on the pale dead face, he recognised his first officer.

Had he save me?

The first officer did not have a survival suit on.

The thunder of helicopter rotors filled his ears along with more shouting. Brusilov heard words of encouragement. Hope filled his heart. He felt hot breath on his right ear and down the side of his face. Someone was dragging him through the black water. Brusilov hovered near death. Suddenly he was moving up into the air.

Brusilov passed out as he saw the belly of a helicopter looming over him.

Damien

Avignon, France
Three months later

Damien finished his espresso, grimacing at its bitter taste. It was not a patch on the Warfighter Coffee he could get in Australia.

Hard to come by in Europe. He held onto the hope that the lads could break into the market and satisfy his craving. He took in the classic architectural lines of the Palais des Papes, drinking in the culture and beauty of Avignon. Damien had often visited the city in the past. He felt calm and relaxed among its ancient streets. In his mind, it was on par with Alaska and the Australian Outback for how it made him feel.

Twisting in his seat, Damien watched his target move swiftly across the court that dominated the entrance to the palace. He checked to ensure the area was secure, then stood up and dropped five Euros on the small table. A large tip the coffee did not deserve, but they'd let him sit in the seat, sipping that single cup of espresso.

Damien looked to his left and right, then strode across the court. His target had their back to him. Damien's black MACV-1 boots whispered on the flagstones. The target never saw him coming.

Closing the distance, Damien looked around casually. He reached forward, and gripped the target's shoulders firmly.

Spinning Grace around, he fixed her with a dazzling smile. Frowning, she looked up at him. Suddenly, her face lit up with excitement.

'I've missed you,' said Grace, nuzzling into his muscular chest. She hugged him like she never wanted to let go. Grace had waited months for Damien to cash in on the promise he had made to her in the Arctic. As the icebreaker *Aysberg* limped into Murmansk, an FSB helicopter had flown out to meet them. Damien stepped on board and told her to be in Avignon in three months' time. He would be there.

'I was always coming,' replied Damien, returning her tight grip, and kissing the top of her brunette hair lightly.

'How long do you have?

'Enough for you to escort me, an avid fan of your discoveries, for a quick thirty-minute tour of the Lapidary Museum. I hear you have secured an exhibition of your excavation on Rudolf Island. A nice memorial for your friends.'

'How did you know?' said Grace, grinning. She took his hand and led him off towards the museum. Winter was gripping the air. Avignon seemed to revel in its freshness. The air smelt clean and crisp. The streets remained mostly deserted. Tourists would not clutter its stone roads for another four months.

'I keep up with all things archaeological now. I have a keen interest,' replied Damien. A happy laugh spilled out of his mouth.

Fifteen minutes later, they arrived in front of the old chapel of the Jesuit college. The building normally housed exhibitions of Greek through to Paleo-Christian collections. The curator had made an exception for Grace. The story of what occurred on Rudolf Island had slowly filtered through the community. Museums were suddenly open to showing her discoveries.

Grace rushed Damien through the other antiques until they arrived in the back corner of the museum.

'In the back?' queried Damien. He was slightly annoyed that Grace's exhibition had not been placed more prominently.

'Any space is good, Damien. People will still get to see what we found. A six-month showing is what they've agreed to,' replied Grace. She could not help but stare at Damien's face. He was pretending to be interested in the pieces of rusting metal and splintered wood under glass on the tables.

'Who really taught you how to shoot?' asked Damien suddenly. He turned to look at Grace. There was a gap in her life he could not find any information on.

'What?' asked Grace, confused by his direct question.

'You have an idea of my past, Grace. I need you to answer that question for me before we go any further.'

'In truth, my brother. I don't talk about him. So, I told you it was my father,' she said simply and held his gaze. She could see the calculating way Damien was processing the information. Grace had only mentioned her father on the island.

'How did he learn?'

'The Legion. He was in the French Foreign Legion for ten years. I don't know what happened to him after he left.'

'Good to know,' said Damien.

He looked at a rusted hook of iron and breathed in deeply.

'Okay,' he said quietly.

'Happy?' Grace asked uncertainly.

'Let's not waste our time on this. Take me through everything,' said Damien encouragingly, spreading his arms wide across the tables. Laughing lightly, Grace explained each item and its history. Damien listened quietly and asked the occasional question.

'That's everything,' said Grace as she came to the end of the exhibition. She felt a sudden sadness. Grace knew Damien was about to leave. 'When will I see you again?' she asked, quietly looking down at the floor for a moment. When she looked up, Damien was staring at her.

'I'll call you. I kept my promise this time. I will always keep my promises to you, Grace.'

'I will hear from you, then,' replied Grace simply. She knew there was no scope for anything other than waiting for Damien's call. 'Will you visit for longer next time?'

'I can promise that. Maybe here again. I like Avignon,' ended Damien.

He leaned down to kiss Grace lightly on her lips, and lingered for a second. When he pulled away he smiled warmly at her, spun on his heel, and disappeared towards the museum's entrance.

Grace watched him go, quietly wishing he would stay.

Pushing the glass doors open, Damien stepped clear of the old chapel. He did not pause as he moved across the stone courtyard. Halfway, his mobile telephone started ringing. Calmly, he pulled it free from his jacket and looked at the display. An unregistered number. Damien pressed the green answer icon and lifted the telephone to his ear.

'Hello, Chainsaw,' came a familiar voice.

'Fuck off, Don.'

'You owe us a favour,' replied Don Murphy calmly.

'You heard me,' said Damien forcefully. He ended the call and tucked the mobile back into his jacket. He continued across the courtyard.

CIEST..

More from Big Sky Publishing

View sample pages, reviews and information on this book and other titles at
www.bigskypublishing.com.au

BIG SKY PUBLISHING

More from Big Sky Publishing

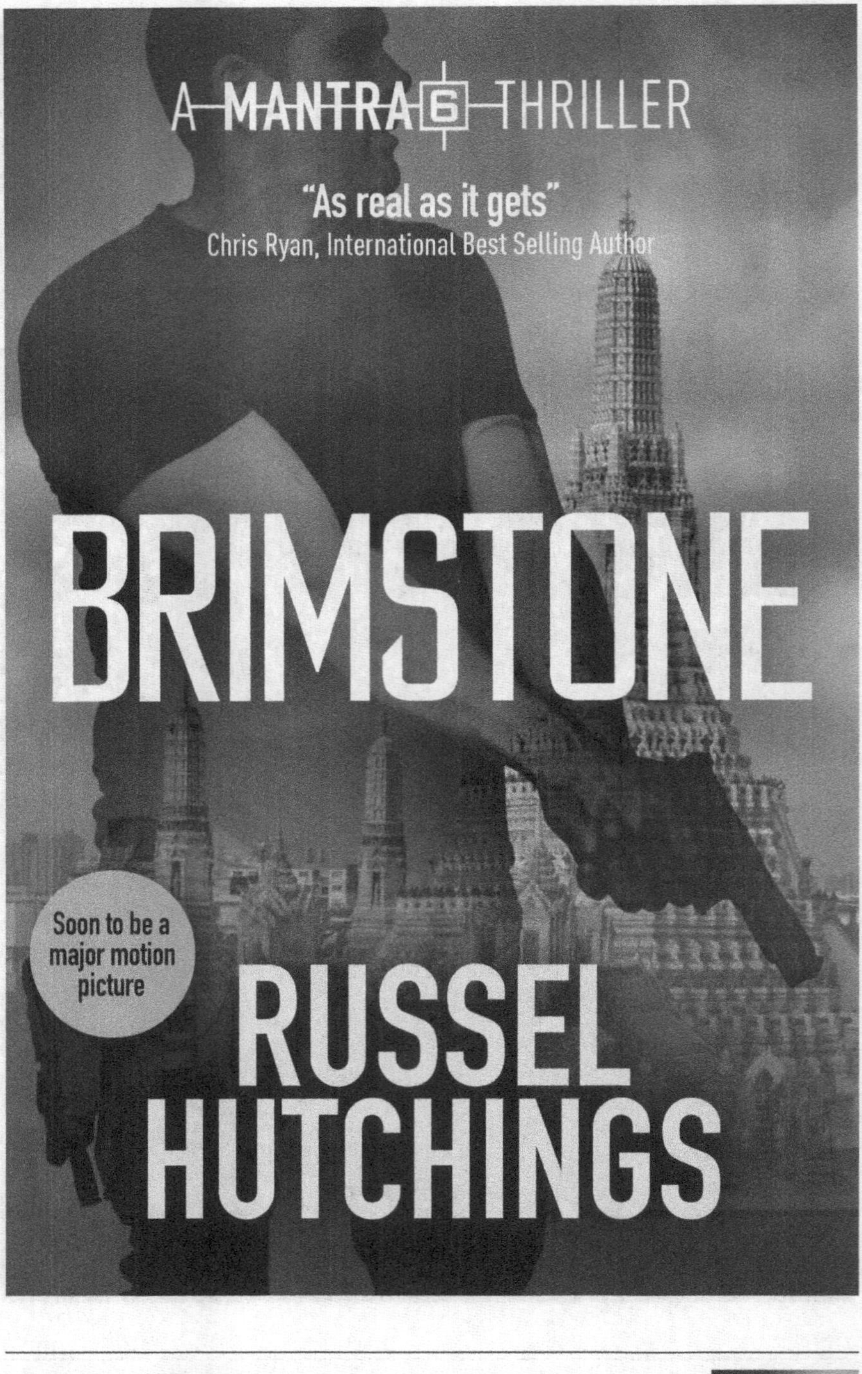

More from Big Sky Publishing

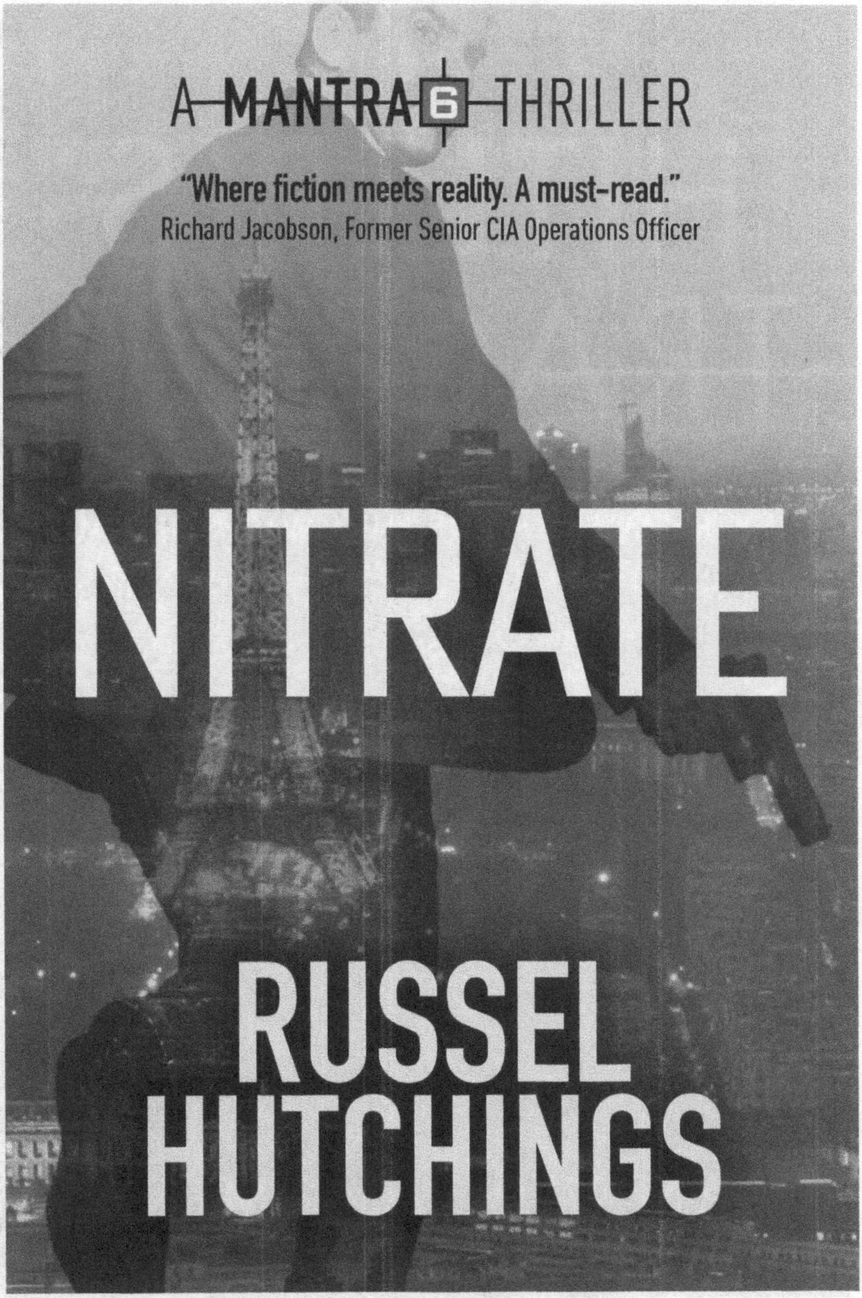